DANGEROUS
ILLUSIONS

DANGEROUS ILLUSIONS

A NOVEL

CAROLYN A. GREENE

ZACH TAYLOR

THE SEQUEL TO CASTLES IN THE SAND

LIGHTHOUSE TRAILS PUBLISHING
EUREKA, MONTANA

Dangerous Illusions

©2014 Carolyn A. Greene and Zach Taylor

Sequel to *Castles in the Sand* (Lighthouse Trails Publishing, ©2009)

Published by:

Lighthouse Trails Publishing

(see back of book for publisher and author contact information)

Scripture quotations are taken from the *King James Version.*

Cover and interior design by Lighthouse Trails Publishing. Cover photos from bigstockphoto.com; used with permission.

Publishers Cataloging-in-Publication Data
(Library of Congress Cataloging-in-Publication Data Applied For)

Green, Carolyn A.
Taylor, Zach
    Dangerous illusions: a novel
1. Greene, Carolyn A. 2. Taylor, Zach 3. Christian--Fiction.
4. Mystery--Fiction. I. Title.
    ISBN-13: 9780989509350
    ISBN-10: 0989509354

813'.6--dc22

Note: Lighthouse Trails Publishing books are available at special quantity discounts. Contact information for publisher in back of book.

Printed in the United States of America

To my husband,
who so generously tolerates,
accommodates, and encourages my
writing cave habits

—Carolyn

CONTENTS

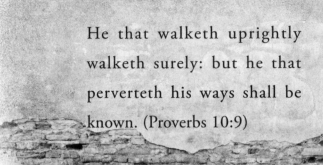

He that walketh uprightly walketh surely: but he that perverteth his ways shall be known. (Proverbs 10:9)

CHAPTER

1

I t was nothing like he'd thought it would be. Rob Carlton walked the narrow brick and mortar path following close behind the robed monk. Hands in his jacket pockets, his neck enveloped by his upturned corduroy collar, and his knitted cap pulled low over his ears, Rob looked up as they passed an old brick office building belonging to the monastery. A certain sacred ambience lingered in the air.

The mountain wind buffeted Rob's back, and the low-lying cloud cover obscuring the knife-edged peaks disseminated late spring snow on both him and the monk. Rob was cold, but he fought the urge to make haste, and in lockstep, paced himself with that of his companion while listening politely to quiet explanations. Rob asked the occasional question while half-wishing he'd never come, yet at the same time, strangely glad he did.

It had been a long one-hundred miles from Birch Valley, and he had plenty of time to think. All week long Stephanie had been insistent that he go, and on the Saturday morning that was his usual day to sleep in late, he found himself packing a small suitcase, listening in veiled irritation as she chattered away while preparing his favorite hotcakes-and-sausage breakfast. After twenty years of marriage, she was an impossible woman to refuse, for she knew all the right buttons to push. And one morning along the way, he awoke, struck with the startling realization that she had evolved into the kind of woman who could make his life quietly miserable while smiling to herself, convinced that whatever she required of him was in his best interest. It was she who was into this monastic mystical stuff, not him. Her quirky yet altogether feel-good theology had lately taken a dramatic turn.

At first, when she had begun traversing what he considered a slippery slope, Stephanie was content to leave him be with his old-time Baptist tradition. She, on the other hand, voraciously read books by obscure authors (ones he'd never heard of anyway) and engaged herself in a wide variety of spiritual exercises.

It was when she began watching the videos that she turned a corner, urging and, of late, demanding he become involved. His joking rebuffs were increasingly met with a self-righteous hostility. "You're an elder of a failing church," she snipped, "and you're not even interested in giving the congregation the shot in the arm it needs."

So he gave in and agreed to meet with the monk. Rob had fumed his first hour behind the wheel, but the more he thought about it, the more he felt she might have a point. His traditionalist mentality was getting Sheep Gate Lane Church, or Sheep Gate as the members called it, nowhere—and fast. To be sure, the old ways were comfortable and doctrinally sound, but the atmosphere of the church was now dry and devitalized. He really did care about the spiritual life of folks he had loved and fellowshipped with for the past decade; he just didn't know what to do to get them interested anymore—or to renew his own interest, for that matter. Lately it seemed as if the entire concept and reality of church life was lacking a certain vitality.

But worst of all, the congregation was thinning out, and it was no longer the life-changing experience it used to be for those who remained. One thing he knew for sure—account books don't lie. Offerings had dropped significantly over the past few months, and at the current drop-out rate, the church would close its doors before the new year began. Given his position as a salaried staff member, he was at risk. The imminent doom of surrendering a comfortable lifestyle for a spot in the unemployment line did not sit well with Rob at all.

And now here he was, following some robed monk down an ancient-looking stone path far removed from anything he'd ever known. He glanced backward periodically, half-expecting to see a reporter from the *Birch Barker Weekly* snapping his photo for the newspaper's next exposé.

Rob had the feeling that everybody in Birch Valley knew precisely what he was up to. Yet it was supposed to be done in secret. "Remember, don't tell anyone you are going up there," Stephanie had reminded him. She had even suggested he not take his iPhone with him at all.

"Tell me again why no one can know," Rob had asked as he zipped his suitcase closed and grabbed his jacket.

"There are people—like Jacob Brown—who would resist changes—the kind of changes I'm thinking about—if he got wind of it. I can just hear him now at some emergency-called, all-church meeting saying, 'This kind of thing is going against the Gospel,'" Stephanie mocked. "How many times have I heard Jacob say something like that! Sometimes I can't help wish Jacob Brown would just . . ."

"Stephanie! Don't even say such a thing!"

"Well, after all, he is getting up there in years."

Rob had left the house with Stephanie still going on. She followed him to the car and continued talking to him through the open car window as he backed down the driveway to the road. After he had gotten out of town and was heading up toward the monastery, he had realized how he hated this cloak-and-dagger stuff. He had wished the weekend was already over and done with just so he could report back to Stephanie that he had given it his best shot and found her ideas to be anything but feasible or doable.

Now, as Rob walked with the monk, he took a closer look at the young bearded man. His rough, brown hood was drawn across his face, and each hand poked into the warm and spacious robe sleeves. A gentleness and serenity emulated from him. Serenity—oh how Rob longed just for some peace.

As the monk's robes whipped every which way in the wind, he led the way to the small tiled courtyard. They paused at an overlook at the edge of the gray stone wall that encircled the area. Speaking in a soft tone, the monk said, "As you can see, it's a most idyllic setting for a retreat. It's early yet, of course, and officially, we don't house people until May, but your wife was so . . . insistent that you needed, well . . . some guidance, and she seemed familiar with our ways. She did say you might have some personal obstacles to overcome regarding some of our teachings, but we understand that not everyone who comes here for refreshing subscribes to our faith. We're very aware, understanding, and accommodating when it comes to such matters. It's the personal journey, not indoctrination, that we're interested in."

"So it doesn't matter that I'm not Catholic?" Rob probed.

The young monk smiled warmly. "Not at all. We welcome people of all faiths here. We've had Protestants, Buddhists, even agnostics ..."

Rob's eyes widened. "Buddhists?"

The monk chuckled. "We often get that reaction from those involved in mainline religion or Christian fundamentalism. But on a more serious note, we believe we—that is, you, me, everybody—can learn from all spiritual paths, regardless of our upbringing or current faith. Up here, amidst this unspoiled solitude, we provide a place of refuge for all who come. We exist primarily to help facilitate an authentic spiritual journey for the seeking soul. Some of our most influential Catholic teachers of the past were involved with Zen teaching. While we don't incorporate everything pertaining to that particular pathway into our spiritual disciplines here, we still believe much of it to be compatible with Christian theology."

Rob leaned against the waist-high wall as he perused the gray, hand-fitted rock giving the impression of a medieval castle, a symbol of both comfort and fortification. The monastery proper included a chapel and connecting monks' cells all built of the same locally quarried stone, giving an appearance simultaneously imposing and retiring—a monument, perhaps, to a bygone yet intensely spiritual era. Rob had to admit it was a pretty place. A blue-green sea of spruce, fir, and pine cascaded downward from the aerie; and the air was rich with the scent of residual winter snow that remained at this altitude. It had taken some fancy footwork, driving wise, for him to get there; and the switchback climb through pockets of mud and dingy snow had afforded him a few moments of high tension. But standing on the edge of the monastery's overlook and drinking in the quiet, Rob reluctantly admitted to himself that it had been worth it. There was something about the place he couldn't quite put his finger on—a prevailing, transcendent, "a way backward is a way forward" kind of atmosphere that brought back fond, childhood memories like fishing for lake trout or experiencing that ecstatic, full of hope and promise feeling so part and parcel of young love. Feeling a twinge of regret, he couldn't remember if he'd kissed Stephanie goodbye before he rushed out the door and sped away. He'd have to make that up to her when he got home.

"Come," the monk urged. "There's something else I'd like to show you." They left the courtyard and walked along a meandering flagstone pathway through what was more than likely a spectacular flower garden during the summer. Next, they passed by thickets of brown stems poking up through patches of snow until they came to a large, circular, cement pattern, roughly thirty feet around and built into the ground. Rob stared. He recognized it from the cover of one of Stephanie's books. The book's title came rushing to the forefront of his memory—*The Labyrinth: Old and New.*

It was an odd thing to see this maze-like structure in real life sitting in the heavily wooded grounds of the monastery. With its circles within circles, it had the distinct look and feel of something ancient. "This is a …" the monk began.

"Yes, I know," Rob interrupted. "It's a labyrinth." He stared long and hard at it, thinking.

The monk regarded him with respectful silence then asked, "Would you like to … ?

Rob shook his head. "Not just yet," he said somewhat sheepishly. "This is all so new and …" He shrugged. "You know."

The monk placed a gentle hand on Rob's shoulder. "Would you like to see one of our prayer huts?"

Rob nodded, and they made their way back to the courtyard and to a small wooden A-framed building. Inside the prayer hut, as it was called, it was warm and cozy, out of the wind, and heated by a small propane stove. Rob looked around in nervousness and wonder, shifting his gaze from a tall, stained-glass window that nearly filled one side of the front entrance wall to the triple-tiered racks of lighted votive candles in the front to the plain wood altar gussied up with a brace of gilt candlesticks. Behind the altar was a large cathedral window, which unveiled a not-too-distant view of fir and pine trees leading up a mountainside. The two A-frame walls were decorated with murals; and one Rob recognized—an ecstatic monk on his knees with his arms outstretched and his hands, feet, and side pierced in accordance with one of his visions. Francis of Assisi. What was it they called it? Stigmata. The actual wounds of Christ, they said. Rob looked up at the center of the wall to the hand-carved crucifix. The figure of the suffering Jesus overlooked the room from its placement above the altar. Rob stared upward, feeling strangely drawn. Despite the modern décor, the room exuded a kind of antiquity reminiscent of another place and time—perhaps dating as far back as a thousand years.

Rob sat down on a large cushion situated on one of the wooden benches that lined the walls. He sighed and gazed out the window. The monk sat next to Rob and said, "Many monasteries that act as retreat centers are more modern than ours. But as a community we felt much could be gained by keeping the atmosphere like it was for the original brothers who established the Order. Don't you agree?" Rob nodded but said nothing. His countenance exemplified the struggle he was going through to rely on logic and reason. For a time, the monk sat quietly, hands folded in his lap, gazing alternately at the crucifix and then at Rob. Finally, he took a deep breath and asked, "Mr. Carlton, what is it you're looking for? Your wife was not very specific, and though we don't normally make it a habit to pry, I'm sensing a feeling of desperation in you that I'd like to help you through. That is, if you'll let me."

Rob studied the face of the young gentle man for a prolonged moment then let out a weary sigh. "I've got trouble, and I don't know what to do." No sooner had the words left his mouth than all he had been feeling came bubbling to the surface with such intensity, he couldn't suppress it: the dying church, his wife's nagging, his own helplessness and uncertainty, and the fear of losing his position. A hundred other things came forth too, all jumbled together. And although he wasn't completely coherent, the young monk seemed to understand.

"It's obvious what you and your people need," he said in a comforting voice. "Renewal. You've languished in dead traditionalism for so long you don't know how to "do church" any other way. Mr. Carlton, that's why we've opened our doors to the public for the retreat. We, that is, the Catholic church at large and our little community specifically, have rediscovered the old ways, the paths that the ancient Christians took in their spiritual walk. It's like I told you. It's the journey that's important. How we get there is personal, and what may look to some as, oh, *heretical* . . ." he said the word with a derisive smile, "is for another a valid tool for finding God. You understand?" Rob nodded.

"I think so," he conceded. "But, again, I'm no Catholic . . ." The monk looked on patiently and spoke as if to a child. How funny it was—Rob was old enough to be his father, but here the "son" was comforting and mentoring the "father."

"Like I said, you don't have to be. The ways in which we teach here, as well as the practices and spiritual disciplines we teach, you can take back to your own church and incorporate. At least try it and see. What have you got to lose? We have many success stories, and most of them began similar to yours." Rob pondered, and the monk stood. "Look," he said, "why don't you just sit here awhile and meditate. It'll come to you, what you should do. I'll pray for you. Come to the main office when you're ready to go to your cell." He turned to leave but stopped and looked down at Rob. "I should tell you though, that by accepting these teachings and putting them into practice, two things will happen: first, your life will go through some dramatic changes, and second, you will face opposition back home. Some won't understand, and others will simply refuse to embrace a liberating spirituality. It's largely out of fear this happens—fear of change—fear of others who are different. You have to prepare yourself for that." He reached down and touched Rob's shoulder once again then took a few steps and went out through the antiquated looking oak door.

Silence engulfed the room, and Rob sat with his head down and hands between his knees. *Opposition,* he thought. "Yeah," he muttered. "Like Jacob Brown. There's no way he'll stand for this. And yet if I decline, Stephanie will make my life insufferable. The house won't be fit to live in."

Rob's mind drifted to the monk. He had such a kind demeanor, so gentle and even . . . well, even soothing. *Jacob is always emphasizing doctrine,* Rob pondered. *Talk about fear—Jacob is afraid to try anything new. But what about charity? Look at this monk. He is kind and seems to have so much peace about him. Just because his beliefs are different than ours, does that make them wrong?*

Then it hit Rob that maybe Stephanie was right. Maybe there was something they were missing. Maybe, just maybe . . . He shook his head and with gritted teeth said, "Man, I don't need this."

Out of the corner of his eye, he spotted a worn, little book within arm's reach on a small shelf built into the wall. He leaned over and took hold of it while at the same time reading the title: *The Cloud of Unknowing.* In parentheses, it said, "Written by an anonymous monk in the fourteenth century." *Hey, I remember seeing that book on Stephanie's desk,* Rob mused. As he opened the book, a cloth bookmark fell out. He let the book fall open to the marked page. Underlined in pencil were the words: "take thee but a little word of one syllable: for so it is better than of two . . . fasten this word to thine heart . . . With this word, thou shalt beat on this cloud and this darkness above thee. With this word, thou shall smite down all manner of thought under the cloud of forgetting." *Take this word, a word with one syllable,* Rob pondered. Stephanie was always talking about her prayer word and how repeating it and meditating on it brought her into the presence of God where she could hear his voice.

Raising his face again to the crucifix, Rob studied the figure there—the crown of thorns, the bleeding wounds on the hands, feet, and side. As he shifted his attention to the wall murals, he found himself drawn again to the painting of Francis of Assisi. "Yes," he said aloud. Rob stood, hurried over to the door, paused, and walked back to the cushion. He reached down and grabbed the *Cloud* book, briefly eyeing it again, then tucked it under his arm. *I have a feeling I am going to need this little book.* Out the door into the fresh air he went. He was anxious to speak more with the monk. And when he had a chance, he had to call Stephanie. Something told him it was going to be an exhilarating weekend.

CHAPTER

2

A multitude of wings flashed in the early morning sun as a small flock of startled pine siskins flitted chaotically through the conifers while Jacob and Margaret Brown trudged to the end of their long gravel driveway. Both had arms filled with baskets of fresh garden flowers as they walked side by side to the little roadside stand. Close behind them and nosing through the grass, wet from the morning dew, a diminutive Jack Russell terrier divided her time between snuffling up the occasional field mouse and barking at the flurry of morning birds.

"Beautiful," said Jacob as he glanced up at the sky. "Not a cloud in sight. Think it'll get hot later today, though." He lingered for a moment and gazed up at the spires of the Rockies, bronzed in the dawn light as they rose majestically above the sleepy foothills of Birch Valley.

From under the wide straw brim of her sun hat, Margaret's eyes followed his. For a moment, she drank it all in. Then, she set down the overflowing flower baskets, sidled up beside him, slipped a slender arm into the crook of his own, and sighed wistfully. In a soft-spoken tone she lamented, "Why can't we stand here like this forever?" then added, "I'm going to miss you, Mr. Brown."

He looked down at her. Smiling, he planted a soft tender kiss on her forehead. He moved to the stand and unlocked the lid on the hinged wooden donation box. Jacob reached inside and grabbed the previous day's earnings—some loose change and a sparse, scattered collection of bills. After a quick examination, he dropped the money into a leather drawstring pouch.

Margaret watched, studying him and committing everything about him to memory. She smiled at the movement of his hands—those callused, weathered hands that had known a lifetime of hard work. How she loved those hands! How they could move so seamlessly from work to tender touch, cupping her face before a kiss, or with a rough fingertip, brushing a single, stray silver hair from her forehead while she cooked meals. They had grown old together, yet his touch never failed to rekindle in her the days of their youth, when everything was new and exciting.

"You'll be busy keeping this stand going," he noted. "It'll seem like a long week, I guess, being here alone, but I made sure to have lots of folks checking in on you. Nathan will be by every day during the week to help with the farm, and Millie's only a phone call away."

Her mind was a jumble of thoughts—Jacob's leaving, the garden, being alone. Each year the garden itself became a little more difficult to maintain, and with it, the roadside stand they'd managed for the past twenty-five years. Row upon row of corn, tomatoes, cucumbers, and squash, along with a separate plot for their kitchen spices and tea herbs, always elicited a gush of admiration from neighbors and customers.

But the years were catching up with Jacob and Margaret now, and although accustomed to hardship and being physically fit, they were beginning to feel the weight of their ages. Nevertheless, they loved the seasons of sowing, tending, and harvesting, and Margaret only hoped they could continue this way of life for the remainder of their time together. It was a ministry, after all, and the donation money they garnered from the vegetables, as well as from the sale of the zinnias, asters, and snapdragons from Margaret's flower garden, all went toward helping a needy family or two every Christmas. The blessing of sharing their good fortune had always returned itself upon them a hundredfold.

There were other blessings as well—their membership in the wonderful assembly of Sheep Gate, volunteering at the local soup kitchen, rescuing many a wayward teenager from an often unfeeling, impartial foster care system . . . it was an impressive list. They had, in fact, become local heroes, a beacon of light for those lost in darkness as well as to those in legitimate need. Have a problem? Talk it over with Jacob and Margaret, for they'll know what to do. Troubled teen? Send them on over to the Brown's place. They'll always make room for one more . . . It was humbling, really. Despite their spotless reputation among Birch Valley residents, they still considered themselves just ordinary folks, or believers in Christ who only did what was expected of them. And sometimes they failed even at that.

"I know it has to be, Jacob," Margaret said. "I just wish . . ."

"Now, now," he gently assuaged her. "We've been over all this."

Margaret forced a smile then frowned, punctuating it with another sigh. "J.B., I have a bad gut feeling about this. Couldn't you just wait until she gets back?"

Jacob shook his head, his jaw set firmly in place. "Time's up," he said. "My decision's been made. I'm done, Margaret. From now on, I wish only to have more time for us and the things we want to do, and how can that be a bad thing?"

She nodded but stood frowning, still disappointed. Jacob couldn't keep from smiling. He hooked the money pouch to his belt then moved closer to his wife. With both hands, he cupped her face. She closed her eyes and melted into the roughness of his hands, reached up to cover them with her fingers, and tenderly kissed each one.

"Yes," she murmured, weary and still very much in love. "I'll manage. 'They who wait upon the LORD shall renew their strength.'"

For a while, they stood with clasped hands, Margaret savoring the warmth of his fingers on her face. She wanted to etch this moment in her mind, to be able to replay it over and over again during the nights he was away. Opening her eyes, Margaret realized Jacob was now looking intently down the road. A light green sedan sat parked on the opposite shoulder about a quarter mile away. She hadn't noticed it a moment ago but wouldn't have been concerned if she had. People stopped alongside the road all the time. It was a scenic drive, and a panoramic of mountains brooding over ranchland was conducive to impulse picture taking. Jacob, however, seemed very focused, provoking in Margaret a vague sense of foreboding.

"Jacob?" she asked, "What is it?" He gave a small shake of his head, yet staring. An uneasiness welled up from deep within Margaret. "The newspaper had something in it a few days ago about break-ins," she said, staring at the vehicle. "You think maybe they're up to no good?"

"Can't say," Jacob replied, giving her a semblance of a smile. "Hey, why don't you go put on the coffee, and I think I'll mosey on over there and see if they need some help. Maybe they're having engine trouble or something."

"You think?" Margaret nodded to herself. Made sense. At least the thought made her feel better. "Maybe you should drive the pickup over there, J.B."

Jacob huffed. "Drive that little ways? Hah! Waste of gas. Besides, that old dog," he said, arching his thumb over his shoulder at Daisy, "could use the exercise. C'mon old gal." Off he went, at a steady clip, the somewhat curious terrier waddling along behind him on her stubby little legs. Somewhere near the twenty-year-old mark, she was still able to follow, even if it was at a slower pace.

Margaret stood and watched. As Jacob neared the vehicle, the driver keyed the ignition, slammed it into gear, did a 180, and squealed off in the opposite direction, leaving a short, double-lined streak of abraded rubber on the asphalt. Jacob stopped cold, arms at his sides, staring after the car. Daisy rattled off a series of halfhearted barks and waddled faster in pursuit, eventually passing Jacob. "No, girl," he called. "Come on back here. They're clear out of the county by now."

He crouched down beside the dog, patting her head as she sat on her haunches, huffing and puffing from the exertion. He stared down the road a minute longer, then stood upright and began the walk back to Margaret, who still stood watching with arms folded. From her vantage point, she couldn't help but notice how he looked back over his shoulder a time or two and shook his head, in bewilderment. "What was that all about?" she called as he approached.

Jacob shrugged, feigning disinterest. "Dunno. A tourist, maybe? They can be funny sometimes." When Margaret didn't respond, he smiled. "That coffee doesn't brew itself," he said. He reached for her with one hand, and they each lifted a flower basket to carry back to the house. Though neither mentioned it, the driver of the car with its accompanying disappearing act, hung between them.

With his second mug of coffee in his gnarled hand, Jacob stood on the porch and gave the property the once-over. From the row of fencing to the outbuildings, the whole place was beginning to look a little run-down. On his earlier walk back to Margaret, with Daisy in tow, he had even noted the fading numerals on the old mailbox and how the mailbox post leaned a little toward the road instead of standing perfectly upright. Things didn't used to be that way, he mused.

It was a good place, this two-story home, the old barn, the acres of meadow grass, and the stands of old growth pines and a variety of other trees. He never tired of looking out toward the foothills either, to the ring of the Rockies, off in the distance. They'd been here more seasons than he could begin to recall: autumn, when the aspens turned gold and shook and swayed in the gusting wind; winter, when the snow lay heavy and quiet over a sleeping land; the flowering of spring, characterized by the earth pushing forth its tender green shoots, trees re-budding, and everything being green again; and finally, the sultry heat all too akin to the dog days of summer. So many memories— some good, some not so good. But all part of God's plan for their lives.

Truth was though, a lot weighed heavy on his heart and mind lately. He had felt tired lately, inside. The Flat Plains Bible College debacle was only a part of it. It had been three years since the rescue of Tessa from a spiritual nightmare there. Since then, he had been involved with the college board and leadership with the job of re-laying a biblical foundation. But for all the good he had wrought, so much still needed to be done, and sometimes it felt like one step forward, two steps backward. At seventy-two, Jacob was tired of sandbagging.

Add all that to the condition of Sheep Gate Lane Church and his feeling like he had to cudgel a church board into growing a spine. As an elder and board member at Sheep Gate, Jacob had always helped with the church load, but the last year of Pastor Glen Davis' life, Jacob was forced into divvying up his time between family, church, the farm, and Flat Plains. That year turned out to be too much for either man. Glen succumbed to physical exhaustion and Jacob to the spiritual kind, and since Pastor Davis' passing, Jacob's involvement with church-related activities had diminished greatly.

The thought of what Margaret would say to selling the homestead made him apprehensive. But it was something he was considering more all the time even though a prospective buyer would surely want a sizeable amount shaved off the asking price. The property was a fixer-upper by modern day real-estate standards. The clematis vine was taking over the south side of the house and the hedges were in desperate need of a trim. Then there was the septic field and the aging in-house plumbing, and a hundred and one other repairs clamoring to be done. The front yard they kept well manicured, however. It was the property's nicest feature.

Standing there on the porch, Jacob realized he had been in deep thought for several minutes. He took a gulp of coffee and watched as the terrier wandered in off the driveway and heaved herself, one step at a time, up onto the front porch, where her long toenails went clickety-clack against the worn wooden planking. She stopped beside Jacob, plopped herself down on her haunches, and stared up at him expectantly. Jacob smiled, reached down with one hand, then stroked her between the ears. Standing upright, he let out a heavy sigh, and shook his head. "Can't do it, Daisy. Nope. I'd sooner be put in a box."

"Jacob!"

He hadn't heard Margaret open the door and step out onto the porch with a plate of fresh-baked bran muffins. "What did you just say?"

Jacob chuckled. "Nothing much. Just talkin' to the dog."

She waved the plate under his nose. "Still piping hot," she said, "eat some and talk to me, instead of the dog!"

"Ha!" Jacob replied. "She listens to me."

Margaret smiled in part, looking deeply and searchingly into his eyes. "You should stop talking so much to the dog and get back to talking to God." She hadn't meant for them to, but her words cut him right to the quick. He turned again to look out over the property, taking another swig of his coffee around a mouthful of warm muffin and appearing unmoved. But he couldn't deny it. Margaret had called it like it is. Lately, he hadn't been walking with the Lord the way He had before, and prayer had become something of a chore. He would not tell her so, but it scared him. And he was at a loss as to what to do about it.

CHAPTER

3

The death of a church is never an easy thing to watch. Two troubled years for the little country church at the end of Sheep Gate Lane left the congregants weary. Sitting on the outskirts of Birch Valley, the small, century-old building seemed rather iconic, a representation of America's heartland. On the outside, it had everything to recommend it—fresh white paint, slate blue trim, and a half-dozen large windows looking out over a peaceful countryside. But its serene exterior masked ongoing, interior turmoil. For a half century, it had been a meeting place for a congregation of serious Bible believers, but like many strong Christians, the founder—Glen Davis' father, Benjamin Davis—could not have foreseen the gradual, insidious infiltration of postmodern "progressive" beliefs.

Pastor Davis had been a strong man—a rock even, but the massive coronary that took his life jolted the congregation into a kind of spiritual numbness. For the first time in church history, church board members were at odds with one another, unable to reach any kind of consensus about a suitable replacement. Months of advertising in congregational magazines and online had produced no permanent prospects, just a few itinerate "preachers," none of whom showed much interest in God's Word. Among the board members, desperation prompted a flurry of unproductive meetings. Even the dependable Jacob Brown was uncharacteristically taking the summer off. Sheep Gate seemed destined to end with a whimper if something didn't change soon.

The arrival of Chip Davis on the scene appeared to be an answer to their prayers. The grandson of the late Pastor Davis and his widow, Ellen Davis, Chip was still somewhat green, even with three years of Bible school and a two-year youth pastor internship under his belt. His plans to help move his grandmother into the Silver Meadows Senior Community took an unexpected detour when he was asked to speak the first Sunday morning he attended Sheep Gate Church with his grandmother.

Much later, if you had asked any member of the congregation just what, exactly, Chip had preached on, they couldn't really give any kind of concrete accounting. It seemed it wasn't so much what he said, as it was how he said it. The good-looking young man with the wavy brown hair and rich baritone voice had a special something, a charisma he projected from behind the pulpit that made folks feel as if he were speaking to them, individually. He smiled a lot during the message, pointed his index finger at a couple of handpicked people a time or two, raised a hand to heaven and seemed to grab a fistful of blessings for himself to pass out to the assembly. No one remembered the gist of the sermon, but the effect of it was electric. The few remaining youth in the congregation were ignited, and clamored for a repeat performance at the youth meeting that same Sunday evening. Chip graciously conceded.

As it turned out, time was on the congregation's side. Closing the sale on his grandmother's neglected house proved to be more of an undertaking than Chip had anticipated, so the young Bible school graduate tacked on some extra time to his original two-week visit. Since he had the time, and the church lacked a permanent shepherd, Chip was approached by the deacon board to preach again. And again. Chip always smiled, blushed a bit, and accepted with an all too apparent humility.

Word got around the Valley about the young minister at the little country church. He might be a bit flamboyant for these parts, folks said, but he sure preached a killer sermon. Visitors began lining the pews, and the congregation flourished as some members who had drifted away returned and brought family and friends with them to Sunday service. Soon, even Wednesday nights were playing to a nearly packed house. And the youth group was bursting at the seams, with kids from the Valley bringing their in-town friends and their relatives along.

All this was not at all lost on the elders' board. Nor did they forget that Chip's last Sunday at Sheep Gate was almost upon them. That Saturday, several of the congregation gathered together in the church basement for an impromptu church meeting.

"I'd like to call this meeting to order," Rob Carlton said. "Okay, can we settle down, please? We don't have a lot of time."

The two other elders, their wives, and a half-dozen congregation members dispersed from around the coffeepot and took their seats at the long foldout table. Rob was glad the room wasn't packed out. He didn't want to appear to Chip to be high-pressuring him, but, at the same time, wanted enough folks present to offer support in case the board met with stiff resistance from their pastoral candidate. A sudden hush fell upon the room as they all pulled their chairs forward, situated their elbows on the hard white plastic table, and drank their coffee or tea, with bated breath, watching Rob.

"Okay," he said, "this is not an official meeting, so we can dispense with 'Robert's Rules' and all that. We all know why we're here." As he spoke, he fixed his gaze upon each one seated, lingered a moment, then moved on. "Our church," he said, "was languishing just two short months ago, and it looked like we were going to fold. Chip Davis came along, preached some of the best sermons to come from behind our pulpit, and the pews are overflowing. It doesn't take a rocket scientist to see we need this guy."

Henry Beam raised a hand. "Yeah, but can we pay him what he's worth?"

Rob shook his head. "Not near as much as some of the bigger churches in the state. He said he's had some really good offers, and we can't match them financially."

Carrie Littlejohn appeared concerned. Carrie had not made it out to many church meetings ever since her husband entered the final stages of cancer. And since the funeral, she had determined in her heart that now that she was the sole spiritual leader of her home she would do her best to be involved in her church. Sitting there now at the church meeting, both feet propped up on a chair after serving customers all day at the restaurant, Carrie asked, "Hasn't any of the board spoken with him? I mean, surely he knows the good work he's started here. He can't just walk out on us now. I can't see how we could lose him and keep the congregation. And my son just loves him. And we have more kids in the youth group than ever now. Even some of the hardcore troublemakers from town are showing up. We know exactly what'll happen if Chip leaves."

Rob lifted a placating hand. "Thanks Carrie, but we know all that. We have talked with him," he said with a tired sigh, "but I don't think he's interested. I—we, the whole elder board—were hoping for some ideas from any one of you. We're fresh out. He's coming here in a few minutes and maybe some of you can . . ."

"Rob?" Elder Bud Clement poked his head into the room from the doorway leading to the upstairs sanctuary. "He's just arrived."

Rob nodded and took a deep breath. "Okay," he said, "ask him to come down, will you?"

A moment later, with Bud leading the way, Chip appeared in the doorway. As he entered the room, he released a broad smile and began shaking hands. Soon, he took the empty seat beside Rob. Rob rose and got right to it. "Chip," he said emphatically, "we talked, and we all agree. We need you here at Sheep Gate. I thought maybe you'd like to hear it from some of the others in the congregation."

One by one each member spoke, earnestly, convincingly, and with deep feeling. And at the end of it, Chip sat silent, eyes on the table before him, looking like he was, in all seriousness, mulling it over in his mind. But the instant he lifted his head to look at them, they knew his answer.

"I'm sorry," he said. "I just don't think this is the place for me. You've all been so nice, and I hate to disappoint you, but. . ." shrugging and apologetically smiling, he continued, "I've considered it, and I don't think it'll work. I'm looking for a position in a larger setting. Small town life just isn't for me. I don't think I'd be happy here. And that would mean you wouldn't be happy with me. I'll be available for the next few weeks, and by that time, my grandmother's house should be in shape for sale. Again, I'm sorry."

A few of them took another stab at it, but they all knew it was a done deal. Sheep Gate would lose the best thing to have happened to it in two years, and the congregation would have to revert back to triage mode to try to prevent the hemorrhaging of the church's spiritual lifeblood. And it would have been nice, some of them thought, to have the grandson of the late Pastor Davis to fill his shoes. But clearly there was no changing Chip's mind.

But the next day at church, Chip's decision was turned on its head. As he took his place behind the pulpit to offer his departing sermon, the words became like a frog in his throat. She had slipped unobtrusively into the last open seat in the back pew, and with one deft hand movement, flipped her thick, brown hair back behind her shoulder, and nailed him with her eyes. Even from that distance, he could make them out, along with the warm smile she offered the other congregants.

And just like that, Chip knew he had to stick around.

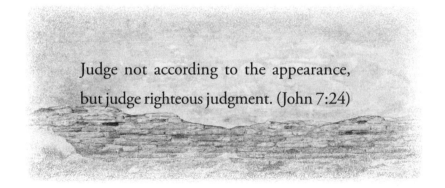

Judge not according to the appearance, but judge righteous judgment. (John 7:24)

CHAPTER 4

The three of them stood in reverent silence over the small mound of fresh earth. Margaret laid a bouquet of assorted roses on the mound and moved back to stand and look on with Tessa, as Jacob positioned a pine headboard.

"Daisy," it read in carved lettering. "Faithful to the end."

Tessa mustered a weak smile. "It's fitting."

Margaret sighed. "Doesn't say enough. It never could. She was something special."

Jacob didn't yet trust himself to speak. Daisy had been *his* dog, really. That hole in the ground was small compared to the one now in his heart. The house would be too big without her underfoot, too quiet without the sound of her overgrown toenails clicking against the floor.

Tessa gave Jacob a hug, and they stood there for what seemed like a long time. "I'm sorry I didn't get a chance to say goodbye," she said. "My plane was late getting in. Connections weren't good, then going through customs took forever."

She had, in fact, only just arrived. Her two suitcases still sat at the head of the gravel driveway, where the taxi driver had left them. She hadn't even been up to the house, stunned to see her grandparents standing under the weeping birch tree in the front yard, Jacob patting the last shovelful of dirt onto the grave. Standing there now,

she suddenly felt that her white dress, picked that morning to em-
ulate life and new growth, a fresh start, was inappropriate or even
an unintended mockery in this place of grief and stillness beneath
the trees. Jacob had found Daisy out on the shoulder of the road
near the mailbox. That faithful old dog had been waiting for him,
as she did every time he left for town. Jacob couldn't tell if she had
been hit by a passing car or had just died in her sleep. She had no
signs of being hit so he chose to believe the latter. He couldn't bear
the thought that she could have been struck down. She had been a
constant companion for so long.

It seemed ages since Tessa had left for Spain. After leaving Flat
Plains Bible College, Tessa told Jacob and Margaret she wanted to
go on a missions trip. Jacob put her in contact with a small Christian
mission organization that ministered in mostly Catholic countries.
Since Tessa had been so influenced by Teresa of Avila while attend-
ing Flat Plains, she felt drawn toward reaching out to Catholics,
particularly in Old World countries. Spain was perfect. A whirlwind
of history, language, and cuisine—the reality proving itself to be so
much more satisfying than the dream. The ministry of evangelism to
Catholics had been extremely difficult. It was one thing, she learned,
to preach the Gospel to sinners who realized what they were; it was
quite another thing to penetrate the hardened veneer of a religious
system that proposed to offer participants a chance at heaven if they
were "good" people who followed the prescribed religious rules.

Now that she was home, there was so much she wanted to tell her
grandparents—how she had grown in the faith, ministered to the poor,
had a burden for the lost—especially those lost in a pseudo-religious
maze, as she had been . . . but it would have to wait.

In one sense, the three of them had already walked together
through Spain and other parts of Europe. The wonders of the Internet—e-mail and Skype, in particular—had allowed Margaret and Jacob to keep current with Tessa's travels. Yet, speaking into a computer
camera and seeing faraway faces on a monitor was not the same as
being there, holding hands, drinking Margaret's famous lemonade,
and downing one hot muffin after another while laughing and sharing
their experiences with one another. Daisy's burial scene made her

feel robbed, in a sense. Tessa knew she was being selfish, but she had been so looking forward to a happy reunion. She had undergone a transformation since those difficult days at Flat Plains and had walked the soil of a foreign country sharing her testimony and the hope of the Gospel with all who would listen. She'd been part of the sadness and the rejoicing of people's lives and had seen God's hand providing in so many ways. Yet, for the time being, she was prohibited by death and sadness from celebrating the glad homecoming that should have been hers. It just didn't seem fair.

Then, looking upon the deep sadness etched into the lines of Jacob's face, she repented, with a deep sense of inner knowing that she was, indeed, at the right place at the right time. There was ministry to do here as well.

After the humble burial service for Daisy, the three of them walked to the house without a word said. Jacob had collected the suitcases and led the way up the front porch steps. He paused once to look back at the grave. "Something always dies," he said to no one in particular then went inside to carry the suitcases up to Tessa's bedroom. Margaret and Tessa exchanged concerned looks. Tessa spoke softly so her voice wouldn't carry through the screen door. "Wow. I've never heard him talk like this. He's really hurting over Daisy."

Margaret bit her lower lip, stopped to consider for a moment whether to reply or not, then motioned for Tessa to come with her to the far end of the porch. She lowered her voice to just louder than a whisper. "It's more than that," she said. "You don't know he just resigned from his position on the board at Flat Plains Bible College."

"What?!"

Margaret waved Tessa quiet, looking over her shoulder at the front door. "Shhh. He'd be embarrassed to know I told you. He'll tell you himself all in good time and when he's ready. But I can't pretend to you." She took a deep breath. "He also resigned from the board at Sheep Gate just before he left for Flat Plains. And he hasn't been to church all summer."

Tessa's mouth hung open, and she looked away shaking her head. "This doesn't make sense," she said. "I'm going to go talk to him."

Margaret laid a hand on Tessa's arm. "No, no, don't! It would humiliate him. He's going through something very personal, and you facing it head-on would only make it worse." She dropped her hand from Tessa's arm and looked out over the fields. "I've been with that man a lot of years," she said, "We've had hard times, easy times, but he's always been such a rock, always seeking the Lord through every trial. But lately, it's like the light has gone out of him. His finding Daisy today was just one more of life's hard blows for him to have to take and deal with.

"I've caught him looking at the house, Tessa, and the barn . . ." She gestured with her hand. "Well, as you can see, they've got that run-down look. The barn and the house both need new paint, and other things are in serious need of being fixed up. He's getting older and can't get to them like he used to. It doesn't bother me much, but I think it vexes him. I'm thinking he feels he can't do his part anymore. Then, there was that scare with you at Flat Plains with the false doctrine and all. It tore him up inside, knowing a college we trusted turned out to be, well, not a safe place for you at all. And to think he and I had placed you directly in harm's way."

Tessa acknowledged, "Well . . . how could either of you have possibly known?"

Margaret dismissed it with another wave of her hand. "Doesn't make any difference whose fault it was honey—even if it was no one's. For afterward, even though we got the victory, he was kind of worn out. Between you and me, Tessa, I think he's just plain tired—life-weary even. And it scares me. Because I love that old man, and he's good and kind, and a man of God. I hate to see him going through this . . . and I don't know what to do . . ." Margaret's voice broke and Tessa moved in close to put her arms around her.

"Yes, you do, Gran," she whispered. "We both do." She bowed her head until it rested against Margaret's snow-white hair. "Oh, Father," she said, "You see what we don't, and You understand the struggles in the heart of Your precious servant, Jacob. In Jesus' name, we ask Your help, Lord, that You would lead us all in the way we should go, comfort us in this struggle, and give us Your strength to keep following Your Son."

As they held each other, a two-door, light green sedan once again cruised slowly on the road by the Brown property unseen by anyone.

O n the outskirts of town, the lone waitress of the Birch Bark Bistro made a pretense of sweeping the outside walkway in order to better examine the unfamiliar person sitting at one of the three patio tables. Myra Kettridge was intrigued. While strangers were commonplace this time of year, to Myra, this one just didn't fit the bill as a tourist or someone in a state of transition.

A lone female, this customer had thick hair piled up and covered with a plain, dark headscarf that even obscured part of her forehead. Not a strand of hair protruded, so Myra was unable to tell the color. The upturned collar of a white jacket covered the woman's neck, so any jewelry she might have been wearing was hidden. Plain, dark slacks ran the full length of her legs, meeting their end with stylish, yet comfortable-looking, slip-on shoes. Nothing from the neck down gave away any specific information about her. But she was a study in contrasts.

To a keen observer of human nature—which all longstanding waitresses are—the woman appeared to be trying a little too hard to be seen as "average." In other words, she did not want to draw any attention to herself. Yet she failed to note the contradictions in her dress. For instance, the top half of her face was shielded by a pair of huge mirrored sunglasses even though the midmorning sky was a comfortable cloudy blue. The remainder of her face she kept lowered into the folds of the town newspaper, the *Birch Barker Weekly*. But she only pretended to read. She hadn't turned to a new page in the past five minutes. Plus, as she held the newspaper with one hand, she seemed to be fiddling with something on the table with the other, using the paper as a cover. This mysterious-looking woman hadn't bothered to come into the diner but instead had just pulled up in her car and seated herself at one of the outside tables despite shivering in the cool morning air. Moreover, she ordered tea in a contrived voice, feminine, to be sure, but strained, like it didn't quite belong to her.

By this time, Myra's internal, human radar device had overloaded, blipping off the charts, to where she found this conundrum of a woman to be nothing short of maddening.

Then, came her one big break.

The woman began talking into her newspaper. Myra drew closer, within a few feet. With the whirling dust Myra sent spiraling upward into the sunlight, the woman coughed, looked up sideways from the newspaper at Myra, and balked. Myra pretended not to notice and proceeded to play the part of an airheaded waitress sweeping out of sheer boredom.

The woman ducked back into the newspaper. "Where are you?" she snapped. Myra was now nearly close enough to touch her. *So, it's a smartphone she's tinkering with,* she thought. Under her breath, the woman growled, "It's day nine. You got that? Day nine! What? You're breaking up . . . say it again, more slowly. . .Yes, yes, now will you listen?!" She continued, "He's back, and so is she. No, no . . . I did see him but didn't hear the conversation. I was too far away." The woman paused then began again, "How soon can you get here? Look, I don't want any excuses. There's a time element involved. I need help, and I need it now. What . . . ? Hello . . . are you there . . . can you hear me . . . hello?" The woman sighed in exasperation as she stared down at the black screen on her phone. She looked up at Myra and grimaced.

Myra smiled an intentional sweet smile. "Can I get you some more tea?" she asked.

"No." The woman tucked her smartphone into her purse, took out some money, and plunked it on top of the now discarded newspaper. In one swift, sharp movement, she pushed back the chair, rose, and walked briskly to her car. Her stride was purposeful, but elegant, like she had long since been accustomed to the finer things in life. She opened the driver's side door and slid inside, keyed the ignition, then drove away.

Myra watched the disappearing vehicle and could not keep from speculating. Movie star perhaps. They can be pretty eccentric. Myra shrugged, and as she reached for the money, she was already thinking of the juicy gossip that would begin with her. Her smile gave way to a frown. "Hey!" She turned sharply in the direction of the now empty road and sighed. *Great,* she thought, *there goes that tip.* She looked ruefully at the colorful crumpled foreign bills laying on the table. *Oh well, I won't be in this town much longer.* Myra had high hopes for life in the big city and could hardly wait to leave. Already her boss had begun interviews for a new waitress.

In the quiet of a late Monday afternoon in Birch Valley, Tessa strolled down the south end of Charles Street. The bright summer sun filtered through a stately row of elms, casting warm shadows on the sidewalk before her and setting the wide residential lawns on fire with an almost iridescent green. Wonderful, old, Victorian-style homes set back from the street held their own with the elms and were inviting to look upon with their open, front porches and bench swings or wooden lounge chairs. From someone's backyard, a dog barked half-heartedly then stopped—an old dog, perhaps, as Daisy had been, sounding off out of a time-honored sense of duty at anyone who might be passing by. The warble of songbirds wafted in from a gentle breeze from every quarter. Spain had been terrific—a great experience, she thought. But this town was home—a place where people still said hello to one another as they passed on the street, where the air was fresh and invigorating, and where classic pickup trucks were a common site.

Pickups?! You know it! How novel it felt to be sitting behind the wheel of Gramps' old 1970 Chevy, with most of its tan paint worn away by years of dust, flying gravel, and blizzards. Before coming into town that day, Tessa had spent the afternoon cruising the backcountry and traversing logging roads that switch-backed into the Rockies. At every bump in the road, the Chevy's suspension squealed like a mechanical banshee throwing Tessa upward from the front seat, flipping her pony tail back and forth, making it look just like her beloved horse Sassy's tail when she was swatting flies. When Tessa finally made it into town, it was almost four in the afternoon. "Don't hold dinner for me tonight," she had told Margaret that morning. "I'll grab something." But other than a couple apples she had taken with her, Tessa forgot all about eating. Now in town, she pulled the vehicle into a parking spot by the town center's gazebo, shouldered the door open, swung her legs out the door, and in one smooth motion, hopped down onto the asphalt. The library was still a few blocks away, but Tessa craved a slow, thoughtful walk through her own nostalgia.

Everything was as Tessa remembered it, but it was as if things had moved, been rearranged, not geographically, but in her mind. Or perhaps her heart. She had seen so much during the time she had been away. She had lived through a variety of incredible (and sometimes impossible) situations and had been to the very land that had been calling to her imagination. Coming back now was almost surreal, dreamlike even. She realized it was not the town of Birch Valley but she who had changed. And she liked the feeling. The old, familiar despising of small-town life, coupled with the imprisoning feeling of being holed up in a remote mountain hideaway—all that had vanished, and she no longer felt the desire to escape or get away. Nor did she feel driven any longer by her hunger for the new and exciting. She welcomed the return to a simpler lifestyle and concluded that the old saying—"you can't go home again"—could not be further from the truth, not for her anyway. She *had* come home, to family, to the place that spurred her forward in her search for true meaning. Work remained to be done, of course, but at least it could be done here. At least here, she could rest in the love of family. As she walked, she felt the heartache of a sad homecoming wash away. "Thank you, Lord," she whispered.

Her return on Saturday had not been all bad. At dinner, Jacob had rallied from his melancholy and they all talked long into the night, partaking of hot muffins for dessert and emptying a couple glass pitchers of lemonade. Huddled together on the overstuffed couch (Jacob's personal afternoon snooze bed), with the goodies on the coffee table before them, they spoke in the most lively and animated of manners as she regaled them with tales of her spiritual "exploits," and as they, in turn, filled her in on the refreshingly mundane details of the farm life she had come to miss. Then there was Sassy, sweet, mellow Sassy, who nickered at Tessa's approach to her stall, whose velvety muzzle stroked her face with horse kisses. For quite some time before going to bed that first night, Tessa had sat on the barn floor with her back to the rough plank wall, inhaling the pungent fragrance of fresh hay and manure while beside her, Sassy contentedly munched her alfalfa.

The only empty spot in the reunion had Nathan's name on it. He had been preaching the last few Sundays in another struggling church in tiny Heaton, fifty miles from the Canadian border. Jacob had said that Nathan always left Birch Valley early every Saturday morning so he could sleep at the church that night and be ready for the Sunday morning and evening service. He took his time during the long drive back to Birch Valley and hadn't yet made it home before nightfall Monday. She had ached to see him but couldn't fault him for not knowing her expedited schedule. Anyway, it would be worth it to see the look on his face when she hunted him down Tuesday morning.

The morning after she arrived, waking an hour before dawn, Tessa had sat in front of the east-facing bedroom window with the lights off, looking out over the night fields, watching the resident gray owls make one final, silent fly-by in stealth mode in their never-ending nocturnal quest for live prey. The day had begun with a lonely, liquid birdsong, just one, followed by a smattering of others in the pines overlooking the fence rails. She watched the distant ring of peaks—at first dark and foreboding—slowly etch themselves against a lightening sky while beginning to glow in an array of cool colors before giving way to a warm yellow. She held her breath while the first probing shafts of sunlight slid between the mountains to touch the pasture below her window. This was one of the things she had been waiting for since her arrival back home—to once again, in real time, witness the light of a new day, as if God were saying, "Welcome home, Tessa."

Yes, with all its current troubles and future uncertainties, it was home sweet home.

And uncertainties there were. The reunion with the Sheep Gate's congregation at yesterday's service had left her elated, and the sermon by the new young pastor had been exhilarating. But it had also been vaguely disturbing, though she couldn't quite say why. Standing on the church's front steps after the service, Margaret furrowed her eyebrows and her gaze was filled with questions. "What did I tell you?" she asked, in reference to that morning's breakfast conversation about Chip. "Pretty potent speaker," she had said over a cup of coffee. "And a nice enough young man. But I find myself on guard around him. Knows lots of Scripture, but . . ." She shrugged and sipped more coffee.

Now, after a serene afternoon driving around in the countryside in her grandfather's pickup, Tessa felt anxious to get into town and make the one stop she had planned to make that day. Already it was after five.

As she walked toward Birch Valley library, she noticed its unimposing structure of red brick that appeared stuck in a time warp somewhere between its founding days and the present. A broken concrete pathway, fraught with renegade weeds in the pavement cracks, led to the single step flush with the library's front door. As she reached for the handle of the big glass door and began to pull, it swung open and a small, balding man darted out the door and brushed up hard against her. Tessa staggered in a backward direction, losing her balance as her legs buckled. Her purse swung from her shoulder in a half-spin, the flap opening, resulting in half its contents scattering all over the walkway. She grabbed the old steel pipe rail to keep from hitting the ground and for a moment squatted not far from the concrete.

The little man exclaimed, "Oh, I'm so sorry!" He reached out his hand to help her up, and she took it. He apologized profusely, his face an embarrassed red. Both he and Tessa crouched down and began gathering up her purse items.

"That's okay, really," Tessa assured him. Her voice sounded a bit shaky. The man grabbed whatever he could with both hands and dumped them unceremoniously into her open purse.

"Oh, I just can't believe how careless I am," he murmured, looking down and scanning the walkway for anything they both might have missed. He stood abruptly, mumbled "Forgive me," then turned on his heel and hurried down the street.

Tessa's lips curled in a half grin, and she shook her head slightly as she swatted dust from her jeans and this time, more tentatively, pulled open the library door.

Once inside, Tessa headed straight to the receptionist's desk where a slender, middle-aged woman worked on some posters behind the counter. She had long graying hair pulled back into a ponytail and rather large glasses that framed her face with the old-fashioned, "I am the town librarian, gone spinster" persona. As far as women went, Tessa noted she was not at all unattractive, but deliberately and intentionally plain. With her hair a different style and thinner, more close-fitting glasses or contacts, and perhaps a touch of makeup, she could be quite "fetching" as Margaret would say. "Man judges by outward appearance," she heard from inside her, "but God looks upon the heart." Tessa felt convicted over her hasty appraisal of this woman. "True, Lord," she whispered. "Forgive me."

The librarian looked up and smiled. "Can I help you?"

Tessa smiled back. "I was told the library has some new computers, and I need to do some research."

"Absolutely," the librarian said. "It's the best tool for that kind of thing. Do you have a library card? I'm sorry, I don't recognize you."

"Oh, I've been gone for quite a while. I just got back," Tessa said, head down and hands sorting through her purse. "I'm going to need a new card. I must have lost mine somewhere along the way . . ."

"Of course!" the librarian exclaimed. "Now I know who you are. Theresa . . . uh . . ."

"Dawson," Tessa said. "You can call me Tessa." She stretched out her hand.

The librarian smiled and took Tessa's hand in both of hers. "Millie Forsythe. And yes, I know you don't know me. I'm pretty new here. Moved to town only a year ago. I love it. Came out here from California. So many laws, you can't breathe, you know what I mean?" She chattered on. "The *Birch Barker Weekly* did a piece on you last week. Picture of you and your grandparents. You're associated with some missionary group that went to Spain, right? First two years you just went overseas for the summer missions trip, and this last year you did the whole twelve-month thing, right?"

Tessa nodded. "Yes, that's right. Boy, you sure keep up on things."

Millie raised a faux-imperious eyebrow. "Well, of course! I'm the librarian," she dispassionately declared. "I know everything."

Tessa smiled but then in frustration sighed. "I'm sorry, I know you must need my I.D. for the new library card," she said, "I'm going to have to . . ." and she upended her purse onto the counter. She shrugged apologetically. "I almost got knocked down outside. Stuff flew everywhere—car keys, loose change, even my wallet, which is where I keep my I.D. . . ." Her voice trailed off, and she looked quizzically at a small, white note. "That's odd . . . I don't recall having a sticky note in my purse . . ."

"What is it, sweetie?" Millie asked, looking down at the purse's contents, now scattered in front of her on the counter. Her gray ponytail fell forward.

Tessa stared. Three words in bold red jumped off the page at her: BE VERY CAREFUL

Millie's eyebrows furrowed as she scrunched up her face. She looked from the note to Tessa and back again. "Could that be from your grandpa? Mr. Brown's your grandpa, right?"

Tessa looked up, puzzled. "Couldn't be," she said. "I saw him this morning, and he didn't mention anything. And why would he put a sticky note in my purse anyway?" She put the note back into her purse, intending to ask Jacob about it later. Maybe he did put it in after all. Finally locating her driver's license, she pushed it toward Millie and in a few minutes was issued a new library card.

"Can you show me where the computers are?" Tessa asked.

Millie came out from behind the counter and motioned for Tessa to follow. They proceeded to an area walled in on three sides, containing a long table with a half-dozen chairs and the same number of computers. "You can have an hour on any one of these," she said, then, in a conspiratorial tone added, "that's the official position. I have to say that when other patrons are around. But . . ." she threw a quick look over her shoulder at the older couple seated by one of the windows, reading, "you go ahead and take as long as you need. It's the least I can do for you as far as a 'welcome home' present goes." She winked and went back to the reception area.

For the next four hours, Tessa remained glued to the computer surfing the Net. At first, she wasn't quite certain what she was looking for and wound up going down a dozen or more cyberspace rabbit trails. When she exhausted those, she clicked out of user mode, leaned back against the cushioned chair, and stared at the now blank monitor, mildly frustrated.

She found herself thinking back again to yesterday's sermon. Chip had proven to be all his supporters claimed of him—full of energy, funny, uncommonly magnetic despite his youth, and he had a way of talking as if . . . as if . . . Tessa had been the only one in the room and he was speaking only to her. His knowledge of Scripture seemed prodigious. He could quote from a variety of books of the Bible without having to thumb through one. His message was one of hope, acceptance in God's love, and the promise of divine help to walk spiritually.

Afterward, Tessa felt motivated; everyone did. And hanging around to meet him after the service, she felt reassured he was a pretty decent sort of guy. He was young, dedicated, and she had noticed (smiling to herself while still staring at the blank computer screen) his interest in her appeared to be less theological and far more personal. Her mind toyed with the idea of that. He was good-looking, seemed like a perfect gentleman, and was a Christian. Those were pretty important criteria for someone who . . . what? *Well . . . maybe someone I could really relate to.* What she meant, even as she thought it, was that she wouldn't mind being asked to go out with him. She could think of worse ways to spend an evening. *Bet he's a great conversationalist, too.*

She frowned. Yes. She just bet he was. Something nudged her as if a phonograph in the middle of a really good song drug clear across a record. Then she got it. For all his sermon yesterday, including all the adrenaline he poured into it, he didn't actually say anything. It wasn't so much that his message was bad or counter scriptural, but it just seemed . . . what was the word? Fluffy. That was it. Marshmallow-like—full of air and tasty but lacking any real nourishment. That's what she had been looking for on the Internet at the library. Sermons like his.

She found some all right, many of them quite good in their own way, preached by experienced pastors and ministry school graduates, many who had attained a certain level of recognition in their field. But all during her research she could feel something was not right, not so much a deliberate commission of error, but perhaps an omission of scriptural substance. It all sounded good, but . . .

"Tessa?" Millie stood behind her with an apologetic expression. "We're about ready to close."

Tessa sat up straight and looked out the window across the room. Darkness had begun to settle over the valley. "Wow. Have I been here that long? I'm sorry."

Millie smiled. "I wish *all* my patrons were so studious."

Slinging her purse over her shoulder, Tessa rose from her seat, thanked Millie, then walked out into the cool evening air. She stood on the front step a moment and took a deep breath, savoring both the quiet and the nighttime scents and sounds. Then she walked to the sidewalk and began the three block walk back to the pickup.

The streets were nearly deserted, just a kid here and there on a bicycle, and one young couple strolling, arm in arm, on the opposite side of Charles Street. She smiled at them, then felt a pang of loneliness. Mission work had always been so time-consuming that she'd rarely even given a thought to an intimate relationship with anyone, but now that she was home, not only thoughts but feelings began to stir deep within her—feelings she had never before had the inclination or time to deal with.

Tessa reached the end of the last street and began the walk across the road to the gazebo where the old pickup waited. As she rummaged through her purse for the keys, an explosion of light blinded her. She froze and instinctively raised an arm up over her eyes. From roughly a hundred feet away, tires squealed, a most unexpected intrusion upon the small town quiet of the night, and a car lurched forward, racing toward her. Tessa's fight or flight mechanism kicked in as she tried to catch her breath. She turned onto the sidewalk while making a run for it, but the vehicle swerved sharply to match her movement. Suddenly, from right behind her, only a few short inches away and too close for comfort, the clean, sleek blur of metal roared by her. The side mirror on the driver's door caught the lower end of her purse strap and snapped it from her shoulders, spinning her around and flinging its contents into the air. She fell hard to her knees, her long hair flying wildly every which way through the cold night air. The vehicle then fishtailed around the next street corner, showing itself to be a light green under the street lamp.

Tessa remained on her knees, shocked and staring at the disappearing car. Her breath came in broken gasps and fear gripped her heart and constricted her throat. The pungent odor of burnt rubber hung in the air. Hurried footsteps sounded behind her, coming from the gazebo. A teenager with a skateboard under his arm knelt beside her. "Are you okay?" he asked, his eyes as wide as saucers.

Tessa swallowed hard, nodding without speaking. The boy helped her to her feet, looking down the road where the racing vehicle had been moments earlier. "I can't believe it. I saw the whole thing. That guy tried to kill you."

Tessa stood motionless, trembling, and unable to make sense of what had just happened. Her excuse sounded lame. Cotton-mouthed, she rasped, "Maybe he didn't see me."

Her knees hurt, and one of her pant legs was ripped with torn away skin protruding from the hole. Without thinking, she stooped and began gathering up the scattered contents of her purse, following their chaotic strewn pattern for almost fifty feet. The boy set his skateboard on the roadway and bent down to help her.

Tessa managed a smile. "Thanks."

Five minutes later, they'd found the last of her things. They stood and the boy threw an anxious glance down the road then turned to her. "You should report this," he said. "I know what I saw. He was trying to nail you."

Now standing in front of her pickup, Tessa hugged the purse to her and shook her head. "I just want to go home," she said. She climbed slowly into the pickup, slipped it into gear, and drove off. The young man watched her pull away and then glanced at the darkened road where the rogue car had disappeared. Shaking his head and shrugging his shoulders, he stood with one foot on his skateboard, then pushed himself off again into the night.

And the Lord shall deliver me from every evil work, and will preserve me unto his heavenly kingdom. (2 Timothy 4:18)

CHAPTER

5

Tessa's knees hurt. The homey, familiar clatter of dishes and the scent of crisp bacon made her feel somewhat better, but what happened last night kept playing and replaying in her mind. Was the boy accurate in relaying what he'd seen? From her perspective, first blinded, then trying to run, she couldn't tell what was going on. She only knew she had to get out of there. That made for a hazy recollection of the incident as a whole. The pain in her knees was real—she knew that. And she also understood how close she'd come to being hit—probably killed. It was impossible, therefore, to dismiss the incident entirely or with absolute certainty, as though it had been a mere accident.

For just a second, Tessa considered the alternative and shuddered.

"Tessa, dear, are you cold?" Tessa looked up from her plate and realized she'd been toying with her food, distractedly pushing it around on the plate. Margaret hovered over her, frowning.

Tessa smiled and shook her head. "No, Gran. Just . . . thinking."

She had hobbled into the house fifteen minutes after the near hit last night only to be fussed over appropriately by Margaret. "Just fell," Tessa had explained, and Margaret had left it at that after applying a splash of hydrogen peroxide and a stretchy knee bandage put her right again. Tessa had also skipped eating a plate of leftovers Margaret had saved for her in favor of going straight to her room.

For a long while, she had lain on her bed in the dark, staring up at the ceiling and wondering about what deeply disturbed her. Even while overseas the past year and the two previous summers, Tessa had never encountered any real danger aside of a few instances of mockery by Spanish locals, and once, a veiled threat from a priest who forbade her to evangelize, but nothing life-threatening to where she felt in immediate danger. Eventually, she had fallen asleep on top of the covers. When she woke, it was a half hour past the break of day.

Even now, hours later, sitting in the kitchen where everything seemed so "normal," she pondered as to why she didn't tell the two of them about the incident. She paused a moment, and her fork hung halfway between her plate and her mouth. It struck her that she referred to it as an "incident," but not an attempted "hit-and-run."

"How are my favorite two girls this morning?" Jacob had waltzed into the kitchen through the screen door, which slammed back into place causing Margaret to look up from her cooking and level a deliberate frown at him. "Sorry, Ma," he said. He took his place at the head of the table. "Boy, I could eat a horse," he mused, "Sassy excluded, of course."

Tessa smiled and forced herself to eat. Margaret dished up a heaping plate of eggs, home-fried potatoes, bacon, and biscuits in front of Jacob, who rubbed his hands enthusiastically. He raised the chipped, empty white mug that was his favorite. Margaret poured ink-black coffee from the old porcelain pot. "Thank you sweetheart," Jacob said, then gave Margaret a wink.

Tessa watched Jacob dig in. It pleased her that his mood seemed to take a turn for the better and be on the upswing the past couple of days. Although he didn't go with her and Margaret to church on Sunday, his initial depression seemed to have lifted for the most part, and it was, once again, as if she'd never left home.

As was his habit, he'd already gotten an hour into his chores and was famished. "Hey," he said around a mouthful of biscuit. He lifted a finger in pausing, then gulped down some coffee. "I'm heading into town in a while. Tractor needs a new belt. You wanna' come? Never know what, or who, you might see there."

He raised his eyebrows and smiled at her knowingly. She regarded him quizzically. "What?"

He took another bite. "Come and see," he replied. She offered a little, confused laugh, but declined. "No, I think I want to hang out here today. I still have some catching up to do with Sassy and the neighbors. I told the Hartmans I'd stop in today. I can walk there. I still have the keys to the pickup, though. Gran, have you seen my purse? I came in this way last night . . ."

"Here it is," Margaret held it up by the broken strap. "What happened?" she asked. "And my, it's dirty."

"Must have happened when I fell," Tessa said lamely as Margaret set the purse before her. Tessa undid the snap and rifled through its contents. Her hand closed in on the keys, and when she produced them, the sticky note she'd seen at the library came up with them. It fell to the table, and she stared, remembering, holding the keys in midair. Jacob furrowed his brow. "Something wrong?" he inquired. Tessa shook her head "no," and with her free hand snatched the note, a little too quickly it seemed, and crammed it back into her purse. She tossed the keys to Jacob, and he caught them in midair. The mood had turned. Jacob went back to eating and Margaret to her dishes, but she sensed them both watching her. She felt heat rise to her cheeks and took another bite.

"I think I will go to town with you after all, Gramps," she said with forced enthusiasm. "I forgot to check something at the library yesterday."

It was good to be back even though he'd only been absent a couple days. Nathan Shepherd slid into a corner seat by the window, hands folded on the table, looking out at the street. The morning sun's rays slanted over the line of shops across the street, leaving the north-facing storefronts covered in shadow. The rays then spilled over onto the south windows of the little corner diner where Nathan sat with a folded *Birch Barker Weekly* on the table before him while he soaked in the morning sun's warmth and let his thoughts wander. The past few weeks had been a blur. Between helping

Jacob with the farm upkeep before he left, then helping Margaret with some of the tasks while Jacob was out of town, and then getting tapped by the pastor-less congregation in Heaton—he had been kept enormously busy. As for the farm, Jacob had let things go lately, and the old place showed it. The neglect was mirrored in Jacob's face, and it seemed he was always tired. When asked, Margaret was uncharacteristically evasive, but Nathan had determined to corner the old man soon and impress upon him the need to open up and share what was weighing so heavily upon his heart. Something was seriously wrong in Jacob's personal life. And surely he'd seen the change at Sheep Gate Church—the same Jacob who first took on and then plowed through the spiritual rubble of Flat Plains would not leave his old congregation to fend for itself. One sermon was enough for Nathan to realize that this Pastor Chip Davis thing was a bad call by a church board. Yet he'd heard of no inquiries made by Jacob. That was contrary to all he knew of the strong Christian man he'd met a few years ago and had come to know so well and respect.

Then there was Tessa.

With Tessa on her full time mission's trip the past year, Nathan had pulled up stakes and engaged himself in traveling whenever his Bible school courses were not in session. He had knocked about the Western states primarily, with the exception of one brief sojourn to the East Coast near the end of winter, just before he headed back to help on the Brown farm during Jacob's absence. He found Times Square and Independence Mall intriguing, but he was still a small town boy at heart, and he could never see himself actually moving there to live. Still, the experience was an eye-opener and educational. During the time he'd spent back east, he had witnessed two muggings and had crossed paths with dozens of bag ladies, homeless men, addicts, pushers, con men, and gangbangers. It was great opportunity there for ministry, but in his heart, he knew it was not for him. On his way back across the prairies, Nathan had stopped to check on his old friends, Katy and her husband Sam at Flat Plains Bible College and found them still at work and happily expecting their first child. Finally, it was on his return to the Rockies when he knew this was where God had led him.

With Birch Valley as home base, he picked a new direction each summer and hit the road. There was something to be said for footloose and fancy free summertime living, but at times the loneliness attached itself to him like a living thing. Nathan had never before experienced the depth of that Scripture, "It is not good for man to be alone" as he came to experience it in his ongoing travels—especially lately. Summers spent working for the Forest Service, working construction, scrounging up minimum wage restaurant jobs, or being hired on-site to dig ditches or split firewood to earn ample "moving on" money seemed exciting at first, but eventually the novelty wore off, and it all too quickly became just another lifestyle that left him wanting. Roots were what he needed, and he loved Birch Valley but had met no one—since Tessa—who attracted him in any sort of permanent or lasting kind of way. Nathan was not an openly sentimental man, but he had kept every one of her letters and, in both his spirit and his heart, had gone with her to foreign lands, vicariously savoring the foods, interacting with the people, and alternately and respectively either enjoying or hating the climate. He wished he could have gone with her but in retrospect believed the separation had been God-ordained. Before she left, they had known each other only briefly, after all, and perhaps this was a time of testing the waters of deep feeling. The last thing he wanted was to rush into a premature relationship. It could wind up hurting them both.

Looking back, it seemed fitting that they had taken things slowly. What began as a friendship blossomed into something just short of a declaration of mutual love. During the school year, they spent as much time together as possible when he wasn't immersed in his studies. Going for walks, reading the Word and praying together, drives out on the highway, or just hanging out at the town coffee shop bonded them with strong but unspoken feelings. And now it seemed that his time away from her had both been long and yet a mere heartbeat. His feelings for Tessa elated and tormented him at the same time. In all that long stretch of time, neither one of them had written or spoken to one another of anything of an intimate nature.

And too, he certainly hadn't allowed himself any kind of hope therein, but yet, in all this time, he still could not get her out of his mind or his heart. Reading between the lines of her many letters, he sensed she felt the same way. He wondered if she had ever stared at the Spanish moon at night, thinking of him watching the same moon over the Rockies. What really drove fear into his heart more than anything, however, was that her markedly different life experience in a vastly different world would certainly work a number on her, perhaps tarnishing her small town girl love of a simpler life. Had the blue jeans and flannel shirts of her teen years been replaced by more sophisticated attire, not only in the physical but in her heart and mind as well?

He would not have long to wait now to find out. Her imminent return both overjoyed and scared him at the same time. He wasn't certain how to address her anymore and feared that their initial meeting again for the first time in over a year would be awkward at best. He shook his head, thinking of the volume of famous love poems he had recently picked up at the local bookstore. Now it seemed a stupid or even clumsy gesture. He had some vague idea of romance at the point of purchase, and yet, sitting alone in a coffee shop found himself grimacing at ridiculous mental images of himself greeting her on bended knee at the bus stop or airport, clenching a rose in his teeth and quoting Shakespeare's sonnets. He wondered which would hurt more—the thorns pricking his gums or trying to showcase his feelings for her in Elizabethan English.

"Can I help you?"

Nathan looked up and smiled. "Yeah, thanks. I . . ." He became tongue-tied and his mouth dropped open. "Katy?"

The waitress returned the smile, but only in part, regarding him with dark, puzzled eyes. "No," she said tentatively, "my name's Zhanna." Then she smirked. "Is this a pickup line? I think I have heard this one before . . ."

Nathan raised his hands defensively and shook his head. "No," he said, "I . . . uh . . . really, you look . . ." He cocked his head to one side and stared. "Are you sure you're not . . ." Zhanna looked down at him in knowing condescension, and with her order book and pen still in hand, crossed her arms. "I know who I am," she said. "I have been me all my life. Now, can I take your order please?"

Nathan softened. "I'm sorry. Really. I'm not trying to, you know, hit on you or anything. It's just that you look so much like . . ." Unable to let it go just yet, "Do you have a sister?" he pressed.

Zhanna shook her head, still somewhat wary of his intentions.

"No," she said. "I am an only child."

Nathan stared, dumbfounded. She could be Katy Buckler, that bouncy roommate of Tessa's at Flat Plains. Or her twin . . . Same styled brown hair, tanned complexion, dancing brown eyes, and dimples. Even the accent was Katy's. "You're not going to believe this," he said, "but you look just like a good friend of mine. I mean, you could be her double."

Zhanna returned his gaze. "You are right," she said curtly. "I do not believe you."

For a moment they regarded each other in silence, then Zhanna smiled big. "Got you!" she said.

Nathan sighed in relief. "You do believe me?"

Zhanna nodded. "Sure. It is too early in the day for me to believe otherwise." She put out her hand. "I am the new waitress and pastry cook, and, as they say, chief bottle washer. I just arrived in town a couple of days ago. They hired me on the spot. That's good, yes?"

Nathan smiled. "Yes!" he said, and engulfed her little hand with his big one. The small brass bell above the front door rattled. An older construction worker sauntered in with a newspaper under his arm and took a seat at one of the rotating stools at the short counter. "I'm glad to know you," Nathan said, "And I won't hold you up any longer. Coffee and a cinnamon roll, please."

Nathan marveled at the startling likeness, but decided he'd better divert his attention to something else. He flipped open his own copy of the anything-but-newsy local newspaper. There was never, for the most part, anything much of immediate interest happening in the small hideaway town of 17,000, and what's more, he had purchased the paper only on a whim. A photo of a nun in full habit flashing a pearly white Hollywood smile took up the entire top of the front page. "Sister Genevieve to Combat Homelessness" it trumpeted and went on to note that the Carmelite nun, an immigrant from Spain, had set up shop on Henley Lane in a small vacant warehouse with upstairs living quarters connected. Located on a side street where many of the economically disenfranchised rented trailers or apartments, The Master's Way would eventually help Birch Valley's homeless and poor. Donations of food, clothing, and household items to be used in the ministry could be dropped off in the back, the story noted.

"She's doing a good thing, yes?" Zhanna set a massive cinnamon roll and mug of coffee on the table before Nathan as he looked up.

"Yeah, I guess," he said.

Zhanna shrugged. "She was in here earlier. You just missed her. She was asking if she could put us on her list for day-old food—bread and pastries, stuff like that—for her mission when it opens. Hal, the owner, isn't here, so she said she'd come back later and ask him. I think she'll get lots of help. This seems to be a friendly town, yes?"

Nathan nodded in agreement while glancing out the window momentarily. He then took a large swallow of coffee and promptly choked on it, coughing and staring. Jacob Brown's old tan pickup cruised by, and sitting in the passenger's seat was a lovely girl with one arm draped over the lowered window and her long brown hair streaming behind her in the breeze. Zhanna craned her neck to look outside, then looked back at Nathan. "You see a ghost?" she quipped.

"Tessa," Nathan whispered. "It's her. It has to be her." He looked at Zhanna with wonder in his eyes. "She's back," he said quietly, then smiled from ear to ear like he'd just won the lottery. He clapped his hands together and stood up so fast, he nearly knocked his seat onto the floor, and asked in a hurry, "Can you wrap this to go? And the coffee, do you have a foam cup I can put it in? I gotta get going before I lose her."

Zhanna collected the erstwhile breakfast and brought it back a moment later as a to-go. Nathan handed her a five. "Keep it," he said, all smiles, and headed for the door. He stopped so sharply his boot soles squeaked, and turned around. "Zhanna," he said.

Already behind the counter with a coffee carafe in hand, Zhanna paused.

"We're having a Bible study on Friday," he said. "We'd love to have you if you'd like to come."

Zhanna smiled apologetically. "I don't' think so," she said. "I'm not really into that scene. I was planning on hanging out with some friends Friday."

Nathan persisted with a smile. "So, you're not into hanging out with the One who keeps your heart beating and holds your life in His hands?"

The construction worker turned to stare at Nathan. From the carafe, Zhanna poured coffee into his mug. "Will you be there?" Zhanna asked, a glimmer in her eyes and a hint of a smile defining the corners of her mouth.

"Of course," Nathan replied. "I'll be leading it."

"Okay, then," Zhanna said, "I'll think about it."

Zhanna suddenly found Nathan's smile quite . . . encouraging.

"Seven o'clock," he called, pulling open the front door. "I'll pick you up here a few minutes before if that works for you." She gave a quick nod, and Nathan dashed outside and headed up the street.

Zhanna stood with the carafe and stared out the picture window after him. She didn't know who this Tessa was, but maybe the two of them should meet. A little competition never hurt anyone.

Tessa stood at the front desk with the small sticky note in hand, as Millie Forsythe leaned over the counter with both elbows and stared at it, shaking her head. "Nooo," she said thoughtfully. "I don't remember any little man in here yesterday. But then again, I was busy working on a bunch of posters most of the day for the writer's symposium next month. Most of the people who came in here yesterday are just a blur to me."

"Thanks." Tessa straightened up and stood idly fingering the little white note. It had to have been him, she reasoned, when he helped her put the stuff in her purse just outside. There was no other logical explanation. She'd ransacked her purse for some remnant Spanish coins just before leaving the farm yesterday—a scrapbook gift to Margaret of Tessa's missions trip. No note then. The purse hadn't left her side the entire time she'd been cruising the back roads in the pickup. She only took it out of the truck cab when she'd parked and walked to the library. The only time—the only time—it was out of her hands had been when she bumped into the little man. No—when he had forcefully bumped into her. She hadn't noticed at the time, but thinking back, the entire incident seemed orchestrated, premeditated even. It was a bit tight, but upon closer examination, there had still been plenty of space for him to squeeze by, even given how fast he was moving. In retrospect, it seemed as if he actually swerved into her, deliberately.

This is crazy, she thought, staring into space. *Why? Why would anyone do that?* And, if that was indeed the case, what in the world did the note itself mean? She tried hard to remember his features, but he was one of those nondescript individuals who blended really well into a crowd. *He was balding and had glasses,* she recalled, *gold,* I think. *No, black wire-rimmed. No. . .*

"Thank you so much." Tessa had been so lost in thought that she had only marginally noticed the habited nun who stood a few feet away, smiling at Millie. A black head covering over a white mantle, a simple drab brown habit reaching nearly to the floor, a silver cross attached by a sliver of chain around her neck—put it all together and she was the quintessential nun. "I'm trying to get the word out," she said pleasantly, "and I'm going to nearly every community building and store in the business district. God will remember your kindness."

Millie beamed. "Anything to help, Sister."

The nun had turned to the large bulletin board off to one side of the glass front door and tacked a colorful poster advertising The Master's Way. A collage of smaller photos danced across the poster front—nuns in traditional garb feeding the poor, offering medical attention, etc. Most of the imagery seemed to portray activities having taken place on some foreign field.

Just what the people in Birch Valley don't need, Tessa thought, and figured that evangelism would be a corollary to the nun's feeding and clothing activities. This was not good. Though she cared for and loved Catholics, she had seen enough pure European Catholicism to know the serious conflicts it presented to the simplicity of the Gospel. Sooner or later, Tessa knew the two of them would lock horns, theologically.

The nun turned and faced Millie again. She presented a gracious smile and extended a slight hand. "Please tell people about us," she said. "Food, clothing, prayer, or any way in which they can be of help."

"Will do, Sister," Millie said with a reciprocal smile. "And, welcome to the community."

"Thank you." The nun then noticed Tessa, gave a half smile while reaching for the door. She stopped and turned. "You're Theresa Dawson, aren't you?" Tessa's heart jumped as she looked squarely at the face in front of her. Tessa felt nervous—the nun's face, she didn't recognize, but something about her eyes were hauntingly familiar. Warm and strikingly clear, they gazed seemingly gently out from a tanned, delicately fashioned face. *Have we met before?* Tessa wondered.

Disconnected from her thoughts, Tessa smiled an uncertain smile. "Well, yes," she said. "How do you know me?"

The nun came forward to shake her hand. "I'm Sister Genevieve. I recognize you from your picture in the newspaper a couple of weeks back, with you and your grandparents. You know? The article said you were coming home from a mission's trip in Spain. Such a lovely country, isn't it? I was raised there. Lived there most of my life. Joined the order in Malaga. I've recently been sent from a cloister in New Mexico to minister here. I'm glad to meet you."

Tessa retained her smile but slightly frowned. "But didn't you just arrive?" she asked. "I mean, you are new here, right? How could you have read the paper if you weren't here?"

The nun waved a dismissive hand. "Oh, that. Whenever they send us out to another community, our superiors always have us read the newspapers of that place for at least a month beforehand, go online to the Chamber of Commerce, that kind of thing, to familiarize ourselves with the people and the town. It gives us a heads-up of an area and some understanding of the local needs."

"Oh . . ." Tessa nodded. "Your English is good." The nun's ultra-feminine voice did indeed betray a foreign accent.

"Thank you," she replied. "I spent many years in the United States before moving back to Spain to join the order. Well, I must be off. So much to do . . . so much to do . . ." Her habit rustled, and the simple black wooden rosary dangling at her side clattered softly with each step. As she turned to go, she waved to Millie and reached for the door.

Before she could think, Tessa called after her in Spanish, "I hope you have a wonderful day, sister. Nice meeting you."

Without skipping a beat, the nun turned with one hand on the door and beamed. "And you, Theresa," she replied in continental

Spanish, "come see me at the mission sometime!" Then she opened the door and strode purposefully down the step to the sidewalk, her white mantle gleaming in the morning sun.

Tessa stood watching, her mind wholly preoccupied with processing what had just happened. She didn't even notice Nathan bound up the single step outside and practically take a flying leap into the library. "Tessa! You are back!"

Tessa's eyes focused on the strong, brown-haired man looking down at her. His smile was infectious. "Nathan," she breathed, and reached for his hand with both of hers. "I . . . I mean . . . oh, it's good to see you! I was going to search you out today!"

"I got the wind knocked out of me when I saw you and Jacob drive by. Good thing everybody drives slow in this town. I ran down the street the whole way, trying to keep an eye on the pickup. I saw it parked outside Garvin's Automotive, and Jacob told me you were here."

"I hear you're preaching."

He nodded, almost embarrassed. "If you can call it that. At a wide spot in the road just this side of the Canadian border. Heaton. Beautiful little place. Great folks. They advertised; I answered. They like me. That's the whole story."

Tessa lightly squeezed his hand and her eyes held his. "They're fortunate."

Nathan smiled and said softly, "I'm the fortunate one. *You're* back..."

Tessa blushed and looked down. "I missed you, too."

Tessa's face flushed even more as she realized they were still holding hands. If Nathan noticed, he feigned ignorance. Instead, he held tight and pulled her to the front door. "Let's go for coffee," he said hurriedly. "We can talk. I want you to tell me everything. Hey, did you know that at Birch Bark Bistro there's a girl who looks just like Katy Buckler?"

CHAPTER

6

J acob Brown muttered to himself as he stamped down the last shovelful of earth around the base of the mailbox. *Second time this week*, he thought, *second time! Well, I'll have a surprise waiting for them next time. I'll bed this baby in concrete. Next time they hit it, they'll be missing a car bumper.*

In the cool of the early mountain morning, his breath formed little puffs of steam around his face. He leaned on his upright shovel, thumbed back his hat, and swiped the back of his free hand across his sweaty forehead. He was getting too old for this. There was a time he could do this kind of thing all day long, and the only thing it would do was give him a better appetite at mealtimes. But now, his body ached like it had a permanent case of the flu or like he'd been run over by a Mack Truck. He felt a twinge in his heart area now and again as well but reckoned it might be more from stress than the actual farm work itself. He'd been at this an hour, replanting his fallen mailbox after the previous night's vandalism.

Everything was changing. He once knew a time when no one would even so much as think to bother anyone else's property, but this new crop of kids just seemed mismatched for decent living. More and more lately he felt like an anachronism, a throwback from a different era, and that he just didn't belong anymore.

Looking skyward, he scanned the breadth of it and felt insignificant and infinitesimal. "Lord," he prayed, "I just don't know what's happening. I'm so tired, and I'm wondering if there's still a place for me in Your plans. Maybe I've outlived my usefulness." He looked down at his muddy boots. "I don't even go to church anymore, Lord. Can't bring myself to do it. I'm just plain worn out, and I don't know why."

He looked up again, and the words nearly choked him. "Help me," he whispered heavenward. "Show me the way. Don't let me dishonor You. Folks keep looking to me for answers, and I don't have them anymore. They seem to think I'm something I'm not. I feel like I'm living a lie. Father. Help me to be faithful to You. Lead me, O Lord . . ."

The hum of an engine cut into his prayer. He looked over his shoulder as a dusty black-and-white jeep pulled into the drive beside the roadside stand. From behind the wheel, a young man with brown hair and a lanky frame donning a cowboy hat and jean jacket pushed open the driver's door and dismounted. Irritated by the interruption, Jacob produced a smile. "Hello, Nathan," he greeted. "I kind of expected to see you here today."

Nathan grinned, extending his hand as he walked forward. They exchanged grips.

"Tessa tells me you two had a great time getting caught up yesterday," Jacob said. "Said you're really enjoying the preaching stint up Heaton way. Could work into something more steady. Lots of little mountain communities don't have a resident preacher. I can see lots of ministry in the circuit thing. The old-line Methodists did that when the country was new. You'd be following in their footsteps."

"Don't think I haven't considered it," Nathan replied with a smile. "But I'm kind of leaning in another direction."

Jacob rubbed his stubbled jaw and pinned Nathan with a steady gaze. "Well," he said, probing . . . "have you thought about maybe putting in for a position at Sheep Gate?"

Nathan responded carefully, "I don't think I'd qualify in their eyes. Besides, I hear they really like their new man…"

Jacob shrugged. "I heard that, too. Margaret went with Tessa the other day. She's been going pretty much every week, even though she just said that this Chip guy is "okay" whatever that's supposed to mean."

Nathan looked at him quizzically. He hesitated. "So . . . you haven't been back to church since the board asked this new guy to preach? It's been two months since then . . ."

Jacob sighed. *Here we go*, he thought to himself. "Haven't felt up to it," he said. "Been pretty tired lately."

"But . . . Jacob, they need you. You should have put in for the position. You know what that church needs better than anyone, and you're the kind of mature pastor they all need."

Jacob raised his hand, with his palm extended outward. "I'm getting too old to keep fighting other people's battles. They've got the tools at Sheep Gate. They just need to use them. They'll do okay."

Nathan looked away a moment, then down at his feet. "Ah . . . I heard you resigned from your position on the board at Flat Plains Bible College. Why Jacob?"

"You heard right," Jacob nodded. "And I resigned from Sheep Gate church board as well. But you know that, too." Jacob's eyes narrowed, daring Nathan.

Nathan shook his head. "I don't understand. Aren't you the one who always said nobody is ever too old for the Lord's work? How can you give up when the church and the college need you more than ever?"

Jacob grimaced. "Put the brakes on it, son. There's a time and a season for everything. Anyway, you're still way too young to fully understand these things."

It was a pathetic excuse, and Jacob knew it the moment the words left his mouth. He also knew it was the perfect way to end Nathan's inquisition. He changed the subject. "So, do you have a line on anything definite on your other ministry applications?"

Nathan nodded, took off his hat, and held it in both hands. "Yes sir." Jacob thought it oddly out of character.

Sir? thought Jacob. *What's with the 'sir?'*

Nathan continued. "I'm considering doing a youth pastor internship this fall. I've put out a few resumes. Got a nibble or two."

Jacob nodded. "Good. You gonna stay in state, or . . ."

"Idaho is home. I'm actually shooting for a small town church somewhere. There's another one way upstate over the other side of

James Pass that's just a speck on the map. I took a drive up there last week. Real little place. Cowboys still ride their horses into town and tie them up at the general store. Lots of working ranches in the area, and a lot of ranch kids. I think I'd really like it there." He hesitated, looked away, and nervously cleared his throat. Jacob furrowed his brows and narrowed his eyes while continuing to look at Nathan, making Nathan even more nervous. "I . . . uh . . ." Nathan continued, ". . . think maybe . . . Tessa would, too . . ."

Going out of his way to hold back a smile and play dumb, Jacob drawled, "So, you think Tessa'd like to see the place, too, eh?"

Nathan nodded. He looked into Jacob's face searching for some sign of approval.

"Well, why don't you ask her? She's still free, no job or anything. She's got time to go. It'd be a nice trip for the both of you. I would think they'd put you up at the church there for a day or two? Maybe Tessa in the current pastor's home? I mean, if they want to make an impression on you to stay and such . . ."

Nathan smiled, opened his mouth to speak, then thought better of it. He then shook his head. "Jacob," he said, "you're playing me. I think you know good 'n' well why I'm here."

Jacob guffawed and clapped a gloved hand onto Nathan's shoulder. "Son," he said, "you remind me of someone from a long time ago. And I was just doing what her pappy did to me. You can't fault an old guy for having some fun."

Nathan grinned, nodded, and chuckled. "Is she up at the house?"

"You bet," Jacob said, still grinning. He leaned close and winked. "She's been waitin' for you aaaallllll morning."

Nathan jokingly pushed him away. He cocked his head and looked at Jacob in earnest. "Well, do I have your blessing?"

"You asked her, yet?"

Nathan shrugged. "Well, no. I mean, we just met again yesterday after so long, and I didn't want to rush . . ."

Jacob shook his head. "Youth is wasted on the young. Son," he said, "nothing I say is gonna make any difference if she turns you down first." He motioned with his chin to the house. "Go find out. Then come ask me."

Nathan positioned his hat back on his head, and with a look of determination, strode up the drive toward the house. He took the porch steps two at a time, knocked on the screen door, and disappeared inside.

Jacob stood leaning on the shovel and watched the door a full five minutes. Nathan's direct nature wouldn't allow Tessa longer than that to say "yay" or "nay." Like clockwork, at the five-minute mark, Nathan poked out his head, all grins, and waved his cowboy hat at Jacob. Jacob lifted his hand in salute as Nathan again ducked inside. Jacob later learned that it wasn't exactly a proposal—Nathan told him he wanted *that* to be something special, somewhere special. But he said he couldn't wait a minute longer to tell her how he felt and in what direction he hoped to go with their relationship. He said he couldn't wait to tell her he'd been in love with her from almost the minute he met her when they sat in his jeep on a cold blustery day, and she cried while drinking hot chocolate.

Jacob raised his stubble overlaid face to the sky again. A faint sadness welled up from deep within him. "Lord," he said, "I've always thought of her as . . . my little girl. But I guess she'll be Nathan's now." He always felt in his heart they would end up together.

Ezekiel Hazlett stood at the head of the soup and bread line, savoring deep whiffs of hot chicken aroma while cradling his paper bowl in both of his dirty hands. From under a forest of gray beard, he licked his dry, cracked lips, while underneath his ratted, long, silvery hair, his head throbbed. Although it was noon, he hadn't yet had his first requisite cup of coffee, and the hangover resulting from last night's unofficial meeting of the "Birch Valley Hobo Society" (or, known by locals as "that bunch of drunks and losers") was, at present, killing him. For the moment, food was optional, but if he didn't get some of that go-juice soon, he'd be waking up on a slab in the sheriff's office basement, and they'd be prepping him for his allotted 3 x 6 feet of American soil—or, as the locals would have it, a "waste of taxpayers' hard earned money."

The back section of the Birch Valley Community Center hummed with inordinate activity to Ezekiel's way of thinking. He didn't recognize half the people behind him, queued up for the noon meal. He considered them interlopers. This was his stomping ground. So many newcomers breezing through town lately and most without means, or worse, unapologetic freeloaders—a term he would have resented had it been applied to him. He'd done his bit for society, he figured, fought for God and country way back when, and now was living off the fat of the land. *After six years of service, a purple heart, and bronze star,* he reckoned, he was owed *at least one free meal a day.* Made him proud to be an American. Land of the free and home of the brave.

The beginnings of a thought occurred to him in the midst of his brain fog. He thought hard to remember the all of it. The effort of thinking physically hurt his brain.

"Well, how's my favorite homeless veteran today?" The sound of Jacob's voice interrupted Ezekiel's conjumbled thoughts. Jacob stood behind the long stainless steel counter, a large metal ladle dangling from one hand. Hot steam from a massive pot of chicken soup curled about his face.

Ezekiel straightened up, squaring the shoulders of his full 5'9" frame and squinted at Jacob. "I am not homeless," he corrected with a subdued ostentation, "I am merely temporarily displaced."

Jacob smirked. "Yeah, and from that red in your eyes, I can see you're also temporarily hung over. Again."

"A mere setback, my good man," Ezekiel said, and held out his bowl with shaky hands.

"Zeke," Jacob urged as he filled the bowl, "why don't you come home with me for a few days? I told you we've got a couch just your size. The missus would be happy to have you. You know she really likes you. She was up at five o' clock this morning making this soup because it's your favorite. And she's on me all the time to get you to come back to the farm with me. You could work off the room and board . . ."

Ezekiel shivered dramatically, hunching his shoulders and making a face. "That word," he said, "is an affront to a man of my—at the moment—indelicate situation. And the name's Ezekiel, my friend.

'Zeke' makes it seem like I've got a brother named 'Bubba' somewhere." He added an apology. "No offense to any Bubba of your own
acquaintance, you understand."

Jacob chuckled a little, shook his head, and waved Ezekiel on, who
by then had grabbed a large foam cup from the stack in front of the
stainless steel coffee urn and depressed the black button. He lifted the
full cup to his varicose nose and inhaled. "That'll do," he murmured
and took his regular seat by the window overlooking a back alley.

Even as he was filling the other bowls, Jacob could feel an approaching rumble pulse through the building and build to a deafening
roar. Just outside the open back door, a Harley pulled up, revved a few
seconds more, then died. Within moments, a massive form filling the
doorway blocked the sunlight. All conversation came to a standstill.

"Uh, oh," Ezekiel breathed. He took another bite, keeping his
eyes on his meal but the corners of his eyes on the stranger. From
beyond the open doorway, the tinny jingle of music from a passing
ice-cream truck seemed strangely out of place.

The biker dude standing in the doorway was a big man, a stranger,
black-bearded with long, oily, dark hair kept in place by a faded red
bandana wound around his forehead. His black leather jacket and
chaps complemented his old Levis and worn cowboy boots. Reflected sunlight shimmered from the checkered stock of his holstered
.45. From under a canopy of dark, bushy eyebrows, his eyes made a
thorough sweep of the room, then he walked to the head of the food
line where Jacob stood watching from behind the counter. The words
"Hell Boys" blazoned in red on the back of his jacket broadcasted his
associations. He gestured to the soup pot. His voice was low, a bear's
warning growl. "That for anybody?"

Jacob nodded, attempting a smile. "If you're hungry, it's here."

The man nodded, grabbed a bowl, and leveled a hard stare at
a young drifter who had been first in line. He extended the bowl
to Jacob who noted the bloody skull and bones tattoo on the top
of his right wrist. Jacob filled the bowl almost to overflowing and
doubled him up on the bread. A long time doing the bread line
ministry had taught him that a man with a full stomach is less
likely to make trouble. The stranger filled a coffee cup then took

a seat at the far end of the room with his back to the wall. He ate in stony silence.

Hushed conversation filtered back into the room. The young man first in line threw a glance over his shoulder at the biker and, with the counter between them, leaned as close to Jacob as possible. "He's got a gun!" he whispered hoarsely. "Aren't ya gonna call the cops?"

Jacob shook his head with resignation. He'd been there before. "No," he said. "First off, the phone's out of order in this part of the building, and I don't have a cell phone; and second, it's not against the law to carry a firearm in public here. Just calm down. Doesn't look like he's here to make trouble."

The youth was incredulous. "You mean he's allowed . . . ?"

Jacob sighed and spoke as if he were addressing a child. "Son, this is cowboy country. Everybody and his brother packs heat. It's just part of the deal."

"But he could shoot somebody . . ."

Jacob smiled intrepidly. He slid back his apron to reveal a .38 snub nose in a little belt holster. "So could I," Jacob said, and looked right at him unblinkingly. "Now, you want to eat or talk?"

The young man backed away in horror and disgust. "This place is crazy. Outta here," he said, and ducked out of line to hurry to the back door. He was followed by two of his eavesdropping friends. Jacob shrugged and filled the next bowl.

In ten minutes, the biker was gone. He had cleared his own table, had offered a curt "Thank you," and a moment later had saddled the Harley and roared off. Jacob stared after him, wondering.

"Could've been close," Ezekiel said from across the room.

Jacob moved from behind the counter, wiping his hands on his apron. "But it wasn't," he said. "And, I was praying the entire time." He smiled. "Who knew that in the winter of my life, I would find myself in such a dangerous line of work?"

Ezekiel chuckled, took the last bite of soup, and chugged the remains of his coffee. "Hear you may be losing some customers," he said wryly, "to that nun across the street, no less. They say she's opening her own eatery for Birch Valley's finest."

Jacob nodded and frowned. "I've seen the posters. Sister Genevieve, I think she calls herself. Can't figure why a nun is setting up shop for "the homeless" here of all places. There are only a half-dozen 'registered' homeless men in this town. It's not like it's a big mission field or anything."

Ezekiel shrugged.

Jacob raised an eyebrow and grinned. "How about you?" he prodded. "Am I going to lose you to the competition?"

Ezekiel chuckled and shook his head. "Nah. I believe in customer loyalty. As long as your wife does the cooking and not you, I'll keep coming back."

"**W**ell, we hired him for the long term, however long that is." The voice on the other end of the phone line was beginning to get a little irritating.

Jacob Brown sat in the black, overstuffed chair in his office feeling the extra soft padding attempt to absorb him bodily, as always. When he shifted positions, one of the ancient springs creaked or perhaps even pinged from somewhere deep within the upholstery. Normally his favorite chair, at the moment it flat out refused to make him comfortable. Jacob leaned his face forward into the phone, his words strained. "You did what?!"

"What did you expect?" Rob Carlton asked, exasperated. Jacob could see the church elder throwing up his hands in disgust. "We needed someone, he was available, and . . ."

"Good reason," Jacob muttered sarcastically.

"Annnndddd," Rob went on, "he's been filling the house. People love him. You probably would, too, if you'd . . ." His voice trailed off.

"Come to church?" Jacob interjected in an exasperated tone. "Yeah, I get it, Rob. But some of us have been doing this kind of thing a lot longer than others. I've sat on more boards than I can really even remember. I'm taking a sabbatical from the whole thing. And yeah, that includes church. I was gone for a while and have been taking some time off church since I got back. This farm doesn't run itself, you know."

Rob's voice was placating. "Oh, Jacob, come on. You know I didn't mean it like that. It's just that, well, we had to make a decision. In fact, we'd asked Chip to stay about a month ago, but he said no then. Just this past Sunday he did an about-face."

Jacob's eyebrows furrowed. "Why'd he change his mind?"

"Said he'd thought it over. I don't know. I'm assuming he prayed about it and was led to accept. We were overjoyed, of course."

Jacob shook his head. "Rob, he's a kid. I haven't seen his resume, but from what you tell me, he's never even pastored a church before. Man, when I was twenty-five, I didn't know zilch. He's got no life experience . . ."

"What kind of life experience does a man need to be able to preach the truth?" Rob asked. "Ezekiel and Timothy were just 'kids,' too. I'm forty, and I sure don't know it all. Neither do you. But that doesn't stop us from preaching . . ."

"That's not the point," Jacob cut in. "I've never even heard of Wayfarer's Seminary. Sounds like a diploma mill."

Rob hesitated. "I . . . guess it went defunct a couple of years ago," he admitted, "so we weren't able to access his records, but," he added, "lack of a long-term seminary education doesn't necessarily mean he's unqualified. If you'd just come listen to him speak . . ."

Jacob nodded vigorously, waving a dismissive hand. "Yeah. I'll give him another try. In the meantime, I'd like to talk with him in person if I could. Just to get a better feel for where he's coming from."

"Excellent idea!" Rob agreed. "In fact, he's in the office right now, and we were discussing that very thing when you called. We can come right over if now's a good time."

Jacob paused, somewhat surprised. "Okay. Yes. Bring him over. I'll ask Margaret to put on the coffee, and we can chat for a bit."

For a few minutes after hanging up, Jacob sat, idly passing the cordless phone handset from one hand to another, thinking. Maybe he was being too judgmental. After all, he hadn't even met the boy . . . young man. He sighed. And who was he to judge, anyway, he who hadn't been to church for the past two months, struggled with his daily Bible reading, and lately offered up prayers to God that were more like the desperate pleas of a frightened child? His ability to discern might not be as sharp. Jealousy, perhaps? A religious prejudice based on looking down upon someone spiritually because he's young? He bowed his head and rested his elbows on his knees, still holding onto the cordless. "Lord," he prayed, "if it is me, if I'm the one standing in the way, or if this attitude is stemming from my own deceitful heart rather than from the conviction of Your Holy Spirit, then show me. Please. I'm . . . confused right now. And really, just a little scared. I know I don't have the right to ask much right now, but lead me, Father, please, in Jesus' name."

Lifting his head, he called out, "Margaret, could you . . . ?"

She poked her head in the open doorway and smiled. "It's already on, dear. We've got some of yesterday's oatmeal cookies to go with it. Think that'll be enough?"

Jacob nodded, smiling but looking tired. "Fine," he said.

The two of them were there in fifteen minutes. Margaret and Tessa buzzed around with coffee and cookies, and though the women disappeared around the corner and left the business to the men, both remained within earshot. Jacob couldn't fault them for eavesdropping. This concerned them every bit as much.

Chip Davis seemed to be all Rob had portrayed him to be— genial, humble, and courteous. He knew his Bible, too. Jacob quizzed him on several key passages, and Chip even rattled off the before-and-after verses. He openly admitted his seminary training was incomplete, but asked Jacob to give him a chance. He made it a point also to remind Jacob that church attendance had dramatically increased in the time he had stepped up to the pulpit. While Jacob couldn't fault him for pointing to his success, something about the way Chip said it was vaguely self-promoting. This troubled Jacob, though he couldn't quite say why.

One more thing gave Jacob cause for concern, and that was the way Chip looked at Tessa. It was not leering, but something resided behind those warm brown eyes that Jacob just didn't like. Or trust. Perhaps it was the grandfather in him, but the same kind of protective spirit stirred in him as it did when Tessa was threatened at Flat Plains three years earlier. Perhaps even more disturbing was the way Tessa returned Chip's gaze. The two of them kept exchanging glances and smiles. All well and good, except for just this morning Nathan had made it plain he wanted to call on her. *Who is to say Chip isn't the decoy sent to divert Tessa from Nathan, the Real McCoy?*, Jacob wondered.

When Rob and Chip rose to leave, Margaret showed them to the door, thanked them for coming, and bid them to come back for a more congenial and lengthy visit. When she returned to the office, Jacob remained seated in his chair, hands locked underneath his chin, eyes focused on something only he could see. "Well J.B.," she probed, "how did it go?"

Jacob smiled wryly. "You tell me. You heard it all."

Margaret looked over the top of her glasses at him. "Is that a rebuke?"

Jacob shook his head. "Not hardly. I'd have done the same thing." He stood up and walked to the other side of the room and gazed out the window to the driveway. "Something's wrong," he said. "Can't quite put my finger on it, but something's not right."

Margaret eyed him closely. "He talks a good talk, said all the right things."

Standing at the window with his hands interlaced behind his back and watching the car disappear down the dusty road, Jacob thoughtfully replied, "And maybe that's just it."

Tessa sat on folded knees on the old braided rug in the attic. It was the safest place to escape the church politics that had just invaded the Brown's sanctuary and remember what life was about. A lifetime of bittersweet memories lay scattered about the old wooden chest, its lid thrown back and tarnished brass fittings exhibiting a broken, burnished golden hue in the late afternoon sunlight that filtered in through the attic window. It was a dingy place—a musty treasure house of long unused items, but it remained the sanctuary of a youth spent with the Browns. Her bedroom, bright and cheery, had seemed almost a mockery and affront to those early years after her parents died. She preferred a gloomy oasis, one more well-suited to the moods of a stormy teenage life and upon discovering the attic, she made it her own little retreat. Here, she could sit on the old two-by-four bed frame and stare out the dirty window, letting her mind drift back to a simpler, happier time before losing herself in the fertile and pristine playground of her own imagination.

Sassy understood. She was the only one, Tessa felt back then, who shared her wildness of spirit, her desire to run anywhere away from fenced pasture. Losing a loved one will do that to you. That much she knew. Losing two at the same time was like being hurled from a cannon into a black hole. In the attic, she didn't have to look into questioning, sympathetic eyes, or listen to one more, "I'm so sorry, dear. But we love you. Let us help."

The Browns did indeed love her, that much she could be sure of. But it was easier to shut them out than to deal with the incurable wound of her twice-broken heart.

Now, sitting alone with the warm afternoon breeze blowing through the wooden-paned window, Tessa felt an overwhelming sense of sorrow. How she had hurt Jacob and Margaret! They were not her birth parents, but blood relatives could not have treated her with more love, respect, and patience. And they had offered her the promise of an eternal security she had denied even existed. How Christ-like they had been to her back then . . . full of compassion, steadfast, and longsuffering. She'd never be able to repay them for all their kindness. But she was determined to try.

It seemed ironic, as she poured over the items on the floor, that this was the sum of her life up until she moved in with the Browns as her new foster family after the accident that took her parents. The old chest, a gift from her mother, was the only link to her past. But its contents revealed little: a couple pieces of clothing (an old dress and a sunbonnet), some fake jewelry, several books, and a half-dozen framed photos.

The one treasure she cherished above all the others was *The Complete Works of William Shakespeare*—a gift from both of her parents on her seventh birthday. It had been old even then. She lifted the massive volume and traced a finger over the worn leather cover and gilt-edged pages. It must have been an expensive book to buy for parents of only moderate means, and surely they knew she would have no use for it as a child. They both had loved literature, however, as was evident at many of the quotes they had put in the book's margins, and it was apparent they must have read it together often. She still knew little of Shakespeare's works, but it sparked an interest in her to read and glean more of who her parents were. Memories were all she had of them now, and even some of those had grown hazy. It dawned on her this book would enable her to gain access to at least one corner of their world and understand them more as an adult, through their eyes, as experienced through Shakespeare's writings.

She put the book aside and returned the other items to the chest just as footsteps sounded on the creaking wooden stairway. Margaret opened the door to the room right before ducking down to avoid hitting her head against the low slanted ceiling. She saw Tessa curled up in a corner on the floor and stopped. "Oh, I'm sorry, dear," she said. "I didn't know anyone was in here. I was coming up to look for something."

"It's okay, Gran. I was just leaving anyway." She flipped the chest lid shut and clicked the latches into place. She held out the book for Margaret to see.

"From your parents?" Margaret asked in an upbeat tone. Tessa nodded and handed the book to Margaret who turned it around in her hands. "Beautiful," she said. "They don't make them like this anymore. This is a real collector's item."

"I never read it," Tessa said, embarrassed. "I was too young and too . . . well, you know. I've been thinking a lot about my parents lately, and I kind of wanted to get to know them all over again. But with a different heart."

Margaret gave her a shoulder hug. "Jesus does that for us, doesn't He? Changes how we look at everything." She squeezed once more and moved across the room to contemplate a stack of cardboard boxes. "So much stuff," she murmured. "I'm trying to remember where I put a book on Birch Valley history. Marlene Hendricks asked about one of the original settlers, and I told her I'd loan her the book . . . Ah! Here it is. Right on top. I can't believe it."

They both left the attic, each holding a book, and filed down the stairs to the second floor hallway. From there they both moved side-by-side down the stairway leading to the living room. The heel of Tessa's knitted slipper caught on a nail in the cracked edge of one of the steps, and she instinctively grabbed at the banister with one hand to correct herself from falling while Margaret reached out a steadying hand. Tessa was saved from a bad fall, but the volume of Shakespeare flew out from under her arm and flipped through the air, gilt-edged pages flashing before it landed on the living room floor with a thud.

"No!" Tessa cried. She ran down the stairs, stooped, then picked up the book off the hardwood floor. Anxiously, she turned it over and over to inspect it for damages. Margaret came quickly to her side and hovered over her.

"Oh, I'm so sorry, dear," she said. "I've been asking Jacob to hammer that stair down into place for some time now. Is the book all right? Anything ripped? Is the binding still intact?"

Tessa moved her hand over the binding, examining the pages; except for a couple of bent leaves, the book still appeared intact. She straightened herself and replied, "No, it's okay." Then she flipped to the back. "Wait a minute," she spoke in a strange tone of voice.

"What is it?" Margaret asked with obvious concern.

The cloth binding on the inner back cover had torn, revealing the corner of a hidden sheet of paper. Tessa fingered the exposed corner, then carefully peeled back the fabric to dislodge the folded sheet. Taken aback, she unfolded the paper and stared. "It's a letter . . . from . . . my mom," she said shakily.

Margaret let out a little gasp, and her hand went to her mouth. She could not stop looking from Tessa to the letter and back. Touching Tessa's shoulder, she said, "Maybe you should read this by yourself. I'll be in the kitchen if you want to talk about it."

She backed up a step, turned, and went around the corner to the kitchen. Between the near fall and the hidden letter, she was shaken.

For an instant that seemed to last years, Tessa stood staring, first at the personalized letterhead—Marilyn Dawson—then at the signature at the bottom of the page. Some of the text in between was blurred. She noted that the ink was only splotched in certain places, distorting some of the text, as if something wet fell onto the paper from above while the letter was being written.

Tessa blinked, trying to hold back tears. She walked to the bottom step of the stairway to sit down. Swallowing hard, Tessa wiped a tear from the corner of her eye and began to read.

Dearest Theresa,

I hope you don't mind my using your full name here. I've always thought it a lovely name and that it suits you, a beautiful, gentle child, a lover of horses. No child can ever know the full extent of his or her mother's love, so neither can you, now, understand the fullness of the love I have for you. Let it be enough for you to know that I would give my life for you, as would your loving father, and we have cherished you since the wonderful day you came into our lives. I hope that your knowing this will make it somewhat easier what I have to tell you now.

I had never believed the time would come to write this letter. I've often thought of telling you, but you are so young now, and I'm afraid of hurting you or destroying your trust in us. I don't think you would understand. My thought is that you will keep this book with you through the years, and someday, somehow, if we are ever separated in this life, you will read what I wrote in the margin of the book telling you about this letter. I pray you will read it through the eyes of your heart and know it was written with many tears. Your dad and I love you, Theresa. Please keep that before you as you read this.

For several months now, I've had a foreboding feeling that makes it necessary to tell you what I never wanted to. Your father and I were childless for years. We desperately wanted children, cried for children, but I could not conceive. So, after many years of heartache, we decided to adopt a child. We put out a discreet ad, and within one day we were approached by a very respectable man, a lawyer, who told us he had a wonderful baby girl who needed a home. The mother, he said, was an unwed young woman who could not care for a child. Though we were sorry for the young woman, whom we were never to meet, your father and I were overjoyed that our greatest wish was finally coming true.

It was a private adoption, and we were granted custody of the child within a week. We knew this was unusual. The process of legal adoption takes much longer and requires home inspections, personal interviews of the prospective adopting parents, stacks of paperwork, and so forth. Much of the process was either bypassed or hurried through. There was an understanding between the three of us (the lawyer, your father and I), that we were not to ask too many questions. We didn't. We only knew that we fell in love with that child the moment we laid eyes on her, and from that point on, she was ours. We were given a birth certificate— which should be in your personal effects, if we should be separated—and a considerable joint bank account was opened in our names, with the money to be used to care for the child for the first two years. Your father and I had always lived frugally, and we knew that if we moved to a bigger house, bought a new car, or bought new expensive things, we would attract attention to ourselves. As soon as we were given the child, we moved across the country, to a quiet neighborhood, to start over. We continued living as before, only with a new baby. We never saw or heard from the lawyer again. Theresa, you were that baby.

Tessa looked up from the letter for a moment. With wide eyes, she sat frozen, realizing she had failed to take a breath for some time. After filling her lungs again, she returned to reading the letter. Deliberately, she took a deep breath then returned to reading.

Oh, dearest child, please forgive us for not telling you. We honestly didn't know what to do, and we decided to wait until you were old enough to understand. But I don't think we will be able at this point to talk it out. I'm assuming that, if you are reading this letter, your father and I have passed on. Theresa, I don't know how to say this, but the reason for writing all this is because I feel that something is very wrong. I have a sense of, I don't know, danger. Not for us, but for you, should anything happen to us. I know now that the way we did this was wrong. But it's too late to undo it. And we do not regret for an instant having you as ours. You are our child, and always will be.

But I've been thinking what would happen to you if your father and I should die before we can tell you face-to-face about all this. I think of this lawyer, even after the five years since we adopted you, five years since we've seen or heard from him, and I realize we knew nothing about him. He gave us his name, but I don't think it was real. And, he was obviously representing someone. Why all the secrecy? And why so much money? But now it's too late to do anything about it, except warn you. I'm suddenly so afraid for you.

You are probably a young woman by now. So please, be careful. And remember that, no matter what, your father and I love you with all our hearts.

With All My Love,
Mom

Tessa started to set the letter down but did not feel it slip glibly from her numb fingers. It rustled as it hit the floor. For a long time she stared straight ahead, expressionless. "My real parents aren't my real parents?" she whispered to no one.

Then a tremor ran through the full length of her body, and from her heart she convulsed with sobs. She did not hear Margaret, who hurried in from the kitchen. She did not feel the arms around her, the rocking of two bodies, the words of comfort spoken. Tessa only knew that her world, or the world as she once knew it to be, was being washed away by her tears.

When my father and my mother forsake me, then the Lord will take me up. Teach me thy way, O Lord, and lead me in a plain path. (Psalm 27: 10-11)

CHAPTER

7

"This is ridiculous." Chip Davis leaned his back flat against the living room wall of his grandmother's house and slid into a crouch. Positioned on crooked knees a couple inches above the linoleum floor, he looked at the wet paint roller in his hand then at his blue-flecked jeans and flannel shirt. He let out a heavy sigh and in the most juvenile manner. He wasn't cut out for this kind of thing—manual labor and the like. And he definitely wasn't like his Bible-preaching grandfather. No, Chip was more like his daddy. *Yeah, well, dad's in prison*, he thought, *so maybe his opinion isn't worth much.* There had to be an easier way, but Chip didn't know what that might be. The old man had always told him that running a good scam took a lot of planning, and at least the appearance of being a working guy often factored into that. Chip examined the work he had already done—kitchen, bathroom, and most of the living room. A new carpet needed to be laid over the ancient linoleum, but at least he could hire someone out to do that job with his grandmother's money.

Sunlight filtered through the three picture windows facing the road. They were in dire need of a good cleaning. "I guess I do windows too," he said to himself out loud. But once the house was done, he'd be able to live more comfortably in it until it sold, and even that might take awhile. Like everything else with regard to the economy, the housing market had plunged, and nobody got their asking price. Plus, he could turn down reasonable offers on the house in his grandmother's name, if he could convince her to give him carte blanche. It could become his base of operation until he sheared these sheep of all he could.

But then, there was Tessa.

"Arrgghhh!" He laid the paint roller in the pan, forcefully pushed himself upright and began pacing. Why did she have to appear out of the woodwork? And what was the attraction for him anyway? Some hometown girl with a shy smile and a pair of hazel eyes that pierced your very soul. He stopped to recall that afternoon's coffee and "grill" at Jacob Brown's house and how Tessa swept gracefully into the room to serve them. She even made something as simple as offering cookies seem like a personal invitation into her life. And she favored him repeatedly with shy, penetrating glances that seemed charged with interest . . . in him. Yeah, those eyes of hers.

Chip vacillated between being miffed to daydreaming to back to being miffed again. He changed clothes and stomped out of the house. *People don't even lock their doors*, he thought with contempt as he slid into the front seat of Mrs. Davis' '81 Lincoln Continental—a classic. He floored the accelerator and cranked the steering wheel hard, the rear tires spewing gravel as he veered onto the road. Coffee! He needed coffee! The coffee at his grandmother's (*These hicks still say granny or 'gran' for short* he thought) was the kind of blasé stuff the old pioneers stocked up on for hard times. Tasted about that old, too.

A mile down the road he pulled sharply into the Birch Bark Bistro. Advertising Wi-Fi, the log cabin coffee shop would be a place he could kill two birds with one stone. He craved the social networking of the Internet, as his grandmother was so lost in the last century she never had her house hooked up. To gregarious Chip, living with such technological deprivation was like going through a serious withdrawal or the D.T.'s.

Chip grabbed a small table with two seats by the window and ordered an almond latte. He was pleasantly surprised that this backwoods coffee shack actually had a decent caffeine bar.

He logged onto "e-Pastor" and downloaded a generic sermon, the kind he could give a fifteen-minute tweak to and put his own personal spin on before memorizing it for Sunday morning. He even found an easy Sermon on the Mount message with a slide-show for youth that he could play up, perfect for this evening's service. The site had everything—hints for rising pastoral stars, an "Etiquette Corner" (to school neophytes in the pastor/layman relationship), and of course, a categorized listing of thousands of sermons, each tailored to a specific congregational profile. Although he doubted that was the site's original intention, it proved to be a tremendous resource for guys running a con—like him. After he picked and clicked, the sermon downloaded onto his hard drive for later retrieval. Business out of the way, he logged onto his uZone account. He did a quick search and nearly melted into the chair.

He hadn't thought to do this before. Tessa's photos from Spain and a few of her with Birch Valley backgrounds took their place before him on the monitor. Her long, flowing hair, her bedazzling smile, and her country girl expression all jumped off the screen at him and made him swallow hard. He was smitten. "Oh," he murmured, his gaze distant and chin resting on one hand, "the places we could go together. The things I could show you . . ."

"I'm game," a cheerful voice quipped. "When can we leave?"

"Huh?" Chip looked up, his eyes vacant. The waitress, smiling, set his steaming latte before him. He smiled back. "Sorry," he said. He blushed. He felt like he had just been caught with his hands in the cookie jar. "I was just daydreaming."

Zhanna came around behind him to look at his laptop monitor. "Nice," she said. "Beautiful country, wherever it is. Is she your girlfriend?"

"Uh, no," said Chip, closing the laptop and folding his arms conspicuously over it. "Just an acquaintance."

Zhanna smiled slyly. "I know her anyway," she said. "She was in here the other day with that other good-looking guy. The one who . . . oh, you don't know about that . . . but he told me I looked like someone he knew. Sounds like a pickup line, yes?"

Chip nodded. "Yeah." He processed that news and appeared despondent. "I didn't know she had a boy . . ." He looked up at Zhanna and attempted the closest thing to a smile. "Like I said, just an acquaintance."

Zhanna backed away and with a wink gave the "OK" symbol with her thumb and index finger. "Sure," she said. "I will forget that look in your eyes when you saw her picture." She made an exaggerated lover's face, with longing eyes gazing heavenward. Chip frowned.

As Zhanna moved back behind the counter, Chip's thoughts raced. *Another guy? Who? She just got back. How could anyone have time to . . . maybe an old boyfriend, someone who'd been waiting for her all this time . . .*

It hit Chip like a ton of bricks that he was jealous. His mouth hung open. How crazy was that? He didn't need complications right now. Really, he didn't even know this girl. Man, he was getting so distracted.

On the other hand . . . maybe this was a coincidence he could use or a happy accident. He was far too practical to believe in fate or divine providence, but marriage—or a relationship prefaced with a proposal—to a pretty local girl could earn him lots of points at Sheep Gate and the neighboring communities. People were already coming in from the outlying areas just to hear him preach. They had even done a write-up in the local newspaper about how the new preacher was flying in the face of the old religious establishment, breaking new ground, and bringing in new churchgoers by the droves. The people adored him. Maybe it wouldn't be so bad after all to cool his jets in Bubba Town for a while. Everybody has to start somewhere.

A poster on the community bulletin board caught his eye. The Master's Way posters were all over town, but he'd never actually read one. Now, from a few feet away, he poured over the text on the sheet, the photos of what looked like missionaries, and finally rested on the nun in full habit. Something about her smiling face made him do a double-take. Like a Rolodex, his memory flipped back through the years. After a moment, his mouth dropped open, he slapped his forehead with his right hand, and his short burst of laughter made the other patrons, as well as Zhanna, turn to look at him. Still chuckling to himself, he waved them off, shaking his head and glancing every now and then at the poster.

Smiling, he sat back in his chair and mulled over a lot of things while sipping away at his coffee and planning.

For the second time in an hour, Margaret knocked softly and leaned close to the door, listening. "Tessa, dear," she called, "are you okay? I've kept supper warm for you. Please come down."

From her seat on the edge of her bed, Tessa looked up at the bedroom door with puffy eyes. "In a minute, Gran," she said but had no idea how she could force both an appetite and a happy face. The entire week's events had sent her mind reeling. Looking around the room, she thought how everything had seemed so right just a few short days ago—so idyllic even. How she had loved coming home to the fresh smell of linen hung on the clothesline to dry, her familiar flannel patchwork quilt, and the antique night table where her beloved old Bible from Jacob lay with a tattered homemade bookmark. And yet now, she felt like more of an alien in Birch Valley than she ever had when she lived in Spain.

She pulled on her knitted slippers, struggled to her feet, wiped her eyes one more time, and threw the crumpled tissue into the over-flowing wastebasket by the nightstand. How could she let Nathan see her like this at the Wednesday evening church service? She dreaded facing *anyone* right now. But seeing no other choice, she opened the bedroom door and headed to the kitchen.

At the kitchen table, she picked at the fried chicken and biscuits with her fork. They tasted like cardboard. Margaret pulled up a chair and sat down beside her with a cup of steaming hot tea in her hand.

"Here," she said, smiling meekly. "This usually helps some."

Mechanically, Tessa took a swallow then sat staring at the cup. Margaret touched her arm. "Listen," she said, her voice sympathetic, yet emphatic, "I know you don't want us to mention anything to anyone, but you can't just do nothing."

Tessa covered her face with her slim and shaking hand. "Gran, please . . ."

"No, no," Margaret chided in a gentle tone. "We can't just not deal with this. I know you've just had quite the shock . . ." She looked away and shook her head. "But your mother thought it was important enough to write a letter that has now come to your attention for such a time as this . . ."

Tessa's voice was flat. "She's not my mother."

"Stop that. No matter what they did, they loved you as their own. You were their own. They gave up their lives in order to have you as their daughter. Could any blood parents have done more?"

"They could have told me the truth."

Margaret shook her head. "You were way too young. At least they thought so. They were trying to protect you."

Tessa turned to look at Margaret through reddened eyes. "By hiding things from me? By pretending to be the very people they weren't?!" She looked away. "And by pretending I was somebody I wasn't?!"

For a moment, Margaret was silent, tracing a finger on the blue-checkered tablecloth pattern. She drew a deep breath and delicately stated, "It doesn't change who you are now. It doesn't change that you are our adopted daughter, does it?"

Tessa rallied and held Margaret's gaze. She looked at Margaret with tenderness then shook her head. She didn't want to hurt Jacob and Margaret any more. "No, Gran. I love you like my own parents. You and Gramps have been like real parents to me—the best ever. That will never change. It's just that . . ."

A tear gathered in the corner of Margaret's eye, and she quickly wiped it away. "I know," she said. "There are a lot of unanswered questions. But that's the point, isn't it? Who was this lawyer fella? And who was behind the adoption? And, most importantly, why? A lot of money was obviously involved, and apparently your real mother was not an unwed teen. It doesn't make sense. I can see why your mom would have eventually been concerned for you. Somebody went to a lot of trouble to keep this all secret. So, again—why? Jacob and I have seen your birth certificate. It's real. And it's on file. I . . . checked with the state while you were in your room."

Tessa looked intently at her, surprised. "You did?"

"Uh huh. Idaho Vital Statistics has the original. Your parents are listed as Richard and Marilyn Dawson. It's not a certificate of adoption, but an original record of birth."

Tessa looked away. A deluge of honest questions contended for honest answers in her mind. "That's impossible!" she said, bewildered.

"It's not if you have enough pull . . . and enough money."

"What should I do?" Tessa asked.

Margaret folded her aged hand on Tessa's. "Get the police involved. At least go on record that you have some concerns. They probably won't be able to do anything because it's been so many years since the letter was written, and without incident . . ."

Tessa's face sobered, and she sat straight up. "There's something I need to show you." And with that, she bolted upstairs and returned to the kitchen a minute later with a sticky note in hand.

Margaret's eyebrows furrowed. "What is that?"

Tessa bit her lip and with a trembling hand gave it to Margaret, who unfolded and read it. She looked up with sudden concern. "What does this mean?" she asked.

Tessa took a deep breath. "I got knocked down hard the other day, when I went to the library," she said. "When I looked in my purse, this was in it. I think the guy who knocked me down did so on purpose, so he could plant it there."

Margaret swallowed hard. "Now I am getting scared," she said.

Tessa's eyes darted away, then fixated on Margaret again. "Those are the same words in my mom's letter." She nervously bit her lip. "And that's only the half of it!" she uttered.

Margaret stared, visibly afraid.

"When . . . when I left the library," Tessa falteringly began, "it was dark. I had parked Gramps' pickup at the gazebo and walked to the library from there. When I came back at night and started crossing the street, a car . . . tried to run me down!"

"What!" Margaret cried. Her face was overtaken with a look of horror and sudden realization. "Your purse?!" she said. "The strap!"

Tessa nodded. "I don't know. It somehow got hooked on the car as it went past and everything went flying. I wasn't actually hit, but I tripped and fell when the car tore the purse from my arm. That's where the scrape on my knee came from. A teenage boy came to help me. He . . . said he saw the whole thing—that the car was already parked near the pickup, then came right straight at me . . . on purpose!"

For a moment, Margaret remained silent, giving little shakes of her head, her eyes conveying utter disbelief. Then she said, firmly, "Jacob needs to know about this." She stood and moved to the kitchen screen door.

"No, Gran," Tessa cried. "Please. Life has been so hard on Gramps lately that I'm afraid it'll do something to him. He worries so much as is!"

Margaret regarded her in utter astonishment. She walked back to the kitchen table and leaned over Tessa. "Do you mean to tell me," she began, angry and indignant, "that we are to keep this strictly between us? My dear girl, for over forty years I have kept no secrets from that man out there"—she pointed her finger toward the door in Jacob's general direction—"and I do not intend to start now. Whatever else may have happened in the past, the fact remains that you are our daughter now, and I refuse to stand idly by and let something terrible happen to you." She leaned in close to Tessa until they were face to face. "There has been an attempt made upon your life!" she said. She stood up and looked heavenward. "This is a nightmare. We've been hit with one thing after another lately. I can't even begin to understand it at all."

Then she clenched her jaw and looked again at Tessa. "But . . ." She stopped saying anything more, strode boldly to the screen door, opened it, and called, "Jacob! Can you come in here, please? Right away!" And there she stood, arms folded, rigid, and determined.

Wednesday night service was packed out, mostly with the younger crowd but with a smattering of middle-aged folks and even older folks who either had already heard Chip preach or had heard glowing reports about him from a neighbor. It was a festive, lively, and charged atmosphere, abounding with much by way of laughing and jostling among the youth and brimming with amicable conversation among the older set—the sum of which was excessively loud as voices competed to be heard. The two huge coffee urns, set on tables behind the last pew, took hit after hit, and the collective caffeine buzz that was in progress amplified the in-stereo party spirit.

Nathan Shepherd stood leaning against the back wall, his gaze alternating from Chip who was standing just below the podium to Tessa. She happened to be wedged between a pair of strapping farm hands broad as haystacks to one side and a pack of slicked-up city kids from Idaho Falls on the other. He wished he could join her, but she was three pews away (and no empty seat besides), and Chip was up front getting ready to preach.

As Chip strode onto the podium, a few in the audience clapped. In what Nathan considered to be perfect showmanship style, Chip paused in his paper shuffling, flashed an ivory-toothed smile at the audience, and waved majestically. Nathan winced. Not a vindictive man by nature, Nathan felt a sudden and focused dislike of Chip. Just then, he was tempted to pray out loud one of the imprecatory psalms, with "pastor" Davis as its object.

From behind the pulpit, Chip spotted Tessa and practically vaulted from the podium the three steps to the main floor making a beeline down the aisle to her pew. All apologies to the haystack brothers, he made enough of an inroad to take Tessa's hand to engage in small talk for a few minutes, bending so close that his face was nearly touching hers. As Nathan watched this scene, his eyes narrowed. Nope. Now he *knew* he didn't like the guy.

Music then began resonating from the overhead speakers, and Chip took it as his cue. In less than a minute, he was up front, and a hush fell upon the room. As if emanating from heaven itself, a blue-white bar of light from a newly installed set of balcony spotters shined down on him. He seemed bathed in an ethereal presence. He bowed his head and stood, silent, appearing to pray while the synthesized music flowed all around him. When he lifted his head and riveted his gaze upon the congregation, he opened his mouth to speak. Employing the use of a high-end, clip-on microphone, his voice was measured, resounding, and confident.

"I'd like to welcome everyone here tonight and thank you for coming. We have a special treat in the form of a short video that I'll be basing my preaching on. There will be a time of Q and A afterward, so if anyone has any questions, I can address those then. I want to give you all a heads-up as well that next week we'll have a special guest who will be speaking. I'll leave the 'who' of it to your imagination, because I hope to pique your curiosity. Hope you join us then. There's coffee in the back for you caffeine addicts, so feel free to partake while we worship or during the message. We're pretty casual here. I think God would be pleased we're comfortable enough to kick back and enjoy. For now . . ."

He raised his hand and pointed a finger upward toward the balcony, and behind him a huge screen dropped down in front of the large wooden cross situated in the front in plain sight. Rock music inundated the sanctuary and kaleidoscopic imagery darted across the screen. Most in the pews rose and hundreds of hands shot upward, like a human wave rising and falling with the heavy beat. Entire pews moved in lockstep to the music. Up front, Chip tapped his feet, spun on his heels, and executed an array of smooth moves while dancing with total abandon as the blue spotlight followed him. The kids went wild. A few of the older folk rose up to leave but could not negotiate their way out of their pews.

In the back, with the other latecomers who couldn't find a seat, Nathan stood transfixed but not without serious reservations. His gaze jumped from Chip, to the crowd, to the lighting effects, and back at Chip again. He felt the bass beat pulsating through him. His eyes searched for Tessa, but he couldn't see her past the dancing teens in the last couple of pews. After about five minutes, the music did a slow fade while seamlessly transitioning into the background for snippets of video showing what Nathan took to be missionaries helping feed, clothe, and build homes for the impoverished overseas. The featured workers in the video glowed as they recounted their experiences of helping others and bringing goodwill to foreign lands, as the camera panned out over the happy faces of villagers in Africa, India, and a tiny jungle island in the South Pacific.

The narrator went on excitedly about reaching out to those less fortunate overseas, banding together in a big brotherhood of man by being the hands and feet of "the Master" and ministering to the poor of the world in His Name. Nathan listened intently, but the fifteen-minute video never did mention which master. The movie closed with an image of Christ, hands outstretched and hovering over the missionaries. Nathan was confused. If this indeed was Jesus they were talking about, why didn't they just say so to begin with?

When the video ended, Chip segued right into the sermon using as his springboard Matthew 25:40, which states, "Verily I say unto you, inasmuch as ye have done it unto one of the least of these my brethren, ye have done it unto me."

He preached with a graduated emotional intensity, first calmly and standing behind the pulpit— then striding toward the podium and pacing back and forth with the occasional finger directed ever so pointedly at the congregation—then finally, building up to the message apogee, flinging off his jacket and rolling up his sleeves while the spotlight made the sweat on his face glisten. His words then came gushing forth in such rapid succession, it was almost impossible to distinguish one thought from another. Without missing a beat, he infused into his message a scattering of random segments on recycling, social justice, and caring for the earth as God's appointed stewards. So," he ended dramatically, "will you share your blessing with those less fortunate? With the least of these? Or do you profess to follow the Son of Man who has no place to lay His head, but ignore the homeless entirely?"

Standing in the middle of the podium, he appeared drained, but was smiling beatifically.

Nathan smirked. He hadn't seen such successful crowd manipulation since the last rock concert he attended as an unbelieving, rebellious teen. He noted that even the older folks who had intended to leave at first, thought better of it, stayed for the sermon and happily remained seated even now.

One of the church elders stepped up from behind a wing of the podium and handed Chip a bottle of spring water. It had become his trademark. "So," he said, "let's open up the floor for discussion."

Nathan raised his hand, but Tessa beat him to it. Chip grinned shamelessly and said, "Miss Tessa Dawson!"

He could only see the back of her head, but Nathan was sure she blushed.

"What about sharing the Gospel?" she asked, feeling a little gun shy toward the idea of suddenly being in the spotlight. "I mean, it's important to feed the hungry and build them homes, but what about the salvation message? What are we really doing for the poor and needy if we only meet their physical needs? What they really need is the Lord."

Chip nodded. "Good question!" He said. "Let me say that if we are to follow the example of the early church, we do need to be more mission minded, and that includes evangelism. But surely you remember how the early Christians lived communally, sharing all their goods so that no one had lack. Wouldn't we do well to follow by example? If we are to bring heaven to earth and build the kingdom, we've got to live more simply, the Jesus way, move away from individualism and consumerism. That means be in community, now. Does that make sense?"

Tessa faltered. *No*, thought Nathan. *It doesn't. In fact, you didn't answer her question at all.* Chip moved on quickly, taking on a half-dozen more questions and rattling off quick answers that were only vaguely referenced in Scripture. He cited parables out of context quite a bit but did it in such a way that it actually seemed to make sense in a Machiavellian, artful dodger, circular reasoning kind of way.

It was nearing eight o'clock, and the teens were getting restless. Chip had advertised free burgers and sodas to all the youth at the Birch Bark Bistro after the service, and when one of them shouted out, "We're hungry!" followed by a chorus of laughter, Chip got the hint.

Chip laughed. "Okay, I hear ya! Church is over. I'll meet you guys over at the Birch Bark in about fifteen minutes." He raised his hand to them in a strange kind of salute. "Remember our mystery speaker here next week," he said, "and don't forget to check out our new website. Peace and justice!"

Nathan threaded his way upstream, through the crowd, making for the podium where Chip was talking with a couple of late-teen girls holding their Bibles. They practically fawned over him, and Chip projected a fatherly shepherd image to maintain respectability. Nathan stood without speaking, deliberately eavesdropping as the conversation revolved around the uZone blogging site that was so popular with the younger crowd. "Come on, you guys!" called a teenage boy from the back of the room, motioning to the girls. "Everybody's gonna get there before us."

Smiling and waving goodbye to Chip, the girls turned to dash down the aisle and out the sanctuary doors with their friend. Chip looked up at Nathan, who towered over him by a half a foot. "Hey bro. How's it going?" He thrust out his hand. "Chip Davis. I'm the pastor here."

Nathan reluctantly returned the handshake. "Nathan Shepherd. Well, I was thinking about your . . . interesting . . . sermon, but first, I couldn't help overhearing you talk about that uZone thing. You think it's a good idea to get others involved with that, as a pastor and all? I mean the site can be misused . . ."

Chip smiled reassuringly. "Hey," he said, "I'm a uZer myself. It's safe and private. And you can have over five hundred subscribers. It's actually a great tool to make non-Christians a lot more comfortable with the idea of 'church.'"

Nathan threw a glance over his shoulder at the rapidly dispersing kids. "You have quite the fan club, Pastor Davis."

Chip grinned sheepishly. "Well, you know young girls," he said, apologetically. "They tend to idolize leaders, but really, I'm just here to serve and point them in the right direction."

"As long as you point them to Jesus and God's Word," Nathan said, forcing some semblance of a conciliatory smile.

"Yes, of course. You saw the film. Following in the footsteps of the Master. Anyway, the kids' world is social networking." He shrugged. "It's the new way. Nothing wrong with using technology to make disciples."

"But it's not the real world, Chip, and uZone is not safe. Nothing's private when it's on the Internet. I wouldn't encourage the girls to use it. There have been security breaches lately, I've read . . ." Chip nervously flashed more of his pearly whites. Nathan wondered if it was a bigger smile or indicative of a wolf baring his fangs.

"Could you please call me 'Pastor Davis?'" he interrupted. "And yes, it's safe enough. I mean, we all take a chance just getting out of bed each day. We can't be afraid of everything. Besides, I'm not their babysitter. I'm only encouraging them to use uZone to invite their non-Christian friends." He took a sudden conversational detour: "So, did you like the film?"

"Not really. I mean, sure, it has some merit, but as a Bible-believing pastor, you do know that fixing the world's social problems is not our sole mandate. Even the world can clean people up. That's a social gospel."

"I know that," Chip said. He was growing impatient. "But the world already sees the church as intolerant and exclusive. We need to be more like the unbelievers, act more . . . normal . . . like Jesus did when He spoke to the prostitutes and tax collectors. Or like Paul, who was all things to all people so that a few might be saved. We need to change the way we've been doing church in order to attract the world's attention and appeal to those who are of the world by whatever means necessary."

Nathan shook his head. "Jesus reached out to unbelievers, but He was never 'like them.' He said we are to be in the world but not of it, and the apostle Paul said that the Gospel is foolishness to them who are perishing. The purpose of the church is to equip believers to go out and make disciples of Christ, not to draw the world's ways into the church. We don't have to be like them in order to win them. We are to be set apart, separate, a light, a city set on a hill and speak the truth in love. And when Paul said to be all things to all men, he was not telling us to become worldly. Paul always taught with the centrality and the righteousness of Jesus Christ in mind."

Chip seemed irritated. "They won't accept that. God is love, and we have to show them that love. Like the monks and nuns who live in squalid villages, that kind of thing."

Nathan pressed. "If we don't share the truth, we are just sending people to hell in clean rags. We have to be wary of introducing some progressive emerging spirituality to these kids. What the kids need is to become spiritually rooted and grounded in the Word of God, and a big part of that involves learning just who God is by studying the Bible."

"Nathan, I appreciate your views," defended Chip, "but who has been given the reins here?"

"Reins?"

"Yes, who is the pastor of this church?"

Nathan spoke with calm authority. "Chip, you are ultimately

accountable to God for where you lead these kids. Hopefully you have given the reins to Him. Christ is to be the Head of the church, not man."

Chips eyes blazed with anger. He busied himself by unplugging his guitar and packing away his equipment. "Excuse me, I don't know where you are coming from, but I've got to lock up and meet a bunch of the kids who have questions. We'll be meeting at the Birch Bark Bistro. You're welcome to come if you like, but I really have to get going."

"I'm coming from Ephesians four, verses eleven to sixteen," Nathan said. "You might want to look that up on your iPhone. We'll talk again. This isn't over, Chip." He started to walk away when he noticed Chip take another swallow from his bottled water. He pointed at it casually. "You really like that stuff."

"Better for you," Chip replied, his demeanor once again congenial. "No harmful chemicals to introduce into the body. Pure alkaline water flushes out the system. I've ordered a bunch for the church. Can I get you one?"

Nathan succumbed to the urge to be a wise guy. "No, thanks. I . . . uh . . . hear you hang out at the Birch Bark Bistro a lot. I wonder if they use chemical free water for their coffee and tea there. I could be mistaken, but last time I checked, I'm pretty sure their water comes right from the tap. Town water is chlorinated and fluoridated, in other words."

A priceless momentary look of distress came over Chip's face. He seemed genuinely concerned. "I don't know," he reflected. "I'll have to look into that."

Nathan headed down the side aisle toward the sanctuary doors while Chip hit the lights and the entire place went dark except for the aisle lights. He could kick himself for missing Tessa. He had wanted to talk more with her, maybe go for coffee with her somewhere for an hour before heading home. He reached the main doors and pushed them open. Sideways rain splattered against the windows of the lobby entrance. From there he could see Tessa across the street, standing by Jacob's pickup as the wind blew her long hair in every direction while she searched in her purse.

Nathan stepped outside. "Tessa!" he called and sprinted across the street.

Chip exited the building at that moment, locked all the doors, then stood under the eaves, watching. He saw Tessa smile, nod, open the truck door, and slide into the driver's seat. At the same time, Nathan ran to his parked jeep only a few yards away.

Chip turned up the collar of his jacket and watched them both drive off in the same direction.

So *that* was the guy Zhanna mentioned. Nathan had come across pretty strong inside the church just a few minutes ago. He showed himself to be a cautious man where the Word of God was concerned. Chip wondered if that caution bled over into other areas as well. If so, that might be a weakness Chip could exploit. He might be able to use Nathan to gain some additional ground temporarily regarding his plan, but Tessa was a personal issue. He had no intention of just stepping out of the way where she was concerned.

"Poor Mr. Nathan Shepherd," he said under his breath. "You don't know who it is you're messing with."

For as the heavens are higher than the earth, so are my ways higher than your ways, and my thoughts than your thoughts. (Isaiah 55:9)

CHAPTER

8

Deputy Sheriff John Akim leaned back in his old wooden chair and felt the slats dig into his spine. He'd petitioned the city council a good hundred times or more for three new chairs for the sheriff's office, and a good hundred times his request had been denied on the basis of "unnecessary expenditure." The present furniture seemed reminiscent of the turn of the previous century—it actually appeared to have been built back then. Like everything else in the two-man office—dinosaur computers, early digital cameras, even their 1960s fingerprint kit—the chairs were ancient relics. Akim loved his job but hated his anything but ergonomic working environment. Even the straight-back chair the young lady sat in across the desk from him precluded any comfort for the bereaved or distraught.

Akim's morning had gone badly. He woke up late, exhausted because of a three o' clock in the morning complaint concerning the Hawley place, where the brothers, drunk as usual, were celebrating the Fourth of July a bit late with a stash of misplaced fireworks they'd found. One defective Roman candle rocketed into the barn instead of skyward and set the hay ablaze, hence the fire department's involvement. Akim crawled into bed at five, leaving the paperwork until the following day. But before work, his youngest awoke crying, with what turned out to be a case of the chicken pox; and the whole time his wife was inadvertently charring his breakfast, she kept grouching at him about getting a raise. To get some peace, he settled for a coffee on the run and a pit-stop at the Birch Bark Bistro for a couple of danishes. To top it off, Sheriff Baker, on leave to deal with a death in the family, wouldn't be returning from Hinton for a few weeks, so anything that came up was in Akim's court.

Now this. Eight a.m. conspiracy theories. They didn't even have the decency to let a man finish his hard won second cup of coffee for the day.

On the desk before him sat the soiled purse. He idly fingered the broken strap. "Sooo," he drawled, feigning interest, "this happened several nights ago. Why did you wait until today then to finally report it?"

Tessa shrugged and looked embarrassed. "Well . . . I didn't want to . . . you know . . ." She heaved a sigh. "This is all new and scary to me and even a little embarrassing. I wanted some time to think it through."

"Why did you choose us instead of the local Police Department? Seems like it's a matter for them."

Tessa shrugged again. "Your office was closer?"

Akim fought the impulse to roll his eyes toward the ceiling.

"We've been friends with Ted Baker for a long time," Jacob explained. "He's gone to bat for us before. We figured he might take a personal interest."

Akim picked up his mug and gulped down some more coffee. With his hands curled around the mug, he set it on the table before him. He appeared to be thinking over Tessa's account. "Ma'am," he said, and looked from Tessa, who was sitting, and back and forth at Jacob and Margaret, who stood on either side of her, "you do know that this sounds a bit farfetched? I mean, after all, we're not New York City or Chicago. We don't get many hit-and-run reports here. As a matter of fact, in the two years I've worked for the sheriff's department here and the previous eight years in other law enforcement positions, I've never had one. I mean, Miss Dawson, you're talking attempted murder. Are you sure it was deliberate?"

Tessa lowered her eyes. "Well, no," she said, "not exactly. But the boy who saw it thinks it was. Anyway, the point is I was nearly killed. That's the truth. And what about that sticky note I showed you?"

Akim nodded wearily. He rubbed his bloodshot eyes and took a deep breath. "Okay," he said, "Here's the situation: you can't describe the car that nearly hit you; you didn't see the driver; you have no idea why anyone would deliberately try to run you down; you have no enemies that you know of; and . . . you just got back into town after being gone for quite some time. You haven't even had time to get anybody mad at you." He leaned forward with both elbows on the marred desktop. "Miss Dawson, we can do the paperwork, but we've got nothing to go on. You don't even know the boy's name who witnessed this . . . incident. As far as the note you showed me, you yourself admitted that even you don't know exactly what it means, or how it got in your purse. It could all be very innocent."

Jacob's voice was polite but hard. "Deputy Akim, are you going to help us file a report, or not? We can come back when Ted's here, if you like, and explain it to him."

Akim held up a hand in surrender. "You win, Mr. Brown." He stood and moved to an old black filing cabinet in a corner of the room, pulled open a drawer, and removed some forms. He sat down, picked a pen from a pencil holder and forced a smile. "Okay," he said with resignation. "Let's take it once again from the beginning."

Outside the sheriff's office, the three of them stood in the morning sun beside Jacob's pickup. Margaret scowled. "Well," she said, "that went splendidly, sarcasm intended. I don't think he took us the least bit seriously."

Jacob looked back at the station and then at Margaret and shook his head in agreement. Mountains emblazoned by the early morning sunlight reflected in the two huge windows fronting the building. "Imported help," he muttered. "They get these guys from Boise or wherever, who are used to "real crime." Chances are, he most likely thinks it was some drunk who just didn't see you, Tessa. And I wish you had told him the rest of it."

Tessa shook her head. "No," she said, emphatically. "I'm not ready for that. It's too soon, and this town's too small. Everybody would find out, and they'd gossip."

Margaret touched Tessa's arm. She was worried. "You fret about what other people will think," she said, "but dear, your life is in danger. Your life, Tessa! The longer we put off doing tomorrow what surely should have been done today, the more we run the risk that something . . . potentially awful . . . unthinkable even . . . will happen!"

"I can't Gran," Tessa replied apologetically. "My thoughts are still in a tailspin. Everything is all jumbled up and I . . . I just can't yet, that's all. I did tell Nathan last night though. We drove up to Benton Overlook and talked."

"You didn't mention that," Jacob said. "You told him everything?"

Tessa nodded solemnly.

"What'd he say?"

"He was kind of . . . stunned, at first," Tessa recounted. "Then, he got mad. A quiet, smoldering beneath the surface kind of mad. He promised"—her face becoming flushed—"he promised he'd protect me, and if anyone wanted to get to me, they'd have to go through him first." She smiled and looked away shyly.

Jacob exchanged glances with Margaret and raised his eyebrows. "Welllll," he said with finality, "I guess yesterday wasn't a total loss." He winked. "Benton Overlook, eh? Nice view of the town lights at night. We've had some pretty nice talks there too, way back when, haven't we, dear?"

Margaret smiled and socked him playfully in the arm. "J.B., this is serious," she chided but welcomed Jacob's attempt at levity.

"Let's go get a donut and coffee," Jacob said, opening the pickup's passenger door for Tessa and Margaret to slide in. He went around the front of the vehicle and got behind the wheel. "Junk food gets my wheels turning." Then he added, on a more serious note, looking at Tessa, "None of this makes any sense, I know, and yet, it all seems connected somehow. We're going to have to do something. Not sure what, but we need to do some brainstorming."

"And praying," Margaret added.

Tessa sighed. "Amen."

"Nice place." Chip Davis let the door swing shut behind him and, with his hands tucked in his pockets, gave the interior of The Master's Way the once over. He nodded to himself. "It has definite possibilities," he noted.

Sister Genevieve stood at the far end of a luncheon-inspired Formica counter, sifting through paperwork and squinting her eyes as she held a document up close to read the fine print. She looked up. "Oh, hello," she said with a smile. "I'm afraid we're not open yet, so there's no food. I'm actually waiting on some assistance from the convent that sent me. We . . . uh . . . still have to gather donations and such . . ."

Chip returned the smile. "I'm William Davis," he said cordially. "Pastor of Sheep Gate Lane Church. Wanted to welcome you to the community."

"Why, thank you," Sister Genevieve said. "I am a stranger here, but people have been so good to me."

"Nice accent, sister," Chip said.

The nun turned a bit red. "Thank you again. I'm French born and raised in Spain, you know, but living in the States for some time now. My convent is . . ."

"Yes, sir," Chip went on, giving the room another thorough sweep. There was not much by way of furniture—only a couple small, round tables—minus the chairs—and a semi-circular counter that ran half the length of the room, which was fitted with late fifties-style padded stools. An antiquated jukebox took up space in a dark corner—a hulking thing that could appear either curious and imposing or bespeaking of nostalgia, depending on the age of the viewer and their knowledge of Americana. A half-dozen south facing windows let in rays of early morning sunlight that created a play of light and shadow over the furnishings of a bygone era and the dust that still overlaid everything. Only the counter where the nun stood had been wiped clean.

The place had, in fact, been a small burger joint back in the day and could easily hold up to fifty or so patrons. It seemed to Chip it most surely would again, once Sister Genevieve's new feeding program got underway.

"Yes, sir," Chip repeated, "I've always wanted to help feed the homeless and clothe the needy. Or something to that effect."

Somewhat mystified, the nun replied, "I don't understand."

"Oh, I think you will . . . Dr. Winters," he replied, flashing a wolf-like grin.

The nun, no longer mystified, appeared flustered. "I'm sorry," she said, in a voice that now sounded strained. "You are sorely mistaken. I'm Sister Genevieve. I have been sent here on a mission under the auspices of my current convent in New Mexico. I've been commissioned by this convent to start a homeless mission here."

"You know," Chip said and nodded, walking casually toward her, "that's pretty good. You've got the accent down and everything. Oh, and the face, Sister, the face! Definitely a hardsell." He held up both hands together to view her through a frame of fingers, like an old-time movie director. "Who could turn down that face?" he said. "You look like an angel, you do. But then again . . . you know that, don't you?"

The nun folded her arms in a defensive posture squarely in front of her habit, tucking each hand, for some curious reason, into a spacious sleeve. She stood before Chip defiantly, completely rigid, and staring at him with what Chip imagined to be daggers in her eyes.

"Admittedly," Chip continued, undaunted and wagging an index finger at her, "I gotta hand it to you, the habit threw me at first, not to mention the veil covering your hair and all. I must have seen a half dozen of those posters you canvassed the town with before it hit me. There was only one telling photo of you in the collage, in keeping with your real life profile, but that was enough for me to connect the dots. Yeah, there's only one Jasmine Winters. How am I doin' so far, doc?"

Any shred or trace of being mystified or flustered had dissolved, and her countenance was one of total indifference. Her eyes, peering out from under the veil, pierced him straight through, as though a look could kill. Chip stopped and weighed her silence. His attention was drawn to her folded arms as his eyes riveted on where her wrists left off. She could be packing an Uzi in those oversized sleeves for all he knew. "Relax sister. No need to get tense."

In a flawless American accent, Jasmine curtly retorted, "What do you want?"

Chip inhaled deeply, savoring the moment, and exhaled slowly. Good. She would not have asked or switched accents for that matter, if she wasn't ready to deal. But he decided right then and there he'd have to always be looking over his shoulder with her. From only a few feet away, she seemed like a coiled snake, waiting to strike at him unaware. "A proposition," Chip said. "A partnership, if you will."

Jasmine smirked and shook her head. "There's always a glitch," she thought out loud and moved past him to the front door and locked it. "I should have done that earlier," she said in disgust, then added, bored, "This way." She glided across the room and walked through an open door into the back room with Chip in tow. Once there, she told him to close the door. She then pulled the wimple from her head. Long platinum hair tumbled from captivity. She tossed the wimple unceremoniously onto the old desktop. "These things are so hot," she said and ran a delicate hand over her sweaty hairline. "I don't know how real nuns do it, to be perfectly honest." She turned and regarded Chip with open derision. "I don't need a partner," she said, then raised her eyebrow. "But, just out of morbid curiosity, how did you figure it out? I was very careful, paying close attention to every last detail, or so I thought."

Chip nodded, admiration pouring from him. "Oh," he said, impressed, "you're good. I thought I was a scammer, but now I think I could stand to learn a thing or two from you. The accent, the garb, the angelic smile—whew! Classic. And, uh . . . yes, you do need a partner." He arched his thumb backward at his chest, recommending himself.

Jasmine placed her hands on her hips. "What makes you so sure?" she demanded. "You seem to think you know something I don't. I'll have you know even the local town cops believe me. 'Yes, sister. No, sister. Just let us know how we can help you, sister . . .' Why, even . . ." She stopped herself. "Again, what makes you so sure I am in need of your assistance or anyone else's for that matter?"

Chip raised both his eyebrows and shrugged with a mock "golly gee" schoolboy look on his face, then chuckled. "Don't feel so bad, Jazz. It takes one to know one. But really, it wasn't anything you did or didn't do that tipped me off. No, you see, I have a gift—a profitable one at that—that allows me to remember things that everybody else forgets. My mind is like a sophisticated filing system. If I've read it or seen it, it gets filed away in my mind. That includes books, words spoken, pictures, scenarios, names . . . or, in your case, faces."

Jasmine's jaw slackened. "Photographic memory."

"Ding, ding, ding . . . we have a winner." Chip leaned up against the counter and watched her. "That's how I can rattle off entire chapters of the Bible. But you don't remember me, do you?" She shook her head, her lips pursed together. "Two years ago," he said, "in Topeka, you were running some kind of transcendental meditation-based gamut when I encountered you. I attended one of your "classes," thinking maybe I could use some of your techniques to further my own . . . plans and make them take shape more quickly. How'd that go anyway?"

Jasmine's upper lip curled in disgust. "Like almost everything else since I lost my position at . . ." Rage mixed with angst exuded from her face. "Did you get anything out of it?"

"Out of what?"

"The class," she said, in a most exasperated tone. "The class! You know. Did you learn to meditate or to go inward?" Her disgusted gaze became that of a probing, almost hopeful one.

Chip laughed out loud and looked at her incredulously. "You're kidding, right? Don't tell me you actually believe that garbage?! I thought you were running a scam."

Jasmine scowled. "You're all the same," she said without explaining herself.

Chip put up his hands defensively. "Ah, c'mon, Jazz. Don't take it so personally. Really, you were good. I actually learned a lot about mood inducement through props and voice moderation. I watched you induce mass hypnosis. I couldn't believe it! The whole crowd. You had those dopes eating right out of your hand. Very smooth. As a matter of fact, you're one of the main reasons I'm here, in this town. You gave me the idea."

When it became all too plain to Chip that Jasmine still did not understand, Chip took the floor. He paced excitedly, hands waving. "It was perfect," he said, nearly breathless. "Made to order. When I saw you back then, something clicked," he said as he tapped his forefinger against his head, ". . . in here. I kept thinking to myself, 'She's doing it, and they're paying her well to do it. So why not me?,' I asked myself. So, I studied. I watched every hokey program put out by televangelists, and man, are they a dime a dozen in this country. I didn't bother with the little guys, however, or the ones who seemed genuine, for they never made it big. They wore the same shabby suits every Sunday. They stayed small, irrelevant, and hidden in obscurity. No, it was the big names I paid attention to—you know, the ones with the ten thousand dollar watches, the solid gold rings, and the mansions in Beverly Hills, or wherever. I watched how they approached the stage, set up their props, did their lighting, how they spoke, and even how they moved their hands. If they showed up in a town close by, I'd actually go and see them in person."

Chip froze, stretched out his hands toward the empty room, apparently visualizing a crowd before him. "Man," he said, his voice filled with awe. "You should see those guys in action. What pros. They work the crowd until it's literally ready to bleed cash. They'd have widows on a pension so worked up they'd be writing their last twenty-dollar check to give to these 'ministers.'" He smirked right after placing added emphasis on the last word, then turned to Jasmine, who stared back at him with penetrating narrowed, disapproving eyes. "I saw thousands," he said, amazed, "thousands with tears streaming down their faces,"—both his index fingers drew invisible lines down his cheeks—"and they were . . . how should I put it? . . . lost in some spiritual reverie. They weren't even really there or present at that point—in the stadium, I mean. Boy were they somewhere else. And they paid to get there."

For a moment, he fell silent then looked up, his eyes searching Jasmine's face. "Just like they did with you," he said softly. "Just like they're gonna do with . . . us."

Jasmine regarded Chip with disgust. "You pathetic man," she said. "You have no idea what you're asking. I'll give you my answer so even the likes of you can understand. No. Not going to happen. I don't want anything to do with your 'rise to fame.'" She turned away and started shuffling through the paperwork again on the counter. "And I could care less about the money, at this point," she added.

"So, what is it?" Chip demanded. "You want converts? Not a problem. Look, I've got the church for it. It's already set up. I'm drawing in the younger crowd by the droves, and they're really into this mystical, esoteric stuff you're so fond of—labyrinths, candles, prayer stations, the whole nine yards. See—I've been researching and doing my homework! Both of us together can go big-time even in a town this small. Look, we can even go live on TV, if you want. You'll have followers all over the country. Come on, Jazz! Think about it. The possibilities . . ."

"You're hard of hearing," Jasmine said. "The answer is still . . ."

"I'll tell."

Jasmine froze right in the middle of what she was doing, with her mouth still open from having just been interrupted. She looked at him in utter disdain once again. "Oh no you won't," she said and with a remarkable degree of self assurance. "You'd be giving yourself away, too. We'd both go down, and you know it."

Chip shook his head. "No way! Not even!" He fixed his gaze on hers. "You're bluffing. Besides, I've been here long enough now. I've laid all the groundwork. These people trust me. They think I'm one of them. But as for you . . ." He chose his next string of words carefully. ". . . I don't think you can risk exposure. You've got something going and can't afford to louse it up. I don't know what it is exactly, but I have a gut feeling it's big. One word from me to the cops and . . ."

Jasmine moved toward Chip, watching him every moment. Framed by her wavy, platinum hair and those penetrating eyes, her face, like beauty chiseled in stone, remained emotionless. *A face belonging to one who had no soul*, Chip mused to himself. Jasmine stopped a foot from Chip. A chill ran up his spine. Suddenly, he felt afraid. Her subtle yet intoxicating fragrance of Jasmine oil enveloped him. Whispering in a low, deep steady voice and without blinking, she said, "Don't—you—ever—threaten—me—again."

Then she turned and nonchalantly strode over to a desk, giving the pretense of being preoccupied with other matters, and without looking at him asked, "When?"

Relief flooded Chip. He exhaled slowly, feeling like he could breathe again. He felt exhilarated, scared, and almost euphoric all at the same time. "Next Wednesday night. One of the elders is after me to pump up the program, and your kind of stuff will fit in nicely. I already told the congregation we had a mystery speaker lined up."

Jasmine smiled, but in a most unaffected manner. "That's me, all the way." Her voice then took on an unmistakable air of authority. "Bring me a program of the night's pre-planned activities. Also, we'll need some time to go over our respective roles with regard to the church service. Meeting here will appear innocent enough to anyone who sees you. You can even tell them I'll be the mystery speaker if you have to and to keep it on the down-low for now. It'll make them feel special."

"You got it," Chip answered.

"You can leave now." It wasn't a suggestion; it was an order.

"Righto Jasmine." Chip moved a few steps to the back-room door and opened it.

"And William . . . That is your real name, isn't it, the one you registered under for the class?"

"Don't call me William. Only my lawyer addresses me by my given name. The name is Chip."

Chip stopped and turned. Jasmine leveled a flat gaze at him. "Well while we are at it, don't *you* call me Jasmine. Only my friends address me by my first name. *We* are not friends. To you, it's Dr. Winters."

Chip gave a slight nod. A moment later he stepped out into the gradually intensifying heat from the encroaching morning sunlight. He shivered and looked over his shoulder at the door. "What an ice woman," he muttered underneath his breath. "You have friends?" he murmured. "You could have fooled me!"

The thought crossed his mind that he may have made a HUGE mistake in coming there. As he headed down the sidewalk toward Main Street, he knew with utmost certainty he'd have to watch his back from that point on.

E zekiel Hazlett pulled the badly soiled sleeping bag away from his face and opened his eyelids just a crack. Groaning, he slammed them shut and laid there feeling the sensation of the cold ground penetrating clear through his tattered foam padding on through his threadbare bag, through three layers of dirty clothing, and finally, directly through the thin skin covering his bony back. The late summer mountain mornings were icy cold, and his makeshift camp under Cutter Creek Bridge remained enveloped in shadow until noon. Shivering, he weighed the merits of getting up and venturing forth from his sleep chamber against attempting to return to the troubled shadow lands of fitful, bone-chilling slumber. He became all too aware of the relentless sensation of someone hammering away on a set of drums inside his head—a solo performance induced by too many shots of whiskey the night before. He decided that sleep was, by far, the lesser of the two evils.

With a nearly dry tongue, indicative of cottonmouth, he licked his cracked lips, grimacing at the dirty sock taste in his mouth. He felt around blindly on either side of his sleeping bag for his antiquated tin army canteen but couldn't locate it by feel and was forced to open his eyes. Somehow it had slipped to the bottom of the bag, and he had to sit up to retrieve it. It was a struggle to sit upright. He propped himself up on one arm and reached for the canteen, sat up all the way, unscrewed the lid, and drank deeply.

As he tilted his head back for a second swig, his eyes caught a human figure above him, standing on the shoulder of the road and looking down, watching him. He was a fine-looking young man with wavy brown hair and a boyish face whose spotless white shirt glowed angelically in the early morning sunlight as he lingered there, just above the bridge. He could have seemed friendly had he smiled. Instead, he stared impassively, and Ezekiel paused in mid-drink and stared back. He lifted the canteen in greeting, but the young man remained emotionless and motionless a moment longer then turned without so much as a word. Ezekiel could hear the retreat of his polished shoes clicking against the pavement.

Stuck up! Ezekiel thought aloud then looked around at his camp. Despite his binge drinking, he kept the area militarily tidy, a habit that carried over from his army days. The sleeping bag was torn and smelly, of course, but what does one expect? There's a reason they call it "homeless." He looked down at his stained olive drab field jacket and pulled a handful of his long, stringy hair in front of him, well within view. He lifted an arm and took a whiff, wrinkled up his nose and shrugged.

Okay, so he was filthy dirty. So what? He was still a man, drunk or not. But he suddenly felt . . . embarrassed.

Lying down, Ezekiel laid the canteen upon his chest, pulled the sleeping bag up to his neck, folded his hands behind his head, and steadied his gaze on a flawless blue sky. "Still a man," he murmured to no one in particular, and through the slow-lifting alcohol-induced fog, it felt like his heart had been pierced through. Once again, he heard the little boy voices, the echoes of distant children's laughter, the death rattle of machine guns and mortar rounds. There was never enough whiskey to drown out the voices or the images. Her timeless face hovered before him, fading in and out while she smiled most reassuringly as she watched them pin on the medals.

"Still a man," he muttered to himself again while a lone tear traced a single line through the dirt on his face, stopping only to pool in his ear.

"I don't believe this." Jacob Brown was not an easy man to impress, nor was he given to exaggeration. Yet, as he stood at the mailbox shuffling through the latest of his mail, he questioned whether the two letters were a joke in bad taste or an actual example of local government control run wild. As he opened his mouth to vent out loud, Nathan pulled up into the driveway in his black and white jeep and came to a gravelly stop, windshield glinting in the early afternoon sun. He opened the car door, stepped out, and strode toward Jacob.

"Jacob," he began, his face determined, "I need to talk to you." He stopped a few feet away. "Wow," he added, "you look mad."

"So do you. It's a good thing you came by. I was just about to give the birds an earful," Jacob grumbled. He waved the latest of his mail back and forth in the air as though he were swatting flies. "More than one somebody really has it in for me as of late," he grumbled. "The one from the City of Birch Valley says I'm in violation of code for not maintaining my mailbox numerals; the other, from the State of Idaho, says I'm in violation of state codes that 'suggest' I'm selling herbs and vegetables from this stand that may be substandard, relative to human consumption. That's a polite way of saying 'possibly contaminated.'"

Nathan's jaw dropped. "With what?"

Jacob gritted his teeth. "That's precisely what I'd like to know. They don't say. Of course. Just that some troublemaker put a bug in their ear, and now they're going to pay me a visit. To 'inspect' and ask a lot of questions about the 'healthfulness' and 'safety' of my 'product.' Doesn't matter to them, apparently, that the proceeds go to help needy families in the valley. Bureaucratic garbage. And I wonder who this anonymous *someone* is who falsely fingered and accused us?! Can't imagine it's anyone in the valley. They're all our friends."

"I'm real sorry, Jacob.," Nathan said with feeling. "It's the age we live in, more or less. Nothing's at all like it used to be."

Jacob refolded the paperwork and stuffed each piece of mail back in its respective envelope. "Well," he said, "you didn't come here to listen to me gripe. You've got your own troubles, by the look of you."

Nathan nodded and took up his angry stance again. "Not just mine. First off, what are we going to do about Tessa?"

Jacob took a deep breath. "That's a big question, son. Ask her. Right now she's put us on hold as far as any official or additional intervention is concerned, except that charade we went through at the sheriff's office this morning. She won't come clean. Not completely. She's embarrassed and confused about being adopted and all the cloak-and-dagger stuff that came with it. Until she gives us the go-ahead, we're stuck in a holding pattern."

"I don't understand this," Nathan shot back. "There's more to this than she's admitting. Or at least more than she's willing or able to deal with. What are we—what am I—supposed to do in the meantime knowing all this? Just wait until something else bad happens?"

Jacob held up a restraining hand. "Listen, Nathan. We're between a rock and a hard place right now. Tessa's calling the shots. All we can do is just sit tight . . ."

"And pray," Nathan cut in.

"Yeah," Jacob said wearily. "That too . . ."

"All right, look, that brings me to the second reason I'm here. Jacob, you've got to check out what's going on at Sheep Gate. Last night was a real eye-opener."

Jacob nodded. "Yeah," he said, "Tessa told me it was 'different.' But I guess it's the first time that Davis fella has done something like this. Maybe he's just trying out some new stuff. You know, trying to better reach this generation . . ." Jacob's voice trailed off. His explanation sounded lame, and he knew it.

Nathan looked disappointed. "That doesn't sound like the Jacob Brown I know. What gives?"

Jacob's lips thinned. "The Jacob Brown you once knew is plumb tuckered out. It's time somebody else . . ."

"Did what?!" Nathan asked, astonished. "Take up the fight?! Have you pass the torch?! I can't believe my ears! It was you who helped put Flat Plains College back on the right path. It was you who helped Tessa know the truth and accept the Lord. Finally, it was you who gave me somebody to look up to when I didn't think there was anybody left worth looking up to."

Jacob sighed, and his eyes showed themselves to be tired. "Don't look up too high, son," he said. "I'm not as tall, spiritually, as you think I am." Nathan suddenly realized Jacob spoke more slowly now and with a tinge of sadness in his voice that could not be named. "I don't know what's happening to me, Nathan. So much has gone on lately—what with the church going 'modern,' this snazzy new preacher, Daisy dying, this bureaucratic nonsense, and most of all, all this business with Tessa. I feel like I'm sinking in the quagmire of it all and like everything's moving way too fast yet in slow motion at the same time. I'm so tired all the time—inside, if you know what I mean. It all just kind of snuck up on me, and it's hard to even pray anymore . . ."

Nathan regarded him with compassion. His voice was firm but gentle. "I know," he said. "I've seen it. You haven't been to church since way before you left to resign at Flat Plains. Otherwise, you'd be fully aware of what has been going on. And this thing with Tessa has me on edge and at my wit's end, too. If anything happened to her, I'd . . . But Jacob, we need you. Men just like you. You're going through some kind of crisis of faith from what I can gather. I've been reading a lot lately about the lives of a number of old saints who experienced the same thing in their own lives. But God brought them out of it stronger than ever. You can't let this thing beat you J.B! We need you. Remember David, in the Old Testament, where he encouraged himself in the Lord. You can do that too Jacob—encourage yourself in the Lord."

For a long moment, the silence hung like a black cloud between them, then Jacob sighed again. He put a heavy hand on Nathan's shoulder. "Okay, partner," he said with a sad, life-weary smile, "lay it on me."

Nathan grinned and let out a long, slow breath. "I knew you wouldn't let us down," he said. "Well, for one thing, the church library. This Chip Davis has been getting rid of most of the books on solid theology and replacing them with an eclectic mix of books by Catholic mystics, New Age gurus, and so-called *progressive* Christians who are teaching outright heresy."

They began walking toward the house. "And, Jacob, you should have been there last night. It was more like a rock concert than a worship service. I felt sick to my stomach by the time it was over . . ."

In a far corner of the Birch Bark Bistro, Chip sat across from Tessa, hands folded before him on the table, eyes averted, looking uncharacteristically shy. From behind the counter, Zhanna caught his eye once and gave him a knowing wink and a smile, and he gave every appearance of pretending not to notice. He was having a hard enough time without a busybody waitress making faces and insinuations. Fortunately, Tessa's back was to her.

Chip wished more was going on to keep Zhanna occupied and out of his business. The bistro was quiet that evening with only a few patrons scattered about the little room. He had hoped for a much busier atmosphere so the two of them could speak without drawing attention to themselves, and he felt it was only luck that allowed him to slip away from the people who were constantly calling and stopping by the church wanting to meet him. He'd have to get right to it because if one of his fans happened by, the personal moment would be over. Frustrating, at times, the lack of privacy purchased at the price of fame. But this was it, so he threw himself into it with a restrained kind of gusto. "Look," he said quietly, "I know this is kind of sudden. For you, I mean. But Tessa, I'm telling you the truth, ever since I first saw you in church, I was . . . what's the old word they used to use? Smitten? I just can't get you out of my mind or stop thinking about you. And now," he added, dramatically averting his gaze, "my heart, too."

Tessa tried to muster a smile, but failed. Nervously, she took a sip of her hot, steamy chai tea. When she ventured here at his invitation this evening, she was still rattled about the pagan-type atmosphere she'd sensed at Sheep Gate's "revival," and naively thought Chip had it in mind to discuss her impromptu flight from the church the evening before. His intimations took her aback. She was frightened and yet oddly exhilarated. Two good-looking men, each charismatic in his own way, setting their sights on her. This was too wild for words. Her head became a whirlwind of jumbled thoughts. Everything was moving so fast, from Nathan declaring his desire to court her, to the car nearly mowing her down the other night, to her mysterious adoption . . . and now this. She had to admit, she was kind of taken with Chip the first time she listened to him. He made a significant effort to speak with her after each service she attended, and just the act, in and of itself, made her feel special. After all, many of the young, unattached women in church were falling over themselves trying to attract Chip. He would be considered a terrific catch by today's modern standards.

Tessa gathered her thoughts and swallowed hard. She hoped he hadn't noticed. "Ummm. I don't quite know what to say, Chip," was all that came out, and she closed her eyes and mentally kicked herself. How about telling him how flattered she was, or that Nathan had already expressed his strong feelings for her, or something like, "Wow, you're actually thinking of me in that way?" But all she could offer was a schoolgirl's stutter.

"Tessa," Chip implored, and at eye level, he locked eyes with hers, "I think . . . I'm falling in love with you."

Tessa found the need to catch her breath. Her cheeks flushed. "Chip," she said haltingly, "you don't even really know me. How can you possibly say something like that and mean it?"

"I know enough," Chip said, his jaw tightening, bound and determined. He looked very masculine at that moment. "All I'm asking for is a chance. I know Nathan Shepherd is calling on you, too." She startled, and he smiled at that. "Yeah, I'm pretty perceptive that way. You and him after church the other night and all. And I hear the kids in the youth group talking. I'm not asking you to dump him or anything. That wouldn't be fair. But . . . isn't there still time for finding out about or exploring the possibility of us . . . maybe? I mean," he shrugged, looking away and appearing all shy again, "I'm not a big, strapping outdoors guy like he is, but I've got some good qualities, too, I think, and all I'm asking for is a chance to show you. We don't have to rush anything. But my intentions are genuine."

His eyes met hers again, and Tessa melted. "Ummm. I'll have to think about it. Okay?"

Chip smiled at her ever so winsomely and let out a huge sigh. Almost a little too huge, but Tessa all-too naively dismissed it in the heat of the moment. "You bet," he said, boyishly. "That's all I ask."

An obnoxious series of engine revving sounded from the street just outside the coffee shop before finally ceasing and desisting. The little bell over the Bistro's door jangled, and a pair of imposing, heavy leather boots, filled by an equally imposing form, sounded across the floor. From the street outside the bistro came the carnival-ride-like music of the ice-cream truck much like a comedy of errors. The legs and base under the padded vinyl on one of the counter stools protested loudly as the fierce-looking heavyweight settled onto it. Chip looked apprehensively at the biker across the room and grimaced. "Uh-oh," he said, with contempt. "There goes the neighborhood."

Tessa looked over her shoulder at the biker who sat at the counter. Black, fringed leather jacket with the name "Hell Boys" blazoned in red on the back, black leather chaps, square-toed riding boots, and a holstered, checkered-handle .45 automatic strapped to his right side. His long, black, greasy hair was pulled back into a pony tail with a dirty, red bandana wrapped around his forehead. A forest of black moustache and beard covered over half his face. Without looking at Zhanna, he said, "Coffee" in a gruff voice, and as she poured him a cup, he slowly turned his body around on the stool until he faced

Chip and Tessa. From behind the dark veneer of his mirrored sunglasses, his obscured eyes scanned the both of them up and down. He reached behind him, instinctively knowing where to lay hold of his cup, and brought it to his lips, sipping his coffee deliberately while keeping his gaze riveted on them.

Tessa turned and leaned over the table. "Chip," she whispered, "He's scary. Let's get out of here."

Chip dismissed her remark with a wave of his hand and smirked. "Just another tough guy trying to impress people," he said. "Look at that gun. Big man." But he spoke in a quiet voice.

The doorbell jangled again, and an elderly stooped-over woman using a cane entered the room. From under a straw sunbonnet, two generations removed, her sparkling blue eyes studied the patrons' faces. She smiled with the gentleness of the aged as she struggled, step-by-step, to the counter, passing up a chair by the door. Stopping by the biker, she looked up and asked, "Would you help me, dearie?"

Hub Morrison stood respectfully and offered his grimy hand. "Sure, ma'am," he said, as she leaned all of her weight into him and laboriously seated herself on a stool right beside him. She beamed her thanks. To Zhanna, she said, "Iced tea, please dear."

The biker re-seated himself at the counter and turned his back toward Tessa and Chip. This came as a great relief to Tessa, who, sensing a prodding, said, "Chip, there is something I'd like to talk to you about."

Chip leaned in close, his elbows on the table. He smiled big. "I'm all ears."

"Wellll . . ." Tessa began, "it's about the church service last night."

Chip tensed. "Oh?"

"Yeah," Tessa went on, "I don't know what I'm trying to say, exactly, but . . . the first one I attended . . . well . . . the whole thing was . . . kinda flashy? Like you were putting on a show instead of an actual church service. Do you know what I mean?"

Chip's voice iced over. "No, not really. Can you elaborate?" he said.

Tessa hesitated. "Well, I . . . ummm." She shrugged and then said, "The lights, the way you danced all over the podium, the thumping music . . . I felt like I was at some kind of rock concert or being entertained at a Las Vegas casino. Then the video—it was all about those missionaries, if you can call them that and how much "good" they were doing. There was no Gospel message of salvation in it at all. I don't know, Chip. God's Spirit within me just didn't bear witness to what was going on. In fact, I felt very uncomfortable."

Chip's eyes softened. "Oh, that," he said. "Tessa, you have to understand. This is a new generation of churchgoers. We have to do whatever it takes to reach them. Just because we keep up with modern times doesn't mean we're not adhering to the Gospel message. The video did speak of Christ, right?"

"Well, yes," Tessa admitted, but was quick to add, "but only at the end. And it was so vague. It could have been any 'Jesus' they were talking about."

Chip frowned. "Any Jesus. What do you mean by that? There's only one Jesus in the Bible."

Tessa nodded. "Yes Chip, but in Matthew twenty-four, Jesus said, 'For many shall come in my name, saying, I am Christ; and shall deceive many.' A lot of people these days, more people than you might think, either profess to be Jesus or claim to be hearing His voice and speaking in His name, when, in truth, they have their own hidden agendas, or they are sincere but sincerely deceived."

Chip took on a more defensive posture. "Are you saying I've got my own hidden agenda? Or that I don't adhere to or believe in the Gospel?"

Tessa's eyes opened wide. "Oh, no! I'm not judging your motives," she assured him. "I'm just saying that we have to be careful when we preach the Gospel. We can't make up our own theology. I mean, wow, last night's service. I hate to say it, but it was a false gospel I heard at church last night. It's got to be the true Gospel that is preached and the real Jesus, or it's leading people along the broad road that leads to hell and their ultimate destruction instead of leading people along the narrow path and pointing them to salvation."

Chip's voice rose a decibel or two as he glowered at Tessa. "Are you insinuating I'm leading people to hell?"

Chip now had gotten Tessa on the defensive. "No, Chip. Listen.

You're misunderstanding me . . ."

"Tessa," he stated with a smug air of superiority, "God has given me the authority to do what I want with this congregation. I'm His appointed shepherd at Sheep Gate . . ."

"What *you* want?" Tessa's tone hardened. "No, Chip. It is Christ's church, not yours. You're called to do only what God says and not to exalt, promote, or implement your own plans above His or in place of His. As a pastor and seminary graduate, you should know that."

Chip was livid now and pulled out all stops. "Now wait just one minute, Tessa . . ."

"Hey mister!"

Chip hesitated, his mouth hanging open. He looked over at the counter where the biker once again sat facing the two of them.

"Don't yell at the lady." His voice was cool, dispassionate, and unaffected.

Tessa froze, her eyes becoming wide with fear. Chip smirked. A really, really stupid move, Tessa thought.

"This conversation, *sir*,"—Chip delivered the last word condescendingly—"is none of your business. We're talking about things you couldn't possibly understand. So, why don't you just leave us alone?!"

The padded stool squeaked again as Hub Morrison stood. Tessa couldn't help but notice how, oddly enough, the old lady's eyes lit up with excitement.

Hub's boots thudded across the linoleum and stopped at Chip and Tessa's table. Chip looked upward, and his face turned a ghostly white as it drained of all color. Hub's mountainous form blotted out the evening sunlight coming in through the windows. He reached down, and with one ham fist, gathered Chip's spotless shirt collar into a handle and lifted Chip effortlessly up and away from his chair. Chip's feet dangled a few inches from the floor. Hub moved his face to within an inch of Chip's, and as he spoke, the whiskers of his beard tickled Chip's face. His breath reeked. "I could leave you alone in the graveyard, little boy," he said.

"Now, b-be cool," Chip replied, breathing shallow. "I've got a big mouth sometimes. Didn't mean to make you mad . . . okay?"

Chip caught his "scared out of my wits" expression reflected in the biker's mirrored sunglasses. After a long pause, Hub smiled faintly. "Yeah," he said and released his grip. Chip fell to the floor, sprawling out lengthways, sending his chair reeling.

Hub walked back to his counter stool to finish his coffee while Tessa helped Chip to his feet. In the meanwhile, the old lady somehow had gotten down off her stool all by herself, without needing any assistance and, leaning on her cane, made a beeline over to Tessa. She bent over to give Tessa a hand. Strangely, she looked exhilarated as she smiled. "So much excitement," she said almost out of breath. "I need to get out of the house more often. This town is much more exciting than I remember."

With Chip now in his seat, looking away in utter humiliation, Tessa reached over to touch his hand. "Chip, let's go."

"In a minute," Chip said, his voice strained. "When I can walk. Just please, sit down now and finish your tea. Don't make a bigger scene."

The old lady left the building without so much as another word, and as the door opened and closed, a bell on the door jangled. Tessa looked around, startled. Something so familiar. That . . . that scent. A fragrance that was like . . . She turned to look at the door, but the old lady had vanished—all too quickly.

Tessa sat thinking while taking a few swallows of her chai tea. A strange expression came over her face. She closed her eyes and tried hard to remember what was so familiar about that woman. A couple of minutes later, she and Chip rose to leave. The room began to spin all around her, and a wave of nausea swept over her. Cramps began to twist her stomach into pretzel-like knots, and she nearly swooned. Chip reached out to steady her. "Not you, too," he said, exasperated. "Wait until I get you outside to faint if you can."

As they moved across the room, Zhanna emerged from behind the counter to open the door for them. The bell jangled several more times as every other patron, save Hub, took their cues and nervously exited the coffee shop. Zhanna stood with her hands on her hips, regarding Hub with a chiding gaze. "Thanks a lot," she said. "There go my tips for the night."

Hub smiled. "You're a tough lady," he said, and reached into his back pocket for his billfold. He took out a twenty and tossed it onto the counter. "This should make up the difference."

Zhanna offered a teasing smile. "You're still a bully," she said, fingering the bill. Looking out the front picture window, she added, "But I do like your scooter."

Hub winked. "Let me know when you want a ride, princess," he said.

"Ha!" Zhanna replied. "I said I like your bike, not you!"

Hub chuckled. Sipping what was at that point lukewarm coffee, he noticed for the first time the corner edge of a slim, white envelope protruding from his side vest pocket. He pulled it out, his eyes still obscured behind his sunglasses, then fished a thin-bladed knife out of its boot scabbard. Easing the razor tip under the gummed edge, he opened the envelope, stupefied as he stared at a pack of one-hundred dollar bills. He looked up to make sure the waitress wasn't watching. He realized at that moment that someone, somewhere had slyly slipped him what he had been expecting to receive in a face-to-face meeting.

> The steps of a good man are ordered by the Lord: and he delighteth in his way. Though he fall, he shall not be utterly cast down: for the Lord upholdeth him with his hand.
> (Psalm 37:23-24)

CHAPTER

9

"**A**rsenic? Are you kidding me?" Tessa sat propped against the raised back of the hospital bed, her mouth agape.

Doctor Charles Meldon stood beside the bed, clipboard in one hand and peering down at her over the rim of his glasses. Pushing seventy, his grandfatherly features were balanced by his professional demeanor. The ceiling light glowed against his bald head. "Well," he said, "you understand that it's just a preliminary diagnosis based on the list of your symptoms. The fact that you're feeling better in such a short period of time rules out the possibility of serious poisoning. Again, I'm only guessing, but the suddenness with which it occurred, and the list of symptoms itself—sharp headache, vertigo, confusion, stomach pains and nausea—well, it's classic." He added, somewhat hesitantly and with a sudden rush of color to his face, "Moreover, I've been doing some reading lately about the effects of various poisons used in murder. I'm a mystery novel aficionado, and the one I'm reading now . . . well . . ."

Jacob Brown's voice developed a hard edge to it. "Are you saying someone tried to murder my granddaughter?"

"Oh, absolutely not," Dr. Meldon assured. "Arsenic poisoning can be induced in any given number of ways, most of them quite accidental."

Then it was Margaret's turn. "With symptoms so quickly?"

Meldon paused, pursing his lips. "The speed at which the symptoms developed is a bit confounding," he admitted. "In theory, it could be accounted for due to a deliberate dose of the stuff. Still, to suggest attempted murder through arsenic poisoning . . ." he offered an embarrassed smile, "really, that kind of thing went out of style in the last century. I honestly don't think you have any cause for concern."

The room went uncomfortably silent. Dr. Meldon shrugged, uncertain. "Still," he offered, "if you'd like, we can do a few additional tests and send the samples to Boise for further evaluation. . ."

"No," Tessa murmured, her gaze far off.

"Yes," Jacob countered. "We need to know."

Tessa's eyes shifted to Jacob. "Documentation," was all he said, and the finality in his voice meant an end to the discussion.

Dr. Meldon nodded. "I'll advise the nurse on duty, and we'll do a round in the next hour. You wouldn't happen to have the cup you drank from, would you?" Tessa shook her head. Meldon smiled and said, "Just a thought. It would certainly expedite things, but we'll go with what we have. You rest, Miss Dawson. I'll let you know when we are to start." He tilted his head and smiled, walking toward the door. "Fascinating," he said, almost to himself. "In all my years of practice, I've never actually seen a case of arsenic poisoning, if that's what it is. I'm sure that's it. I'd even stake my life on it."

When he left the room, Tessa looked from Jacob, whose countenance registered anger, to Margaret, whose eyes registered fear. "I'm scared," Tessa said in a small voice.

Margaret reached over the bed railing and patted her hand. "We are too. Tell me, do you have any idea who could have done this? I mean, if it really was attempted . . . poisoning?"

Tessa's erratic thoughts raced, impeded only in part by her now receding headache. The vertigo was lifting, but she was still fighting confusion. She closed her eyes, wracked her brain, and shook her head. But then, she tensed, and her eyes flew wide open. "You don't think it was Chip? He was at the table with me the entire time."

Jacob chewed on that and discarded the idea. "What motive could he possibly have unless he's a complete nut? And how would he slip it into your cup unnoticed?"

Tessa shrugged retiringly. "I don't know. Several people could have done it, I guess—the waitress, one of the customers . . . hey!" She sat straight up in the hospital bed. "The old lady. She was right beside the table when she helped me with Chip."

Jacob and Margaret exchanged worried glances.

"No, really," Tessa insisted. "I know it sounds crazy but, thinking about it now, something just didn't seem at all right about her. And there was something else—a fragrance, a certain scent."

Margaret raised her eyebrows. "A scent?"

Tessa nodded then groaned at the pain. "Yes," she said, wincing. "It was . . . I recognized it . . . from somewhere." She rubbed her hand against her forehead. "I just don't know where, exactly . . ."

"Okay, kiddo," Jacob said, leaning over the bed and placing his big hands gently on her shoulders. "That's enough for now. Like the doctor said, you need to rest. We can talk more about this in the morning." He depressed a button on the bed remote and the mattress lowered to a more reclining position. Tessa looked imploringly at both of them. "Are you leaving?"

"Not on your life," Jacob said, then went wide-eyed with apologies. "Didn't mean that. Dumb thing to say." They looked at each other a moment, then burst out laughing. Tessa groaned again, hand on forehead, but smiling still. It would be a long night.

Jasmine Winters sat facing the old dresser mirror, pulling bits of face putty from around the bridge of her nose. She scrunched it up and wriggled it, enjoying the sensation. She hated being encased in makeup for hours on end, but it often took that long just to prepare for a relatively short-lived outing. Who knew that, years down the road, her youthful stint with a traveling theater group would come in handy in such a big way.

"Ouch," she said as she eased the false gray lashes away from her stretched eyelids. She placed them carefully in their tiny cubicle in the small wooden makeup box next to the sets of fingernails then leaned her face close into the mirror. "Looking a little peaked, aren't we, dearie?" she mumbled, swabbing away some eye wrinkles with a damp facial sponge. When she was all done removing the war paint, she placed the box next to the large suitcase that held both the wigs and another hinged box containing a veritable palette of makeup of varying shades. With a little primping, she could become anyone, don any persona, and with her fluency in five languages and her talent for synthesizing dialect, she was not restricted to commonplace English.

One final time, she picked up the long pink comb. The sweaty knots in her hair were the worst part of the charade, the whole top of her head imprisoned in a tight bun wig for hours. After a dozen or so passes, the comb's teeth slid smoothly through the thick platinum strands. The soft yellow glow from the twin tapered candles on either side of the dresser gave the hair, tumbling over her shoulders, a halo effect. She hated the hard light of the bare overhead bulb and never turned it on. Candles were so much more conducive to self-pampering, reflection, and meditation. The incense stick to one side dispensed a slow burning, curling thread of smoke, a visible fragrance that enveloped itself about her, so that she viewed her reflection as through a haze, or veil, framing her with an aura of mystery. The flicker of light and shadow played across her near perfect features. Had it not been for her eyes—calculating and hard—she could very well have been the model for many a Victorian-era angel painting.

"How'd you like your coffee, tonight, Miss Tess? Or was that tea you were drinking?" she said to the reflection, removing a topaz ring from the middle finger of her left hand and tossing it onto the dresser. Another prop. A good one. The stone was set so that it could be flipped up on a miniscule hinge, revealing a tiny empty compartment. Tessa's sickness was easy enough to instigate—just a bit of old fashioned rat poison tipped into Tessa's drink while she helped Chip to his feet. Although Jasmine didn't hang around for the onset of the symptoms, she had a pretty good idea that at that moment the Birch Valley emergency room was treating yet one more patient and that the Brown family would get no sleep tonight.

"That's one for our side," she murmured and touched her fingertip to the bare belly of the little gold Buddha beside the incense holder. She smirked at the figure's jollity. The icon's hypocrisy was not lost on her. For a religion supposedly promoting a slavish king of self-restraint, a self-indulgent Buddha with a prodigious belly seemed a bit of a dichotomy. No wonder he was laughing.

"Tisk, tisk," she remarked when she examined her fingernails, dulled from scrubbing countertops and appropriately peeled to the quick like a good nun's. The loss of their customarily aesthetic and exquisite appearance weighed on her like the death of a friend. What she wouldn't give for a month's growth, a good coat of polish, and a good buffing from a professional.

Looking into the mirror, she removed her dark brown contact lenses. Tilting her head from one side to the other, she both admired and felt disgust at her reflection. How she hated hiding her beauty, slumming with a class of people who wouldn't merit a place even on the bottom of an R.S.V.P. list. Slamming the comb down onto the dresser, she leaned her chin into the palm of one hand and with her elbow on the vanity's stripped, wooden top, brooded.

So, this is what she'd come to. A one-room apartment (two if you count the small back room for storage) over an empty 1950s food joint, a tiny box kitchen with only sometimes running water, a rust-stained shower stall the size of a telephone booth, and a single, old bed with a sunken-in-the-middle mattress. What a cruel joke. Well, anyway, she had been letting the locals know she would begin hiring for major renovation in two weeks. *Two weeks,* she thought. *Then it will be over.*

Had it really been three long, lousy years? What a waste of a life. She could have accomplished so much at Flat Plains College and beyond by now, and it had been, at the time, tantalizingly within her reach. Respect, honor, submission from inferiors . . . all well within reach, and all so unfairly snatched away from her in a moment. And the irony—the irony—that her old foster parent, somebody old enough to have been dead for several years, pulled the plug on her. And with his own adopted granddaughter having been Jasmine's protégé to boot. Talk about a twist. If it had happened to someone else—anyone else, she'd have been hysterical with laughter.

The smartphone on her bed buzzed, and she lunged for it so forcefully the chair clattered to the linoleum several feet away. She shoved the little rectangle to her ear. "You!" she nearly yelled. "It's about time. Where are you? Do you realize I'm trying to get this thing off the ground and I—Need—You—Here?!"

With eyes blazing, she listened only a moment. "Hurricane? I don't care if you've been caught up in Typhoon Mary," she hissed. "You were supposed to be here already. I can't do this alone. We agreed. Remember? Remember? You're in this too, and if you do anything to sabotage it, I'll . . ."

She listened again and took a deep breath trying to regain a sense of inner calm. "New York," she said, relieved but still angry. "Okay, so, I'll expect you tomorrow, then? Right? I said, 'Right?!' What?" She pressed her ear to the phone and leaned forward. "You're breaking up. Are you there? Hello? Hello?! Aaahhh!"

She drew back her arm, aiming for the wall. In her mind's eye she could visualize the tiny black box detonating against the cracked drywall but couldn't bring herself to complete the maneuver. That smartphone was her lifeline, the only material hint of awaiting freedom and a necessary link to her employer. Jasmine sighed, her shoulders caved, and she settled into a sitting position on the bed. She listlessly looked over at the nun's habit overlaying the blanket and looking out of place on the sunken-in bed. "Morons," she muttered, "him and that little fake preacher twerp."

There would always be unaccounted for hitches and glitches to even the best-laid plans, she knew. The people in this town were nothing more than wrenches thrown into the mix, either grinding things to a screeching halt or forcing a detour. She wished she neither needed a partner nor stood in danger of being exposed. She'd already made one potentially fatal mistake when she accidentally left some Spanish bills at the Bistro when she first got into town. The whole thing was a tightrope walk. But the simple fact of the matter was, she didn't desire swift vengeance. No, a long, drawn-out process was more her speed—building the tension, breaking down her enemies one incident at a time, like just enough arsenic in coffee to sicken and cause fear—this made the snail's pace, the inherent danger, and all the wild cards that had come into play and still might come into play very worth her while. It was not just the destination that mattered to her but the journey. If it were all over with a wave of her hand, she'd never be able to savor her victory. Still, there was a timeline to which she needed to adhere, and Chip Davis had thrown a significant wrench into it. The longer she was in Hicksville, the more in danger she was of being found out. Her masquerade was professional, but, like everything else, it had a shelf life. She needed to think and figured if she could make it work for one more week, then she'd disappear. This time for good.

Jasmine felt overcome again by a black surge of inner rage while she stood up and moved again to the dresser to continue with her makeup removal. "Won't be long now, Jacob Brown," she hissed. "Remember me? I'm coming for you. This time I'm going to get you where it hurts."

She looked at her reflection in the mirror and gasped. Her seething hatred from within had disfigured her from without. Jasmine Winters was ugly.

He sat by the guardrail that wrapped around the overlook, surveying the now-flickering lights of Birch Valley, but his mind was far away. As sunlight gave way to darkness, a breeze that filtered its way down from the mountains had a bite to it, driving away the heat of the day. Leaning back up against the sissy bar's backrest, he stretched out his legs as much as possible on the big Harley. He'd parked there more than an hour earlier, and aside from the occasional passing pickup, the road behind him was empty. A young couple pulled up next to him when he'd first arrived but decided Hub was best left alone so they drove off. Hub didn't feel glad about it exactly. He never felt any kind of joy over much of anything. But he was relieved the couple had left on their own initiative. He would have had to oust them had they decided to tough it out. And, oddly enough, Hub wasn't in the mood to fight. He needed quiet, and this was a quiet place.

Hubert Morrison was tired. Not that he was getting too old for a freewheeling lifestyle—being in his thirties still left him much of future road time—but lately it seemed that no matter how many countless places across the country he had roared in and out of, they all began to look unremarkably identical—the same old music played in every bar and saloon; the same redneck types foolishly challenged him to fight; the same uptight law enforcement cowboys continually ran him out of their towns. Even his colors sometimes got him into altercations with brethren of other biker clubs, but generally they left him alone. He wasn't even a Hell Boy anymore, per se. He hadn't ridden with them for the past year, having struck out on his own, well . . . just because.

No, that wasn't exactly true. Fact was, they asked him to leave. Politely, but at the point of a .45. Hub was a loose cannon, and even among a breed that lived outside the law by gun, knife, and fists, he was still in a class by himself. Crazy, they thought, taking chances no sane man would consider, and in doing so, repeatedly jeopardizing his fellow brothers-in-arms. Last year's fiasco with the California state police was, for them, the last straw. He'd been on the move ever since. Going nowhere, doing nothing in particular, earning bread money through dealing or spot construction—a skill learned from his father.

Hub sighed. The old man and he had been tight in the early years, more like brothers. A semi-reformed biker, Tate Morrison had shaved, gotten his long hair cut off, found him a wife who turned out to be no good, and finally packed the saddlebags on his old monster scoot (he never could bring himself to part with it). With a bedroll on the bike and an extra pair of foot pegs, he slid his six-year-old boy onto the seat in front of him and roared off into the sunrise. He grew out his hair and beard again, and in his shades and faded denim vest, he was freedom personified. Hub adored him.

Man, the places the two of them had seen. The road was a long and winding stretch of what Hub knew to be his life, and every chunk of real estate a road threaded through belonged to them as far as they were concerned. Hub's upbringing wasn't much, by moral standards, but Tate tried hard to protect his son from the underworld in which he earned his daily bread. The old man had been a wheeler-dealer—an outlaw entrepreneur who dealt in drugs, guns, and shakedowns. He was careful to always leave Hub in the care of trusted friends—other bikers who lived in real houses and held legal work—whenever he had a "job," but his son was as sharp as a tack and connected the dots early on. Hub took mental notes and fell into the biker way of life as smoothly as turning onto an off ramp. When Hub was only fifteen, the old man finally met his match: another woman, who set him up as part of a plea deal. Tate took a half-dozen slugs from police automatics in a job that went terribly wrong.

Tate's brethren gave him a full biker funeral. Standing over the upturned earth, looking down at the old man's grave, something in Hub snapped. The normal functions of conscience shut down, and he became wholly driven to become the worst of an already bad lot. "Wolfman," they eventually named him, and it not only fit, but the name stuck. Funny. Tate had tried so hard to keep his son from the biker way of life. Sitting on his scoot and staring off into the night, Hub recalled a snippet from one of the conversations they once had, something about "the sins of the fathers." Hub didn't know what that meant exactly, but lately it had been eating at him.

Despite the circumstances of his betrayal, in his entire life Tate had exercised a somewhat odd or uncharacteristic kind of chivalry. He had never defrauded or threatened a decent woman and had only involved himself in some fights that were none of his business in order to protect them, and impressed that attitude upon Hub from an early age. Hub pondered that maybe that was why he faced down that punk in the coffee shop earlier. Pretty girl, but dumb. Couldn't see she was being taken in by some sweet talk and boyish mannerisms. What was her name? Tessa. Short for Theresa. Where had he heard that?

Her face materialized before him, wide-eyed and lovely, but also very much afraid. They were all afraid of him—the good ones, that is. He'd had an old lady once, but she was junkyard-dog mean, and after a year of constant fighting, Hub had left her standing on a desert road a mile out of Barstow, California. He could still hear her harpy voice screaming at him as he gunned the scooter to get as far away as he could from her. Hub sighed. Sad, but that's the best he ever rated. He'd never have . . . what, a wife? Not like her, anyway, that . . . Tessa. For the hundredth time he pulled the photo from the envelope the old lady had given him. It was her all right. The thought of killing the innocent angel he'd seen at the bistro the other night sickened him so much it had sent him riding every mountain road around Birch Valley for days. Any excuse, just in case whoever hired him was watching. All the while his soul, if he still had one, was vexed to the core. He had pulled over at every lookout point he passed just to think, until they all looked the same. The only thing he could see was Tessa's face. What kind of man could take her life for a stack of green bills?

Suddenly, it hurt all over again—losing his father, the miles upon miles of empty roads, the cowboy bars, and the abject loneliness. He slid his hand into an inside pocket of his vest, pulled out the envelope and thumbed the money. Bills, and a lot of them—five thousand dollars worth. He mulled it over for a long time. Then, Hub Morrison did the only truly decent thing he had ever done in his life. He said, "No!" out loud.

Although he wasn't quite sure why, he wouldn't do it. The old lady who contacted him—how did she get his name, anyway?—the same one who slipped him the envelope, could rot in hell, for all he cared. He flat out wouldn't do it.

Now, the money, that was another thing entirely. Hub considered it traveling expenses. He figured he was safe enough if he took it and ran. What was she going to do—call a cop? He chuckled. "Sorry, granny," he said. "Life's a gamble, and you lost."

He'd hang around another few days to give the impression he was planning the job then split at night sometime. Hub had taken on some of the worst dudes on the West Coast. He figured he could handle one seemingly sweet little old lady who turned out to be neither sweet nor a high-quality lady after all.

He woke to being dragged from his sleeping bag by a pair of big, rough hands on his shoulders. Then, amidst the morning-after fog, he felt another pair lay hold of his ankles, and suddenly, he was weightless, swaying hammock-like while being carried at either end. A switch flipped inside of him, and before he knew it, he was back in Nam as his Cong captors toted him off to yet another camp. He kicked viciously and shouted, "No!"

The two men let him go. He hit the ground rolling and, in one smooth motion, lunged upright into the nearest one's midsection with a head butt to the stomach followed by an upward head snap that connected with the man's jaw. The man crumpled without a sound. The other one came at him, swinging bare fisted, but Ezekiel's forearm parried the blow, and he used a leg sweep to cut the man's legs out from under him. His attacker fell hard onto the damp earth with a thud and in a spray of dead leaves. As he lay there, he looked up at him with fear-filled eyes.

"Whoa! Don't kill anybody!" Another man, younger and in a spotless white shirt, came skidding down the slope to Ezekiel's camp, bracing his body against the short descent with his hundred-dollar shoes. He approached Ezekiel slowly, palms outward, smiling in a placating kind of way, but keeping a respectable distance from him. "Take it easy, my man," he said in a reassuring tone. "Guess we went about this the wrong way. Peace, huh?"

The two big men on the ground had struggled into a standing position and stood there dazed. Ezekiel, in a crouching position with knifehands poised, blinked hard several times, his eyes searchingly scoping out his immediate surroundings. He frowned, setting his focus on Chip Davis as he returned to the present. He stood upright. "You," he said simply. "The other day." He jerked his chin. "You were the one up there on the road."

Chip nodded, no longer holding his breath and started breathing in and out again. He waved the two men off, and they headed up the embankment to a white rental van at the side of the road. They stood leaning against the vehicle, rubbing their affected areas and talking among themselves.

"Man," Chip said with admiration, "we sure had you pegged wrong. What are you—commando or something?"

"Or something," Ezekiel muttered. His head pounded and he ran a dirty hand over his eyes. His voice was gruff and dismissive. "What do you want?" he said, as he walked to his bedroll, sat down pulling his knees to chest, and began rocking. From the churning in his stomach he felt he must have imbibed some really bad whiskey the night before. He hadn't felt this rotten since he'd hit rock bottom drinking Tennessee moonshine decades ago.

Ignoring the other men, Chip crouched down beside him. "Proposition?" he asked, arching his eyebrow.

Ezekiel eyed him suspiciously. "How much?" he replied.

Chip smiled a crooked smile. "Oh," he said, thoughtfully, "maybe . . . two hundred dollars and a quart of your personal favorite thrown in?" Ezekiel smirked, but Chip now had his undivided attention.

Then Ezekiel asked, only half joking, "Who do I kill?"

Chip grinned a big grin. "Now you're talking," he said and leaned conspiratorially close. He wrinkled his nose, and Ezekiel's face turned to stone. "We need somebody to ah, well, clean up, and present to the public, so to speak. When I saw you the other day, I knew you were perfect for the part."

Ezekiel threw back his head and raised an eyebrow of his own. "Why?" he sneered, "Because I'm so dirty?" He looked Chip up and down. "You don't look like you're hurting for bread. Why the come-on?"

"That's my business," Chip said. "All I need from you is to let us fix you up some, and you'll be paid. A ten-minute public appearance, and the money's yours. What do you say?"

"I don't do scams," Ezekiel said flatly.

Chip smirked. "Sure you do," he oozed. "You're over there at Jacob Brown's food kitchen every day, making them all think you're some poor slob who's down on his luck." He leaned in close again. "They don't know the real you, though, do they? The fighter I just saw. Bet you've got a pretty impressive military background too. But you wear a mask, like the rest of us. You've been running a game of your own for a long time." Ezekiel pretended to ignore him, but Chip closed in for the kill. "You think they care about you, man? Anybody? How many of them 'nice folks' come to visit you here? Nah, you know the score. It's number one all the way. You're already scamming them, bro. Why not take it up a notch or two and come out on top? If nothing else, two hundred dollars can buy a lot of self-respect."

Ezekiel stopped rocking and closed his eyes. Chip couldn't tell if he was considering the offer or about to throw up. He drew back, tensing his leg muscles for a quick maneuver, just in case.

Without opening his eyes, Ezekiel asked, "Ten minutes, huh?"

Chip had him. He grinned. "That's it. Then you can go your own way. We don't know each other."

Ezekiel nodded and winced at the effort. "Okay," he said.

Chip sighed triumphantly and stood. "Excellent," he said. "You know the new soup kitchen in town, the one that's not open yet?"

"The nun?" Ezekiel asked.

Chip nodded. "That's the one. It's one o'clock now. Be there by three. That should give you time to feel better. Go around to the back, and don't let yourself be seen. She'll let you in. I'll be there. We don't have a lot of time to do this, so you need to be there on time." He turned to go, stopped, and then said over his shoulder, "And, ah, you'll keep this to yourself, OK? That's part of the deal."

Ezekiel nodded and said, "I ain't no fink." As Chip climbed back up the embankment, Ezekiel opened his eyes, riveting them on Chip and yelled out, "Hey!"

Almost to the top, Chip turned and stood looking down at him. Beneath his beard, Ezekiel's mouth was firmly set in place. "The name's Ezekiel. And I'm a man," he said. "Don't you ever forget that."

Chip nodded, looking confused. "Yeah, sure, whatever," he said and made it to the shoulder of the road, climbed into the van with his thug friends, and drove off.

Ezekiel sat alone on his bedroll, rocking again, battling his acute nausea and wondering why he was even still alive.

The thief cometh not, but for to steal, and to kill, and to destroy: I am come that they might have life, and that they might have it more abundantly. (John 10:10)

CHAPTER

10

"If any of you lack wisdom, let him ask of God, that giveth to all men liberally, and upbraideth not; and it shall be given him. But let him ask in faith, nothing wavering. For he that wavereth is like a wave of the sea driven with the wind and tossed."

Jacob closed the Bible after reading the fifth and sixth verses from James 1. He bowed his head. He had been deeply pondering this Scripture. "Lord, I've been like a wave blown back and forth by the enemy's winds." He looked upward, past the ceiling of his study. "But I think I'm ready to stand now. I've been out of the fight, but . . . I want back in." The strange (and even dangerous) things that were happening to Tessa woke Jacob. He realized he had not been trusting the Lord lately, and it was time to set things right. "Lord, please forgive me for not totally trusting in You with everything. And please give me—us—wisdom. Nathan's convinced there's something afoot in our church not of You. Help us to see clearly, and lead us in the way we should go. I pray this Lord, in Jesus' name. Amen."

Jacob had been to the last Sunday morning and evening services where a diverse mix of young and old filled the sanctuary. Jacob thought Chip's message had been rather blah but nothing really heretical. Still, the sermon was punctuated with nuanced references to the goodness of man, the duty to be a good "steward" of the environment and, when referencing the Scripture, "to keep oneself unstained by the world," Chip had flipped the meaning of the verse to now mean keeping the body pure and "toxin-free" when in actuality this verse was referring to the immorality of the world. The wording was very different from what Jacob was used to hearing in sermons, but he had determined to keep an open mind while keeping his spiritual guard up. He had planned on approaching Chip after the sermon to pick his brain on his word usage, but the young minister had deftly slipped out before the congregation itself had completely cleared the building. No matter. Jacob knew that Wednesday night services were mainly geared toward the youth, and it was also the opportunity for a more casual pulpit approach. From what he had been told, Chip had incrementally introduced changes into both the format and the Wednesday night teachings.

Last week, Chip had announced a mystery speaker would be at the church tonight. Chip's choice for pulpit sharing would help openly demonstrate his core beliefs. This night, Jacob was sure would settle the issue once and for all and help him plot his next course of action if one was needed.

With a start, Jacob looked up at the old clock on the mantle. It was about to chime six, and he felt the need to hustle. The Wednesday evening service was usually packed out from what he'd been told. Jacob stood, tucked the Bible under his arm, breezed into the kitchen, and gave Margaret a quick goodbye kiss. He started for the screen door, turned, and returned to where she stood watching him. He towered above her and, for a long moment, their eyes held each other's heart. Then he leaned down, kissed her tenderly this time, and turned for the door. "I'm praying for you," Margaret called after him. She moved to watch him through the screen as he hopped into the front seat of the old pickup with an agility she hadn't observed in a long time. As she watched him pull out of the yard to the driveway, she could tell (knowing him so well) that after a difficult and trying season of pronounced battle fatigue, her man had finally picked up the sword again. She had never been more proud of him than she was at that moment. A Scripture from Isaiah forty came to her mind. She knew it by heart for it always reminded her of Jacob, and she said it quietly, "Even the youths shall faint and be weary, and the young men shall utterly fall: but they that wait upon the Lord shall renew their strength; they shall mount up with wings as eagles; they shall run, and not be weary; and they shall walk, and not faint."

A somewhat harried Nathan was waiting for Jacob on the front steps of the church. When he saw Jacob pull up a half-block down the street (all the parking close by had long since been taken), he took the church steps two at a time and, with Bible in hand, sprinted to the pickup. "The service is about to start," he said quickly. "Tessa's already inside. I've been waiting nearly half an hour. Where've you been?"

"Reading the Word—Nehemiah four—and praying," Jacob replied as they hurriedly walked shoulder-to-shoulder toward the church. "I wasn't about to go into a fight without armor." He shot Nathan a confident look. "We've got a battle to fight," he said, "The Lord is with us."

Nathan grinned. "Glad to have you back, preacher Brown," he said.

The place was packed out, mostly with younger people, many of whom brought their non-believing friends. The two of them wound up standing all the way in the back, wedged between the sea of bodies that kept flowing in and out of the sanctuary into the church's receiving area. Nathan pointed out Tessa to Jacob, who sat in the third row from the back, but there was no way to get closer to her.

The opening hymn was an old one, a standard that had been sung at Sheep Gate since its inception. Jacob looked quizzically at Nathan, who held up his hand in a "wait one minute and you'll see" gesture. But five minutes elapsed, then fifteen, and all was hymns and heartfelt sharing of prayer needs—with Chip as the mediator, of course—and Jacob and Nathan were beginning to look outmaneuvered. The wind had been taken out of their sails. Nothing out of the ordinary at all.

And yet, something was different. There was a prevalent mood, an unmistakable shift in the overall atmosphere, something that gave the old sanctuary an entirely different "feel" to it. When Chip took the podium, quoting the sixth chapter of Galatians, he began, "Bear ye one another's burdens, and so fulfil the law of Christ. For if a man thinketh himself to be something, when he is nothing, he deceiveth himself." Jacob was glad to at least know that Chip's earlier request to the elders to switch to a modern paraphrase instead of using the Bible translation Sheep Gate had always used hadn't been granted yet.

"So," Chip boomed, "we need to be the hands and feet of our

Lord, and minister to the hurting, bear their burdens, and affirm their humanity." The last three words set Jacob's ears burning. He felt in his spirit the need to brace himself for what was coming next.

Though up until this point, the sermon sounded borderline authentic, Chip suddenly cut it short. "Last week I promised you a guest speaker," Chip said dramatically, and, stepping back from the pulpit, he said, "Let's give Sister Genevieve a warm Birch Valley welcome" as he pointed to a seat in the front row, and the town's only nun stepped up onto the podium. The room fell silent. The angelic nun smiled and, extending her hands toward the congregation spoke strongly and clearly, "Peace to you all!"

The youth, who comprised most of the congregation, erupted in cheering. Word had gotten around about the vibrant nun who had come to help the homeless and the poor, and even those in Birch Valley who hadn't met her liked what they had heard. The cheering continued as the nun sweetly laughed, stepped sprightly down from the podium, and went from row to row, shaking hands and touching shoulders, moving among them like an old friend. Many reached out, if only to touch her habit as she passed.

Nathan leaned close to speak directly into Jacob's ear. "This is crazy," he exclaimed over the din. "First Chip and now her. And she only just got here!"

Jacob's nod was grim.

Lifting the hem of her outfit, Sister Genevieve hopped back up the podium steps, extended both hands again, and waited for the crowd to quiet. "Pastor Davis tells me he's been speaking to you about getting out and becoming involved in the community, in people's lives," she said in a Spanish accent, "like the missionaries we're all called to be. The Bible tells us to 'do unto others as you would have others do unto you,' so, in conjunction with Pastor Davis, I am here to show you what living by that spiritual maxim means!"

Beaming, she turned to Chip, who smiled magnanimously while beckoning with one hand toward the front left row. A well-dressed man stood and rather haltingly ascended the podium steps, and, facing the congregation, moved to stand between Sister Genevieve and Chip. He was an older man, not very tall, but rather distinguished-looking in a three-piece suit, polished shoes and salt-and-pepper hair neatly combed. His clean-shaven face revealed a strong cleft chin.

The huge screen behind them descended slowly, obscuring the big wooden cross.

"We found this man living in squalor by the bridge on the edge of town," Chip said melodramatically. "Soiled, unshaven, and uncared for." Chip nodded. The screen blazed with the image of the man as homeless. Chip looked over his shoulder and pointed at the image. "This . . . is what he has been for years . . . and this . . ." he draped his arm over the man's shoulder and drew him into a sideways brotherly hug, ". . . is who he is now!"

The congregation flew into a wild frenzy. Jacob gasped involuntarily. "Ezekiel!" he exclaimed loudly, though no one heard him over the roar. Jacob and Nathan threw exchanged knowing glances. Both looked around, and the faces, primarily of the youth, were ecstatic. Some cheeks glistened with tears.

"With a little help from others, this man," Sister Genevieve shouted over the crowd, "is a new person! He is now seeing himself as God sees him—beloved, precious, and unique. As you all are. With our help, he is beginning to see the light within himself, the divine spark that makes us all one in God! What you see is a direct result of that revelation, and that revelation came as a result of people getting involved and connected with one another. Remember that Jesus taught, 'I was hungry, and you fed Me, I was thirsty and you gave Me drink, a stranger and you took Me in . . . as you have done it to the least of my brothers, you have done it unto Me. This man was the least, and by ministering to him, we have ministered to Jesus!"

Releasing Ezekiel, Chip shouted into the head mic, "It's time to do as it says in Ephesians and break down that dividing wall of hostility between us—Catholic or Protestant—and to work *together* to bring the love of God to the poor and needy. "Jesus said, 'The kingdom of heaven is within you,' and we need to come together and put aside man's dividing doctrines and those isms which cause schisms and allow God's TRUE kingdom to manifest from within us and actually establish it on earth." He pointed again to Ezekiel, who smiled wanly. "Here is your proof! Are you ready?"

"Yes!" the congregation roared in unity.

Chip shouted, laughing, "I said, 'Are. You. Ready?!'"

The thunder of voices swept over the sanctuary, and the congregation simultaneously stood at once, while a flickering collage of images played over the wall screen and music from the hard rock band "Alive Again" flowed from the overhead speakers. Specially filtered lights from above moved back and forth continually and alternately over the podium, bathing the group hugging trio in a kaleidoscope of color. The scene was reminiscent of a disco dance floor illuminated by a spinning glitter-ball or a New Age or Far Eastern ashram awash in prismatic sunlight.

Chip repeatedly thumped his fists against the podium while shouting the name, "Je-sus! Je-sus! Je-sus!" in tandem with the music's beat and pacing back and forth. The crowd fell in lockstep with him until the name became a thunderous chant. With horrified amazement, both Jacob and Nathan watched as one person after another was swept up in the melee. Mostly, they could only see the backs of countless heads, but the thrashing of hair, the gyrating of bodies, and occasionally the tear-streaked eyes kept their feet riveted to the floor and only furthered their resolve to the real reason they were there.

Sister Genevieve took the pulpit, motioning with her hands for everyone to be quiet, as the hardcore music slowly faded, receding slowly into the background until it was replaced with faraway ethereal flute music, seamlessly picking up where the other music had left off. The crowd slowly became so still and quiet, you could hear a pin drop, and with extended hands reaching out to the congregation, the nun said softly, "Now, let the name become a breath, if you will—like a gentle breeze that comes from eternity, for God has set eternity in the hearts of ALL men and longs to move right into your very souls. That's it. Breathe the name in . . . breathe all your doubts and concerns out, in . . . and out, until it becomes part of you . . ." The congregation obeyed, mouthing the name in a collective whisper that filled the church sanctuary. The looks on the faces of those present went from that of wild abandon to a calm repose. Some wept, lifting their faces heavenward; others, with eyes closed, seemed to go blank. One young woman in the last pew, swooned. Jacob pushed forward to catch her from behind but could not reach her through the wall of bodies. Her shoulders hit the pew hard as she collapsed into it, her head bobbing like dead weight over the pew back. She sat, unmoving, with her mouth agape.

"This technique was known to the desert fathers a millennia ago," Sister Genevieve softly continued. "Our modern world has discarded so much of the spirituality that was common practice to them back then. But now . . . now we are re-entering the age of the true and altogether authentic Christian spirit, and you—YES YOU—will lead the way as Christ followers. The future of the church belongs to the youth of this world. Before, we have led you. But now, you must lead us."

Nathan caught a glimpse of Tessa struggling to vacate the pew. He shouldered his way to her, grabbed her hand and politely, but forcefully, plowed a way back through the crowd, heading for the door, with Jacob bringing up the rear. They left to the sound of Chip echoing Sister Genevieve's instructions on focusing on their breath then urging the congregation to visualize themselves standing in front of Jesus at the Sea of Galilee.

Once outside, Tessa leaned up against the outer church wall and, with eyes closed, breathed as deeply as she could of the cool mountain air while Nathan stood close to her with a comforting hand on her shoulder. "You okay?" he asked, his face alarmed.

Tessa nodded without speaking. Nathan's attention turned to Jacob who stood to one side of the door, his countenance a mixture of shock and anger. Jacob's voice was low and measured but filled with righteous indignation. He spoke almost to himself. "I can't believe I've been so blind. God forgive me." He turned to Nathan. "I'm making some phone calls. I'll insist on an emergency meeting of the church board tonight. I want you to come with me."

Nathan nodded. "I'll be there, Jacob."

Chip sat sprawled out on the old, blue, overstuffed couch in a back room of the Master's Way. The furniture was a bit moth-eaten as it was a castoff jokingly dubbed a "donation" from one of Birch

Valley's "upper crust," but it was at least comfortable in a shabby sort of way. A little longer sitting there and Chip would nod off, but the sooner they all met and dispersed, the safer it would be.

He felt totally wiped out, but it was a happy exhaustion. He—well, they—had run a good game tonight. Not only was he now a local icon among the church youth, he was heading in the direction of becoming a wealthy one as well. Little ol' Birch Valley was only the first stepping stone toward a national "ministry." All those years of schooling were finally paying off. Oh, if the old man could see him now, he'd be so proud.

While his mind wandered to bigger and better things with regard to his future, Chip idly watched Jasmine, still in full habit, doling out the pre-agreed upon amount to Ezekiel as the two stood on the other side of the dimly lit room. Chip chuckled to himself at the thought. Backroom deals. The only thing missing was a muscle-bound bouncer guarding the door and a pall of cigarette smoke polluting the airspace and creating an overall hazy effect. Then again, Jasmine's incense could create that effect every bit as well, he silently mused. He listened as "the nun" counted out the bills to Ezekiel while meting them out—part of the booty from the service's "offering." Two-hundred greenbacks wasn't so much to part with, Chip thought, for all they had accomplished tonight.

"You did good, Zeke," he said sleepily. "They never knew what hit 'em."

Jasmine moved behind the scarred, wooden desk. That and the ancient spindly chair behind it was all that remained of the official office furniture. A smothering of spray wood polish had removed the dullness, but the finish had long since been worn away. The chair creaked as Jasmine settled into it and began sorting through the remaining bills. "Be quiet," she said without looking at Chip. "I'm counting."

Chip ignored her. "How much, you think?"

Jasmine shrugged while Chip reveled in the sound of the soft rustle of currency. "I don't know. Maybe a thousand dollars."

Chip's eyes opened wide in surprise. "Wow. From a bunch of kids and hicks?"

Jasmine marveled at Chip's shortsightedness. "Some of those kids have rich parents. Anyway, it's chump change," she murmured.

"Ah," Chip mused, "It's just the beginning. You know, we really pulled it off. Even I didn't believe it would go so well. And you—oh, man, you were born for this kind of work. Think there'll be some fallout from the church board?"

Jasmine shrugged again. "Will you shut up? And yes, probably. If experience is any guide . . ." She stopped abruptly and looked at him.

Chip's eyes narrowed, and a Cheshire grin took its place on his face. "So, some of the mysterious lady's past comes out," he said. "Go on, Sister. Fill us in. I do so love a good story."

Jasmine scowled and resumed counting. Chip focused on Ezekiel, who stood in total silence, looking down strangely at the money resting in his palm. "What about it, Zeke?" Chip asked, smiling. "How's it feel to be reformed? Doesn't even look like you tippled tonight. I thought you would have already been celebrating."

For a long moment, Ezekiel stood there motionless with an odd expression on his face. When he looked up at Chip, his eyes registered revulsion. "You people make me sick," he said in disgust.

Jasmine halted in mid-count, looking up from the desk. The smile erased from Chip's face. "You bought in, buddy-boy," Chip said, deadpan. He nodded to the money in Ezekiel's hand. "You got yours." He lightened up. "And hey, who did we hurt, really?" he said. "The kids had a great time, we made some pocket money, and you got a bath, shave, haircut, and a new suit." He shrugged. "Everybody got what they wanted."

Ezekiel's gaze moved from Chip to Jasmine to the payoff in his now clenched fist. He opened his fingers and the money fluttered from his hand. It settled to the floor at his feet. "I don't want it," he said, and shook his head. He turned and went out the door, closing it unsuccessfully behind him to where it bounced back open again. Both Jasmine and Chip listened as his footsteps receded across the linoleum in the dining area and faded from earshot as he exited the building and disappeared into the night.

Chip sat upright on the sofa, suddenly tense. He shot Jasmine an uneasy look. "You think he'll say anything? I mean, he wouldn't blow the cover, would he? He'd go down, too. Nah, he wouldn't talk

. . . or, would he?" For what seemed like an eternity, Jasmine didn't respond. Her eyes bore holes into the office door, and her face was one of tight-lipped hatred.

"He'd better not," she said finally, slowly. "It'll be the last thing he'll ever . . ." She stopped and directed her gaze deliberately at Chip, who sat staring with a disturbed look on his face. He ran a tongue over a dry bottom lip, then stood and walked to the door. With his hand on the doorknob, he turned and regarded Jasmine as if laying eyes on her for the very first time.

"You know," he said, not taking his eyes from her, "working with you, I could almost believe in a real devil."

He opened the door and walked out, closing it quietly behind him.

"Will you please calm down?!" Worry laced Rob Carlton's voice. He had a big problem and had no idea how to handle it. Looking around at the other elders and their wives made little difference. They weren't about to get caught in the middle of it unless they had to. The emergency meeting after the youth service had turned the church basement into a theological battleground, and Rob didn't like it one bit. Jacob Brown and Nathan Shepherd stood side-by-side with arms folded and faces etched with the most frightening determination Rob had ever seen. He knew Jacob could be stubborn, but this was different. The way it appeared to Rob was that the old man was itching for a fight, and young Nathan, now that he was officially courting the granddaughter, was bound by prospective family ties. Rob, ever the diplomat, knew that, although they had a major problem, running roughshod all over the situation and each other was never a good idea either.

"Well," Jacob growled. "What are you going to do about it?"

Rob waved his hands and paced the floor. "Give me a minute. Let me think."

"What's there to think about?" Nathan added. He pointed upwardly with his index finger at the basement ceiling. "Tonight we witnessed full-blown heresy in that sanctuary up there. Five centuries of Reformation work undone, and to top it off, some New Age practices added. This 'new monasticism' stuff is dangerous! You should have been there. The place was a madhouse." Nathan scanned the dozen or so faces in the room, but most of them purposely avoided his gaze.

"Doesn't anybody here remember that 'River' movement from a few years back?" Jacob queried, amazed. "Slain in the spirit, 'holy' laughter, and people acting like animals? One of the hallmarks of that so-called 'move of God' was that the youth were being 'raised up' to be the last mighty generation before the coming of the Lord. 'The young will lead the church like some glorious army,' they said, 'to conquer Satan and all his hosts.' You all know how that panned out. What we witnessed tonight was reminiscent of some of the practices of that movement. It looked like mass hypnosis, or something just like it. It was mixed up with other heretical stuff, like 'ecstatic union' and breath prayers, but it was there. We saw it. Doesn't anyone here care?" By the looks on their faces, they didn't even get what he was talking about.

Bud Clement spoke up, hopeful. "Paul said to Timothy, 'Let no man look down upon you because you are young,'" but his voice trailed off, and he looked down at his hands.

"Things were going so well," Bill Stafford lamely offered.

Jacob grimaced. "No, they weren't—not even close! None of us were paying attention, that's all. With church attendance up, offerings through the roof, and everybody smiling, we just let our guard down, stopped exercising our God-given ability to discern and called it good." He sighed. "And I'm just as guilty as the next guy."

Rob piped up and said, "We'll talk to him. We'll just ask him to tone it down, or maybe back off a little . . ."

"Back off?" Nathan was incredulous. "How do you 'back off' teaching heresy when a little leaven leavens the whole lump? How about full-blown repentance, instead? Right in front of the congregation on a packed Sunday morning? How about Chip admitting what he did was sin, followed by Chip asking for forgiveness, along with a promise to abandon any and all heretical teachings. Finally, how about Chip stepping down from ministry until such time as it is determined he's theologically sound?"

Rob's eyes widened in total alarm. "Now, hold on. We can't go commando on all this. I agree he has made some mistakes, okay? Bringing in that nun maybe wasn't the best idea."

Jacob shook his head in disgust. "Nice one, Rob," he said.

Rob continued, hurriedly, ". . . but we'll ask him not to do that again. He's . . ."

"Why bother 'asking' him?" Nathan cut in. "You're the board. Have you read the doctrinal statement of this church lately? Catholic teaching and modern ecumenism are clearly forbidden . . ."

Pete Call stood up, angry. He pointed an accusing finger. "You," he said hotly, addressing Nathan, "aren't even a member here. We don't have to listen to you badmouth our pastor. And as for you, Jacob, you resigned as a board member some time ago. If you had wanted to continue influencing church policy, you should have stayed on in that capacity."

Jacob could feel his face becoming flushed and stepped toward Pete. He addressed Pete in a strong, low tone, choosing his words carefully.

"I don't have to be a board member to bring concerns to this church. I am a member here, as is my wife and granddaughter, and it's my right—my duty even—to remind you of your sworn responsibility to protect the flock. Or doesn't the word 'duty' mean anything to you?"

Pete became indignant. "I spent four years in the military, Jacob. I know what the word means."

"Semper Fi," Jacob said, the timbre of his voice intensifying. "Marines. Eight years. And I can spot a lapse of authority from a mile off."

Pete lunged at Jacob, but two of the other elders laid hands on his shoulders. His eyes burned into Jacob. Rob hustled over, waving a hand. "Please, Pete. You're not helping the situation."

Pete turned and slumped into a chair in a corner of the room.

Rob thought a moment more, sighed, then nodded to himself. His gaze met Jacob and Nathan's. "We understand your concerns," he tactfully began, "and we'll talk with Chip. I'm sure it's just a misunderstanding on his part. In the meanwhile, we don't want to get overzealous and make a mess of things."

Jacob's eyes hardened. "I seem to recall the Savior making a mess in the Temple. Overturning the tables of the moneychangers, chasing them and the animals out with a whip He Himself had made. I believe it is in John two, verse seventeen—'And the disciples remembered that it was written of Him, "Zeal for Thine house hath eaten me up." It seems to me Jesus was a bit 'overzealous' at times, too, eh, Rob?" Jacob couldn't help the sarcasm.

Rob was quietly placating but remained unmoved. "We'll take care of it, Jacob," he said with finality. "It'll be all right. You'll see."

"Yeah," Nathan added, shaking his head. "We wouldn't want actual repentance to damage church attendance . . . or church income . . ."

Henry Beam shot straight up from his chair. "I resent that!"

"Or more like resemble that!" said Jacob sarcastically as both he and Nathan moved toward the basement door to the street exit. Before he pushed it open, he turned and faced the elders again. "Just remember," he unequivocally stated in a voice most chilling, "you get what you pay for. You have sown to the wind, and you shall reap the whirlwind."

He pushed open the door, and both he and Nathan disappeared into the moon-lit night.

It was going to be that kind of night. Tessa shifted positions a dozen times, recited Psalm 23, and sporadically prayed, but nothing worked. Finally, throwing off her patchwork quilt, she stared up at the dark ceiling, her eyes roving over the shadows in the plaster and her mind flitting fast and furiously from one subject to the next.

It had been the kind of day when Murphy's Law proved a disquieting reality. She had continued to feel a bit queasy all week long from the residual effects of the poisoning. To take her mind off it, she had puttered around the house, sometimes sitting on the porch and ruminating about Marilyn Dawson (she couldn't yet bring herself to call her "mother" again), and about love, life, death, and faith. This evening's fiasco at the church had triggered a flood of memories of her having come under spiritual attack at Flat Plains years ago. She had nearly forgotten how bad it had gotten being Jasmine's protégé.

To top it off, after the wacky Wednesday youth church ser-vice, Nathan had shown up with Jacob after their late night sortie against the church board and were still having a heated discussion at the kitchen table after sending Tessa to bed. She had finally informed Nathan of the poison attempt but only after Jacob's insisting. He responded to the news with the appropriate and to-be-expected kind of horror and anger that he hadn't been told the night it happened. It hadn't exactly amounted to a blow-up or a knockdown drag-out fight, but the resultant emotionally charged conversation left them both feeling confused, emotionally drained, and not knowing how to proceed. She couldn't fault him, really. She'd left him out of the loop for fear that the man in him would take over, and he'd bully his way around town seeking answers and wind up getting himself arrested for harassment. It was stupid thinking, she knew, but then, she hadn't been thinking straight since the odd series of events began. Before she went up to her room that night, Nathan had put his arms around her and held her. That had made her feel considerably better on the inside, but they were still left with no real answers.

Why? That was the resounding question that kept boomeranging through her mind. The not knowing was the worst part of this insane situation. Why on earth would anyone want to harm her? She was nobody special, nor had she gone out of her way to make enemies. Per-haps she overestimated her own generic sweetness, but she considered herself to be generally good-natured and non-confrontational. She couldn't think of a single person she'd interacted with who would have any reason to . . . Tessa shuddered. The word itself—murder—seemed so inane. In real life, this kind of thing just didn't happen. It was as if she had been scripted into a most nightmarish mystery whodunit movie—of which she desperately wished she knew the ending.

"Help me, Lord," she whispered into the dark. "I don't know what to do. And I'm really scared. Please, please Father, show us the way, and protect us. In Jesus' name. Thank you." She smiled. "And thank you for Nathan and for a great family. Even . . . if I don't yet know or may never know the all of who my biological family really is. I love you, Father."

The muffled hooting of a great horned owl could be heard through her slightly open bedroom window. A night breeze moved through the stand of pines by the driveway and ruffled the lace curtains, causing cool air to settle over her. The chimes of the old mantle clock drifted up from the living room and comforted her. Tessa lost count as she drew the blankets up close, and her eyes grew heavy. *Sleep*, she thought. *Oh, how wonderful.* Then, just before drifting off, she put her finger on it. A . . . fragrance. I know that smell. A nun's habit. A white-haired old lady . . .

Tessa's eyes flew open, and she bolted up nearly falling off the bed. "Jasmine!" she gasped. "It's Jasmine!"

> Now the Spirit speaketh expressly, that in the latter times some shall depart from the faith, giving heed to seducing spirits, and doctrines of devils. (1 Timothy 4:1)

CHAPTER
11

"**A** nun?" Deputy John Akim struggled to mask his disbelief and incredulity, but it was a waste of time, and everyone knew it. The look in his eyes betrayed all his police training in poker-face interrogation techniques, as he looked from Tessa to Jacob to Margaret to Nathan then back to Tessa. "A nun is trying to kill you?"

It had been one of those days for Akim. The instant he glanced out the window close to midnight and saw the headlights of an old tan pickup pull into the parking spot, he had that sinking feeling that his long day was about to get much longer. A black and white jeep had pulled in with the pickup, and along with the family, a young man Akim recognized approached the glass door. This time they had brought backup. The other deputy working a computer keyboard on the other side of the office noticed as well and grinned slyly and made an irritating gesture as if to say, "Have fun."

Akim took the initiative and procured the same three chairs the older folks and the young girl had used and set them in order before his desk. The young guy would just have to stand. Even as the group entered the office, Akim had taken his seat and with a steady gaze and hands folded on his desk, he awaited the inevitable. So far, it had been more than even he had bargained for.

Tessa pursed her lips as she drew her blanket tighter around her shoulders to cover her butterfly pajamas. She felt ridiculous but had to speak the truth. "She's not a nun. I just told you that."

"Okay," Akim said, with hands defensively raised. The old office chair creaked as he leaned back, folded his hands on his stomach, and marveled, his eyes on Tessa. When he spoke again, all bets were off. He was not going to pretend anymore, and professionalism be hanged. "Miss Dawson," he said, slowly, "this is a pretty incredible story you've just told me. Try to see it from my point of view—you say there is a new nun in town who is not actually a nun but is masquerading as one, who also happens to be your old spiritual formations professor, who is also a little old lady who both tried to poison you and run you down with her vehicle because she has a several years'-old grudge she is nursing against you and your family for getting her fired from her job. This professor is also fluent in five foreign languages and is so well-financed, she sets up a front in the form of a church mission to the poor for her plans to kill you . . ." He took a deep breath. "You see where I'm going with all this?"

Tessa blushed out of sheer embarrassment and looked down at her hands, her fingers nervously intertwining and releasing. "I know it sounds crazy, but it's true . . ."

Akim tilted his head and eyed her intensely. "And your proof is the familiar scent of some, what do you call it, Jasmine essential oil, which your college professor wore, and a cup of . . . what is it—chai latte? I don't even know what that is. Anyway, it's virtually nothing to go on."

"Deputy," Jacob interjected, "there's a simple way to prove this." He handed Akim a poster advertising The Master's Way.

"Yeah," Akim said, and shrugged. "I've seen these. You want to go online to check out their website?"

"I've already done that," Jacob said. "They've got a mission statement, some short videos, lots of photos of nuns and their work, that kind of thing. Nothing out of the ordinary."

"So it's legitimate?"

Jacob shook his head. "I didn't say that. Anybody can build a website. I can say I'm the reincarnation of George Washington and ask people to contribute to my cause of replanting cherry trees, but that doesn't mean I'm genuine." He leaned over the desk and pointed. "But there's a phone number we can call."

Akim shrugged again. "So, why didn't you just do that at home?"

"We wanted witnesses," Jacob said pointedly. "In law enforcement, your word would carry weight."

Akim nodded. "I think that's an excellent idea, Mr. Brown. Maybe we can lay this thing to rest right here. But you do realize the time, don't you?"

"Doesn't matter," said Jacob. "It's a fake phone number. You'll see."

He reached for the cordless phone, squinted at the small number on the bottom of the poster, and hit the respective buttons. As the connection was made, he punched the "Speaker Phone" button on the miniature phone console. The room went silent at the sound of a ringtone, and everyone's gaze was fixed on the voice box. At a click on the other end of the line, a young and pleasant sounding voice answered, "Convent of Our Lady of the Roses. This is Sister Veronica. How may I help you?"

Instantly, an astonished look passed over the faces of everyone—except Deputy Akim—and the family and Nathan exchanged confused glances. Akim leaned forward toward the speaker phone. "Yes," he said politely, "this is Deputy John Akim from the Birch Valley, Idaho Sheriff's Department. Terribly sorry to bother you so late in the night, sister. Could I speak to ah . . ." he looked quickly at Jacob and whispered, "What's the chief nun called?"

"Mother Superior," Jacob whispered back.

". . . the mother superior," Akim continued, resisting the urge to roll his eyes and shake his head.

"No apology necessary; God's faithful servants work on His time clock. One moment, deputy," Sister Veronica said. "I'll see if Mother is available."

After a pause, another, older sounding woman's voice said, "This is Mother Angelina. What can I do for you?"

Akim's eyes passed knowingly over Jacob, Margaret, Tessa, and Nathan. His face registered vindication. "Yes, ma'am," he said into the phone. "I was wondering if I could ask you some questions regarding one of your nuns—a Sister Genevieve? She's here in Birch Valley . . ."

"Goodness!" Mother Superior replied, breathless. "Nothing's happened to her, I hope. They said you were from the sheriff's department . . ."

"No ma'am," Akim assured her. "She's fine. I just wanted to get some information about her, if I could. Has she been with your convent long?"

"Why, yes," she said with concern. "For about ten years now. I'm sorry. I don't understand the reason for this call. Has Sister Genevieve done something wrong?"

"Well," Akim haltingly replied. "No. Not exactly. We simply have some questions regarding her, um . . . legitimacy? I'm sorry, ma'am. I'm being as delicate about this as I can. It seems there have been some reasons to believe she's not who she says she is. I just really need some confirmation from you. To start with, can you describe her to me?"

The older nun laughed lightly. "My! This sounds rather conspiratorial. My sisters aren't usually involved in cloak-and-dagger scenarios."

Akim shot Jacob an annoyed look.

"Well," the old nun continued, "she's about five feet nine, rather slender, with a semi-dark complexion—she was born in France but speaks with a Spanish accent due to her being raised near St. Theresa of Avila's convent, you know—oh, she has brown eyes, is energetic, and extremely friendly. Which is one of the reasons she was sent out of the cloister by special order to establish a mission to the poor."

"In Birch Valley?" For once Akim responded with a cop's intuition. "Pardon me, sister . . . 'er, mother . . . but there aren't a lot of homeless folks in this town. Why here?"

"It is a crossroads, is it not?" Mother Angelina noted. "Kind of a 'just passing through' locale to larger towns and cities. If I remember our research, Birch Valley has its share of transients, especially in the summer, when travelers down on their luck have no money to go any further. Plus, there is a bad section of town, "across the tracks," as we put it, where Sister Genevieve has set up headquarters for ministry. Surely those people are entitled, as God's little ones, to love, food, and clothing. And . . ." she added almost coyly, "there is no Catholic presence in Birch Valley. Surely you wouldn't forbid us our chance to minister there, deputy?"

"Oh, no ma'am," Akim replied. The thought of a religious discrimination or harassment lawsuit entered his mind. "You and your people are welcome here anytime. And I've met Sister Genevieve. Real nice lady . . . or nun . . . I mean, sister."

The older nun laughed again. "I'm sure she'd appreciate that," she said. "I don't usually give out this kind of information over the phone, but I understand your position. Let me assure you that Sister Genevieve is one of ours. I have known her personally for ten years now, and I have every confidence in her. I can pull her file, though, if you think you need additional reassurance?"

"That won't be necessary, ma'am," Akim said. "You've been very helpful. Thank you for your time."

"Certainly, deputy," the nun said. "Feel free to call us anytime. Goodbye."

"Goodbye sister." Akim pushed the "End Talk" button and let his eyes rest on each of them in turn. "Well?" he said.

Tessa appeared visibly shaken. "I was so sure . . ." Standing behind her, Nathan placed a large, comforting hand upon her shoulder.

Jacob was unmoved. "Then how do you explain away all the other things—the warning note in my granddaughter's purse, the skateboarder eyewitness, the doctor's report stating that it was arsenic?" Jacob wasn't going to back down.

Akim spoke, intentionally calm, "We tried to find that boy that your granddaughter claimed she spoke with . . ."

Tessa's eyes flared as she looked up at Akim. "Claimed?"

Akim relented. "Okay—the witness to the car incident. But we couldn't find him. You never got a name or gave us a description . . ."

"I was almost run down," Tessa said defiantly. "I was a little too upset at the time to take notes."

Akim shrugged. "Granted. But it still leaves us little to nothing to go on. And I spoke with the doctor at the hospital. He repeatedly told me that you could have ingested the poison accidentally from any given number of sources. As for the note in your purse, I spoke with Millie at the library, and she remembers it all right, but she couldn't say whose handwriting it was . . ."

Akim's voice trailed off tellingly, and the room went quiet. The deputy sitting at the other desk stopped working the computer keyboard and pretended to be studying the monitor.

Tessa looked right at Akim in utter disbelief. A look of consternation and outrage washed over Jacob's face while Nathan's hand curled into a fist.

With narrowed eyes, Margaret brusquely asked, "Are you inferring . . . that my granddaughter has somehow fabricated this entire story or done all this . . . to herself?"

Akim paused for a moment, leaned forward to rest his elbows on the desk, then spoke. His voice was gentle, but firm. "Look," he said, addressing Tessa, "you've had a real upset, finding that letter in the back of your book from a woman who admitted she wasn't your mother. That would do a huge number on me, too. Frankly, I wish you had told me about this the first time you came here. Anyway, all of this riding on the heels of a lengthy, exhausting missions trip . . . well, stress can really do a number on a person, and . . ."

"You're saying she's lying? Or crazy?," Nathan interrupted. He pushed forward, glowering at Akim. Leaning forward, he slammed both of his tightly curled fists onto the desktop.

Akim wagged his finger at Nathan. "You need to back off, Mr. Shepherd," he said, quietly but firmly. "You're behavior is menacing."

The deputy at the other desk turned in his swivel seat to watch.

Nathan regained his composure to an extent and backed away.

"Look," Akim said gently, "I know this is hard, but it's how I read it. There's no evidence whatsoever to back up any of your claims, Miss Dawson, and I can't pursue this any further without it. My hands are tied."

"There's one thing," Jacob said quietly and thoughtfully. "Her hair."

Tessa's face lit up. "That's right!" she exclaimed. "How could I have forgotten about that?"

"You lost me," Akim said, looking confused.

"Bear with me," said Jacob. "Jasmine Winters has long, platinum blonde hair—dyed, but beautiful. Real nuns get their hair cut as part of their vows. Not Jasmine. She'd never let a pair of haircutting scissors come near it. She's too vain about her beauty. All we have to do is . . ."

Akim held up a hand. "Whoa," he said. "I see what you're driving at, and the answer is 'no.' No to you, and no to me. I don't know much about nuns, but I do know that their head covering is some kind of sacred thing to them. I can't go ordering a nun to remove her habit or whatever it's called, just to see the color and length of her hair."

Jacob shrugged. "Can't we just ask her?"

"Absolutely not," Akim repeated. "And if you go near her, you're gonna force me to play hardball with you all. I really don't want to do that. As far as I'm concerned, the conversation with that Mother Superior, through a bona fide telephone number that checked out, more than settles the issue for me. Now, I don't know for sure what else is true about all this and what isn't, but Sister Genevieve is the real thing, and you'd better leave her alone."

Once outside in the cool night air, the lot of them quietly fumed. "I wanted to deck him," Nathan murmured. "You hear what he called Tessa?"

Tessa clasped his hand in hers and forced a smile. "My hero," she said, and Nathan softened and planted a light kiss on the top of her head.

"There's one thing that puzzles me about all this," Jacob mused.

"Only one?" Margaret quipped.

He rubbed his chin with a gnarled hand. "Don't know how, exactly, but I believe Chip Davis is mixed up in this as well. His decision to feature Jasmine as the mystery speaker at church last night may prove itself to be more revealing than either one of them realizes. It's not just his false teaching that's involved here. There's a whole lot more going on behind the scenes than what we can see at the moment."

Tessa beamed at Jacob. "Jasmine," she said. "You called her Jasmine. You believe me!"

Jacob smiled tenderly. "Of course I do," he reassured her.

"Well J.B.," Margaret said, "what are we going to do? Trying to go through official channels is getting us nowhere, fast."

"Dunno," Jacob murmured, shaking his head in disgust as he stared blankly at the mountains in the moonlight—every bit as towering and dark as this situation was becoming.

Margaret could see the wheels turning in Jacob's head. "Yes, you do," she said with a smile.

Jacob chuckled. "You and Tessa head on home. I'll be there shortly. You know what to do in the meantime." Jacob took Margaret by the shoulders, bent over, and placed a quick but tender kiss on her lips. He turned to Nathan. "Give me a lift?"

"Sure. Where to?" Nathan inquired.

In response, Jacob smirked. "Where do you think?"

Nathan's eyes lit up. "Let's roll!" he said and moved to the driver's door of his jeep while Jacob went around the other side.

Tessa shot Margaret a worried look. "But the deputy said . . ."

"Yes, I know, dear," Margaret replied, "but he was just superseded by a Higher Authority. We'll be praying," she called to Jacob, who flung open the jeep door, jumped inside, and waved as Nathan backed out and headed straight into town.

Five minutes later, the jeep pulled up at the curbside in front of The Master's Way. Being such a late hour, it was odd that the old glass door stood wide open propped against a big rock used as a doorstop. Even though the windows were covered with brown butcher paper, Jacob could see some of the Spartan interior that was somewhat illuminated by an old lamp in the corner. He didn't see the nun, but someone must be there. He felt a sudden, vague apprehension come over him. It seemed too convenient—the open doorway—as if he were expected. For a moment, he seriously considered telling Nathan to drive away, but from the corner of his eye, he noticed Nathan regarding him with grim enthusiasm. He couldn't back out now. Nathan would think him a coward.

Both men simultaneously exited the vehicle, but as Nathan stood with his body between the open door and the front seat, Jacob leaned his arms on the hood and said, "No, you wait here. We've got a better shot at this if I go it alone."

Nathan opened his mouth in protest, but Jacob cut him off. "Please, Nathan. She'll feel cornered if we both go in. Alone, I might be able to smoke her out, and maybe just get her to leave town. I think that's the best we can hope for at this point."

Nathan sighed and nodded reluctantly as Jacob shut the jeep door and disappeared into the mission doorway.

It was the first time he'd been in this cafe since it closed decades earlier. The old burger joint brought back memories, and he stood for a moment and gave the room a thorough going over. Not much remained from its heyday. His attention was drawn to the impossible-to-miss hulking old jukebox. Memories of him and Margaret, both young and wildly in love, slow dancing to the tunes of the day flooded him.

Jacob took a few steps toward the center of the room. A dimly lit floor lamp in the corner revealed the back door that led to what Jacob remembered as an office and storage area. He approached the door, and just as he reached for the tarnished brass knob, the office door swung open and with a surprised gasp, a habited nun ran into him. Jacob instinctively stopped them from colliding into each other by placing both hands gently on her shoulders. He backed up a respectable distance, and for a second, neither spoke. In that moment his eyes probed hers, scanned her tanned face, and looked for traces of protruding hair.

"Oh, excuse me!" the nun said, breathless. "I wasn't expecting a midnight visitor. Oh, aren't you . . . Mr. Brown? Theresa's uncle . . . wait . . . I mean, grandfather? I saw your photo in the newspaper with Theresa and your wife."

Jacob smiled knowingly. "Hello, Jasmine," he said quietly. "You're looking well after all this time. You know, I've often wondered what happened to you after Flat Plains."

The nun smiled—with a faint serpentine curl of her lips. "I think you have me confused with someone else, sir," the nun said with a Spanish inflection. "I am Sister Genevieve, hailing from, as of late, the Convent of Our Lady of the Roses in New Mexico. But I am pleased to finally meet you. Your granddaughter is so . . . charming."

Her last word, "charming," was to the spoken word, what Jacob deemed a snake was to the word, "slither." She was milking this for all it was worth.

The nun looked to each of her shoulders, then back to Jacob who realized his hands were still on her. Feeling suddenly awkward, he let them fall to his side and backed up another step. "You can stop pretending, Jasmine," Jacob said with finality. "It's over. We know why you're here, and it won't work. Why don't you quit before you get into real trouble?"

The nun turned from him and walked over to the counter, running her hand across it absentmindedly. "Jasmine," she murmured, almost meditatively. "Such a nice name. Don't you think?" She turned to face him and examined his unshaven face.

"Dark brown eyes," Jacob said. That's not the color of eyes you were born with Jasmine. Not the eye color you had when you came to Margaret and I as a young foster child so many years ago. Light brown is what I remember. Colored contact lenses? Gotta hand it to you. You went to a lot of trouble to get to us."

"Oh," she purred, "you mean my ministry to the poor?" She walked closer to him with the soft rustle of her robes. "No trouble at all. That's what I'm all about. That's what people like me do . . . amongst other things."

Jacob's face hardened. His eyes narrowed and he moved closer, towering over her. His voice was like a distant, approaching thunder. "Look. I'll only say this once. You're in way over your head. All this stuff has been documented—the attempted hit-and-run, the poison, the note. We've been to the sheriff's office . . ."

"Twice," she said casually and turned back to the counter. "I also know about the unfortunate accident. Poor little doggy. Tsk tsk . . . shouldn't have run across the road."

A wave of fear and horror swept over Jacob. He watched with growing trepidation as she traced a fingertip idly over the counter's surface. Not much scared him, but the fact she appeared so unphased was profoundly unsettling to him. Looking back upon previous times in his life where fear gripped him the worst, he recounted how he had been caught in enemy crossfires, had smoke jumped into forest fires, had faced down bears, had taken on thieves, and even took out a calf-eating mountain lion he'd tracked twenty miles into the hills. But this situation was unlike anything Jacob had ever experienced before. Jacob found himself in uncharted territory. His voice betrayed uncertainty. "How?" asked Jacob as he advanced toward her. "How do you know?" In a louder, more commanding tone of voice, Jacob pressed Jasmine harder for an answer. "Why are you doing this? Do you hate us that much? Don't you realize Tessa could have been killed?"

The nun ignored him, gazing out the window facing the street and leaning an elbow on the countertop while resting her chin in one hand. "I have work to do," she said. "Would you please leave?"

Jacob breathed a momentary sigh of relief. *If nothing else, I was right about who she is. This much I do know, especially how she just chose to not remain in character, her Spanish accent gone,* noted Jacob silently to himself.

In a sudden burst of fear mixed with anger, he impulsively reached out and with both hands again on her shoulders spun her around to face him. "Stop this!" he demanded. "Stop this now! I'm warning you, Jasmine . . ."

She laughed in Jacob's face, low, taunting, maliciously, a whisper of a laugh only he could hear. Clenching his teeth, he released her, backed away, and, shaking with anger, turned and strode purposefully across the yellowed linoleum and out the front door.

Outside, he leaned both hands against the jeep's hood for support and stood hunched over unmoving like an ice statue under the street light. Alarmed, Nathan hopped out of the vehicle, walked around to the passenger's side and pulled open the door for Jacob. He stood next to him in standby mode with the door ajar. "Jacob!" he said, wild-eyed and stunned, not having the slightest clue what just took place. "What's wrong? What happened?!"

The dissonant music exuding from an ice-cream truck as it drove past was even more of a mockery of Jacob's current encounter than it ever was with Hub Morrison making his bad-boy entrances. Jacob jumped into the jeep and onto the seat with a gusto that surprised even him. "Who in the world sells ice cream at this midnight hour? I think the devil himself has moved into the neighborhood. Let's just get out of here," he brokenly rasped. "I'll tell you about it on the way home."

"This is unbelievable. We're never going to be able to fall asleep tonight." Margaret sat at the kitchen table, her hand over her mouth and fear exuding from her eyes. "She's out of her mind."

Tessa sat beside Margaret, holding her hand and herself near tears. Nathan stood by the screen door, back against the doorframe, a tan Stetson in his hand, with his gaze fixed on the ceiling. Jacob paced the floor, motioning in thin air with his hands. "Stupid!" he yelled out loud at himself in a self-deprecating manner. "I should never have gone in there alone. No eyewitnesses." He turned to Nathan. "You were right to want to accompany me, for I knew in my spirit God was warning me not to go into her . . . lair." He turned to Margaret with an incredulous look. "She was lying in wait for me. She somehow knew I'd go directly from the sheriff's office to her fake 'mission'" (he said the word as if spitting). He then had a sobering thought. "Does that mean she's got someone working for her in the sheriff's office? A plant, perhaps?"

Margaret looked up at him. The thought of it terrified her. "If that's the case, we're playing right into her hands . . ."

"What is going on here?" Tessa whispered. "Am I right in understanding she actually has people working with her to destroy us? Destroy me! Who are they and why?" She put her head in her hands, and Nathan moved to sit beside her. He put his arm around her shoulder.

"It'll be all right," he assured her, but his voice said the opposite.

Jacob stopped pacing and looked at Tessa. "Yes," he said, suddenly calm, "that tells us more than we knew before."

Nathan looked up at him. "What are you driving at?"

"Okay," Jacob said, excited. "So now we know she's not working alone. She has connections, at least at the sheriff's office, and God only knows where else. Those kinds of people don't work for free. She's paying them for their services. Plus, she's eating regularly, has a car she's hidden somewhere, and is able to afford the rent plus deposit on a vacant building. She's got money—big money, I'm thinking. That's the only way such a complex scheme could work. But from whom? And why would anybody finance a vendetta against us? There's something a lot deeper going on here beneath the surface of which we're only seeing the tip of the iceberg. Knowing this helps, but, in having said that, I'm not really sure at this point how to proceed."

Nathan stood up abruptly. "Well, I know what I'm going to do," he said grimly. "I'm heading down to New Mexico to see this 'convent' for myself. I'll talk to this mother whoever-she-is and get to the bottom of this. At least as far down to the bottom as I can. If I hurry, I can catch the red-eye flight to Boise and onto New Mexico."

Jacob nodded. "That's a great idea. You'll need some money." He pointed toward the counter. "Cookie jar," he said. "There's a few hundred there. Take whatever you need."

"Seriously now?" Nathan said, grinning. "The old 'save it for a rainy day' money in the cookie jar routine? I always thought that was an old movie or old TV show cliché." He lifted the lid of the old blue-patterned porcelain jar, pulled out a wad of bills, and rifled through them, counting them. "Sorry," he said, holding up a portion and putting the rest back. "I don't have much of a bank account these days. But I'll get this back to you as soon as I can. Just need the price of a round trip plane ticket and some money for food and incidentals. I'll try to make it back by tomorrow sometime.

Jacob dismissed Nathan's honorable intentions. "Forget it," he said. "You're doing us a big favor. Everybody's got a part to play in this. The rest of us are staying here and going into some serious overtime prayer. You get going. If you hurry, you can catch the red eye and be there before the sun comes up."

"On my way, with God's help," Nathan said, positioning the cowboy hat on his head and bounding for the door. With the door halfway open, he stopped and made an about turn, looked at Tessa, and in three big steps was at her side. She looked up at him, and their eyes locked. As he leaned his face in close to hers, he looked sideways at Jacob and Margaret. He removed his hat from his head and held it for a moment as a screen between him and them. Then, with a dreamy look, he shoved it back onto his topknot, yanked the brim down over his forehead, turned, and disappeared out the door. He returned a moment later, opened the screen door, and said to Jacob, "I know you've probably already thought about this, but don't let her be anywhere alone." Jacob nodded. Nathan let the screen door slam, and he sprinted for the Jeep. They listened to the slam of his Jeep door and the spray of driveway gravel as he gunned it toward the road leading to the town airport.

At the same time, both Jacob and Margaret turned to look at Tessa. She sat with her hand lifted, two fingertips pressed lightly against her lips, and a smile that told all. Jacob stood not far from Tessa, smiling a smile all his own, punctuated by raised eyebrows. "Well?" he queried.

"Jacob!" Margaret chided, but he leaned in close to Tessa anyway.

With a distant, wistful look, she gazed out the window at the road leading to the town airport. "He said he loves me so much."

CHAPTER

12

The dramatic change in Ellen Davis, the late pastor's widow, was nothing short of incredible. The Silver Meadows Senior Community had worked its wonders on the aging woman's daily outlook. No longer did she sit in a darkened home looking out the dining room window to her neglected flower garden, living in a happily married yet bittersweet past. The facility's invigorating agenda of community mealtimes, outings to a rich variety of parks, and Boise shopping trips, as well as movie and game nights—all together renewed her in ways she hadn't felt renewed for such a long time. The house had become like a millstone around her neck. Although she loved the familiarity of her surroundings (e.g., her furniture and timeworn, handpicked knick-knacks), as she aged and her physical abilities deteriorated, the house had become a mere shadow of what had once been, and all too reminiscent of a past that was long gone. Many older folks clung to their homes as a lifeline. Ellen, on the other hand, had finally severed what had been to her a tether to a time that would never come again. In this new atmosphere of structured, planned enthusiasm, she thrived.

Jacob had arrived an hour before breakfast and apologized profusely for intruding on Ellen's early morning quiet time. Sitting across from her in the warm greenhouse patio at a round, glass-topped patio table (festooned with the bouquet of the day's vase of fresh wildflowers), he smiled and made small talk for a while. Ellen was, in fact, so cheerful that he kept deliberating about bringing up the real purpose of his visit for fear of triggering in her the same deep depression she had left behind on her doorstep months ago. She radiantly beamed in the morning sunlight—her snow white hair creating a soft halo effect around her face and her eyes twinkling brightly, a blue reminiscent to a clear blue sky on a spring day. She must have been breathtakingly beautiful in her early years, he reckoned. Although she was a good fifteen years his senior, neither wrinkles nor faded hair color could readily obscure the looks that had once made her such a head-turner.

In a lively manner and with an animated expression on her face, which was such a welcome departure, to Jacob's way of thinking, from the despairing woman she had become before discovering this whole new world outside her window, she chatted on and on. She was so happy for the visit and eager to let Jacob know that her new life suited her quite well indeed.

"You know," she mused, "I just can't believe I waited this long to move here. It's not at all the death sentence I thought it would be. Actually, I feel alive again, and I'm being shown so many open doors, I don't know which one to walk through first!" She chuckled at the thought of it and sipped her morning tea. "Are you sure you won't have a cup?" she asked. "It's the real thing." She leaned over the table, and furtively glanced at the other residents sitting nearby and said with a wink, "They've only got decaf here, but a couple of us smuggled in some of the real stuff." She laughed quietly. "It's a hoot bucking the system."

Jacob grinned and patted her free hand. "You look great, Ellen," he said. "I'm so glad I came here today. It's so good to see you smiling."

"You have to keep the mind active," she said firmly. "I'd forgotten how good it feels to engage the brain. I'm beginning to blossom again as a teacher. Seems like forever since I've taught public school, but next week I'll be holding classes right here in 'Beginning French.' The week after that, it will be a creative writing class."

A quiet settled over her, and she sat back in her chair, cupping her delicate chin with one hand and regarding him intently. "Jacob," she said, her voice soft, "I'm really touched that you came for a visit, but I have the sneaking suspicion there's something else on your mind besides friendly chit-chat. You're trying awfully hard not to tell me something."

Jacob leaned forward with his elbows on the table and looked down at his big hands. Pursing his lips, he took a deep breath and said, "Ellen, have you been to church lately?"

For a moment she did not respond, taking a sip of tea and looking off toward the mountains. "No," she said, wistfully. "Not for the past month."

Looking searchingly into her eyes, Jacob asked, "May I be so bold as to ask why?"

Ellen sighed, shook her head at a thought, and cradled the cup in both hands, her eyes avoiding him. "I didn't like what I saw there," she said. "It's not the same church I've known the last forty years."

"And that's because . . ." Jacob let the words hang.

Ellen's gaze met his. "Let's stop tip-toeing around the matter Jacob," she said. "You and I both know it's because of my grandson. The whole church has changed since he took over. I saw the way he ran things right from the start—from his first sermon no less, but I kept trying to convince myself otherwise. Chip has definite plans in place to make his mark or to make a name for himself. Fact is, he's . . . a fake. Always has been." She hesitated then added distantly, "Just like his father."

Jacob tensed. "Ellen, I'm sorry, but I have to ask this. Too much is riding on your answer for me to . . . well . . . respect your privacy. Forgive me. But you've rarely mentioned your son. Hank, I think is his name. In all the years you've lived here, I've heard you speak of him only in passing. I've never met him or even so much as seen him. And I've always gotten the feeling that you're . . . hiding something?"

Ellen swallowed hard and looked down again fidgeting with her hands. "Jacob," she said softly, "I know you and Margaret have never had children. Of your own, I mean, you know . . . I'm sorry. But there's no greater sorrow for a parent than to know that you are a failure. That's one of the reasons I holed myself up in my house for so long. My marriage to Glen was wonderful, but my child . . . my only child . . ." She looked up at Jacob, and her eyes were moist. "He's in prison, Jacob. He's been in and out of prison for the past twenty years."

Jacob sat, stunned. Mercy welled up in him, and he draped his calloused hands over her two frail ones. "I'm so sorry," he said. "I had no idea."

Ellen shrugged and threw her hands up in the air. "You just never know how they will turn out," she said. "Your kids, I mean. You pour your life into them and try to teach them right from wrong, but sometimes it's just not enough. No matter how many tears you cry or how much you beseech and entreat or, God forbid, in some instances yell or . . ." She shrugged again, looking away. "In my case, it just wasn't enough . . ."

Jacob's heart broke for her. She suddenly looked old again, and he faulted himself for bringing this on her. Images of Tessa raced through his mind—of her time with them prior to her salvation. If she had continued on with her worldly course . . . A sudden horror swept over him, which afforded him a telling glimpse into Mrs. Davis's grief. "Please help me to understand," he said, his voice gentle. "What is your son in for?"

Ellen blinked, and a tear rolled down her cheek. She quickly brushed it away with the back of one white-knuckled hand. "He's what you'd call a *con man*," she said. "Always trying to defraud and swindle people out of their money. His last con was a big one—five hundred thousand dollars in insurance fraud—and he was given a five-year sentence. Pretty lenient, actually."

She laughed bitterly and sparingly. "Prison life agrees with him," she said. "He's in his element there. He says everybody there "runs a game." No doubt he's picking up new tricks all the time. When he gets out, I'm betting he'll be quick to try them out on the first hapless, unsuspecting soul who comes along . . ."

"And Chip?" Jacob hadn't realized until the words left his mouth that his tone was biting, betraying the intensity of his dislike.

With sad eyes, shaking her head, Ellen looked up at Jacob apologetically. She had caught the inflection. "William is his given name. He's his father's boy," she said, as her lower lip trembled a little. "Everyone started calling him Chip when even as a toddler it was evident he was like a chip off the old block. If anything, he's even more of a smooth operator, for he uses religion as a front.

Everybody thinks he's the greatest thing since sliced bread. He's tried other cons but this one at Sheep Gate is his forte. He's got everybody going. As for me . . ." she said, while fingering the petal of one of the wildflowers, ". . . I just stay away. He doesn't even visit me here, and I don't want him to. I'm embarrassed to have others know he's my own flesh and blood."

"But why?" Jacob pressed. "Nobody knows what he's really all about. Like you said, everybody loves him. I'll bet there are residents here who go to church just to hear him preach."

"Yes," she said, wistfully. "I hear them talking, and they tell me how 'wonderful' Chip is. But they don't know him like I do." Before continuing, Ellen, in a tight-lipped and determined manner, went on to say, "Sooner or later it will all fall apart, and the center will not hold. You can't sow in sin without reaping a harvest of wickedness at some point. God will not be mocked. A man reaps what he sows. Pride goes before a fall, and Chip will fall. The Scriptures say this is a certainty. And when it happens, God forgive me, I don't want to be around. I already feel so much guilt for the way both he and his father have turned out as it is. I don't want others to know how bad a mother and grandmother I've been. I couldn't take that."

Jacob's eyes softened, and he smiled a kind smile. "Oh, Ellen," he said, soothingly, "in all the time I've known you, I've seen a gentle, kind, devoted woman of God. Dear sister in the Lord, you have no guilt to shoulder. People make their own decisions and stand before God and God alone for what they've done. And I know you still pray for Chip. Who knows how it will all turn out?"

She nodded. "And Hank, too. I know that 'With God all things are possible.'" Her eyes were pleading. "Maybe I'll live to see them turn around yet," she said.

Jacob nodded and squeezed her hand, saying, "That's the spirit." A curious look came over his face. "Wait a minute," he said, "if Chip's a complete fake, how does he know Scripture so well? His memory of Bible chapters and verses is phenomenal. It's clear he has no spiritual understanding of the actual verses, and yet, he can rattle off entire chapters without looking at his Bible."

Ellen brightened and attempted a smile. "Oh," she said. "That's easy, for that's his one good quality. He's got a photographic memory. Looks at something once, and he's got an indelible mental picture of it in his head."

Jacob's mouth fell open, and he leaned back so hard in his chair, he nearly fell backwards. He slapped his hand to his forehead. "Of course," he said, thinking out loud, amazed. "That's how he does it! What better way to complete the counterfeit preacher profile?! He can memorize entire online sermons! The Internet is a treasure trove of such things. All he's got to do is look up a topic, read it, then put his own personal spin on it. Tree hugger rhetoric and the like . . ."

Jacob stood. "Ellen," he said hurriedly, "I'm sorry I have to leave like this. But I'll be back, and so will Margaret. I'd love to spend more time with you under a happier set of circumstances as I'm sure Margaret would as well." He leaned over and planted a kiss on the top of her head. "God bless you," he said. "I'll be praying for you. And for the boys."

Ellen looked up at him. "God bless you also, Jacob," she said.

Jacob turned and made haste while vacating the patio, taking the flagstone footpath hurriedly to the parking area. Ellen watched him go. "I have a feeling you're going to need it," she said quietly.

Hub Morrison took up one full side of a booth way in the back of the Gold Dredge Saloon, blending in with the shadows and knocking back his third beer in the past two hours. Hub preferred this vantage point where he could have his back to a wall and keep a wary eye on the front door both at the same time. His position to one side of the "Gents" and "Ladies" rooms also allowed him to monitor bathroom traffic for a seemingly benign trip to the restroom was sometimes used as a smokescreen to come up behind an intended victim. Borderline paranoid perhaps, but Hub had no intention of ending up a statistic.

He got up once in a while when the coast was clear only to feed the jukebox, preferring, at least for the moment, to wallow in the misery of country-western, cry-in-your-beer songs. He wasn't sure if he was trying to forget the futility of his existence or make himself feel better that, at least for the moment, he wasn't the victim of being scorned in love like those dopes were in the songs the artists kept singing about.

Hub wasn't really sure what he was still doing in town. His decision already made, logically he should have put a few hundred miles between himself and Birch Valley by that time. He'd been here a week too long. Still, he had no reason to feel threatened, either with exposure or harm, should he delay his exit. He wondered, too, if the old lady was watching, and pondered, between swallows, what kind of mean old hag would take out a contract on a sweet young girl. Maybe he wanted to meet with her again, just to revile her to her face. Maybe he wanted another look at Tessa, to remind him there was still good in an evil world. He chuckled ruefully. Maybe he just wanted to get drunk and forget for awhile just who and what he was.

It wasn't just because of the cool but humid night that the sweat stuck his shirt to the inside of his leather vest. It was infuriating, but he had begun to closely examine a lot of contrasts between the obvious innocence of this girl he didn't even know and the murky quagmire of his own life. To make things even more troubling, a tape kept replaying in the innermost recesses of his mind that repeated the same two segments from a single Bible verse: ". . . visiting the iniquity of the fathers . . ." followed by ". . . upon the children . . ." Despite his bad boy persona, Hub had been well-educated in a variety of home-school scenarios and had a rather extensive vocabulary.

He knew that "iniquity" meant "sin," and it sorely vexed him and to some extent even grieved and struck fear into Hub's heart that his father's sins could also be his portion, whatever that was supposed to mean. He only knew he didn't care much for that idea and distinctly sensed that his freewheeling lifestyle was leading him down a one-way road marked with a dead-end sign. Last night he had dreamed of standing at the edge of a high cliff with the ground crumbling beneath him. He awoke bathed in a cold sweat. Hub's conscience was being pricked to such an extent he was of the conviction that whoever God was He would require an accounting. For the first time in his life, Hub Morrison was afraid to die.

All his honest self-appraisal went right out the saloon's picture window when she waltzed in.

Hub paused in the middle of taking another swig of beer, his gaze fixed on the tall redhead who seemed to glide across the dirty wood floor to a padded stool at the end of the bar counter, an arm's reach from Hub. She was all class—a royal blue, calf-length dress that had to have cost no less than several hundred dollars, polished black stiletto heels and slung over her delicate shoulder, a designer purse that cost more than Hub normally earned in a good week. Add to that, muted pink glossed nails that, though unaccountably sanded down, augmented her air of striking femininity. And that hair . . . long, loose, and reddish gold with highlights that shimmered even under the dim overhead lighting.

Sliding onto the stool she motioned to the bartender with a deft wave of her hand, and he responded like he had peeled her grapes all his life. Hub vacated the booth and took a seat on the stool right next to her as the bartender came into direct view. "I got that," Hub told him, and without even so much as looking in his general direction, the lady yawned in apparent boredom and in an aloof manner replied, "Diet cola."

Reaching into her purse, she uncapped a cherry-red lipstick and touched up. She didn't use a mirror. She didn't need to.

The bartender set a glass of cola on a coaster, and Hub tossed a five-spot on the counter. "Keep it," Hub said, his eyes still intently fixed on the woman. She sipped from a straw on her soda like she didn't have a mind to matter, still looking straight ahead.

Hub smiled. "What, no 'thank you?'" he prodded.

Without looking at him, she replied dispassionately, "Should I?"

Hub shrugged, looked away and downed another swig of beer. "Real friendly sort. My mistake."

He began to stand, and she turned to face him. In the reflected light of her dress, her eyes were a startling blue. "You give up far too easily," she said smiling and looked over her shoulder at the booth. "Is that your spot?"

Hub grinned, bowed theatrically and extended his hand like a true gentleman. She ignored his gentlemanly overture, glided over to his booth, and gracefully slid into the booth. To Hub's utter chagrin, she sat on the edge, giving him no choice but to sit on the opposite side. He smiled anyway and with bulging arms on the table between them and his bottle clasped in both hands said, "Sugar, what's uptown doing downtown? Me, I belong here. Not you. Unh-uh."

She teased him with a smile and daintily sipped again, "Complaining?"

Hub held up a hairy hand in protest. "Not me. Not even curious, if you don't feel like going there."

"I saw your bike outside," she countered, "and wondered to myself, 'Now what kind of man would belong to a bike like that?'"

Hub leaned forward. "And?"

She shrugged. "Not sure yet."

"Well," Hub said, "So what would make you sure?"

"Oh," she mused, "maybe when you do the job you were paid to do."

Hub froze. His eyes narrowed, and a look of utter astonishment came over his bearded face.

"What's that supposed to mean?" he quietly asked.

She wasn't buying it. Catty and cool the moment before, her voice now changed to calculated and hard-edge. "Tomorrow night," she said. "It has to be done quietly. Then get out. After that, I never want to see you again."

Her alter ego knocked the wind out of Hub's sails. He leaned back against the padding and encircled the neck of his beer bottle with his index finger and thumb and began turning the bottle in circles, eyeing her with caution, working all the angles to best determine whether she was an undercover agent or his actual contact. After deliberating as much as he dared, he threw the dice and asked, "How much?"

"Don't try to strong-arm me," she hissed. "You've already been paid in full and five grand is plenty. Not one penny more."

Okay, so she panned out, Hub surmised. He leaned forward again, elbows on the table. Like poking her with a stick, Hub said, "Changed my mind" and waited for her reaction. He wanted to see what she was made of.

He didn't have to wait long at all. She leaned abruptly forward and with a grip that was unexpectedly more firm than her hand was slight, laid hold of his leather vest and yanked him forward across the table. Much to his complete surprise, Hub allowed the move. His face was only inches from hers. She smiled so that to onlookers her doing so would give the appearance of her being the aggressor when it comes to pursuing a man but her words, spoken beneath her breath, struck him like strategic blows. "Then you change it back," she said. "I don't have time to play games. You came highly recommended, and I expect you to . . ."

Hub continued toying with her. He thoroughly enjoyed the exhilaration that accompanied the risk.

"No," he reiterated. "Ain't gonna."

The redhead's face immediately turned bright red. The whites of her eyes flashed, and her eyes became like daggers. "Then you have something that I believe belongs to me," she said flatly.

At first Hub led on like she had him over a barrel on that count but then thought better of it and smirked. "Way I look at it," he said offhandedly, "we can consider that traveling expenses. It's worth that much anyway just to make me keep my mouth shut. I figure we're even."

The redhead quietly spat, "Need I remind you *that* money is *not yours* to do as you please with!"

Hub shrugged. "Call the police," he said smiling sardonically.

The redhead's face turned the whitest shade of pale imaginable and lost all semblance of her having a soul. Her voice was devoid of emotion. "You were paid," she said, slowly and deliberately, paying close attention to her delivery so that her words would have maximum impact, "to do a job, and I expect you to do it. You will do what you agreed to do, or I promise you . . ."

Hub laughed derisively. "Yeah," he said, "or you promise to do what?!" He laid hold of her small hand in his own ham fist and pried it away effortlessly from his vest then squeezed just hard enough to get the point across. He froze instantly at the sight of her eyes dead ablaze, peering soullessly and treacherously into his own, and the click-click sound from underneath the table. *Funny how a sidearm brought to full cock can stop a big man in his tracks*, he thought. He released her hand and eased back into the seat staring at her in disbelief. He shook his head. "Man," he pondered aloud, "they don't make 'em any meaner."

The redhead softened, leaned back against the padding, and slid something into her purse. She smiled, a beguiling gesture but one that chilled Hub to the core. "Look," she said sweetly and insidiously, "there's no need for any unpleasantness. I'd like to keep our business arrangement amicable. Agreed?"

Hub nodded, still staring, but his mind raced. "Who *are* you?" he asked, filled with fear, awe, and disgust. She ignored the question.

"Remember, nine o'clock tomorrow," she said thinking out loud, "and don't be late! Don't miss your appointment with destiny." She stood, adjusted the purse on her shoulder and smiled down at him. "Hmmm," she said with a satisfied sigh, "that went well. Don't you think?"

When Hub did not answer, she leaned over him, her long hair falling away from her shoulders, a musty flowery fragrance enveloping him. Like tentacles, he imagined. "Don't let me down, dearie," she murmured then turned and breezed across the floor and out the door. The bartender ceased polishing the glasses to lean one hand on the bar counter and watch her go.

Hub didn't know how long he sat there after she'd left. "Dearie," he muttered sarcastically under his breath, and his mind suddenly reverted back to the Birch Bark Bistro and the little old lady he had been so quick to aid. He peered out the window to see if he could still see the red head walking down the street and in what direction before disappearing altogether. The paid killing of a sweet, young girl at the behest of a woman of many faces who packs heat and works for . . . who? His gut instinct told him she was not in this alone. This whole thing was crazier than anything he'd ever been involved with.

Men with fists and knives he could understand, even murder for hire, but this whole scenario was something out of a spy novel or a suspense thriller. And he wanted no part of it. He wished he had just handed the money over and been done with it, but she was gone, and he had no idea who she was or how to get in touch with her. Whoever was behind it all had something in mind way beyond Hub's ability to figure out.

Hub was done. He was getting out tonight. The open road with all its inherent survival challenges and raw simplicity was actually beginning to look really good right about now.

Bone weariness had settled on Jacob. The weather mirrored his troubled spirit—clear blue skies giving way to a thickening gray with the sun nothing more than a nearly opaque smudge behind a veil of cloud. The air was heavy with the promise of rain. Jacob was not a superstitious man. Nevertheless, the change in the weather gave every appearance of being a harbinger of evil tidings soon to come.

The drive back to the farm seemed to take forever, and the jolts and bumps from the truck's poor suspension jostled his insides a bit more than usual. They were reminders of the vehicle's age and of his own age too. This was work for a younger man, he felt, and spending the day in town querying scores of people about their thoughts regarding the alleged "Sister Genevieve" had wrested away any hope from him that he'd ever find anyone who could speak a disparaging word about her. Everybody liked her. Even those who had never met her had been swayed by the good reports of friends, and a large cross-section of believers and unbelievers alike were impressed by both her and Chip's positive effect on the community. Business owners were happy about it also. Stores that had previously been closed on Sundays now had opened their doors to cater to a new clientele.

The whole ordeal was incredibly frustrating. No one would have believed him had he tried to make the truth about her common knowledge. Taking this new development to the church board had been inconceivable until last night, but the congregation was sold on Chip's theatrics. Even at the emergency meeting, which had been the shortest on record, all the elders stood firmly on Chip's side and, by mere association, on Jasmine's as well. For anyone who was a friend of Chip's was a friend of theirs. Even the one person who should be inherently suspicious by nature—a sheriff's deputy—seemed wholly convinced of the counterfeit nun's legitimacy. *Chip Davis' grandfather must be rolling in his grave right about now,* thought Jacob.

But no matter how much Jacob kept mulling it over in his mind, it was becoming all too apparent he had nowhere to go and no one left to turn to for help. He couldn't help but wonder at this point if Akim was in on it. Maybe that's how Jasmine knew of Jacob's movements.

They were waiting in his driveway when Jacob returned.

In the cool of the morning as the sun was attempting to burn off the ominous cloud blanket, John Akim stood leaning up against the closed door of his cruiser, arms folded; and from under the brim of his western hat, he watched Jacob intently as he pulled in from off the road and pulled up to the other side of the driveway. Jacob exited the vehicle with a mounting level of trepidation, his eyes darting back and forth between Akim and the other nameless deputy who stood on the cruiser's passenger's side also watching him closely. Jacob closed the pickup door, walked around the front of his vehicle, and closed the gap between himself and Akim as Margaret dashed out the front door. "Jacob," she called as she quickly descended the porch steps. "They're going to arrest you!"

"What?!" Jacob came to an abrupt standstill and with a bewildered look on his face watched as Akim sighed, pushed himself away from the cruiser, and shook his head, apparently to himself.

Facing Jacob, he pushed back the brim of his hat and said, "Mr. Brown, I warned you about starting trouble. I did now, didn't I? You're gonna have to come back to the office with me. I gotta place you under arrest."

Jacob's jaw dropped as he looked at Akim. "On what charge?" he pressed. "I've done nothing wrong."

The deputy was not in the mood. "Mr. Brown," he said wearily, "did you or did you not go to that Catholic mission and harass Sister Genevieve, and did you or did you not lay hands on her and threaten her?"

Jacob's eyes darted back and forth between one deputy and the other, then to Margaret who had intertwined her arm in his. He hated how scared she looked, and he patted her hand in an effort to comfort her. "I didn't threaten anyone, deputy," he said looking Akim squarely in the eye. "I confronted her, sure, but I never harassed her in any way."

"Did you touch her?"

Jacob struggled to remember. Clearly he hesitated, and it made him look guilty. "Well . . ." he said as thought carefully, "look . . . yes, I put my hands on her shoulders, but I didn't . . ."

"Shake her?" Akim asked.

"Well . . . I . . . I honestly don't remember. I was a little hot under the collar about things at the time and feeling very protective. But she's . . ."

"Mr. Brown," Akim said deliberately and firmly, "Sister Genevieve's brought a complaint against you for assault, and I'm afraid that what you just described fits that criteria. She also wants you charged with harassment because you accused her of being malicious and a fraud."

"But she is!" Jacob exclaimed brimming over with anger and fierce determination. "I tell you that woman is not a nun. She is Jasmine Winters, a former professor at Flat Plains Bible College, and she has been trying to harm my granddaughter!"

Akim sighed again. "Let's go, sir," he said and reached out a hand to pull Jacob toward the car.

Jacob balked while clenching his jaw. "Deputy, you're making a *huge* mistake! Surely we are both just sleep deprived, it's been one of those nights. You've got the wrong person. She's the one . . ."

"Mr. Brown," Akim said firmly, "don't add 'resisting arrest' to the charges." The other deputy moved around the front of the cruiser to assist, but Akim waved him off. He yanked a pair of handcuffs from the back of his utility belt and held them up. They gleamed dully. "Am I gonna need these?"

Jacob's shoulders slumped, and he turned to look apologetically at Margaret. "Hold down the fort, kiddo," he said, "and see if you can get a hold of Will Pierce downtown. We'll need some legal help. And talk to Tessa right away. I don't want her to find out about this secondhand from a stranger before she even gets home." Margaret bowed her head and hugged him tightly even as Akim was gently pulling on his arm. "Let go now, Margaret," Jacob soothed, "it'll be all right. Just do as I ask, okay?"

Margaret nodded, her eyes tearing, her face afraid and pale, and one hand covering her mouth.

Akim swung open the cruiser's door and helped ease Jacob into the back seat, placing a gentle hand on his head to force it below the car door frame. The other deputy quietly walked around the front of the car and slid into the front passenger's seat and closed the car door with a resounding thud. Akim turned to look at Margaret, and his stomach knotted at seeing her tears. Then she heaped burning coals on his head even more when she quietly said, "I forgive you," touching his hand with her own.

"I'm really sorry, ma'am," he said sheepishly. Averting his gaze downward, he found it difficult to, once again, look her in the eye. Conflicted, he walked over to his car, slid into the driver's seat, then eased the car toward the road back into town. As he pulled away from the farmhouse, he caught a glimpse in the rearview mirror of Margaret, falling to her knees, crying out with hands clasped in prayer.

Opening his eyes a crack, the brightness of a harvest moon peeking out from wispy clouds made Ezekiel cover his face and roll over. The movement made his hung-over mind reel. Groaning, he then noticed, with a slow-gaining interest, the double line of railroad tracks spreading out before him into the distance. From the sharp angle of the tracks, he surmised, rather imperceptibly through his brain fog, that he was lying in a prone position with both his legs draped over one track, while his torso sprawled across the ties as his head lay on the other. One semi-clenched fist retained the previous night's empty bottle, still wrapped in the obligatory brown paper sack. He released it and flexed his stiff fingers, blinked several times to see straight, then struggled to push himself into a sitting position. Just the effort of sitting, all by itself, drained him and made everything blurry all over again. Still able to taste on his tongue the residual coating of cheap alcohol, he realized, with a start, that he could have purchased a lot of high-end medication with the two hundred dollars.

Licking his parched lips, he began fishing around with one hand in the pocket of his suit jacket, the one they bought for him, *what— yesterday, a year ago?* He couldn't recall. His hand came in contact with just two pennies and a liquor store receipt. He laughed to the point where it made his head throb for that was all he'd ever been worth. Just a few cents and an empty bottle. Even if he had taken the money, it would have been long gone by now, whenever "now" actually was. Didn't matter anyway. Though it would have been the most money he had seen at one time in years, sure as shootin' he'd have tossed it into a whiskey river and waved goodbye as it floated away.

With his head clearing in waves, Ezekiel surveyed his surroundings. He was in the woods, somewhere out of town. Low lying clouds hid most of the stars making it difficult to determine direction or time, but by the horizon's pale indigo, he reckoned it somewhere in the neighborhood of an hour or two before dawn. He ran a dirty hand over cold, polished steel and, as far as he could reckon, concluded the steel must belong to the set of rails the freight trains use to transport goods to Birch Valley. The depot was just a mile outside of town, but at the moment, he couldn't remember which way that was. He listened, but could hear no town traffic, so he must have wandered pretty far afield in the throes of his drunken stupor. How he did so without either getting beat up by local punks, seriously injured in the woods, or mauled by a wild animal was just a hair short of miraculous. He looked up at a darkening sky and lifted one hand to his forehead in a halting salute. "Thank you, Sir," he croaked.

And then, much to his horror, he remembered it all.

It was beyond humiliating standing on that church podium. All those people staring, applauding, shouting acclamation—at him. He had felt an overwhelming case of the old P.T.S.D. coming on, and it was only his own sheer iron will, birthed in torture by his Cong captors that restrained him from plowing through the lot of them and running out of the building. And those two . . . fakes . . . who used him . . . He wanted to puke just thinking of them. Them? Hah! Him too! He was no different—worse, even. Because he knew better. And he saw Jacob Brown in that church. All the way in back. He could feel the old man's eyes on him, accusing, it felt like. For the first time in many years, people had lauded him a hero, but this time it was a total sham. Like everything else about him. Uncomfortable on the splintered railroad ties and gravel, Ezekiel stared straight ahead into the dark void that was his life.

He felt the tremor in the rails long before he heard the train. An intrusive thought said, *Do it, go ahead. There's no point anymore. You're worthless and you know it. End it here. Stop the hurting . . .*

Worthless. Ezekiel nodded. So right. His usefulness died when she did so many years ago. He looked both ways along the tracks. The vibrations grew stronger underneath him. Now he could hear it, a behemoth rumble of machinery that kept surging ever closer. Leaning on one arm, he lowered himself again into a prone position, resting the back of his head on the rail. He closed his eyes. The metal drummed against his throbbing skull. The rumbling increased until it became a part of him.

"For God so loved the world, that He gave His only begotten Son, that whosoever believeth in Him should not perish, but have everlasting life . . . John three, sixteen."

Ezekiel opened his eyes to look up at the dark, nearly starless, sky. *Where did that come from?* he thought. *Jacob. At the soup kitchen.* On autoplay, it was as if Ezekiel's mind had begun to replay every sermon he'd ever heard Jacob preach in his apron, right down to his every encouragement from an open Bible. At each meal, for the past month, Jacob had spoken that particular Bible verse to him and had repeatedly told him to remember it when he got to the end of himself. He didn't know what that meant at the time, but after staring up for what seemed like an eternity, Ezekiel finally understood. The end of himself. He had no place left to go . . . but to God.

But why? What possible reason would God have for wanting a poor excuse of a wasted life like his? He was no good. God only wanted good people, he had always thought. Then more of Jacob's best-loved passages came to mind and sprung up like a fountain of cool, clear, refreshing water from deep within him.

"Come unto me, all ye that labour and are heavy laden, and I will give you rest."*

"All? Does that mean . . . me?" Ezekiel whispered to himself, astounded at the revelation.

"All that the Father giveth me shall come to me; and him that cometh to me I will in no wise cast out."**

"You mean, I'm not an outcast?" he called out, looking up at the sky. "You want me? Jesus? Me?"

"But as many as received him, to them gave he power to become the sons of God, even to them that believe on his name."***

---

* Matthew 11:28   ** John 6:37   *** John 1:12

As the verses flowed, it was as if God was pouring living water into Ezekiel's very soul reviving his parched spirit.

The rails groaned loudly under the weight and movement of the oncoming train. Blinking hard to fight back the tears, dirty, smelly, homeless Ezekiel Hazlett rasped through gritted teeth, "Okay."

As the dam of self loathing and pride broke, a deluge of tears poured out from him in earnest—a wellspring of decades' worth of pent up and profound inner pain—with each heaving sob representing a wasted year here, a misspent moment there, or a loving word left unsaid. Then suddenly, his deep wound, which he had deemed incurable for so long, gave way to joy and laughter, unlike anything he had ever known before—the kind that cannot be contained. And while still lying there, with upraised hands, he praised the God Who had been waiting for him ever so patiently all those years. At that moment, Ezekiel's brain fog lifted, and the effects of his hang over disappeared. He was clear headed—really, for the first time in years.

"Thank you Jesus! I'm a new man!" he shouted as the train whistle shrieked. Ezekiel instinctively sat upright and hurled his body forward as the train blew past him, the heavy blast of air propelling him with even greater intensity, causing him to roll down the embankment like a windblown tumbleweed. He found himself sprawled out over a patch of dead weeds with his new slacks noticeably shredded. He lay there laughing so hard it hurt and not quite knowing what to make of the pleasant, novel sound of his own laughter mingling with the endless, rhythmic clacking of locomotive wheels.

A good name is rather to be chosen than great riches, and loving favour rather than silver and gold. (Proverbs 22:1)

CHAPTER

13

Marlene Hendricks shed her heavy jacket and handed it to a smiling Lucille Fallon who took it to her master bedroom and added it to the pile of others already there. Marlene was always cold these days, at least when the sun wasn't shining. Pausing on the entry mat just inside the front door, Marlene stopped and reflected briefly before standing her wooden cane in a corner. Those two simple actions were a shadow of what she was once capable of before she took such a bad fall and broke her hip. Even after a painful half-year of physical therapy, she was only just getting used to the idea of slowing down. She had always loathed the word "spry" in reference to the elderly, but it had described her well enough.

Until she took the spill down the stairs, she had been a dynamo, hopping like a little bird from one project to another, never missing a church meeting, and a frontrunner in local seniors' activities. It grated on her, having to admit to herself that those days were a thing of the past, and something as simple as walking a floor unaided was a never-say-die statement of her independence. She had, in fact, walked that overcast morning the quarter mile to Lucille's home for the weekly book discussion and had every intention of making it known. She smiled to herself. Her minor heroics would fit right in with their book series on "Brave Women of the Bible."

With her purse draped over one shoulder, Marlene carefully negotiated the living room furniture with a smile, nodding to each of the nearly two dozen women present. She kept one ear cocked to hear the latest small town chatter. "Mountain telegraph" in these parts was more reliable and far more interesting than a read in the *Birch Barker Weekly*, and it was hugely entertaining to hear each woman give a different perspective on the same event. She chuckled to herself, thoroughly convinced from past experience that a story revisited amongst a gathering of Birch Valley women would invariably result in numerous different opinions. She noted that only every other person was someone she knew from Sheep Gate, but in her time away, the church had undergone some dramatic changes, the congregation's size being just one of them.

Marlene couldn't understand the fuss over the new young Pastor Davis and his energetic but entirely lacking in spiritual substance sermons. Despite the theological hype, his hopping around on the podium and his use of genuinely funny one-liners, the mid-week service (the first she'd attended since her return to Birch Valley) had left her hungry and empty inside. For all the prior buildup she got from other Sheep Gate members, she was gravely disappointed that "Chip" had more the look of an entertainer than a true shepherd.

There was something else, too, an undercurrent to Chip's doctrine that ran through the one sermon she had listened to. Something deceptive, unholy even. The "Jesus" he presented was different from the biblical one—more like a pal who tells you only what you want to hear. His sermon touched on neither sin nor judgment nor Christ's atonement for our sins but instead oozed of ear-tickling, feel-good anecdotal and warm fuzzies and gave one the sense that man could somehow redeem himself if he got involved enough with social issues and doing good works. Plus, the grunge-inspired modern music, the excessive use of a large video screen, and congregational praise all directed at Chip rather than Jesus left a bad taste in Marlene's mouth.

Marlene had really been looking forward to being refreshed and rejuvenated at this informal fellowship at Lucille's house. The atmosphere was certainly more conducive to intimate heart-to-heart talk about their Savior and the ageless truths found in the Scriptures.

The scent of hot coffee and fresh huckleberry muffins led her straight to the large circular kitchen table, laid out as it always was at these gatherings with a white lace-edged tablecloth, fine bone china, and real silver silverware. She smiled. *Half the fun of these gatherings,* she thought playfully, *is that the atmosphere lends itself to learning and yet without anyone getting hot under the collar.* With a plate of muffin and a cup of coffee in hand, Marlene retraced her steps and sat in the only empty seat in the room.

Stephanie Carlton, Rob's wife, called the meeting to order. She was a younger woman compared to some of the others, still in her early forties. She was attractive and well dressed and exuded a no-nonsense air about her that welcomed friendship but on her terms. Marlene had always wished for one of the older women to lead as instructed in the Bible, preferably one who, unlike Stephanie, had raised children and had perhaps a grandchild or two. She inwardly bemoaned the scarcity of women aged in the Lord and saw that the church suffered for it greatly. Yet, she was grateful someone had taken it upon herself to lead the book study.

Stephanie was a proud woman, subtly so, and her characteristic use of proof texts to back up her opinions on any subject proved to be an ongoing annoyance. Still, it was the gathering that mattered, the "forsaking not the assembling of yourselves together," as the writer of Hebrews put it. Marlene was glad to be in a position again to be there weekly, and she had noticed that hot huckleberry muffins, strong coffee, and animated conversation afterward helped anesthetize her to such minor irritations.

But now, however, she stopped chewing midstream. For Stephanie, sitting on a straight-backed chair and framed by the gas fireplace behind her, had just held up a thin volume in one hand, high enough for everyone to see the cover. Marlene stared at the picture of a young woman, bowed as if in prayer with a light emanating from the crown of her head. "As you can see by the title, *God and the Inner Woman,*" Stephanie said, "we are going to delve into and explore the authentic you, the woman God created you to be. So often, we don't know who we are because we allow others to mold us—our fathers, husbands, or even our employers—instead of looking inward to where God Himself already resides. When we do that, we'll have our heart's eyes opened to see the beauty of God in us. Our lives will be transformed."

Marlene swallowed hard then squinted through her bifocals to confirm the book's author was who she thought it was. She raised her hand. "Ah, Stephanie?"

Stephanie smiled. "What is it, Marlene?"

"Well, um, I'm not trying to be contrary—and heaven knows I can be without even trying—but I noticed the author of that book is Mattie Heldstrom. Isn't she that writer who holds seminars all over the country to get people involved in meditation and other New Age practices?"

The room grew quiet, and all eyes were now on Stephanie. "Ms. Heldstrom is a Christian, Marlene," Stephanie replied, confident. "She hails from a Baptist background and has a Ph.D. from North Bitterroot Baptist University right across the border in Montana. She is a Spiritual Formation professor and for fifteen years has been a respected member of the faculty at Samuel Holt Bible College in Houston. She does come at things from a different spiritual perspective, but rest assured, she is a follower of Jesus. Now, I'm going to hand out . . ."

Marlene cleared her throat. "Ah, yes, I understand all that, but . . ."

The room again grew quiet enough to hear a pin drop, and a dozen sets of eyes fell on Marlene. Stephanie's facial expression tightened just a bit. "Yes?"

"Well," Marlene continued, "oh, please excuse the interruption again, but didn't she learn these prayer techniques from a Catholic monk who promoted Buddhist teachings? A monk who pilgrimaged to Tibet, no less, and sat under the Buddhist monks there and even claimed he could see the Gospel in the Buddhist scriptures. I mean, do we really want to learn to follow Jesus from people who believe those kinds of things? And really, the author must believe them too, if she quotes him so much."

Every head turned toward Stephanie now who smiled ingratiatingly while she hesitated in answering. Marlene could see her mind racing. Stephanie tried a different approach. "You know," she said in a placating manner, "I used to get scared about that sort of thing, too, but I've been learning much in the past few months, and I've reached the point where I see nothing wrong with exploring differing routes to God because truth is truth no matter where it is found. That doesn't mean I necessarily believe all that I read, but I'm open to seeing how God moves in religions different from my own. We have to be careful that we don't put God in a box or throw the baby out with the bath water. I get truth wherever I can, not just from the Bible. Some of these techniques Ms. Heldstrom speaks of may have counterparts in Buddhism and what-have-you but they originate from the Desert Fathers. And we all know or should know that at least they were authentic Christian men and women. These doctrines Ms. Heldstrom discusses have been a part of the Christian tradition for more than a thousand years. I hope that answers your concerns, Marlene. Now, if we can . . ."

"Well, actually, I already read the book, dear," Marlene interrupted and smiled apologetically. And I've seen some material that shows how the Desert Fathers learned those meditation techniques from people of pagan religions. They didn't originate from them."

Stephanie sighed and appeared placid, but underneath her cool exterior, she was on the brink of open exasperation. "Oh, you've read this book?"

Some of the ladies began giving Marlene *the look*, complete with raised eyebrows. Others, however, appeared genuinely concerned—worried even.

"Yes," Marlene continued, pausing to sip her coffee. She needed to wet her whistle, now dry from sheer nervousness. "A friend was interested in my opinion of it. All the parts about using candles, icons, and images to pray with was, how should I put it, a bit . . . idolatrous?" She attempted a smile. "I told her it was trash."

An audible gasp went up from several ladies, and Marlene herself, still sipping coffee, nearly choked on it. Where had that come from? Over the rim of her cup, she could not help but notice Stephanie sitting stoically, framed by the blue-yellow light of the faux fireplace, with the look of an angel. *A fallen angel, more like it,* Marlene thought.

"Marlene," a dark-haired newcomer said, "I'm so glad you shared." She smiled and her lovely, porcelain-doll face was offset in a macabre way by teeth and lips stained blue from huckleberry. She was another forty-something one, and by the look of her clothes, a wealthy, conspicuously out-of-place individual in a ranch town like Birch Valley. "You know," she said, appearing thoughtful, "it's a modern world, and we need modern approaches to meet as Christ followers on the common path. And although we may not glean the whole truth from other religious traditions, as long as we gain some truth, surely there's no harm in that. We are still Christians, after all."

Regarding her warmly, Marlene said, "Oh, hello. I don't believe I know you. Are you new in town?"

The woman smiled hollowly. "I'm Mala Grovsner. Of the Boston Grovsners?" She looked pointedly at Marlene and shook her head. "No? Well, anyway, we, that is, my husband, daughter, and myself, arrived last month. I would never have guessed anyone in this cozy little group would have reservations about different streams of Christianity. Even your pastor approved the nun doing some classes with the youth."

Marlene was perplexed. *Nun?* she thought. "What nun?"

"I invited Mala to Sheep Gate," Stephanie interjected, "after we met a few months ago at a silence retreat."

Mala nodded approvingly. "We were told that your little town," she said, "and that Sheep Gate Lane Church, in particular, was the place to go for spiritual refreshment. My daughter Charisse has been going to your youth group sessions for the last two weeks. Anyway, I do understand your concerns. I was where you are a couple of years ago, but then I began to grow spiritually and found real maturity when I learned to glean from God's truth wherever it could be found. I really don't see anything wrong with Christians using an all-inclusive approach to these other belief systems."

"Even if they're contradictory to Scripture?"

"Even if they might appear that way."

Every woman in the place knew that save for the skillful brandishing and wielding of actual swords, in a manner of speaking, a definite crossing of swords was underway. Smiles notwithstanding, iron will clashed with iron will over coffee and muffins.

"Appear that way?" Marlene asked, incredulously. She took another sip of her now cool coffee, realizing it was high time for a refill. "I am of the conviction that 'centering prayer' as put forth in one of the chapters is overtly contradictory to the Christian faith, and I'm sure some of you here would agree. And, um . . . could I see your copy, Stephanie?" Stephanie gave Marlene a look as if to sarcastically say, "Be my guest." Marlene quickly flipped through the pages, skimming. "Ah, yes! Right here in chapter eleven is how to incorporate what is called the Rule of Life into your daily laundry routine. If I know the Catholic belief system—and I assure you I do for I was raised a strict Catholic and remained one for thirty years before coming to Jesus—these are fixed hours of prayer, like the Benedictine monks practice. You know, in monasteries, where they chant and repeat prayers to dead saints." She continued, smiling politely. "Now correct me if I'm wrong, but isn't this the same vain repetition that Jesus, in the Gospel of Matthew, told us not to do?"

Mala sighed and shook her head while trying to project an air of spiritual superiority and level of enlightenment the other ladies, except for Stephanie, seemed to be lacking. "Oh, Marlene," she said, looking heavenward, "we have nothing to lose and everything to gain if we just open our minds and learn to celebrate God's presence in other ways that He chooses to reveal to us, not just in the Bible but apart from it as well. We must stop putting God in tight boxes of our own constructs. He longs to reveal Himself in fresh new ways to each generation."

"Oh, I don't think the Scriptures would agree with you, Mala," Marlene said sweetly. She thought how sometimes it paid to be a spry (at least still in spirit, although not in body), harmless little old lady. "God revealed Himself to us through His Son, by His Word and by His Spirit. In John fourteen, Jesus said, 'He who has seen Me hath seen the Father.'"

"Oh, but dear sister," Mala implored, "His Spirit is everywhere and dwells in everyone. We are all children of God. Instead of trying to change people to believe our way, we are changed when we focus on this deep unity of faith."

Marlene looked at Mala sideways and regarded her curiously. "First of all, just because we are ALL created in God's image does not automatically make us God's children, but it does give us the potential to become children of God when we put our faith and trust in Jesus Christ to be our Savior and Lord, according to God's terms, not ours. And with all due respect, Mala, there is no unity of faith if the Jesus we preach is not the Jesus of the Bible. The Bible does warn about a false Christ and "another gospel."* Unity at the expense of truth is an abomination. Remember, he who has the Son has life and he who does not have the Son does not have life."**

Mala rolled her eyes at the ceiling and interjected, "The idea of hell is so outdated."

Marlene's smile faded. "Not to those who are there."

Mala laughed lightly. "Oh, that's so theologically patriarchal. I would have thought those in the church more mature and farther along by now."

"Careful, dear," Marlene said with a renewed smile, "your feminist . . . oh, what do they call it . . . ?" Her countenance brightened. ". . . ideology is showing."

She knew she shouldn't do it, but Marlene surrendered to temptation and lightly batted her eyelids for effect. It worked. Mala's huckleberry blue smile gave way to a look of utter contempt.

"Could I ask someone to hand these out?" Stephanie cut in nervously and unapologetically—her voice, now agitated, edgy, and an octave shriller. Amidst an uncomfortable exchange of glances and the occasional whisper, another newcomer obliged Stephanie. Marlene took one and began looking it up and down. Its roll call of pagan mystical techniques cloaked in a veneer of pseudo-Christian phraseology would serve as hard evidence. Marlene had considered leaving the house in disgust but decided, being she had just put such heroic effort into simply getting herself there, to sit it out. *Just this once,* she thought, *I'll stick around for this presentation and observe its effects on these women.* After replenishing her cool coffee with some more piping hot coffee and grabbing herself another muffin, she sat back down, dug a pen out of her purse, and began scribbling away furiously on the back and in the margins of the handout. The elders would be interested in this. At least, she thought they had better be.

---

* 2 Corinthians 11:4
** See John 3:36, John 10:10, and 1 John 5:12.

Carrie Littlejohn depressed the driver's seat lever and pushed backward. The seat tilted and lowered as she stretched her five and a half foot frame nearly full-length. It had been a long day, and she wished it had ended a lot sooner. With eyes closed, she unwound for a moment to the sound of nothing—no cell phones humming, no customer complaints, no demands on her time. Only the intermittent sound of footsteps faded in and out of her quiet bubble. Anyone glancing at the petite blonde haired driver in track pants and a t-shirt might have thought she was one of the youth with her small but sturdy build. Carrie was certainly fit, but it had been a long day, the kind that began with spilled coffee on clean clothes followed by a mad dash to drop off Matt at school late, only to acquire a flat tire on the way to work, culminating in a half-hour of making up for lost time after closing. She should have called in sick, she thought, as her downward spiral of a day took its hapless course. But she was feisty, and her work ethic was as strong as her determination. When she got a text from her son that the youth were going to stay late after the midweek service for a midnight summer prayer meeting, instead of crying from fatigue, Carrie had wept silent tears of joy. After working late and then power cleaning her kitchen, she had folded laundry and passed the time listening to some old Bible teaching tapes on Ephesians by Pastor Glen Davis whom she missed so much. She'd temporarily gotten her second wind, but when it finally came time to pick up her son at Sheep Gate church just after midnight, she was ready to call it a day. "Over with," she murmured, "finally."

While she continued to debrief, the muted sounds of the outside world grew strangely dim and blurred as she felt her breathing slow to an even pattern akin to sound sleep . . . that is to say, almost.

The van door being jerked into a wide open position jolted her awake. Sitting up, she saw teenagers spilling out the front doors of Sheep Gate Lane Church and onto the church sidewalks. Yelling and laughing, kids dashed across the parking lot to waiting cars. Carrie sighed and resumed an upright position while looking back over her shoulder. A tousle-headed Matt vaulted into the van, momentarily brushing up against the back of the seat and scooting himself all the way to the far end. A pretty girl, close to him in age, give or take a couple years, followed his lead. With a toss of her head, her lush dark hair tumbled over her shoulders and halfway down her back. She flashed a smile. "Hi Mrs. L."

Carrie smiled back and tried to remember who she was. "You know me, but I don't know you." She looked at Matt, winking, and coyly asked, "Who's your friend?"

Carrie's question caught him totally off guard. He had intently been watching his pretty friend run a comb through her hair. Matt blushed and looked up. "Um, Charisse Grovsner. She goes to our youth group too. Her parents were busy so I told her you'd give her a ride home."

"Nice to meet you, Charisse," Carrie said, her vivid blue eyes scanning the girl's face. "You must be new in town. I don't recognize you."

"Mo-om . . ." Matt melted before Charisse's bedazzling smile. *Perfect teeth*, Carrie noted, *to go along with her perfect hair and perfect ivory roseleaf complexion. Not a blemish in sight.* Carrie felt an immediate growing dislike arise in her toward Charisse . . . yet she couldn't quite pinpoint it. Was it envy possibly? *No, that can't be it,* she thought to herself. *There's something about the way this girl acts.*

"Oh, it's okay," countered Charisse and said to Carrie, "We moved here last month from Idaho Falls. My dad's a lawyer, and he got sick of his practice or something, and he quit his job, and here we are. He's not working and neither is my mom, but we really don't need the money right now anyway. My mom's from a rich family. Anyway, Dad's taking a year off so he can find himself. Mom's already totally into that so she's helping him. They do all kinds of spiritual stuff together. Pastor Chip said they could teach next week's youth group. They've taught classes before in other places. Pretty cool, huh?"

"Oh, well, 'er . . . that's nice," Carrie stammered while thinking "information overload." She then added, "So, I'm the chauffeur, huh?" wondering why she was involuntarily drafted for the position, what with Carrie's parents being so well to do and not having to work. She faced forward and keyed the ignition. "Yes ma'am. Where to?" she asked facetiously, trying her best to curb the impulse to be openly sarcastic instead.

Matt rolled his eyes.

Charisse giggled. "Gilded Drive," she said. "Mom thinks that name suits us. I guess we're in the good part of town."

Forgetting herself, Carrie winced noticeably while she took a closer look at Charisse in the rearview mirror. *Good thing she can only see the back of my head, for the most part,* she thought. At first glance, she hadn't noticed Charisse's haute-couture clothes. Sitting beside a rather plainly dressed Matt, she appeared somewhat over-dressed for a youth group meeting but unaware of it. "Yes," Carrie said, "I know where it is."

Neither teenager noticed her having grimaced. Carrie knew she was probably overreacting, but the young girl's demeanor cut deep. Her casual flaunting of wealth stood in stark contrast to their own incessant financial struggles. As a single mother for the last few years, ever since Ken died, Carrie kept herself and Matt barely afloat. They always had enough but never were able to get ahead, and it grated on her nerves to hear of families who could live in relative ease—especially without having to work for the money because their money worked for them. *You're being petty Carrie*, she thought to herself, but the wound was open and raw and would likely remain as such unless their situation changed. It was an area in which God was dealing with her, but change, more often than not, doesn't happen overnight. Maybe, she thought, with a sigh, He intended to use people like Charisse to achieve that end in her.

"So," she asked, picking right back up where she left off with razzing Matt, "I guess youth group is going well, huh?"

Matt nodded while exchanging periodic glances with Charisse. "Yeah," he said, "lots of new kids, too. From other towns, even. Pastor Chip is really popular. Not boring like . . ." he threw a sudden, wary look Carrie's way.

"Like what?" Carrie asked, now wary herself.

Matt shrugged. "Well, like the old stuff, you know . . . church hymns and stuff."

Carrie raised her eyebrow. "So, Pastor Chip does it different then? In what way?" She had only been to the first youth group meeting a couple of months earlier, liked Chip's engaging manner, and left feeling good about it. And, tired as she usually was, she only periodically had attended service since Chip filled the pastorate. Since then, attendance at the meetings had mushroomed.

Matt perked up. "Like the prayer night tonight. We got a portable prayer labyrinth as a gift from the speaker, and we all got to help set it up in the church basement. Pastor Chip didn't have time to show us though. He said we could try it out while he had to go see Sister Genevieve."

"Sister who?" asked Carrie, her alarm bells ringing.

"The special speaker at the service. She was awesome! Then we watched the DVD that came with the labyrinth about prayer and the ancient pathways. You know, the old ways of the earliest Christians, the Desert Fathers, and things I never heard about before. So then Mrs. Carlton came down and helped us—that's when I sent you the text. We picked our word tonight to pray with and tried it, all of us. Then we lit candles and walked the path, just like the ancient Christians did."

Carrie's face could not hide her confusion and grave concern. "I don't remember anything about Christian practices involving—what is a labyrinth? Doesn't that have something to do with paganism? I don't mean to be critical, but none of this sounds Christian at all."

Charisse cut in. "Sure it is. My parents are both Christians, and we have a stone labyrinth at home, in our backyard. They're awesome. Mom and dad use it to center themselves. We do breath prayers and meditation, just like in youth group. My parents say it's about time the church has come full-circle again."

Carrie's heart skipped a beat, and she went numb inside. "But . . . what about Jesus?"

Charisse replied nonchalantly. "Oh, yeah. Him, too."

Carrie's eyes widened. "Too? As in, He's just an afterthought?!"

Matt's tone was conciliatory. "Mom. Mom. It's okay. They talk about Jesus at youth group all the time."

Carrie's eyes narrowed. "And who else do they talk about?"

Charisse beamed. "Yeah, Mrs. Carlton would love my mom. She talked about 'converging streams,' that all meet in God. My mom knows about that, like Jesus, Buddha, Lao Tzu, all the great teachers, who all lead to God."

Carrie's foot slammed down on the brake so hard the tires locked and skidded. Charisse grinned from ear to ear. "Hey," she said laughing. "You're pretty cool Mrs. L. We're here, and I didn't even tell you my house number yet. How did you know?" Without waiting for an answer, she grabbed her Bible and hopped out of the van, only to poke her head back in to say, "Thanks!" before sliding the van door close with a thump. With her hair bouncing, she ran to the wrought iron gate barring the way to an expansive, multi-level home. She swung open the gate, skipped down the well-manicured footpath leading to the steps. Soon she disappeared through the front door.

For some time Carrie sat, unable to move or speak, her mind in a tailspin.

"Mom?"

Carrie blinked and half-turned to look at Matt. She drew a deep but shaky breath, exhaled slowly, and in a firm voice said, "I want you to stay away from that girl."

Matt's mouth dropped open. "But, mom!"

Carrie gritted her teeth and said, "You heard me."

Matt sputtered and protested, "But . . . but mom . . . she's cute! And she likes me!"

As she turned back around in the seat, Carrie recalled a saying spoken by her favorite grandma. "Poison comes in pretty packages," she said, and as Matt sulked and folded his arms across his chest, she added, "I need to talk to the church elders."

Standing just below the barred window, he stared up at the slice of darkening sky visible to him and fought back the urge to scream.

Jacob Brown was all talked out. No one was left who would listen. Akim thought him a criminal, the church board considered him a fearmonger, and everyone else he had spoken with either believed him to be crazy or simply didn't care. As the arrested party, he had one phone call coming to him but didn't even know who to call at that point. His one hope of legal intervention, Will Pierce, was still out of town for the week, and he would not be appointed public counsel until he was processed, which Akim didn't seem to be in any hurry to initiate. Exactly why, Jacob didn't know. But one thing was certain—the longer he remained here, the more imminent the danger to Tessa. Even outside, he didn't know exactly what he could do, except stand guard over her, because there was no way of knowing who would do the job. Certainly not Jasmine, not directly anyway. No, she would have a solid alibi accounting for when Tessa was to be killed, which he was entirely convinced was a certainty at this point.

The sheer thought of it made him sick right down to the innermost core of his being. It was one thing to come face to face with a death threat against a loved one; it was quite another thing entirely to be locked up and rendered totally impotent to do anything about it.

At least Margaret was home with Tessa now, praying—that and the fact that together they were a united front spiritually. The only Bible verse that kept coming to mind and managed to give Jacob a semblance of peace was in Deuteronomy 32. He softly spoke the words, almost just mouthing them, "How should one chase a thousand, and two put ten thousand to flight, except their Rock had sold them, and the LORD had shut them up?"

He only wished now that Nathan had remained behind to stand guard.

In the midst of Jacob's inner turmoil, God quickened his heart with another Scripture, this one from Ephesians six. He knew this verse so well and had turned to it many times in his life: "For we wrestle not against flesh and blood, but against principalities, against powers, against the rulers of the darkness of this world, against spiritual wickedness in high places."

It was then that peace flooded his soul. "Yes, Lord," he said. "There's a time for war and a time for peace. I'm ready to go to war now, Your way."

With that, he knelt by the single cot, bowed his head, and went to battle.

The woods had grown as black as pitch, especially under the dense tree cover, as clouds swallowed the last light of the disappearing moon. Ezekiel stumbled repeatedly over exposed roots. Branches lashed his face, and once he went down scraping the skin off his outstretched hands on a rock outcropping. Now he leaned tiredly against an old growth pine, surveying what little he could see and feeling all hope drain out of him.

It was pointless to continue. To put it mildly, he had gotten himself totally turned around. To put it simply, he was lost. An eerie black gloom made it next to impossible to distinguish tree trunks blending almost seamlessly into the night. Without daylight to guide him, he was trapped inside a forested maze, running in circles until either utter exhaustion set in or an accident involving losing his footing stopped him dead in his tracks.

He stopped momentarily to determine what his next move would be. Another five or ten minutes and he'd call it quits, he decided. If he still hadn't made any progress at that point, he'd have to, of course, set up base camp by throwing together a leaf bed next to the upwind side of a boulder and hunker down amongst the leaves until daybreak. It would have to be a dry camp, as he was matchless, but that was standard old army routine, and he still had the constitution for it. With hands outstretched to deflect potential unseen branches, he stepped away from the tree and carefully felt his way around by searching the ground beneath and before him alternately with the toe end of each boot first before gliding into each step with his full weight. In a sheltered cleft of the rock, he decided to curl up on some thick feathery moss with tree boughs as his blanket until daylight.

After what he decided was the best sleep of his entire life, Ezekiel woke up refreshed to birds singing and the hum of traffic. Traffic? He sat upright and to his utter amazement realized it was late in the day. It was a miracle. He had slept for at least a twelve-hour, uninterrupted, blessed sleep without a single bad dream and the usual nightmarish sweaty awakenings. It was like the sleep of a new baby, Ezekiel pondered with gratitude as he remembered his new birth on the railroad track during the night.

Five minutes later, he cleared away a grove of low lying bushes and slowly and carefully stepped out onto a raised area that jutted out. He smiled from ear to ear as he rubbed his stubbly five o'clock shadow. He missed his old beard, but at least they hadn't taken his mustache from him. Roughly a hundred feet below he could see highway, and just beyond that, he could see the glow of town lights against a darkening late afternoon sky. Looked like a storm was brewing as he laughed out loud and began zigzagging his way down the fairly steep incline in slalom formation to prevent himself from losing his balance or gaining too much momentum as he made his way to the asphalt.

Halfway down, his right foot caught a tree root, causing him to be hurled headlong down the embankment only to find himself sliding downward at breakneck speed. As he continued gaining momentum, he encountered rocks and brush head first before encountering the sudden, excruciatingly painful blow to his head sending what his brain perceived to be a flash of light followed immediately by an all-engulfing darkness.

Beloved, believe not every spirit, but try the spirits whether they are of God: because many false prophets are gone out into the world. (1 John 4:1)

CHAPTER 14

It was still dark when a much younger looking Jasmine arrived at the mission. A flickering street light reflected off of her black leather jacket, and her retro mod boots clicked against the alleyway gravel as she made for the side entrance. With her nun's duds wadded up and stuffed into a roomy, but chic, designer tote, she rifled through her bling-accented jeans pocket for her keys, failing to notice the shadowy form that began making its way from the wall on the alley's far side, approaching her quietly from behind. "Jasmine?" Her heart skipped a beat while she caught her breath and spun around, her hand already pointing the snub-nose .38 right at the stranger's forehead.

The silhouette of a man stumbled backward into a pile of garbage. Bottles clanked loudly against each other displacing other rubbish and discarded cans. "No, Jazz no!"

Jasmine froze. "Frank?" she asked and stepped cautiously forward, her gun still staring him right between the eyes. She marveled at him in utter astonishment and promptly withdrew the firearm, pointing it up and back, then hissed, "You idiot! Are you trying to get yourself killed? Don't you ever do that again."

Slipping her set of keys into an outer pocket of her tote bag, with both hands free, she helped Frank to his feet and stood shaking her head and looking at him in total disbelief as he brushed himself off.

Though his face was still hard to fully make out, his voice gave him away. "A gun!" he said, incredulously. "What are you doing with a gun?" He swatted his clothes another time and reached down to retrieve a bundle of goods.

Jasmine slid the compact firearm back into her jacket pocket and scanned the alleyway. "Not out here," she said underneath her breath unlocking the side door. "And stop talking so loud!" She opened the door, and they both stepped inside. Closing the door, she motioned to him in the darkness and said, "This way," and headed for the windowless back room. She flicked on the light switch and set her tote bag on the old desk.

The "bundle" turned out to be Frank's backpack, but at first glance, she hardly could tell it was Frank. He was a far cry from the polished, self-acclaimed college president of a few years ago. Long, stringy hair, left unwashed for an entire month or so, it seemed, sprouting out in a disheveled manner from underneath a dirty baseball cap. Add to that, a dark, wiry, curly beard covering most of his face and throat. Smudged with unidentifiable stains, his clothes were an odd pairing of casual American and exotic indigent—including a homespun maroon tunic, jeans, and hiking boots.

"What's with the get-up?" Frank asked staring intently at her. Jasmine tugged at the lush brunette wig and tossed it onto the desk. She unpinned her hair and shook it free, pretending not to notice Frank's admiring gaze. "Still gorgeous," he attested with a puppy-dog look.

Jasmine regarded him in a most uncomplimentary manner. "Did you bring your rock along?" she asked.

A baffled look came over Frank's face. "What?"

"The one you crawled out from under," Jasmine exclaimed. She shook her head and looked him up and down. "You are an unqualified train wreck."

Feeling snubbed and put on the defensive, Frank retorted, "I came straight from the mountains of Tibet, thank you very much. You wouldn't believe everything I've gone through just to get here. I'm so beat, and I need some decent food and a good night sleep."

Jasmine wrinkled her nose. "And a bath," she added. "You could have at least changed into more decent attire. I'm surprised they even let you on the plane."

"If it makes you feel any better, they gave me a hard time at airport security in London. But I made a big deal about 'discrimination,' and they waved me aboard." He smiled devilishly. "Hey, the system works. Political correctness is our friend."

Jasmine gave a dramatic sigh. "Well, at least you came," she said.

Frank's countenance became more serious, and his voice softened. "I'd go anywhere for you. You know that."

Jasmine's eyes flickered. It was fleeting but Frank caught it. Something akin to . . . gratitude, perhaps? Certainly not love. That would be out of character and maybe even out of the question entirely.

"Anyway," she said, in a dismissive manner again, "I'm not sure I even need you anymore. Things are picking up speed now and have taken on a life of their own to where, at this point, you might just get in the way."

Frank's eyes bugged out. "Are you serious?! I came all this way . . . and went through all I did—most of which I haven't even shared with you yet—only to be told you no longer need me or have use for me?! Come on, Jazz! What am I supposed to do now?"

Jasmine engaged her signature "shoo fly" maneuver, as Frank called it, and it had always irked him. "Oh, quit whining," she said. "And let me think for a moment. Ah, yes . . . that's right. I was going to make you a monk . . ."

"I *am* a monk!" Frank shot back.

Jasmine had to stop and think about that while placing her hands on her hips. "Tsk, tsk now. Not the Tibetan Buddhist variety mind you," she assured him. "I mean Catholic. You know, how nuns sometimes have monks of the same order oversee them."

Frank smiled, feeling useful and needed once again by this treacherous woman. "You mean, I could tell *you* what to do?"

Jasmine snickered. "Don't let it go to your head. You know who runs things."

Frank shrugged. "Okay. So what do I do? You were very cryptic over the phone, and I have no idea why I'm here. The whole thing is bizarre. You pay for my plane ticket and send me a thousand grand in expense money. Where'd you get all the cash? Could you please tell me what's going on? And what's with the gun? Are you going to ice somebody?" He was only being facetious but backpedaled when she gave him a look that sent chills up and down his spine. "Hey," he assured, "I was only kidding."

"I'll tell you your part in this Frank," Jasmine countered. "And that's all you need to know."

"You said there'd be a lot of money involved too," he reminded her. "I want to go back to Tibet. I was in the process of learning so much there, and I want to continue to flourish spiritually." He looked around. "Maybe in my reincarnated state I'll be on a higher plane both materially and spiritually . . . well . . . compared to this one."

Jasmine glared at him and stated, "You'll be paid handsomely. And here I thought money wasn't important to a monk." As an afterthought, she added, "Greed will bring bad karma on you, you know."

Frank shrugged, wondering how else she expected him to get back to Tibet. He'd definitely risk it. "So," he said, "what now? Where can I sack out?"

Jasmine smiled disparagingly. "Are you kidding me? A man sleeping in the same building as a nun? That would be great for my reputation, wouldn't it now? No, there's a youth hostel about a quarter mile down the road. You can stay there and blend right in. Come see me in the morning. But, by ALL means buy some new clothes, first. And please shave."

Frank was taken aback and put his hand to his beard. "But . . . but . . ."

Jasmine rolled her eyes. "Oh, okay. What a baby. Trim it, then. And please take a shower. I want you looking at least halfway decent. You're going to be a monk, not one of the Desert Fathers." She turned from him and stopped cold. "On second thought," she added, biting gently on her lower lip as she often did when considering carefully, "keep the beard as is. And, as much as I hate to say it, stay smelly. Forget the monk idea. For the time being, you're an over-the-hill, just-passing-through hippie seeking Nirvana. The Browns and Tessa will then not be as apt to recognize you. You being recognizable could blow the lid off this whole thing." For a moment, Frank stared at Jasmine in awe but mixed with fear.

"Blow the lid off what thing? What in the world is going on?" His stomach growled, and he began to feel uneasy. "Um," he probed, "I'm starved." He looked around the room. "This place was a diner, right? Does the kitchen still work? You know, they're pretty stingy with the food at the monastery. I haven't had a plate of decent pasta since I joined the order."

Jasmine smirked. "Some enlightenment! I would have thought your most basic of inner cravings would have been replaced by self-realization and a more disciplined and abstinent inner spiritual life by now." She shook her head in utter disdain. "Nevertheless, there's a Stop 'n Shop a block away. Buy all the food you want there and cook it at the hostel. It'll help you make friends more quickly. Transients and ramen noodles go well together."

Frank had long since grown weary of standing and now appeared melancholy as he hunched over on one of the stools. He had gone through so much to get here. "I thought," he began, "well, you know . . . that, while I eat, we could maybe just sit and talk . . ."

Jasmine cut him off. "Forget it. There's a single little electric hot plate here, and it'll take forever just to heat a pot of water. Anyway, I'm dead on my feet. And you have to get out of here. I don't want us seen together. Not like this, at any rate."

After giving him directions, Jasmine hit the light switch and led the way through the semi-darkness back to the side entrance. She opened the door, poked her head outside, looked both ways, then beckoned to Frank right behind her. In the doorway, Frank paused. His voice faltered in a childlike manner. "I was thinking . . . I mean . . . when this is all over," he began, "maybe you'll want to check out Tibet, too. It's really awesome. I mean, we could learn together . . . you know?"

Jasmine gave him a gentle shove out the door. The backpack on his shoulders momentarily wedged in the doorframe, and he stumbled. "Get going," she said, "before somebody sees us. We'll talk tomorrow."

Frank nodded without saying anything and trudged off down the alley. Jasmine closed the door, leaving it open only a crack as she watched his form grow smaller yet brighter the closer he got to the alley entrance and to what few streetlights were on just beyond it. He turned the corner, and soon even the sound of his footsteps faded.

Jasmine closed and locked the door and climbed the stairs to her small apartment where she lit some candles and incense then slid to the floor into her favorite Yoga position She stared straight ahead, going over and over everything in her mind as she worked through each situation, right down to the last detail.

When her need to control every possible outcome her mind could come up with was satisfied, she let out a frustrated sigh and extracted her legs from the Full Lotus position. "What a busy day!" she mused. A few more impersonations and she'd lose track of her own individuality entirely. This multiple personality approach had the one inherent flaw of becoming thoroughly confusing and more difficult to keep straight the further she went and the more she developed each persona. With every disguise, she had to remember the storyline, past conversations, and who she spoke with and why. So far, during her short stay, she had played an old lady, Sister Genevieve the innocent with the youth and the suspect with Jacob Brown, Dr. Winters of "Winters and Davis," partners-in-charity scam, and just a few minutes ago, the femme fatale with that dirty biker in the bar.

After all that, she had to do her "sweet young thing" disguise for her half-mile walk to the all-night garage out of town where the car was parked, just to make sure it was still, as of yet, undiscovered. For a few minutes, she had to engage in conversation with the old man who owned the place and put up with his old-timer attempts at flirting with her. And now, finally, at long last, in the upstairs diner apartment, she was Jasmine again. The Machiavellian role playing and chicanery she found to be so entertaining initially, had, by this time, become thoroughly exhausting. As brilliant a mastermind as she deemed herself to be, how she coveted Chip's photographic memory. Then she'd never tire of the theatrics required to pull everything off according to her exacting specifications.

Jasmine stood up and stretched every muscle she could, then idly paced the floor, repeatedly passing through the intoxicating, spice-laden cloud of incense smoke that hung heavy in the air. Her shape-shifting-like movements cast grotesque shadows upon the faded wallpaper in the flickering candlelight—shadows that loomed and menaced, fled, then menaced again. After a while, she lifted up the room's only chair and placed it beside the open window. Seating herself, she closed her eyes and tried to let herself become one with the cool night breeze wafting down and in from the snow-capped peaks of the Bitterroots. That didn't work, either. A wasted half an hour trying to work herself into a transcendental state and now this. Bad karma had run interference on the entire evening.

She wasn't quite sure what she was going to do with Frank—either in the plan she had just formulated, or, as much as she hated to even consider it, in her personal life. The two of them once had a borderline "something" for a couple of years after their dismissal from Flat Plains Bible College and prior to her stint in Spain. It became a relationship she would never have characterized as romantic, but something just the other side of platonic. Her feelings toward him ran the way of a rather rampant ambiguity—from open derision to (rarely) an embarrassing, sisterly kind of fondness for the guy, and all points in between. She had her deep reservations about the wisdom of involving him, partly because of their former semi-relationship, and partly because he was . . . well . . . weak and easily manipulated. That trait could work either in her favor or against it. She didn't have much confidence in his ability to stay the course should the sailing get rough. But she finally decided to exploit his feelings for her, however distasteful it was to her, because he would literally do anything she asked.

Still, even in that respect, Frank didn't warrant her full trust. A simple scam or even a high-level one was something she knew he might buy into, but a revenge killing (she refused to use the word "murder") and a wholesale destruction of lives would be something else to Frank's way of thinking. For despite his many faults, he still had a somewhat intact conscience, to where she knew he would be nothing short of horrified if she actually were to make him aware of her plans, and he would try to persuade her of a far less drastic course of action.

And this was the thing. For all his talk of spirituality, Frank just didn't get it when it came to things like karma and the universe. Jasmine figured this plan had been set into motion by the cosmos, long before either she or Tessa had been born. This had to be Tessa's karma too—her and Jacob's payback in return for the great and unprovoked wrong they'd both done Jasmine. And now Jasmine was simply participating in a plan of which the actions and consequences had already, long since, been mapped out. What else could it possibly be after all that had happened?

Jasmine reflected back to two months prior—a time she could only call an "awakening." On her sparse funds, an overseas trip was possible only in winter, but that was okay. It was a quieter time of year, and tourism would be at low ebb, allowing her the opportunity to savor the country's spiritual climate minus the hard-sell tactics of religious hawkers. And she found just what she was searching for. The little retreat house connected to one of the convents in Avila had been a refuge she would always recall with fondness. She had learned much about Catholic mysticism prior to her stay there—things she had unsuccessfully attempted to impart to the students at Flat Plains Bible College. But under the more personalized instruction she received from nuns well-versed in Teresa of Avila's vision of divine union, Jasmine had been renewed, recovering from one of her recent bouts with depression—a melancholy that kept resurfacing ever since Jacob Brown put her out of a job. In that little stone retreat, where she was treated not as a respected college professor, but as a confused, lost soul, she had begun to lay hold of a kind of inner peace. In her "cell" every night, she incorporated what she'd learned into her other spiritual exercises. The journey had proven to be far more life-changing than she had originally anticipated.

Then, he came along.

He was not an imposing figure, by any means, and even now she struggled to remember exactly what he looked like. He had that kind of face that blends right into a crowd, average and unremarkable at best. It was the kind of face which the wearer of it feels invisible. Jasmine could not help but think to herself how a man like this could commit the most audacious crime in broad daylight, before a crowd of witnesses, and no two people would be able to offer the police the same description of him or account of what actually happened.

Near the end of the retreat, Jasmine ventured into one of the town's parks, stopped at a local café, and sat at a patio table underneath a red-and-white striped awning overhanging the sidewalk in front. Sipping herbal tea and basking in the unseasonably warm Spanish sun, it was there she first noticed him, staring. He was a smallish man, regarding her from behind stylish, gold-rimmed glasses. His business suit was exquisitely cut to form and complemented by a spendy hat with a brim that rode low over his forehead. He was alone, and somehow it seemed to fit him.

At first caught off guard but then irritated at his steady gaze, she leveled at him one of her own. Instead of demonstrating an appropriate or to be expected embarrassment, he smiled, touched his fingertips to his hat and, toting a small but expensive briefcase, made his way over to her. And so it began.

In the past several months she had replayed their conversation that day over and over in her mind, each time attempting to remember more of it than the time before. Each time she failed, but in that drab apartment above the empty diner, she could not help but make every attempt to remember the entire conversation again. "Excuse me," the man said with a smile. His voice was cordial but reserved. "May I sit down?"

Jasmine noted that his smile spoke of a secret knowing, a trait that both intrigued and annoyed her. Without answering, she motioned to the seat across from her. If he was a pickup artist, she mused to herself, he was going about it entirely the wrong way. And he definitely had the wrong prospect.

"Ms. Winters," he began, and Jasmine froze.

Pausing in mid-air with her cup of tea, she replied, "How do you . . ."

"Oh," he said, "I know quite a bit about you." Without missing a beat, Jasmine put on her poker face and made every effort to look composed. Police, maybe? Her mind wildly backtracked. Nothing in her past would warrant that, nothing recent anyway. That car she had stolen and crashed as a teenager . . . the statute of limitations had long since run out . . .

As if reading her mind, the man said, placatingly, "I have no connection with law enforcement, Ms. Winters. You can rest easy."

Jasmine opened her mouth to speak, closed it, slowly placed the teacup on its saucer, and stared hard at him. "Okay," she said, with cautious resignation, "I didn't realize what I was thinking was that obvious. Let's put all our cards on the table. What do you want?"

The man nodded. "Good," he said. "I like that. Neither of us has time to waste, and I've often considered these introductions awkward. I've been waiting for a few weeks now for the opportunity to find you alone. I would like to speak with you about a personal matter. I can assure you our conversation will be to your benefit. Exceedingly."

He stressed the last word leaning forward slightly. Jasmine noted that his smile, though now rather broad, did not extend to his eyes. His eyes retained a coldness as if a wall stood in front of them that she could not see beyond. She ventured, "And you are?"

He waved a dismissive hand of his own. Jasmine noted that his manicured fingernails looked better than hers. "My name's of little consequence," he said and brought the attaché up onto the table. Rifling through his suit pocket, he produced a tiny key and unlocked both clasps of his case. He peered out at her from over the case before actually opening it. With one hand, he produced a manila envelope and placed it unceremoniously before Jasmine. Her suspicious gaze moved from the packet to him then back to the packet. "Go ahead," he prodded, "open it. You'll find the contents . . . interesting, to say the least."

She'd often wondered, since that day, if she should have gotten up at that point and just walked away. Had she done that, she might still be in Europe, learning, progressing, and maybe even mentoring others in their spiritual walks. But her curiosity had gotten the better of her, and she could not just leave that envelope sitting there, un-opened. Perhaps at the time, she had thought that, no matter what was inside, she could still opt out and have it be as though having made his acquaintance never happened. If only . . .

For a long moment, Jasmine stared at the envelope. It was still a crisp golden color as if to suggest the contents therein were hot off the press too. The longer she stared at it, the more inexplicably drawn to it she became. She reached out, pulled it toward her, sliding her fingers over the sealed flap. She looked once more at the man. With a nod, he gave her the "go ahead," and she eased a long fingernail under the gummed area, lifted the flap, and slid out the contents. Dumbfounded, she stared.

Spread out on the table before her was her entire life—photos of her as a child, as a teenager, and even from her stint at Flat Plains Bible College. Foster care documents corroborated the photos. Along with older photos of her mother Cecelia Winters were also more recent photos of Tessa, Jacob, Margaret, and one of someone she'd never seen—a dirty looking mountain of a man astride a mammoth motorcycle, his black "Hell Boys" vest reflecting a glare from the hot desert sun. There were a lot of other papers too, detailing her life as a Spiritual Formation professor, and papers that disclosed details of Tessa's life that even she hadn't known.

Jasmine found herself overcome by unnamed fear and a sense of dread. Holding the documents in both hands, she looked up and said with a mix of anger and confusion, "Where did you get these? And what gives you the right to intrude upon my life like this?!"

The man lifted his small hand, palm outward. "I'm terribly sorry," he said still smiling. "It's always like this in the beginning."

Jasmine's thoughts raced. "What are you—C.I.A. or something?" It seemed the only plausible explanation.

For the first time, the man appeared genuinely amused. "Oh, certainly not!" he said, and he chuckled. "But that does seem to be the standard reply I get from our prospective, ah, operatives."

Jasmine stared with raised eyebrows. "Operatives?"

The man leaned back in his chair, folding his hands in front of his chin, regarding her with a cool expression. "My . . . employer has conscripted me for the task of running a rather thorough investigation on your life, Ms. Winters. My employer thinks he can be of some service to you . . . in return for some services of your own . . ."

He let the last part of his sentence hang, dangling like bait, she thought, but she took the bait anyway. "So, there's actually something in this—whatever this is—for me, right? There'd better be, after you've put together an entire dossier on me."

"Would one million dollars be sufficient?"

Jasmine's mouth dropped as she was momentarily rendered speechless. Finally, trying to find her voice again, she whispered, "A million dollars?" She exclaimed under her breath, "You can't be serious!"

"Quite the contrary."

Dumbfounded, she fell back into her patio chair. After coming to her senses, she eyed him suspiciously. "What if I still don't believe you?" she said, testing him. She gestured to the photos and documents. "Even with all this. I still don't know who you are or what this is all about." She leaned forward again. "Talk to me," she said with finality. "Or this conversation is over."

The man's smile never completely left his face. From an inside suit pocket, he produced another envelope—a thick, white one—every bit as crisp as the other, and placed it on the table before her.

Jasmine looked at it. "What's this?"

"Open it and find out," he said matter-of-factly. Jasmine opened the sealed envelope and inspected the contents therein. Her lovely caramel eyes bugged out. "It's fifty thousand dollars," the man explained. "Expense money, not to be deducted from your final payment of one million. If you agree to the terms."

Jasmine's throat had gone dry. She swallowed hard, and she raised her eyebrows. "And just . . . what are the . . . terms?"

Dropping the congenial façade, the man's demeanor changed in an instant—his countenance hardened. Leaning all the way forward, placing his elbows on the table, and keeping his hands clasped, his eyes pierced hers. She recoiled. In a strong, low, monotone voice, he stated, "Before I relay to you any of the particulars, you must know that once I make known my employer's terms, you automatically agree to them. There will be no backing out and no changing your mind. It won't be tolerated. Decide now."

Jasmine hesitated. The man offered a bit more encouragement. "I can tell you this much," he said, "you will be afforded a once-in-a-lifetime opportunity to act upon a personal vendetta against Jacob Brown."

"Jacob Brown! What does he have to do with this?!" Just hearing the name caused Jasmine's heart to race, and an overwhelming coldness came over her. No, not coldness . . . hate. The bitterness and anger toward Jacob Brown had transformed her heart to one of pure hatred.

The man sitting across from her sat back gesturing with his hands. "Think of it. Your dismissal at Flat Plains Bible College was so unfair. You were only trying to help those poor unfortunates reach a higher spiritual plane. And for that, you were persecuted, dismissed, and now have a permanent blemish on your professional record that will never go away." He paused. "Unless my employer, of course, has it expunged."

Jasmine stared at him with a kind of childlike hope. "He could do that?"

The man cocked his head. He had her now, and he knew it. "My employer could have you set up in one of the most prestigious universities in the world or in the United States if you prefer. Just imagine—not only a professor again, but a faculty head, no less. You could set your own standards of teaching and be looked up to . . . no telling how far you could go in your chosen field. Plus, in addition to your payment, you'll have an annual salary that will help you live in comfort for the rest of your life."

Jasmine's thoughts began to race. Everything he said was true. She had been maligned, and her career—no her life—had been destroyed. To call it unfair was an understatement. She had been reduced to mentoring people in small home groups and living only on a fraction of her former earnings. Maybe karma was finally bringing everything full circle on her behalf. Though she sensed a sinister nature to what she was getting herself into even then, she dismissed the feeling, persuaded that she could not let this one-time chance pass her by. Whatever it was, she would agree to it. Hugging the money envelope close to her, she said, "What do I have to do?"

The man took a deep breath, nodded, and said, "Very good." His voice grew softer. "Theresa Dawson has become a . . . liability. It will be your job to, ah, eliminate her from the equation."

Jasmine's face drained of all color. Trying to get her bearings, Jasmine countered, "Whatever do you mean?"

"Use your imagination, Ms. Winters," the man said dryly. "She is in the way. Remove her. Permanently."

His words stunned her. She had suspected something dramatic, but . . . killing? She didn't care much at all for Tessa and clearly hated Jacob, but . . .

"Remember what I said, Ms. Winters," the man reminded her, giving her a grim look. "You are now 'in.' There is no getting 'out.'"

She tested him. "Suppose I just get up and walk away? Leave your money and forget I ever saw you? After all, I still don't know who you are!"

The man pursed his lips and shook his head. "I wouldn't recommend that," he said. "There's no place you could go to walk away from this. We found you this time. Quite easily, I might add. We can find you again, I assure you. You're not exactly untraceable. And my employer doesn't like loose ends. Anyway . . ." He smiled at her again, ". . .you won't. It's karma, you know. You can't defy karma."

Jasmine thought, then gave a slow nod. "Okay," she said, "Where do we start?"

"I knew you'd see it my way," the man responded, and this time, he smiled with his eyes.

A nd so it had begun. The man had the fifty thousand dollars transferred to the United States, and Jasmine had access to it as cash only, through a third, nameless party. More would be forthcoming should she need it. She had been issued a new passport, under an assumed name, to match her new driver's license, social security card, voter's registration card, and the like. She was also given a plane ticket back to the United States. The plan had already been conceived, utilizing Jasmine's talent for languages and theatre, and Hub had already been contacted prior to her making his acquaintance. *How odd*, she thought, *that they had been so certain she'd go for it.* All she had to do was fulfill her end of the deal, and payment would be wired to a Swiss account, to which she had been given the identification number. Once the assignment was completed, the money was hers. They had also set up a website of her "convent," and all phone calls to the number on the poster and website would be routed through a relay house, and the appropriate person would answer the phone. Mob operatives did it that way all the time, she knew. Hard to prove and virtually impossible to trace. Even an attempt at tracing would require a court order, and that would be approved only with enough evidence to convince a judge. And evidence there was none, except against Jacob Brown.

Once the job was done, both she and Frank were to make their way directly to a safe house where they would be secured overnight until being airlifted by helicopter to another part of the state. With falsified passports to take them back to Europe—the very place she wished she had never left—they would be far from the "scene of the crime."

Whoever her employer was (she knew it was a man and that's all), he had plenty of pull and a vast network of global proportions. Obviously a lot of personal wealth was involved, and with that invariably came immense power. Even Jasmine herself retained a healthy fear of him. Who has the resources, time, connections, and power to track a slandered professor who is a nobody halfway around the world? But even more baffling to her was why Tessa Dawson was so . . . troublesome and needed to be eliminated? She too, was a nobody, in the eyes of the world—just a sweet, innocent kid who went out of her way to avoid trouble. Why in the world would someone like Jasmine's nameless, faceless employer want Tessa dead? So many unanswered questions that Jasmine would, more than likely, never know the answers to, and maybe didn't want to. There was a time in Jasmine's life when she would have found the proposal utterly absurd and horrendous, but Jasmine had changed—oh how she had changed.

Her deep meditation experiences had taken her to new levels, beyond what she could have ever imagined, affecting her psyche and her values—yes, even her very soul. And the voices—help from the other side that she thought of as her spirit companions—talked to her and guided her. Even now, as this sinister plot was brought to life, a special presence that identified itself as "Jesus" comforted her and told her, "It is for the best, and I, too, sacrificed my life that others may be benefited. Also you'll be doing Tessa a favor. She can move into that realm of eternal oneness and not have to suffer anymore in this life." Jasmine had read something like that in a popular New Age book where it said that Hitler actually did the Jews a favor by ending their lives.[1] So when one of her voices spoke these words, it was not too abstract or far-fetched for her to believe.

Including Frank was her idea, although she wasn't entirely quite sure why now. Perhaps she needed some "moral" support. Originally, she had entertained the idea of him donning a monk robe and acting in the capacity of an overseer sent from an American monastery. That way he and she could mingle freely as they allegedly prepared for the mission's grand opening. But she had been afraid he was lacking in the ability *she* had to do a superb acting job and might botch everything. And now he was almost too late. Perhaps, she thought, she should still pursue that part of the plan. But his assistance in other ways might be irrelevant. By tomorrow night, it wouldn't matter anyway, as Hub would have already done the deed. Frank would go ballistic if he found out the whole plan, but even at that, he'd support her. And maybe that was enough.

Hub. She hoped he would fulfill his part of the bargain. The meeting with him an hour ago had not been, at all, what she was expecting or had hoped. Perhaps he was simply toying with her. Guys who are rough around the edges like that have alpha-male tendencies and like to throw their weight around with the ladies—could be it was just a game to him. It had better be just that. She thought it might be a good idea to keep a watchful eye on him all the same. Still, she couldn't force him to do it. Jasmine peered intensely into the penetrating darkness. "He'd better not mess this up," she thought aloud. "We're too close."

At least Jacob Brown is behind bars for the time being, she thought, a slow smile tugging at the corners of her perfectly formed, red lips. The look of horror on his face at the mission had been priceless. Quite a different look than the stern ones he often gave her when she snuck out past curfew as a headstrong teenage foster child, living in his home so many years ago. A hollow laugh, then, instantly, her lips pursed. Another image, this time the memory of Jacob's steely-eyed, unflinching stare jolted her with its startling clarity. Jasmine shuddered as she recalled the humiliation she'd suffered that night at Flat Plains Bible College. Everything she'd worked so hard to achieve—the recognition, the honor, the acclaim—her carefully laid-out, noble plans to teach naïve young college students how to be more "spiritual"—everything that mattered to her, destroyed in an instant by Jacob's unrelenting determination to stop her ambitious dreams. She had even been on television, the prima donna professor—a shining star that fell from the heights of fame. She would never forgive Jacob for that. Never! NEVER!! That narrow-minded, fundamentalist Christian thought he'd won. *But look who's winning now,* she thought with a self-satisfied smirk. Revenge is sweet. *Oh, so sweet indeed,* she gloated with immense satisfaction. And as the bile of bitter hatred rose in her throat, an almost imperceptible sound, like a snarl, rose up with it.

With Tessa out of the way—as per the agreement with Hub—Jasmine could disappear under the pretense of heading back to the New Mexico convent for one reason or another. And yes, of course, it could look a bit suspicious in the eyes of the law since Jacob had declared "Sister Genevieve" to be Jasmine. But then again, Tessa's erratic behavior—like thinking a nun was trying to kill her—might make the law more inclined to arrive at the conclusion that the poor, young Tessa had finally "lost it" completely and vanished of her own free will. And once gone, there would be no way of connecting the dots.

It wouldn't matter at any rate since a brand new identity had been part of the deal with her employer all along. Jasmine Winters would no longer exist. She would even be given a new set of finger-prints (digitally processed and placed on file) as well as a new birth certificate, social security card, voter registration, and the whole nine yards. She didn't yet know who she was going to be, but she had a strong feeling she was going to like it.

Out on the street, two stories down, a young couple strolled hand-in-hand, their double footsteps on the sidewalk and hushed conversation triggering a loneliness in Jasmine that, in times of stress, reared its ugly head. She looked on at the couple wistfully. Once upon a time, she'd been like that—all starry-eyed and gullible, easy prey for any good-looking would-be pursuer with a knack for using just the right words and making all the right moves to get what he wanted. Of course, she would use them also, saying all the things she thought they wanted to hear.

There had been one man in her past in which the situation had been entirely different. But he was the one at fault, not her. For years, she had yearned for a little plot of land to homestead in Montana, a few acres to start off with and a small cabin that two young hippies could call home and add onto as the children arrived. It was such a good life she had envisioned in her mind. He, however, had just used her, and true to his free-love principles, when she finally called his bluff, he refused to step up to the plate. Instead, he moved on to another hippie commune, leaving Jasmine to face a scary future alone.

Without thinking, Jasmine's hand instinctively touched her stomach, and she looked down. Her child would have been in his or her thirties by now. *My child.* A rush of emotion welled up from deep within her, and her lower lip trembled. "Not my fault," she whispered. "There was nothing else I could do." She wanted to add, "Forgive me" but choked on the words.

A tear emitted from the corner of her eye, and she quickly wiped
it away with the back of her index finger. Her face hardened, and the
intermittent glow from the flickering street light fell across her embittered
features. All men were no good, she knew. Love was a cruel joke, played
on the unsuspecting. How often she had tried to love, but they had failed
her—every last one of them. Not a one knew what to do with a woman's
heart. Losers. She reassured herself that it was none of her doing, nothing
lacking in her, and no glaring flaw or personal failing of her own that
brought her consistently to the end of all her relationships. She had tried
until trying was no longer an option and had wept until the once thought
to be bottomless well of tears had, at last, run dry.

Just like Cecilia Winters, she remembered, before Cecilia immersed
herself in a bizarre spirituality and went off on a pilgrimage to India or
some such place, nearly thirty years ago. Jasmine used to think often
of her mother but now only occasionally and always with remorse that
it should have been different. They could have sought truth together,
but men problems had driven her mother to escape in the only way
she knew how. The disconcerting tape, like mother, like daughter, kept
playing in Jasmine's head, but Jasmine refused to listen. Her seeking
had not been the crazy kind. And she was done with "relationships."

"Who needs them?" she asked rhetorically. Enter Frank. The irony
was staggering. For all the men she had known, only Frank—good ol,'
reliable, weak-kneed, nondescript Frank—had stuck with her, even
despite her many attempts to push him away. She shook her head. If
that was the best she could do in the relationship department, maybe
karma from a previous existence had already caught up with her.
Sowing and reaping. Jasmine sat up straight in the chair, surprised and
even somewhat startled at the thought. Where had that come from?
Something Jacob had told her, long ago. Something about sowing "to
the flesh" and "reaping" the consequences of one's own choices to sin.

Jasmine frowned. All her advanced training in spirituality had
taught her there was no such thing and that sin was merely a construct
of an unenlightened mind. She felt she had progressed far past the idea
of a need for "repentance"—so much so that it had become a faint echo
of her former life. Or lives. Jacob's Gospel was too simple—receive his
Jesus for forgiveness of sins, and suddenly you're "new?" What was it he'd

said?—"old things are passed away?" "Couldn't be," she said aloud, for all her spiritual teachers since had taught her that the universe and her place in the divine was much more complex. To reduce it to a childlike acceptance of the Bible's message of salvation was inconceivable to her. Where were all the steps a seeker needed to take on the way to enlightenment? Certainly, there were no exact rituals or methods in place to follow or adhere to "religiously," that were in keeping with the fact everyone is different and requires varying approaches in their journey to find truth. Jasmine's training impressed upon her that the Bible was only "a" way, useful, but not exclusive, nor universal. How could one book or one set of ancient writings be the end-all, be-all to one's lifelong pursuit of truth? How could anything be that simple? To Jasmine's way of thinking, any predilection toward unswerving adherence to the Word of God on the part of any professing Christian, rendered any and all Christians borderline fanatics.

The strolling couple on the street below had long since passed, and even the sound of their footsteps had faded into the night. Wearily, Jasmine arose. She stretched again and snuffed out the flame of a nearby burning candle but allowed the incense stick to smolder. She walked over to the bed and lay down. For some time, before closing her eyes, she stared out the window, observing the play of light and shadow where the street lights stood as they flickered out in dawn's early light. She then turned her focus to the ceiling. Faces materialized on the stucco ceiling—Tessa, Jacob, and the ever patient Margaret. Without thinking, she whispered into the gloom, "What if they're right?"

No one answered, not even her voices, and not even amidst the whirlwind of her own thoughts or in response to the inward cry of her own irreparably broken and jaded heart.

This wisdom descendeth not from above, but is earthly, sensual, devilish. For where envying and strife is, there is confusion and every evil work. (James 3: 15-16)

CHAPTER 15

Carrie Littlejohn sat in her kitchen not far from the muted light of the oven hood fan with both hands locked around her favorite coffee mug and her feet propped up on a chair while she stared out the window into the darkness. It was much too late for an infusion of caffeine, she knew, but the conversation in the car just hours ago effectively cured her of any tendency to adhere to a routine. She glanced at the wall clock. 2:00 am. It was a good thing she had the day off tomorrow. It would be a long night.

A gusty wind had kicked up, and she listened distractedly to the incessant sound of branches wildly brushing up against the house siding. The sudden change in wind pattern signaled a weather change and lent itself to an atmosphere conducive to in-depth, personal introspection and contemplation.

Contemplation. What a word, she thought, in view of recent events. And no, she self-edited, it was not just earlier that night. This contemplative deception had been going on for some time now at Sheep Gate, and she wasn't the least bit sure that a handful of apparently confused and deceived church elders could or even would bring the runaway train of pagan spirituality that had plowed through Sheep Gate to a screeching halt. How in the world had everything gotten so far afield from the Bible in the first place?!

Weren't the elders supposed to be the gatekeepers protecting the flock from stuff like this?

It was all too easy to point fingers. And yet, she realized she was just as much to blame as anyone else. *What a failure,* she thought with disgust, *as both a Christian and a mother!* She should have seen it coming. She did, actually, but only lately discovered that the skill at passing the buck was not strictly delimited to corporate or political arenas. How often she had thought how it wasn't her job to police the pastor, pick apart his sermons, or find fault with those he brought in to assist him in teaching and shepherding. What single mom has that kind of time? That's what they have an elder board for, or so she thought. How simple it had always been to just go with the flow, ignore the scriptural injunctions, and dismiss the spiritual nudges and red flags that went up at each violation of God's Word.

Chip Davis was a fast talker, a man of smooth speech, winsome in all his ways, and with his infectious enthusiasm, he roped the entire church into his pseudo-religious agenda. It was like they were all high on something, a spiritual elixir of some kind that dulled critical thinking and lulled the spirit to sleep. And there was no denying Chip's church growth program actually worked. Attendance had skyrocketed over the past few months, and Sheep Gate's influence was felt far outside their own little valley. Folks had come from sixty miles away to get "tapped in," and the dramatic spiritual change in even some of the wilder youth was a strong selling point for the parents involved—including Carrie.

"Stupid," she muttered, swallowing the lukewarm remains of the first batch of late-night joe. The water in the coffee maker behind her began pressurizing from the heat, beckoning even, but she ignored it while sifting through a morass of self-condemning thoughts. It was only earlier that night when she realized the clear and present danger to Matt—her son—that she finally awoke from her stupor. And now, guilt was having a field day in her heart as the faces of other parents, just as duped as she had been, passed in front of her. Worry etched itself into her tired features. How could she survive another fight? First cancer in the family, now spiritual cancer was spreading through her beloved church family. Now that she knew, the ball was in her court and she had to act. And unfortunately, it had to begin with Matt.

That was the hardest part—figuring out how to tell her son, who adored his pastor, that Chip was, at best, in serious error, and at worst, a false teacher. He probably wasn't even saved. And the nun, "Sister What's Her Name," . . . was she part of Chip's hidden agenda, if indeed it was a deliberate ploy by him? Or was she a sincere believer in her own methods yet just another lost soul who genuinely attempted to help others find her version of God? ? Even if so, why would he allow elder Carlton's wife to teach the youth mystical meditation techniques at midnight in a labyrinth at Sheep Gate Church? In fact, Matt had told her quite defensively, it wasn't the first time she'd taught them how to practice the "presence of God" with breath prayers by emptying their minds and repeating the name of Jesus or some other holy name. Carrie didn't know what that even meant, but she knew one thing for sure—none of that was in *her* Bible.

In the end, it didn't matter, as it was all an elaborate deception from the get-go, and Sheep Gate Lane Church was on a fast track to a no-man's land ecumenical dead-end. Well, she thought firmly, she wasn't about to hop along for the ride. Nor was Matt.

Carrie craned her neck to better hear down the narrow hallway to Matt's room. The door was still closed as it had been since he'd jumped out of the car and stormed into his bedroom and slammed the door. He hadn't even spoken to her since arriving home. Carrie felt badly all the way around, and it weighed heavily upon her now that she would have to tell Matt the truth about his beloved mentor. Just like the rest of Matt's youth group, Matt idolized Chip. The thought of the pedestal her son and the youth of Sheep Gate put Chip on made her cringe. Just like with Saul's conversion experience in the Book of Acts, scales had fallen away from her eyes as the horror of it struck her. Chip Davis had done more than just gain supporters—he had made disciples of himself. He had become a surrogate "Jesus" to these kids, a virtual mediator between them and God. To them, and to many others in the congregation for that matter, Chip's word had not only become law, it was, to his hearers, immutable truth . . . no matter what perversion came out of his heart by way of his mouth.

Carrie removed her feet from the chair cushion and leaned forward with both elbows on the kitchen table. "O Lord," she whispered, "help, please. My God and Father, help me. Show me what to do. Give me Your words that Matt needs to hear. Lead me by Your Spirit. How can I best tell him that Chip is not what he appears to be? Please don't let him reject me, and even more importantly, don't let him reject You."

But even as she prayed, she began rationalizing: *Maybe tomorrow I'll tell him the truth about Chip. Maybe tonight's not such a good idea, what with our argument and all. Maybe I should just go and tell him I love him, and leave it at that, and he'll understand and ask for Your forgiveness . . . Maybe . . .*

Carrie scooted her chair back and stood up, setting the empty mug by the coffee maker and flipped the switch to "off." The coffee maker burbled, clicked internally, and fell silent. She padded down the hallway in her slippers to stand before Matt's bedroom door, listened for a moment, shook her head, and made her way to her own bedroom. Closing the door, she lay down on the bed, still fully dressed, and totally exhausted despite the coffee, she fell into a restless sleep.

She awoke with a start, and for a few moments, stared at the ceiling. Something was not right. She sensed beyond the stillness someone or something moving through the house, quietly, and a paralyzing fear swept over her. She looked over at the clock sitting upon the nightstand to her right. The cool blue digital clock readout said 3:00 am. Without making a sound, she sat up and swung her legs over the side of the bed and reached for the aluminum Little League baseball bat she kept by the bed. But it suddenly seemed like such a pathetic and inadequate way to effectively confront an intruder.

Standing, she quietly enveloped the cold doorknob in her free hand and turned. It creaked, and she clenched her teeth while slowly edging open the door. Tightly gripping the bat with both hands, she extended it before her, probing the darkness. In the doorway she waited, listening, but heard only the faint ticking of the kitchen wall clock. In the hallway, she paused, looked up and down the short hallway, and turned to Matt's bedroom.

Pressing her ear lightly to the door and gripping the bat singlehandedly, she raised her free hand to knock and paused again, catching a whiff of fragrance, sweet, spicy, and exotic. Perfume? No. Incense. She cleared her throat and knocked, lightly at first. "Matt?" she whispered. She knocked again. "Matthew!" she rasped, more loudly this time.

She tried the doorknob. It turned quietly, and she opened the door just enough to poke her head inside. "Honey? Are you awake?" She pushed the door open wider and stopped dead in her tracks.

On a small breakfast plate Matt had nabbed from the kitchen, a thin stick of incense burned, its black as coal end emanating a sinuous thread of hazy smoke. On either side of the room, a couple of votive candles glowed. In the middle of the carpeted floor, Matt knelt, his face uplifted, his hands folded, his eyes closed and mouth open—all signs indicative of a trance-like state. Carrie's entrance into the room caused a slight flicker in the small candle flames, and serpentine shadows moved across Matt's teenage face.

The hairs on the back of Carrie's neck stood on end. She sensed, or more like felt, another presence in the room—different from anything she'd ever encountered before. The bat slipped from her hand and hit the floor with a dull thud. Her throat constricted involuntarily. "Leave," she said, her voice a suffocated whisper. "Get out of here in Jesus' name."

At that moment, Matt opened his eyes and blinked, turning to look at her with bleary eyes. "Mom?" he said faintly, then with a stifled cry, he inhaled sharply (as though someone had been strangling him but had finally let go), fell backward onto the floor, and shook uncontrollably. His eyes rolled to the back of his head.

Carrie fell to her knees and frantically pulled Matt to her, clamping her arms tight around his convulsing body. Strong as she was, it was all she could do to steady his heavy frame, her breath coming in broken gasps. "Jesus!" she called out, utterly terrified. "Help us!"

A flood of Scriptures handpicked by God for that very situation came rushing to the forefront of her mind, washing away the fear, and putting to flight the evil presence. Carrie spoke them aloud, timidly at first but then with increasing boldness.

"He that dwelleth in the secret place of the most High shall abide under the shadow of the Almighty."*

"I will say of the Lord, He is my refuge and my fortress: my God; in him will I trust."**

"The thief cometh not, but for to steal, and to kill, and to destroy: I am come that they might have life."***

"Blessed be the Lord my strength, which teacheth my hands to war, and my fingers to fight:"****

In seconds, the spasms left Matt, leaving him limp and peacefully asleep. And there, on the floor, cradling her son's resting body, Carrie rocked and cried, hugged, and leaned her face over his, wetting the hair of his head with her tears. She sobbed in repentance and tasting the salt of her weeping said over and over, "No more lukewarm, Lord. No more, no more . . ."

And no marvel; for Satan himself is transformed into an angel of light. Therefore it is no great thing if his ministers also be transformed as the ministers of righteousness. (2 Corinthians 11:14-15)

---

* Psalms 91:1;   **Psalm 91:2;   *** John 10:10;   **** Psalm 144:1

CHAPTER
16

Dawn's early light made inroads into the distant, hazy-blue peaks and spilled out over a scattering of dilapidated buildings whose roofs were already beginning to shimmer from the heat. Every window had gotten, at some point, a rock thrown through it, or had been blown, piecemeal, from its framework from the yearly stormy winds. Most of the metal doors, which had a ghetto look to them from paint that had long since been blasted off by sandy desert winds, stood ajar, propped open by sand piled up against them or a thicket of spindly plants. Here and there a scrawl of spray paint on an outside wall marked the passage of vandals. Some of the structures had collapsed upon themselves, but many of them remained upright and in reasonably good condition, structurally at least. In this land of little moisture, the metal doors and supports were largely without rust. On the compound's far perimeter, the turret of an aviation tower pointed three stories above the desert floor. The place was obviously an outdated, small military compound and in its heyday had seen light plane traffic. Long since abandoned, it was now even too far away from anything for even the idlest and most listless of vandals to bother with.

A thoroughly confused Nathan Shepherd stood at the far end of an asphalt runway in bad repair, with fissures running through it in too many places to count, shot through with a myriad of desert plants. The map of the area, already looking very used just from the many times he had to keep referring back to it, dangled from his hand at his side, and as he gave the deserted area and the vicinity another good three-sixty going over, he simply couldn't figure where he'd taken a wrong turn. In the final analysis, it was the only explanation that made sense. Somewhere along the way, he must have hung a left instead of a right. There were so many nameless dirt roads branching out in all different directions into the New Mexico desert that the potential for getting lost was magnified greatly in the pre-dawn darkness in which he had traveled from Taos. To make matters worse, he would have to fuel up again before embarking on another wild goose chase, after having backtracked—a delay he hadn't exactly bargained for.

He checked the map again, scratched the back of his head, and grimaced. No—this was the place. It had to be! He'd spent enough time in the Idaho woods to know how to read coordinates, and the description of the convent's location matched this one. This was the spot where the cloister was supposed to be.

Only . . . it wasn't here.

A shiver ran up and down Nathan's spine, and the hair on the back of his neck stood on end. Of course. How could he—all of them—have been so stupid? If "Sister Genevieve" was a fake, then so was her convent. He didn't know exactly how a scam like this worked, but he had heard of how a phone call could be routed through an office used as a front, and an "operator" answered at the other end and said whatever they were paid to say. The "mother superior," et al, had been nothing more than an actress. That meant two things: this kind of front was a gamble in the long run (as sooner or later someone like Nathan would research the convent's validity); and such a gamble only made sense in the context of a short-term operation. It was never meant to be a long-term kind of set-up, in other words. Which meant that the danger to Tessa was immediate and that the previous two attempts on her life were a prelude to the real deal.

Fearing for Tessa's well-being and with no time to lose, Nathan immediately reached instinctively into his pants pocket for his cell phone and looked at the signal readout. His heart sunk. No service. He was in a dead zone with no telling how far he'd have to go before being able to contact Jacob and relay the disconcerting news. He surveyed the far end of the compound where his blue S.U.V. rental was parked. It took hours to get to this place. "Oh, Lord Jesus, help!" he prayed aloud as he shoved the phone back into his pocket and made a mad run for the vehicle.

He had just swung open the door of the rented car when a buzzing overhead caught his attention. A tiny speck of red, brilliant against the cobalt sky, obliquely approached the compound. Suddenly, he had an idea. He ran to the edge of the runway, looking up, jumping up and down, frantically waving his hat and praying fervently. Immediately, the plane tilted, banked, and began its descent. A few suspenseful moments later, the wheels touched down on the hot tarmac, and Nathan backed away as it roared past, shielding his face from grit kicked up by prop wash. Near the end of the short runway the plane's engines died and, as Nathan ran to it, the pilot shoved open the cockpit door and poked his head out. "You okay?" he shouted. "Are you stranded?" He moved so half of him was visible in the entryway.

Nathan's chest was heaving as he reached the plane. He leaned one hand against the plane and replied, "I gotta get outta here. Can you take on a passenger?"

The pilot, in his late-twenties and with an unruly tuft of red hair scrambling out from underneath a backward baseball cap, made a time-out sign with his hands. "Hold the phone," he said, "Hang on. I'll radio for help. What's the problem—out of gas? You tourists should know better than to get on some of these desert roads." He shook his head. "Then you rely on guys like me to land on airstrips like this. Good thing I keep it cleared for my own use—and that I just happened to be flying by when I saw you."

Nathan shook his head. "No, you don't understand. I need your help. Someone's going to be killed, and I need to get back right away. I don't have time to drive back to Taos and wait for a plane. When I saw you overhead, it occurred to me that you could take me. Possibly."

"To Taos?"

"No, Birch Valley, Idaho."

The pilot shook his head, and his voice lifted an octave. "Dude, you're looking at almost a thousand miles. Even if I could, I'd have to stop to refuel before we actually headed north."

"Would we have to keep stopping, or does it hold a lot of fuel?"

"At maximum fuel capacity, she'll fly as far as you need to go," the pilot said. "Barring bad weather, we could get there without having to land twice for refueling. About six or seven hours flight time. But look, why don't I just take you to Taos? We can make it that far, easy, on what I've got right now. From there you can hop a commercial jet."

Nathan shook his head. "No good. There's no way of knowing how long I'll have to wait at the airport, even if a plane is going that way today. Then, in Boise, I'd have to hop a puddle jumper on top of it, just to get to Birch Valley." He tapped the plane's hull. "How fast can it go?"

The man smiled like a proud new dad. "She tops a hundred and thirty five miles per hour on a good day." He glanced skyward. "This is a good day. At least right here."

Nathan looked at him, hopeful. "Well?"

Through mirrored sunglasses, the man eyed Nathan cautiously. His right arm moved behind him and slowly brought up a double-action revolver, which he held nonchalantly across his chest. "This all sounds pretty crazy," he said reticently. "I don't know you from Adam. You could be an escaped convict for all I know. Hakinnett State Prison's a day's walk from here, but you could've done it. You look strong and able enough."

Nathan reached out and gripped the man's forearm. "Do I look like a prison escapee?" He pointed behind him. "And what about the car? I didn't walk—I drove here."

The pilot shrugged. "Stole it, for all I know."

Nathan groaned. "No, it's not like that. It's my fiancée. I'm telling you, someone's going to try and kill her. They've already tried twice. We took it up with the sheriff's department and the small town deputy there thinks we're nuts. But I'm telling you the truth. As I said, there have already been two attempts made on her life, and they'll get her for sure next time. Don't you understand that I need to be with her? I can't be a thousand miles away when they try again."

The pilot eyed him carefully. "So what are you doing way out here?" With the gun's muzzle he gestured to the empty buildings. "This isn't exactly close to your girlfriend, now is it?"

Nathan reached up with both palms and pressed them to his temples and sighed heavily. He looked up, pleading. "I'll tell you the whole thing on the way there. Please—there's no time."

The young pilot thought for a moment. He looked at Nathan sideways and with a hint of sarcasm said, "It'll cost you. Fuel is my biggest recurring expense, then there's maintenance, and my hourly rate . . ."

Nathan reached into his back pocket, took out his wallet, opened it and removed the wad of money he had grabbed from Jacob's cookie jar and thrust it toward the pilot. "There's over five hundred dollars in there," he said, "and I'll double that when we get to Birch Valley. A thousand dollars for six hours work."

The pilot thumbed through Nathan's wad of cash, eyeballed him briefly one last time, then nodded. "Okay, I'm sold, more or less," he said. "I can see by the amount of cash you have on hand you came prepared, and I'm inclined to think you're for real. Either that or you're an exceptional actor, and I'll wind up dead." He slid the revolver onto the pilot's seat. "Either way," he said, "get in. We got a lot of miles to cover. What are you going to do about the car?"

"I'll call the rental place and tell them where to pick it up."

Nathan climbed into the cockpit beside the pilot who offered a hand. John Adams," he said, "like the president. But everybody calls me 'Mike.' And don't ask."

Nathan smiled and shook his hand. "Nathan Shepherd. And do I have a story to tell you . . ."

"**T**his is all your fault!"

Chip stood in his bathrobe looking at Tessa through sleep-filled eyes. The pounding on the front door of his grandmother's house had jarred him awake, and his first thought was to check the time. His mind could not grasp the idea of anyone's need to see him at ten o'clock in the morning. When he undid the deadbolt and opened the door, Tessa stormed in, thrust an accusing forefinger at him and leveled a barrage of accusations at him, only half of which he understood or was able to even begin to wrap his brain around being he was still half-asleep. In tandem with her venting thoughts, she rattled off each accusation seamlessly, with one pouring right into the next. "My fault?" he blurted. "No way! Wait—what's my fault?"

Tessa glared. "I told you, you're a liar! And you're in it with her."

Chip blinked. "Her? Who? And in what?" He scratched the top of his head through a patch of tousled hair. "You're not making any sense." He cupped his hands dramatically over his ears. "And stop shouting. It's too early in the morning, and I haven't had any coffee yet." He collapsed on the couch.

Tessa took a break from her tirade for what she deemed to be a long enough moment, taking deep breaths while she was at it. She then riveted her gaze upon him again before picking right back up again where she left off. Whatever it was, Chip thought wearily and warily, he was in trouble.

"Like I said," Tessa adamantly stated, "I just left my grandfather at the sheriff's office jail. The deputies say he assaulted Jasmine Winters."

The mention of the name, and Chip was wide awake. A twinge of fear surged through him, but survival instinct took over and he feigned ignorance. "Who?"

Tessa smirked. "You know very well who," she said, with a bold assurance that was unnerving. "Your fake nun. You and Jasmine have been quite the team lately. Your "revival" is reeling them in. And last night's youth group . . ." She paused for a moment and looked him squarely in the eye. "I'm not really sure why you both got together, except you're probably planning on making a lot of money off this show you're putting on. That and making a name for yourselves, too; that's something Jasmine always wanted."

Chip feigned a yawn, but his mind raced. He rubbed the back of his neck to vie for time. When he looked up, Tessa regarded him icily. "Hey," he finally said, hoping to placate her to some extent, "I really don't know what you're talking about, Tessa. I'm sorry about your grandfather—this is the first I've heard of it and, no doubt, the charges are ludicrous—but I'm clueless as to why you'd think I have any knowledge of this."

Tessa walked over to Chip and standing over him stared him down. Her aggressive demeanor scared him far more than he led on. He had never seen this side of her before, found it to be completely out of character, and had no idea she was capable of such anger. He couldn't help but think to himself that maybe it was a good thing she had chosen Nathan over him. "Here's some news for you, pastor, that maybe Jasmine forgot to tell you. She tried to kill me, twice. She almost ran me down in her car the other night, and she also slipped poison into my drink. I spent a night at the hospital after that one. We've gone to the police, and it's all on record. And now my grandfather is in jail on a trumped-up charge. She's trying to destroy my family, and I'm not sure why, but this one thing I am sure of—you're in it up to your neck, and when she goes down, you will, too." Her gaze sat on him like lead, and she leaned her face intimidatingly close. "This is going to break wide open, Mr. William Davis," she said as if savoring every word, "and you'll find yourself in some of the hottest water you've ever been in. You should have learned a lesson from what happened to your father."

Another icy chill coursed through Chip's frame, but he continued to wear a poker face. His thoughts raced. How did they find out about the old man? Grandma must have . . .

Tessa turned and moved to the still open front door. A blast of cool air, heavy with the promise of imminent rain, blew into the living room and rustled a set of sermon notes on the coffee table. She stood a moment in the doorway and with a strange, sad expression looked over her shoulder at him. "And to think I liked you, once," she mused aloud. "If it hadn't been for Nathan, I might have fallen for you. I'm glad I dodged that bullet!"

She walked out of the house, and Chip listened as she got into Jacob's truck and pulled out of the driveway and thought, *Ditto.*

Chip then exploded from his chair. He kicked the door closed and pressed his temples with his lower palms. Back and forth he paced across the living room floor and voiced out loud his rapid-fire thoughts. "She knows! I can't believe it. She knows. What am I gonna do? *What Am I Gonna Do?!!*"

He stopped himself cold and exclaimed, "Jasmine! Maybe I can talk her into dropping the charges." He hurried to the bedroom to get dressed. "Yeah, that's it," he reassured himself. "No police, no courts, no investigation . . . it'll work . . . Maybe she should leave town for a while. Maybe I need to leave town for a while. . ."

Jasmine Winters sat up in bed, wide awake. It wasn't the approaching thunder pealing in the distance or the gusts of wind that lifted the curtains away from the open window. No, it was something else.

Hub. The name came rushing to the forefront of her mind along with a surge of anger. He was leaving . . . and taking the five thousand with him.

Her companions in the spirit world were always looking out for her. Like when she knew, both times, that Jacob had been to the sheriff's office. And that the second time, he would head immediately to her mission to confront her. She just knew he'd be there and used that knowledge to set him up for the perfect fall. There were other times, of course. Lots of them that had given her an edge when she needed it most. It was a sign of her spiritual advancement and discernment, she reasoned, and the feeling was delicious, like being told forbidden secrets by a close friend.

Jasmine threw aside the comforter, leapt out of bed, and wiggled her way into some clothes well-suited to her wig, dabbed on some makeup, and freshened her lips with a cherry-red gloss. She then stashed her nun's outfit and some makeup remover in a tote bag, for the change afterward. Making sure her real hair was tucked carefully under the hairpiece, she gave herself a quick once over, grabbed the bag, and headed for the bedroom door. It wasn't perfect, but it would have to do.

Halfway down the stairs, a tentative knock sounded on the side door. She stopped in mid-step. "Ahhh! Not now!"

Frank. It had to be, she thought. She hurried down the rest of the steps and moved to the door, undid the latch above the knob, and swung it open. Before he could say a word, Jasmine reached out with one hand and grabbed the flap of Frank's open jacket and pulled him inside.

He had taken a shower but looked almost as grungy as the night before, beard and hair still long and scraggly looking. "Now look, Jazz," he apologized, as a look of confusion came over his face. "You are Jasmine, aren't you?" he asked, then without waiting for an explanation added, "I need to know what's going on. I came a long way and . . ."

"Yes, fine!" Jasmine cut in. "Go back to the hostel and meet me here later."

"But . . ."

"Do it!"

The unlocked side door burst open, and in rushed Chip, face flushed and eyes wide. "Doc, we need to talk," he said then skidded to a halt when he saw Frank. "Who's he?"

Frank looked at Jasmine. "Who's he?" he echoed.

Jasmine covered her eyes with her hands. "I don't have time for this!" she protested then said, "Frank, meet Chip. Chip, meet Frank. We're all one big happy family here, okay?" Then to Chip, "What are you doing here? I hope no one saw you?"

"No," Chip replied, "I . . ." His iPhone rang, and he rolled his eyes reaching into the inside pocket of his suit coat.

"Just don't answer it," Jasmine protested.

Chip waved his hands in frustration. "I have to. I can't just not answer it." He pressed it to his ear and said, "Jerk," then in irritation tossed the phone on the counter, sheepishly. "Telemarketer," he said, and to avoid an "I told you so" from Jasmine quickly added, "Hey, did you know that Jacob Brown is in jail?"

Frank gasped. "*The* Jacob Brown?!"

Chip looked quizzically at Frank. "You know him?"

Frank nodded, making a face. "He got me fired. And her . . ." motioning at Jasmine. Chip's face registered surprise.

"Frank," Jasmine warned, "Shut. Up."

Frank shrugged and looked away.

Chip cut to the chase, pointing an accusing finger. "He said you put him there. Something about assault. Is that for real?"

Jasmine waved a dismissive hand. "We'll talk about it later," she said, heading for the side door. "I need to take care of a little problem."

"Wait a minute," Chip said, flustered. "Tessa knows who you are and that we're running a game. She's getting ready to blow us out of the water!"

"She'll never get the chance," Jasmine said almost to herself. She opened the door, scoped out the alley before proceeding, and was gone.

Frank and Chip stared at the closed door a moment longer. Without looking at Chip, Frank mused, "I wonder what she means by that."

Hub gave a quick last look around the motel parking lot and wished he had left the night before as originally planned. He started his bike, and the chopper's sudden roar felt like a searing hot knife through a skull already hammered by a hangover—a remnant of last night's long pondering at the bar about life, death . . . and the lady of many faces. For all his mental acuity, Hub was still a simple man at heart. When things became too complex, he did what he always did—straddled his motorbike and rode off into a new day, leaving the past behind.

Before he pulled out, he looked skyward. Low lying, slate gray clouds hugged the Bitterroots and draped themselves across the horizon line. White lightning flared, and the rumble of thunder, now only a few miles away, echoed in the valley. *Looks like rain,* thought Hub, *and lots of it.* Although it would slow him down some and make a mess of his gear, it would also keep his pursuers, if any, at bay until he was out of the personal hazard zone. *Nobody tails people in the rain,* Hub thought. He kicked his bike into gear and eased out of the parking lot.

He did not notice the green, two-door sedan pulling up behind him a block away.

Chip Davis got behind the wheel and high-tailed his grandmother's classic Lincoln Continental out of town. He wasn't sure where he was headed, but anywhere as far away from Birch Valley as possible seemed like an extraordinarily good idea at this point. He wondered how the congregation would deal with a suddenly empty pastor's office. Surely, when he didn't show as he always did at least sometime during each day, they would attempt to locate him. When his iPhone would remain unanswered with his grandma's car gone and a house search would reveal some missing personal items, the elders would sound the alarm. He only hoped no one would hit the panic button and call him in to the cops on a missing person's report.

Chip sighed, dejected. *There goes the revival,* he thought.

The two suitcases packed with his clothes and a few books looked pathetically sparing on the wide-cushioned back seat, mocking him and his dreams of success. Maybe he was no better than his dad after all. At any rate, he was going to be long gone by the time Jasmine rendezvoused with Tessa. This was turning out to be far more than a *harmless* con job. These were dangerous illusions they were playing with, and nobody was going to pin a murder rap on him.

A holographic vision of Tessa's face hovered, like liquid glass, in front of the windshield before him. Chip swallowed hard. He had been so infatuated with her, had conceived such great plans for the two of them, and now it had all gone south. And whereas before he wasn't entirely certain of the true nature of Jasmine's hidden agenda, now he knew, beyond all doubt, her plans were suspect, and he knew he was powerless to stop her. The woman was crazy! To continue to remain involved at this point would be to set himself up as an accessory to the crime. And yet, in not reporting Jasmine's plans to the authorities, he realized that made him a co-conspirator. Chip was torn. The man in him wanted to protect Tessa, but the cowardly con in him said to run. "I'm sorry, Tessa," he murmured. "But I can't. I just can't risk it. Anyway," he said trying to convince himself, "this crazy plan of Jasmine's probably won't even work. I'm sure Tessa will be fine."

He caught a glimpse of himself in the rearview mirror. No, of course he wasn't being cowardly or neglecting his duty to look out for the welfare of another and do unto others as he would like to have done unto him; had the tables been turned he would expect the same to be done for him. No sir, just playing it smart by not ending up in prison like his father. "Sure, you keep telling yourself that," he said to no one in particular, wholly disgusted with himself.

He buried his anguish as the first few, heavy raindrops began splattering against the windshield.

"**O**h great!."

Nathan looked at Mike curiously. "What's the matter?"

Mike studied the control panel then fooled with the radio dials. "Hmmmm."

Nathan was getting worried. "What gives?"

"Radio's out," Mike relayed. "Something in the electrical system's been playing hide-and-seek the last few days. Thought I had it under wrap, but I guess not."

"So, what does that mean for us?" Nathan pressed. "Will we have to land somewhere?"

Mike said lightly, "Can't. We're over the Rockies right now, and there's nowhere to land anyway. I'm bending all the rules, but if we steer clear of cities and towns we shouldn't have to worry about air traffic. I just need to keep my eyes peeled, and it wouldn't hurt if you'd be my second set of eyes."

Nathan gulped and nodded. "You bet. You won't catch me sleeping." He peered out the cockpit window at the lowering visible portion of sky.

"Everything else seems to be in good working order," Mike assured. "Just can't contact anyone. It's kind of a big deal, but short of making a pit stop to run some tests, we'll just have to wing it." He turned to Nathan with a grin. "That's a pilot joke, son." Nathan forced a smile. "It'll be interesting when it comes time for a simulated runway landing," Mike went on, and when he noticed Nathan bristle said, "Relax, dude. I earned my wings flying as a bush pilot in Alaska. I've gone with no instrumentation before, and I'm still alive. We'll make it OK—that is, if we don't fly head on into a mountain in this thick fog."

He looked sideways at Nathan and grinned.

"If we don't fly into a mountain in the fog. Very funny," Nathan retorted. "I die," he said, with attitude, "then you don't get paid."

Mike chuckled. "Won't need it, then. It'd be my pleasure to stiff the bank that has a lien on Lizzy." He lovingly patted the dash.

Nathan peered out the cockpit window. Mountains, many still ringed with perpetual snow from last winter, rose and fell on the horizon line spreading out underneath them. He noticed a thick, hazy gray cloud-like covering enveloping the peaks farther off, and pointed to it. "Is that something we should be concerned about?"

Mike had already noticed. "Wasn't gonna say anything. Probably just a squall. But I never checked the weather report for this far north. I wasn't planning on flying to Idaho."

If Nathan could have stood, he'd have kicked himself. He should have called Jacob while they'd made their one refueling stop. Now, with the radio out, he couldn't even have Mike call ahead to the nearest tower to relay the message. "Please, Lord," he murmured. "Get us there in time. Keep Tessa safe. Give Your angels charge over her to keep her in all her ways. Give her a way of escape out of any and every situation."

Fixing his gaze straight ahead at the approaching storm, Mike asked, "You prayin'?"

Looking out the window, Nathan nodded. A formidable bolt of lightning flashed within the farthest cloud bank.

"That's good," Mike said, his voice solemn. "I got a feeling we're gonna need it."

Parker Henlin held the wheel in a death grip. On the backseat behind him, his young wife inhaled air sharply with each new contraction then took quick short breaths as she had been taught in the birth coaching classes. Their physician had already been notified, and he would be waiting at the hospital upon their arrival, which suited Parker just fine because he was a Mr. Fix-It, get 'er done kind of guy, and helplessly waiting for resolution on anything, even the birth of a new baby, put him on edge. This was their third child, and Parker had thought he would be an old hand at this instead of sweating it out as if he were a parent for the first time. "We're almost there Nance," he said, trying to reassure Nancy and himself both. He eased up only slightly on the accelerator as he expediently rounded a bend in the highway.

The vehicle was nearly upon the homeless vagabond when the man sauntered down the remainder of the incline into the ditch and staggered onto the dirt shoulder then out onto the road itself. Parker forced the steering wheel as hard to the left as he could and barely steered clear of the hapless soul just as he fell face forward onto the asphalt and lay motionless and sprawled out. Parker pulled sharply onto the dirt shoulder and slid to a gravelly stop, eliciting a sudden exhalation of air from his wife while her next contraction coincided simultaneously with the sudden skid. As Parker exited the vehicle, he threw a quick apologetic look over his shoulder and with a "Sorry, love," sprinted to the middle of the road where the man lay.

Kneeling down in the onset of drizzling rain, he rolled the man face up and gasped at the huge plastering of caked-on blood on the older man's scalp. The rain had washed the blood down the side of his head, matting his short gray hair with red. "Ezekiel?! Where's your beard? And what's with the suit?" Then Parker's voice changed from one of surprise to anger, "Drunk again! And to think I stopped for this."

"Jacob Brown," Ezekiel muttered almost unintelligibly in response, sounding totally inebriated. "Need to see . . . Jacob Brown . . . Take me . . . to . . ."

The rain now began to come down in torrents. From the car, Nancy called Parker's name. A slight man, Parker pursed his lips, took a deep breath, gritted his teeth, and hoisted Ezekiel up against his back side and draped him across his spindly shoulders. He faltered under the dead weight but made it to the car somehow, positioned himself to pull open the door, and winced, "Sorry, hon.' Could you move over a little? Got an injured man here."

Looking frightened, Nancy Henlin pulled herself fully upright and quickly slid to the far end of the seat as Parker eased Ezekiel down onto the seat while putting him in place as best he could. When she saw the blood, she said quietly, "You poor man" and reached into her purse for some tissue. She carefully dabbed at the wound, comforting him with, "You just hang on. We're almost there. They'll fix you up."

Parker smiled to himself as he propelled the old station wagon forward hoping to get his pregnant wife and the injured man to the ER in double-time to make up for lost time. *What a woman*, he thought.

Hub veered onto the highway and gunned it as fast as he dared and could safely manage but only because of the all-too real danger of hydroplaning. He set his face against the wind and rain. The rain felt surprisingly good on his bearded face considering the circumstances—cleansing even, and drummed against the old-style helmet he still wore in memory of his father. The chaps and his heavy jacket would keep most of him fairly dry for the next hundred miles or so. By then he'd be at some truck stop or hotel, no longer under the weather—and starting his entire life over again.

His Harley rumbled and hummed contentedly beneath him and with a smirk and a symbolic backward wave of his hand, he happily paid his last regards to Birch Valley.

Next stop—anywhere but here.

The windshield wiper action of Ellen Davis' car whisked continual sheets of rainwater away from the windshield as Chip fiddled with the radio dial for something worth listening to. If he could just get his mind off all this drama. He heard the familiar roar of a motorcycle and anxiously glanced in his rearview mirror. His eyes widened. The biker from the Birch Bark Bistro was coming up fast. Chip hunched down with his head barely above the steering wheel as Hub came alongside. *My sunglasses*, Chip thought wildly, *where are my sunglasses? I wish I had a hat . . .*

But the chopper jutted out to the left of him, swung wide, and whipped around in front of the Davis car with Hub entirely oblivious to Chip's presence. Chip laughed nervously out loud. "What an idiot," he exclaimed, "the guy didn't even see me."

Hub revved and gunned the bike again and shot further ahead on down the highway.

Jasmine Winters felt an impotent rage seething inside of her, coursing through her veins. Pressing her foot down on the accelerator, she inched it more and more. The sedan surged forward smoothly just behind a gold, classic older vehicle. The voice inside her head kept goading her, compelling her to keep ripping down the highway faster and faster. *He thinks you're a fool. Used you like the rest. That's my money he's taking. I won't let him get the last laugh.* "He'll see I'm no fool," Jasmine whispered, through a clenched jaw. Jasmine had murder in her heart. She had become unrecognizable.

Tightening her grip on the steering wheel, Jasmine's knuckles whitened. She rammed her foot on the gas pedal, flooring it, and the back tires squealed. The car swung across the broken yellow line, and for a moment, came right alongside the Lincoln Continental.

Chip heard the whine of tires against the slick asphalt and grimaced. All he had wanted was a quiet, unobtrusive drive out of town with nobody watching or taking note. Where was everybody coming from this late in the afternoon? Or maybe he should ask, where was everybody going?

A ruler's length to his left, a green, two-door sedan was now neck and neck with Chip's car in a passing maneuver. Instinctively, Chip looked over at the driver . . . and froze. In that split second, Jasmine turned her head and locked eyes with Chip with her eyes dead ablaze. Chip swallowed hard. Jasmine then looked straight forward again. The car sped past his, swerved into position in front of him, and began closing in on the motorcycle just several hundred yards ahead.

Hub sensed someone was now following him—sneaking up on him from behind. He could not shake the feeling that this same someone was quickly gaining on him. Something about living on the edge his entire life afforded him a highly developed sixth sense, like a distant early warning system that resonated even louder than the deafening rumble of his bike. Making sure the coast was clear in front of him, he quickly looked back over his shoulder and felt the color drain from his face. Even though it was a totally different persona, there was still no hiding or mistaking in Hub's mind who she was.

Chip's mind went blank, and he drove on autopilot. In abject horror, he watched Jasmine's car shoot forward, bank, and swerve deliberately into Hub's rear tire.

Hub felt the bike's rear wheel take control as he spun into a one-eighty. Through the blur of spinning roadway, he was vaguely aware of the green sedan whizzing past. Immediately Chip's car was upon him, and Hub flew up against the gold classic's windshield while his bike, with an array of sparks, was dragged under the car.

Long afterward, Chip would wake from the hundredth replay of the same nightmare. It never varied—Hub's face, a snapshot of unsurpassed, helpless, abject fear—his mouth a dark opening in a mass of windblown beard, the whites of his eyes flashing under his scraggly wet hair.

In a suspended moment, their eyes locked, in a state of mutual, simultaneous mortification. Chip's foot slamming down on the brake caused the Lincoln to fishtail with a deafening squeal. It wasn't until much later that Chip realized the squeal had actually been the sound of himself screaming.

Upon sudden impact with the classic, the bike died as if it had been fatally shot and wounded, its big motor gasping under the crunch of heavier metal.

When Hub's face struck the windshield, he stared at the driver, through the cracked glass, in the midst of his head trauma, thinking, oddly enough, "Hey, don't I know you . . . ?" before everything went black.

Chip felt the Lincoln plow over the bike and drag it down over the asphalt in a show of sparks. The nauseating smell of burning rubber and free-flowing gas swirled around him. Instinctively, he jammed down harder on the brakes. The brakes grabbed, the car stopped abruptly, and the face on the windshield disappeared as the biker's body was hurled backwards from the car's crumpled hood and flung into the tall grass in the ditch.

*Z*hanna Hargraves took it all in without thinking—the old gold classic with the shattered front end turned sideways in the road and with a bedlam of crushed motorbike under the front tires, the pronounced black rubber streaks leading up to the car's rear wheels, and the junkyard of debris all over the road. Dozens of greenbacks, stuck to the slick asphalt and littering the knee-high, roadside grass, gave the wreck an almost celebratory air. The air was thick with the smell of spilled fuel.

She brought her 1980s minivan to a screeching stop on the highway's dirt shoulder, yanked the automatic's stick into "Park," and turned on her emergency lights. Throwing open the driver's door, she jumped out of the vehicle as if she had been ejected, and leaving the door open, sprinted through the downpour to where Chip, clutching a handful of sodden hundred-dollar bills, crouched in the wet grass beside a jumbled figure of a man.

Her hand covered her mouth. *That biker from the coffee shop! The one I pretended not to like.* Hub was a bloody mess, his arms lying limply off to either side of him as though he were dead. His bearded face, lacerated in a dozen places, had swelled up terribly.

Zhanna looked frantically at Chip. "Is he . . . ?"

Drenched and disheveled, Chip did not respond. His eyes vacant, he continued to squat and stare at the sprawled out, seemingly lifeless form. He seemed to be in shock.

Zhanna leaned over and grabbed one of his shoulders. "Is he dead?!"

Chip still did not respond. Zhanna crouched down herself and reached out a tentative hand, pressing her fingertips against Hub's neck. The warm pulsing of blood underneath the skin nearly made her cry for joy. "He's alive," she said, smiling through tears. She turned to Chip and asked, her tone desperate, "Do you have a cell phone on you? We need to call 911."

Chip crouched unmoving, staring, and a flood of anger rose in Zhanna. "You!" she yelled. "Do. You. Have. A. Phone!?"

"No," Chip murmured, shaking his head only vaguely as he looked at her. "Yes," he said, still detached, "yes, I do."

"Give it to me! Hurry!"

Chip rummaged through his jacket pocket and came up empty. He patted himself down, looking confused, then realized he must have left his iPhone at Jasmine's. "I don't have it. I don't know where it is," he lied. He looked back down again at Hub, anxiously this time.

Zhanna gasped and stood, thinking furiously. "Listen," she said. "I have to go get help. I don't have my phone with me either. I left it at work accidentally yesterday. You stay with him, yes?" She pointed. "And get that car out of the road if you can, okay?"

Chip nodded and stood, more like a mannequin than a man. He then slowly made his way over to his grandmother's smashed Lincoln.

Zhanna raced back to her minivan and jumped in. She jerked it into gear and gunned it back toward town.

> How precious also are thy thoughts unto me, O God! how great is the sum of them! If I should count them, they are more in number than the sand: when I awake, I am still with thee. (Psalm 139: 17-18)

CHAPTER

17

Hub dreamed he stood at the edge of a cliff alone. Extreme darkness enveloped him roundabout like a palpable physical presence. Far below, a seething cauldron of molten orange and yellow stretched away from him as far as his eyes could see, and the thick and sickening smell of burning sulfur hung heavily in the air. The loose earth began to give way beneath him as an agglomeration of little stones began falling downward. A sickening fear gripped his heart.

An audible voice shattered his dreamscape. "Sins of the fathers . . ."

Hub looked around. "No!" he shouted.

"Sins of the fathers . . ."

"Get away!" He yelled, swatting the air. The ground beneath his feet shook.

"The sins of the fathers are visited upon the children . . . that means YOU!"

Hub adamantly cupped his palms against his ears. "No! Not me! Not me! I'm not goin' there! I'm gettin' outta . . ."

The cliff's edge crumbled and gave way with the heavy landslide of earth taking Hub with it. He skidded partway down on his back, rolled over onto his stomach in the shifting dirt, and clawed viciously at the ground. Sliding faster, pulled downward, he screamed . . .

He shot upright in bed with a wild-eyed look and his fists clamping down hard on the handrails.

"Hub, no! Nurse. Nurse!"

Sudden and excruciating jolts of pain surged through him—his head especially—and he collapsed back onto the bed, intensely groaning. With his eyes clamped tightly shut, it took him a full minute of countenancing his head-to-toe pain—his head especially—for the voice to register and to feel the comforting caress of a smallish hand. "Take it easy, Hub" a soothing voice entreated. "You want to hurt yourself more? No, right?"

Hub partially opened his eyes. A worried Zhanna sat at his side, her arm over the handrail and her fingers around his big right hand. She squeezed. He looked around at all the white, the tubes in his arm, and the oxygen hose leading to his nostrils. A swath of bandage covered his head. Every muscle was on fire. His face felt like a balloon. "You," he rasped. "I . . . can't . . . remember . . . your . . ." he said slowly. Speaking took so much effort.

"Zhanna," she prompted with a smile. "That's okay. I could not remember my own name if I had just been in an accident like you."

His eyes moved randomly. "Oh, yeah. Yeah." His top lip curled in an effort to smile through sutured lips. "I'm alive. How 'bout that, huh?"

Zhanna nodded. "Yes, Hub. They say you'll be okay . . . after a while."

An older man in surgery scrubs—surgical cap included—strode into the room, saw Hub awake, and smiled. "I'm Doctor Prague," he said. "And you, Mr. Morrison, are lucky to be alive. I honestly don't know what kept you in one piece."

"Am I busted up bad, doc?"

Prague raised his eyebrows. "No internal injuries that we can tell. It's the closest thing to a miracle I've ever seen. Lots of torn muscle tissue, broken nose, and you may be in rehab a while, but we'll worry about that later. In the meanwhile . . ." he reached for a hypo and plunged the needle into a vial of clear liquid. "I prescribe sleep and a lot of it." He turned to Zhanna. "I'm afraid you'll have to say 'night-night,' miss. Mr. Morrison's going to . . ."

"No!" Hub interjected, eyes widening. "No sleep. I don't want to go to sleep." If he slept, that nightmare might continue.

"But . . ." Hub sat up in bed again and yanked one of the tubes from his arm. "I'm outta here." He groaned again and Prague, first restraining him, gently eased his massive frame back onto the bed. "No sleep, doc," Hub pleaded. "I can't go back there."

Zhanna shot the physician a frightened look. "That's how he woke up," she said. "Screaming, yelling about fire."

Doctor Prague attempted to console with a smile. "Hallucinations," he told her. "Very common after this kind of trauma."

"Help me," Hub whimpered. "I'm goin' to hell."

Zhanna squeezed his hand again. "It'll be all right, Mr. Morrison," Doctor Prague said, loading the syringe.

Hub rolled his head back and forth, in pain and afraid. "A preacher. I need a preacher," Hub said, almost childlike. "Somebody get me a preacher."

Zhanna brightened. "Wait, doctor, please. There's a pastor out in the hallway." She turned to Hub. "I'll go get him," she said, attempting cheerfulness. "It will be okay. You'll see."

She made a break for the door and poked her head outside. "Pastor Davis," she called into the hallway. "Pastor Davis, come here."

At the nurse's station, roughly twenty yards away, Chip stood with a Birch Valley police officer, repeatedly nodding his head and looking tired as the cop wrote up a report on the accident. He looked down the hall to see Zhanna waving to get his attention, and without a shred of enthusiasm, waved back and gave a "one minute" signal. Zhanna gestured for him to come inside the room, and she went back to Hub's side.

Five minutes later, Chip entered the room, dragging his feet and running a finger through his now neatly combed hair. Despite the accident, not a scratch marred his handsome features. "What a day," he said, his eyes bleary. "I'm wiped out. That was the third cop who wanted my version of the accident. It's like I'm public enemy number one or something. For the love of Pete, why do they think it's called an 'accident?' I didn't do it on purpose. I'm a victim too. Man! You'd think they'd be out catching real criminals."

Zhanna, holding Hub's swollen hand, waved Chip over. "He wants to talk to you," she said.

Chip gave Hub a wary-eyed look and bit into his lower lip as he shuffled over. He held his hands out, placating. "Now, it wasn't my fault, man," he insisted. "It was that chick in the car behind you. I . . ." Through puffy lids, Hub saw Chip move to his bedside and furrowed his bushy eyebrows at Chip. "You?" he queried, in total disbelief. "You're a real preacher?"

"Well, uh, yes," Chip stammered then sat upright. "Of course I am. I'm an ordained minister of the Gospel."

Hub's free hand shot up and clamped onto Chip's jacket. Chip gasped and attempted to draw back.

"No, no," Hub assured. "I just need you to tell me something. I know I'm going to hell and . . . I'm . . . scared. I don't want to go there. No way. Tell me how to stay out of hell. You're a preacher. You know, right?"

Perplexed and looking at both Doctor Prague and Zhanna for a way out, Chip finally rallied and sat down in another chair beside Hub. In an attempt to comfort Hub, he reached up to pat Hub's beefy fist, which was still gripping Chip's jacket. "Now, now," he said in his best stage voice, "there's no need to be afraid. You're not going to hell. Hell is just a state of mind. You know, like being laid up here in this hospital room." He smiled at Hub who clearly did not understand.

"Well, what I mean is," Chip went on, "you see—God forgives everybody. He's not into punishing us for . . . things like . . . well, being what and who you are or what and who you aren't." He looked from Zhanna, who looked at him funny, to Prague, who regarded him with one raised eyebrow and a shake of the head.

"So," Hub probed, his voice quiet, "I'm not going to hell, then?"

Chip smiled with fatherly condescension. "No, no, of course not. Some pastors talk a lot about hell, but, you know, I think . . ."

"Get this guy outta' here!" Hub roared, shoving Chip from the chair. Chip scrambled to his feet and made a beeline for the door.

"Sorry doc," Chip said hurriedly. "This is your baby." And he disappeared down the hallway.

Hub covered his face with his hands and moaned through his battered fingers. "Can't anybody tell me how to stay outta' hell?"

"I can tell you, bro." The voice came from behind the curtain separating Hub from the bed next to him.

Hub turned and struggled again to raise himself.

"Mr. Morrison," Doctor Prague said firmly, the syringe still in his hand, "you've got more stitches in you than a little old lady's quilt. If you don't hold still, we're going to have to do this all over again. Is that what you want?"

Zhanna helped Hub lower himself back onto the bed a third time while Doctor Prague moved to the long, white curtain separating the beds. He pointed at Hub and said, "You stay put." With that, he pulled the curtain back on its circular rod, took a breath, blew it out through puffed cheeks, and said with a shake of his head, "Hub Morrison meet Ezekiel Hazlett."

Ezekiel's head, partially shaved and heavily padded with gauze, turned toward Hub. Ezekiel fixed his gaze on Hub in the form of a friendly, yet unwavering stare. Hub immediately sensed a peace coming from his injured roommate. "Are you a preacher?" Hub asked. "A real one?"

Ezekiel's smile was like a splash of warm sunlight on a winter's day. "I hadn't thought of it that way," he mused, "but yeah, in a sense I guess I am. I'm kinda' new at this, but I can tell you what I know."

Hub's face became flushed with something he'd never felt before—hope. Through all the bar-room fights, long, lonely highways, and drunken binges, he'd never gotten past the sense of the immediate. Only today mattered, because tomorrow was always too uncertain. Only now, in the light of Ezekiel's unwavering gaze, did Hub finally catch a glimpse of not only tomorrow, but the day after, and the day after that . . . on into eternity. Hub struggled with the words. "Tell me, please. I had a dream . . . a nightmare—I think it was what hell is like."

The room became hushed. Zhanna leaned forward to get a better look at Ezekiel, and Doctor Prague regarded him with a personal interest that eclipsed the professional.

"Well," Ezekiel's smile popped out from under his gray mustache, "up until yesterday, I was a drunk and a flat out failure. And I don't know much. But this I do know: "For God so loved the world, that he gave his only begotten Son, that whosoever believeth in him should not perish, but have everlasting life . . ."*

Frank hurried out of the office as Jasmine entered the building through the mission's alleyway door. She breezed right past him and headed for the stairway to her bedroom. Frank stared after her, worried. "Jazz," he ventured, "you okay?"

Halfway up the stairs Jasmine stopped and looked down at him. Something was wrong. She just didn't look right. It wasn't her wig, matted to her head by the rain, or even her disheveled clothes soaked through. No, it was her eyes. Normally penetrating and direct, they were now empty windows as if nothing of substance lingered behind them. Frank's concern gave way to trepidation. "Jazz," he said, "what's the matter? What happened?"

Her natural caramel eyes shifted from Frank to the huge picture window overlooking Henley Lane. "He's dead," she intoned. "It had to be done." She turned and continued walking up the stairs, and Frank listened as she opened her bedroom door and went inside.

Overtaken and compelled by mounting fear, he took the steps leading upstairs two at a time, quickly traversed the short, narrow hallway, and pushed open wide her bedroom door.

"Don't you believe in knocking?" she snapped, and Frank looked at her in total astonishment. This was the old Jasmine again. Like nothing had ever happened.

A torrent of rain hammered the roof, and the room was dark. Frank looked around anxiously. Rife with the smell of mold and incense, the storm-darkened room was overhung with a dungeon-esque-like gloominess.

Jasmine removed her wet jacket and hung it on an antique coat rack, pulled off the soaked wig and tossed it onto the solitary chair. At the dresser, she fingered the belly of the little laughing Buddha and smiled. "Two for us; them, nothing."

---

* John 3:16

Frank advanced toward Jasmine hesitantly a couple of steps, "Jazz," he said, "who . . . who's dead?"

She shrugged. "Does it matter?" She reached into the top drawer of the dresser and pulled out a manila envelope and handed it to him. "Read this," she said decisively. "Memorize it, then get rid of it. Don't put it in the trash. Burn it, then stir the ashes."

Frank looked cluelessly at the envelope in his hand. "What is it?"

"Instructions," Jasmine said curtly. She walked toward her open closet door and undid the latch to her old steamer trunk of wigs and stage makeup. "Follow them to the letter," she said over her shoulder. "And do not deviate." When Frank did not answer, she stopped rummaging around and shot him a look. Staring him down, she asked, "What did I say? Repeat back to me what I just said."

"Do not deviate," Frank replied, parroting her. He stared at her strangely.

She nodded and went back to her searching. "Stop staring," she said, although she had her back to him and hadn't seen, for again, she was clairvoyant.

Still holding the envelope, Frank walked over and stood before her. "Jazz," he asked quietly, feeling more and more gripped by fear, "what is going on? You haven't explained . . ."

"Oh, cut it out," she said, "We're running out of time. I've eliminated two major problems, but still have the biggest one left to take care of." She stood, holding the nun's habit and the plain, abbey-approved shoes. "I hate these things," she said with utter disdain. "But this should be the last time." Bemused, she looked out the rain-soaked window and wondered, "You haven't seen William, have you? I wonder if he ended up in the ditch, too." She laughed coldly. "His congregation should give me a medal."

"You mean that young pastor guy? No," Frank said, "but he may be back. He left this behind despite the fact he seemed to be pretty attached to it."

Jasmine turned to look at Frank, and her eyes flashed when she saw the iPhone in Frank's extended hand. Reaching out, she snatched it from him and gazed at it as if it were a priceless gem.

"That's it," she said to herself. "Now we have the ways and means."

"The ways and means to do what?" Frank pressed. "Jazz, you're not making any sense."

Her gaze moved from the phone to Frank, and although she smiled, the vacant look had returned. "It's all coming full circle," she posited. "Tessa dies, Jacob is destroyed, I have a new life."

Jasmine looked right through Frank oblivious to the mortified look on his face. "No," he breathed, shaking his head and placing his hand on Jasmine's arm, loosely gripping it. "You didn't bring me all this way for this. Please tell me you didn't bring me all this way for . . . no, not this . . . *not this!*"

Jasmine sneered and yanked her arm away. "Grow up, Frank," she said. "All the money we could ever want and the time to pursue our goals. Have you forgotten already that this is what we wanted more than anything—life itself even—when at Flat Plains?" Her face immediately softened, and she attempted a smile with an almost pleading expression adding, "It's got to be this way, Frank. You see, don't you? It's karma. It all comes around, and now it's finally coming around to us. Tessa's just playing her part. It's the natural order of things. You know . . . don't you?"

Frank was unable to respond, staring back at her with the whites of his eyes more visible than ever and his chest heaving in and out as though he were hyperventilating. Jasmine's eyes narrowed in contempt. "Go back to Tibet, Frank," she condescended, "you've got a lot more learning to do."

"**Y**our seatbelt fastened?" Nathan looked nervously over at Mike, whose face had become set like stone, and nodded. "Good," said Mike. "Cause we're goin' down."

For the last half hour, the plane had been buffeted by a fitful wind jarring them with a turbulent ride reminiscent of Nathan's jeep along a mountain switchback. They had already lost too much time surrendering to a sky impinged by descending storm clouds, skirting peaks so closely they could make out mountain goats huddled in the crags. With each show of lightning around the tiny aircraft, thunder boomed and rumbled, coursing through the hull and right through them—a succession of resounding peals that made them feel like they were one with it. Rain and hail pelted the windshield as the plane flew through first one dark cloud embankment and then another, until through an opening in the sky they glimpsed a wall of boiling pitch before them.

Praying for their safety, Nathan asked, "Are you sure we have to?"

Mike pointed with his chin. "I'm not flying into that. Anyway, we're on the brink of flying on fumes."

"Where will we land?"

"Not sure yet. We gotta get outta these clouds. I just hope we have at least a little byway of clearance between us and the ground."

Nathan felt the plane drop, a sharp maneuver by Mike that left Nathan's stomach feeling displaced and tied up in knots. "How high are we?" he asked.

"About two hundred feet," Mike replied.

"Are we out of the mountains?"

"I think so."

"Do you know where we are?"

"Exactly, you mean?"

"Yeah."

"No. But somewhere just south of Boise, I think. I'll have a better idea in a . . ."

The view below them opened up suddenly, and they shot through a rift in the cloud cover skimming over a forest canopy. The tops of old growth trees scraped the plane's underbelly. Nathan sat up perfectly straight and as stiff as a board as his fingers dug into his seat's armrests. Much to Nathan's relief, the forest finally gave way to a wide, drenched valley lined with ranch style fencing. "There's where we want to go," Mike said.

Nathan regarded Mike with open incredulity as he saw him pointing to an open road. "A road? You want to land on a road?"

"Highway 93, if I'm not mistaken," Mike said in a startlingly unaffected manner as though this kind of thing was routine for him. "We find a straight and open stretch of road and land this thing." Without taking his eyes off the clouded landscape, he added, "Oh, and, uh . . . keep on praying, will ya'?"

The tempestuous thunderstorm raged outside a wall of picture windows that looked out on a slick, rain pelted section of roadway. Rain fell steadily, pouring off the corners of eaves and spotting the glass, not quite able to completely drown out the voices—first raised and excitable then muted and tired—coming from the other room. With eyes fixed on the closed bedroom door, Rob Carlton and Henry Beam lounged on the couch and sipped strong coffee, wondering why they had been called on a weekday afternoon. It was serious, whatever it was. Down-to-earth Bud was not one for theatrics, and his summons in the middle of a heavy thunderstorm gave the interior atmosphere a kind of ambiance reminiscent of that in a mystery novel or suspense thriller.

A moment later, Bud Clement entered the living room in silence, his face an indecipherable blend of emotion. He sat down wearily in the nearest empty chair and stared.

Rob and Henry straightened up immediately, Henry spilling hot coffee in his lap. With a napkin, he patted at it instinctively as Rob demanded, "What is it? Did someone die?"

"He's in jail," Bud said rubbing his red eyes. "Jacob. I just got off the phone with his wife. They arrested him last night."

Rob and Henry exchanged sharp glances, and Henry asked, fearfully, "Why? What did he do?"

Staring, Bud shook his head. "Don't know. Margaret wouldn't say."

Rob stood and as was his crisis-management custom began pacing the carpet. "It's gotta be something dramatic—what with him and his grandstanding." He put his hand over his face, shook his head, and sighed pronouncedly. "This is crazy. I knew it. I knew he'd go off the deep end and do something stupid sooner or later."

Bud looked at Rob soberly. "We don't have the facts, yet," he said indignantly. "Maybe he hasn't done anything wrong at all. Maybe he was falsely accused."

Henry looked uneasily from one to the other. "Yeah," he offered, "but of what? They don't just arrest a guy for nothing. And why didn't Margaret call us sooner? That doesn't make sense."

"Sure it does," Bud corrected. "She didn't trust us after that confrontation with Jacob in the church basement. Can you blame her? Anyway, she didn't call. I did. I got an earlier phone call from Carrie Littlejohn at four o' clock this morning, and I've spent the last few hours in prayer over her concerns about the church—something I should have been doing far more of these past few months. Just before you both got here, I thought the best thing to do would be to get Jacob involved and meet with us. He knows more about this stuff than we do. He's dealt with it before. That's when Margaret told me."

Rob turned to face Bud, but directed his words at Henry as well. "Didn't trust us? That's a cop-out. Sounds like they're hiding something."

Bud stared at Rob in disgust.

"Hold on," Henry said to Bud. "What stuff? Why did Carrie call?"

Bud stared at the floor, shook his head at the thought, then regarded them both with troubled eyes. "You're not going to believe this, but she had a . . . visitation . . . last night, a . . . spirit, if you will . . . that seemed to have targeted Matt."

Henry's mouth dropped open. "You mean . . . an evil spirit, like a demon or something?"

Rob looked on with disdain and retorted, "Oh, come on."

"I only know what she told me," Bud replied, fixing his gaze on Rob. "Matt was doing one of those 'meditation exercises' he learned in youth group. I guess . . . something went wrong . . ."

Rob's hands flailed in the air. "Great. Just what we need. First Jacob gets busted and now Carrie imagining devils underneath rocks. Just when things were going so well."

Bud sneered at Rob. "So quick to judge when you haven't even spoken with either one of them. And things aren't going 'so well' with the church, obviously. Which is why I asked both of you here. We need to talk. Truth be told, Carrie's experience with Matt scared the wits out of me. And it came right on top of Marlene Hendrick's call just now."

Rob stopped pacing. "Oh? Don't tell me . . . Marlene and some of the older folks are complaining about the music again? Or the move to replace the pews? That was my idea, you know, and a good one, I think. We have to keep up with the times. Stale traditionalism—colonialism, if you will—in worship doesn't pay the bills. We have more and more young people showing up . . ."

"I have a question," Bud cut in out of sheer exasperation. "Have either one of you attended any youth group meetings lately?" Neither man answered. Bud shook his head again. "Me neither. But the nun incident last night was the last straw." He paused. "Either of you know what a labyrinth is?"

Henry shrugged.

Rob waved a dismissive hand.

"Carrie said her son told her they had a labyrinth at youth group last night," Bud continued, "a portable one, and the kids walked it while praying . . . repeating words over and over." He suddenly straightened, for something had just occurred to him. "You knew," he said to Rob accusingly. He stood up slowly and stared at Rob incredulously. "You talked to him already, didn't you? Chip, I mean. He brought in this abomination with your full knowledge and consent, did he not?"

Bud stepped forward in an abrupt anger, and Henry nervously stood up to intervene in what he thought would become physical. Bud's blue eyes were piercing, but his face was grief-stricken. "Why?" he asked. "I really need to know. Is this guy so important that he should be allowed to literally do anything he wants with or without elder approval and without being held accountable? You have to know the pagan roots of things like the labyrinth. You have to."

Rob's face hardened, and he glared back at Bud. "Don't play innocent Bud. You knew what he was like before Jacob and that Nathan guy came and confronted us about the nun last night at Sheep Gate. And you didn't bother talking to Chip about it, either. You can't lay all this on me. Somebody had to do something."

"Like you."

"Why not?" Rob straightened, taking on a defensive posture. "None of us wanted to go back to what we had before—empty pews, a dying congregation. Every month we wondered how we'd pay the water and electric bills. Now look. So Chip invited the nun to speak. So what? So what if her beliefs don't quite match our church's constitution, doctrinal statement, and all that . . ."

"Our doctrinal statement and all *that* . . . ?!" Henry stood aghast.

Rob hurried on. "I didn't mean it that way. Anyway, it had its problems, too. And I think it went too far in one direction. Maybe it's time to meet somewhere in the middle. Oh, Bud. Who's to say we're right or have a corner on the truth? The biggest churches in the country today are the ones that give some leeway when it comes to beliefs. Ecumenism isn't all bad, you know." He alternated his gaze from one to the other and let his inner diplomat kick in. "Look," he said, conciliatorily. "I know this is a little different from the course our church has taken over the years . . ."

Bud grimaced. "A little?!"

"Okay, okay," Rob agreed, "A lot. But look at what Chip's accomplished so far. He's brought the Gospel back into the community, and from here we can reach the world and make it a better place by ushering in the kingdom."

"It's not our job as the church to change the world, Rob," Bud said, his voice adamant. "You know that. Nor was it ever to be all about the numbers game. Our mission is to save the perishing by preaching the true Gospel and making disciples versus preaching the social gospel and leading people astray. For that is God's way of making the world a better place, one person at a time, versus this new, ecumenical, en masse approach to 'saving' the world."

Rob extended his hands, pleading. For a moment, Bud thought he looked like Chip up on the church podium. "But why just that?" Rob asked. "What's so wrong with building relationships while proclaiming the Gospel? What better way than through the narrative of learning from each other and telling our own life stories. Chip is great that way."

Bud chuckled bitterly. "Yeah, Chip's a good storyteller all right. I imagine there are some tall tales in the resume he submitted to the church board way back when."

"The point is . . ." Rob continued, sighing, "we had better come to grips with the idea that the church is entering a new paradigm, a way of thinking that is not restricted by two thousand years of tradition. We can't be stuck in the past. Right now, we have the opportunity to reach people who would never have entered a place like Sheep Gate Lane Church ten years ago. We can help put morals back into the community, then the country, so we can reconstruct society. It's all about how our efforts can bring in the kingdom, to enact and model the Christ consciousness . . . I mean, Christ . . ."

Bud glared at Rob. "What did you just say?" He and Henry exchanged startled glances.

"I don't know what "gospel" you're talking about, Rob, but the one I believe in is the power of God unto salvation, made effective by the shed blood of Christ Jesus. The only Christ."

"There are other aspects too, Bud," Rob quickly added. "World hunger, home-building, education—all tied in with the spiritual. There's nothing wrong with that."

Henry stared, disgusted. "Except that it's, *again*, a social gospel, and it's anti-biblical."

"As I understand it," Rob tried to correct, "it's written in Scripture that if you say 'be warm and be filled, but don't give the person raiment, food, or shelter' that you are the problem and not the solution. The social gospel you're so hell-bent against enables you to be a part of the solution and is also about the here and now, too, Henry. It's not just about heaven and something that happened long ago. We can get so spiritually minded we're of no earthly good. Chip's got his faults. We all do. But when he talks about caring for the earth, recycling, treating all men like brothers, and tying that in with the Gospel message . . . look, that's powerful, and it makes perfect sense to me. And yeah, contemplative prayer is a way to reach that goal."

Bud narrowed his eyes. "Do you drink Chip's specially bottled water now too, Rob?"

Rob retorted angrily, "So what if I do? These are the only bodies we have, right? Aren't we supposed to take care of them and treat them as a temple? The Gospel will do us no good if our bodies are sick, and meditation will help both body and soul."

Henry shook his head and lifted his hands helplessly up in the air. "I . . . I don't believe what I'm hearing." He turned to

Rob, amazed. "I thought we were a church that stood for biblical principles! You know how many saints have gone before us, paying with their blood to stand for the truth? Does it mean anything to you? Anything at all?"

"Oh, come on," Rob snickered. "You're the ones acting like the Inquisitors or the Crusaders. And you're both playing the innocent card a little late. Okay, so I happen to think a little contemplative spirituality injected into this congregation might be a good thing. There. I said it. It's certainly boosted tithes and offerings, and attendance is through the roof. And everybody likes Chip. Including me. The nun's okay, too. I've spoken with her. It's not like we're teaching Catholic doctrines like the transubstantiation Eucharistic stuff, so what's the problem?"

Bud eyed him, hesitated, then spoke carefully. "Your wife teaches that ladies' Christian book study doesn't she?"

Rob looked at Bud suspiciously, wondering where Bud was going with that. "So?"

Bud probed, "Marlene says she's promoting some New Age material."

Rob's tone became derisive. "That's nonsense. It's a little different, that's all."

"Thought vibrations, healing energy, self-affirmation . . ." Bud said. "None of that is scriptural."

Dumbfounded, Henry looked from one to the other.

Rob rolled his eyes. "I don't know how many times I have to explain this," he said as if speaking to small children. "It's just different names for practices that have been part of authentic Christian tradition for centuries . . ." Rob took a deep breath and leveled a hard look at them both. "Okay, I gotta say it. You guys are sounding just like Jacob. Dealing with him is an adventure in frustration. He's not open to anything new, even if it's old."

Bud frowned. "So, you're saying exactly what?"

Rob drew in another breath, and they could tell he chose his words carefully. "I went someplace last April. A monastery." He grimaced at the shock on their faces. "Yeah," he said, sarcastic, "Be still, my heart. Look, last spring we were going nowhere fast as a congregation. This church was on its deathbed. I went to a Catholic retreat center looking for answers, and I'm telling you I found them. As much as I respect Jacob, the two of us are on completely different planes now. For him, everything comes from his head, all about doctrine and what he calls 'truth.' But I learned what's called the 'prayer of the heart,' like the ancient monastics, and the time I spent there, in the presence of God, gave me a new understanding. I realized then how doctrine often becomes the main stumbling block to unity."

Bud stood with mouth gaping. Henry bowed his head and sat down on the couch, folding his hands in front of him.

"You really, honestly, just don't get it," Bud muttered in outright astonishment.

Rob glared. "You had your chance to address things, Bud. You both did. You blew it."

Bud nodded, and he let his shoulders droop as he turned away. "Yes, I did. I saw it coming and dismissed my gut feelings and reservations regarding the matter. I failed to protect Christ's flock."

"Me, too," Henry added, his voice tinged with deep remorse and regret. "We all did. Some shepherds we are. Hirelings, more like." He covered his face with both hands. "Oh Lord," he whispered, "I'm so ashamed."

Sue Clement stood in the doorway to the kitchen, coffee pot in hand, silent and staring. She looked as if she was about to cry. "Anyone for some more . . . ?" she ventured, and Bud smiled sadly, shaking his head. "Not now, love. Thanks."

She turned and disappeared into the kitchen. Bud's gaze fixed on the last spot she stood, and he closed his eyes at the sound of her muffled sobbing.

For a moment, no one moved, then Rob shrugged his shoulders and lifted his hands. "Well? Is the meeting adjourned? I think it's pretty much all been said. Are we going to keep going round and round . . . ?"

"Oh shut up Rob," Henry murmured through his fingers.

Rob sat motionless, appearing shocked. "Hey, I don't have to take . . ."

"You're right," Bud cut in, his voice firm. "You don't have to take anything anymore. You're out."

Rob's mouth dropped open. "As in I'm no longer an elder?!"

"You got it."

Rob approached Bud, jabbing him in the chest with his index finger. "You have no authority to remove me. I was voted in by the congregation, and only they can vote me out."

Bud drew a deep breath. "You're right on that count at least. But I think we can wrangle up enough votes, especially once it comes out in the open just what you've been up to all this time."

"And you, too, Bud—you and Henry both. If I take a fall, you both do."

Bud nodded. "Maybe it's best I go anyway. I've certainly failed in my responsibilities. Could be I'm not elder material. I'll leave it up to the congregation to decide."

Henry stood. "That goes for me too. I'm through giving the enemy too much ground. I'd rather be told to leave eldership than continue to live a lie."

Bud reached out and patted Henry's shoulder. "In the meanwhile . . ."

Henry nodded. "Yeah. Let's go see Jacob. We've got some repenting to do. I've got a feeling God's not done with Sheep Gate Lane Church yet. Not by a long shot."

Deputy Akim quietly swung open the heavy metal door separating the office from the jail area and found Jacob still on his knees. The image of Margaret praying was still fresh in his mind, and now the husband was at it. He watched the old man awhile, took note of the peace of his aging, rugged features, and felt oddly intrusive, as if he were not the one with the authority in that place. "Mr. Brown," he called gently.

Jacob looked up, stood, and moved to the green-painted barred door of his cell and waited. Akim strode the length of the narrow hallway and stopped. His voice was no longer patronizing or one of a skeptic or cynic but rather strangely respectful. "We haven't heard from Sister Genevieve yet," he said, probing. "I was just wondering how you felt about . . . your accusations of her."

Jacob smiled. "The very same," he said, understatedly confident. "Her name is Jasmine Winters, and she's no nun."

Akim sighed and passed a hand over his tired eyes. "This is getting us nowhere," he said, frustrated. "Look, do you want to do time?"

"Why am I even still here, deputy?" Jacob prodded. "I should have been processed long before now."

Akim's troubled gaze met Jacob's peaceful one. "I was hoping a night in jail would cool you off," he said. "Maybe get you to retract, or . . . something. Then I could go talk to the sister and ask her to drop the charges. I'm pretty sure she would. Good PR and all that. The charges haven't been brought to the district attorney yet, so there's still some wiggle room. I had hoped we wouldn't have to go the full nine yards with it."

"Deputy," Jacob said, and his words were sad but firm, "my granddaughter's life is in danger, and you can do something about it. Keep me here, if you want, but get to that 'nun' before she gets to my Tessa!" Reaching through the bars, Jacob laid a fatherly hand on Akim's shoulder. "It's all yours now, John. I've turned it over to God, and you will have to answer to Him when it's all said and done."

Akim opened his mouth to protest, but the phone rang. He walked over to the desk and hit the speaker phone button. "Deputy Akim speaking."

"Crandall calling sheriff's office. John?"

Akim leaned over to speak more directly into the phone. "This is John; go ahead," Akim said reticently.

"Yeah, uh, we got a plane on the highway over by Henderson's ranch."

Akim raised his eyebrows in disbelief. "A plane landed on the highway?"

"Exactly. Pilot said the radio was out, and he was flying blind. And get this—the guy who was at the office the other day with the Browns is a passenger."

"You speaking of Shepherd?"

"Roger that. He says he has some information and wants to talk with you, pronto."

Akim squared his shoulders, switched from speaker phone to the handset, and put the phone to his ear. He bristled. "Put him on."

"Deputy Akim?"

"Yes, Mr. Shepherd. What is it this time?"

"Look, I just need to tell you, there is no convent, Deputy Akim. Do you hear that? It doesn't exist. There's nothing there but an abandoned military airstrip and some empty buildings. I saw it for myself!"

A look of utter consternation came over Akim's face. Having a hard time believing someone would go this far to prove a point, he found himself becoming suspicious all over again. "You actually went to New Mexico?"

"I went there last night and saw it this morning—then caught a plane out of there—a whole other story. But your 'Sister Genevieve' is a fake. There is no convent. I repeat, there is no convent."

As the realization of the truth hit Akim, his eyes narrowed in anger, and he said, "Let me talk to the deputy." Akim waited only a moment before he heard the deputy's voice on the other end of the line. "Yeah, Pete," he said hurriedly, "call the highway boys and have them take care of this airplane thing. Direct traffic until they get there. Then bring Shepherd in here as quick as you can. You got that?"

"Consider it done."

Akim slammed the phone down, spun on his heel, strode to a wall panel, and pressed a button. Immediately Jacob's cell door slid open smoothly. Jacob stepped out, hustled to the outer office, and laid a hand on Akim's arm. With a huge grin, he asked, "Well, deputy, where to?"

Akim was determined. "To that mission on Henley Lane," he said, grabbing his Stetson and leading the way to the front door. "We're gonna find out what color hair 'Sister Genevieve' has."

Car doors flew open, and Bud and Henry hit the pavement running, hunched against the rain as they sprinted across the parking lot to the sheriff's office. As they reached the front door, it burst open with a blast of stale, inside office air enlivened only by deputy Akim and Jacob Brown nearly plowing them down. Over the torrential downpour, Bud said, "We were just coming to see you! We thought you were jailed."

"I was," Jacob replied with a grin, "but I had some divine intervention."

"Look," Henry said, "we came here to apologize. And repent. We don't know what you're accused of, but we're with you in this. Anything we can do . . ." Akim proceeded to his parked cruiser, pulled open the driver's door and called, "You coming?"

Jacob nodded and gave Akim a "one minute" signal, then, with one hand on each of their shoulders, he said, "I knew you guys wouldn't let me down. Contact anyone in the church you think you can trust and tell them to pray. It's all going down, right now."

He hustled to join the deputy. "What's going down?" Bud called after him.

Jacob pulled open the door and slid inside, rolled down the window, and replied, "Tell you when I get back. In the meantime, you know what to do!"

Akim put the car into reverse and spun out of the parking lot.

Margaret rejoiced, and Tessa crammed her face close to her grandma's to press her ear to the phone. "Okay, my love," she heard a newly liberated Jacob say with a laugh, "we're heading over to the mission right now. Sister Genevieve has some explaining to do. You both stay close to home and, Lord willing, we might just tie this whole thing up tonight. I'll call you as soon as we know something."

The two of them held hands while dancing in circles on the

kitchen floor, overcome with schoolgirl giddiness. "It's over," Tessa exclaimed. "Jasmine is so busted!"

By her purse on the kitchen table, Tessa's phone buzzed and she made a dash for it, telling her grandmother, "Maybe Jasmine or Chip confessed. Wouldn't that be wonderful?" A text message on the phone stopped her short. Margaret walked over to get a good look at the script:

> Meet me at my grandma's house right away. I have something very important to tell you.

"It's Chip all right," Tessa mused. "It's his name on the screen. It's coming from his phone." Tessa and Margaret exchanged glances and, biting her lip, Tessa said with an abrupt determination, "I'm going," and walked over to the wall hook where her jacket hung by the screen door.

Margaret hesitated. "Jacob said for us both to stay here," she said. "I don't know why, but I don't have a good feeling about this."

Tessa slipped into her jacket, slapped on one of Jacob's extra Stetsons, and slid her purse strap over her shoulder. She went over to Margaret and squeezed her arm. "It'll be fine," she said. "Maybe Chip's going to come clean. We need all the evidence we can get to put Jasmine out of commission, don't we?"

"Well . . . yes . . ."

Tessa opened the door, and as she sprinted out into the rain, she called out, "I'll phone you from Chip's grandma's." Mud splashed up her jeans nearly covering her boots as she dashed across the unpaved driveway and swung open the door to the old pickup. She jumped into the driver's seat, keyed the ignition, then backed out and swung around heading for the driveway entrance in a spray of mud.

Margaret watched the truck turn onto the highway and disappear down the road. "Lord," she prayed, her voice quiet and fervent, "protect Tessa." She let the screen door close. Her brows were furrowed, and she felt troubled. "I don't think Jacob would have let her go, not alone anyway."

Frank was halfway down the alley, ducking his head against the rain as he headed blindly into town. He had no idea where he was going. He wanted out, but it was far too late for that. Even then, he couldn't leave Jasmine. A year without seeing her had dulled some of the pain of separation, but the instant he saw her in the dim office light, the feelings he had for her all came rushing back. He was trapped and knew it. And, ironically, as unconscionable as it was to consider, a part of him wouldn't have it any different.

"What do I do? What do I do?" Frank whined softly. Jasmine had left only a moment earlier, ignoring his wild protests, spewing venom at him, and saying she wished she'd never asked him to come to Birch Valley. Truly, he too wished she hadn't. He could be in a quiet Tibetan monastery right now, chanting or spinning his prayer wheel, or meditating on anything other than . . . murder. He couldn't bring himself to believe it yet. He was still in a complete state of shock. It was like a nightmare he kept wishing to wake up from, only to find it was *real*. Revenge he could understand, especially where Jasmine was concerned, but—killing? Where was the good karma in that? Then there was that "dead" nameless, faceless person. Had she already killed him for certain? And then there was that look in her eyes, like . . . like . . . someone else was there, a stranger. He had no idea how, but he had to stop her.

He froze as he saw before him the sheriff's cruiser swerve in from the road and slide into a parking spot in front of the mission. He could not see the front of the vehicle, as that part of it was hidden by the alleyway side of the building, but he heard two car doors open and close in quick succession.

His first thought was to double back in the opposite direction, but an uncharacteristic bravery prompted him to quickly proceed and assess the situation. He'd have to tell Jasmine something, or he'd catch it from her later. Hugging the alley wall, he wound around upended trash cans and empty beer bottles until he made it to the sidewalk where he stood fifteen feet from the tail end of the cruiser.

His stomach flip-flopped. Hunching against the rain, a sheriff's deputy and Jacob Brown tried the front door, pressed faces to a section of one of the front windows where the brown butcher paper had fallen down, then trudged right past Frank—he looked like just another indigent hippie—and raced down the alley to the side entrance. They pulled on the door and hustled inside.

Frank heard himself groan. He'd forgotten to lock the door. Stupid, stupid, stupid! If they went upstairs to Jasmine's room, the game would be up.

Feeling sick to his stomach, Frank hurried to the hostel to get his gear.

"I don't have a warrant to do that."

Akim stood at the foot of the stairs while Jacob took them two-at-a-time. At the top of the stairs, he turned, pointed a fore-finger heavenward and said firmly, "Deputy, you might not have one, but I've got all the warrant I need" and disappeared down the narrow hallway. Leaning on the handrail, Akim waited while the brim of his Stetson dripped rainwater onto the ancient linoleum.

From an unseen place, he heard Jacob say in a subdued voice, "John, you'd better have a look at this." The deputy's curiosity finally got the better of his law training, and he bolted up the stairs. In the single small bedroom, Jacob stood by a large closet with sliding doors looking down at an antique steamer trunk with the heavy lid thrown back. Akim whistled, thumbing back his drenched Stetson and shaking his head in disbelief.

An assortment of wigs of varying hair colors and lengths, make-up cases, and theater accoutrements filled the trunk to the brim. They both exchanged glances, and in a quiet voice while handing his cell phone to Jacob, Akim said, "Call your granddaughter again."

Jacob's fingers flew over the phone number pad, and he held it to his ear. "Margaret?" He said. "Can I speak to Tessa?" He frowned. "I wish she had stayed put like I asked. I'll head on over there with John Akim." Handing the cell phone back to Akim, he said, irritated and worried, "She got a text message from Chip Davis. Said he had to talk to her about something important." He shrugged. "Maybe he's going to fess up."

Akim's face drained of all its color. "Jacob," he said, his voice soft, "Chip Davis is at the hospital after an accident. An officer over at Birch Valley PD told me he didn't have his cell phone on him to call for help. A young girl had to come into town to report it. Davis didn't send that text."

Tessa was miffed and even a bit confused as she stood on the open front deck getting thoroughly soaked. Chip's grandma's car was not at the house, but when she found the door unlocked, she went inside. She walked to the middle of the living room and called out, "Chip," though she knew it was pointless. Curious, she wandered into the dining room and then into the kitchen.

Rain pelted the outside walls and drummed on the roof as the storm intensified. The afternoon sky darkened as though it was evening, and the house interior was plunged into an eerie semi-darkness. A shiver worked its way up Tessa's spine. Something was not right, and her gaze flitted from one gloomy doorway to another. *Forget it, Chip. I'm outta here*, she thought and began to make her way back to the living room toward the front door.

As she crossed the living room, she struck her already sore knee against a coffee table, winced, and crouched down to rub the bruise.

"Tessa."

The whisper, like the sigh of faraway wind, lingered in the air from behind her. A wave of nausea swept over Tessa, and the fight or flight response compelled her to abruptly jump up. She anxiously glanced about the room and was finally was able to make out a silhouette standing remarkably still in the nearest bedroom doorway. A hooded figure, slender, and dreamlike, in flowing robes and frontally swathed in darkness, stood motionless. She could feel the eyes on her, watching from beneath the shadowed hood. "I . . . I . . . was just leaving," she said, her throat constricted, then more firmly, "Pastor Davis isn't here. I was supposed to meet him . . ."

From out of the darkness came a soft humorless chuckle. "No you weren't," the figure said. "I sent that text. Glad you could make it."

Tessa grew tense with fear. "You stay away from me," she said, adamantly. "I'll call the police." Stepping backward toward the door, she tried to remember where any knickknacks or other throwable objects might be located. She reached behind her for something, anything she could wrap her hand around to throw or use as a weapon.

"Don't," the voice ordered sternly.

"Who are you?" Tessa asked, breathless.

"Oh my," the mocking voice chided her now. "It hasn't been that long, has it? C'mon now. Surely you remember your old . . . teacher."

The figure advanced closer until only a dozen feet away. Jasmine reached up and touched the edge of her hood with her hand, lingered there a moment for effect then casually brushed her hood back. The head covering—actually not a hood at all, but a nun's facsimile veil—fell away. A tumble of platinum hair spilled out over narrow shoulders. In the half light, Tessa could now see the full smile, mocking and confident.

"Jasmine!"

Tessa stepped backward instinctively then stopped, her eyes on the small dark tube protruding from underneath the other voluminous sleeve. Jasmine shook her head no longer smiling and said, "Uh-huh," her eyes unblinking in the scant light.

Her voice was flat, toneless, and detached. "I wanted your grandfather," she said, "and I got to him. Through you. How's it feel?" When Tessa did not answer, she went on, "Biker boy was supposed to do the job, but he sprouted a terminal case of conscience. I sent him to the morgue. Or to the hospital, but even if he's alive, he won't talk. He was well paid, and he's an accessory . . ."

Tessa shook her head. "You must be crazy," she said with resolute certainty. "Oh, Dr. Winters . . ."

The nun suddenly lost it. "Crazy?!" she shrieked. "Me, crazy?! Who do you think made me that way? Your fake and monster of a grandfather, that's who."

Tessa trembled, startled and immobilized by Jasmine's outburst.

Dr. Winters began pacing, waving her gun wildly. She shook her head, her hair cascading down below and over her shoulders. "I had my future all planned out," she said with amazement. "It was all there, everything within reach. Just a little further to go. I'd have been in charge by now. And . . . not only that . . ." She turned to Tessa with a genuine look of both shock and offense. "I . . . was just trying to do some good. Teaching people to find themselves, look inward, find that divinity within, become who they were meant to be . . . is that so bad?" Her voice became shrill at the tail end.

Tessa was searching for the right words, anything to buy her some time. Unfortunately, it was too early in the evening to be missed, so no one was looking for her. She had to stall Jasmine and try to use reason instead of emotion. "Listen, Dr. Winters," Tessa anxiously began, her mouth now dry. "We can work this out. It doesn't have to be this way . . ."

Jasmine laughed derisively. She strode over to Tessa and got eyeball to eyeball with her. "Dr. Winters," she said cuttingly, then backed up in rage, wildly tossing the hair out of her eyes. "As if that means anything anymore. Nobody—nobody will ever hire me for that kind of position again. Not under that name. Do you know how many applications I put out? Do you have any idea? Hundreds!" she shouted. Then, under her breath, she seethed, "Hundreds. Years of rejection. Years. Nobody wants Dr. Winters anymore." She smiled again. "But they might want the other me, whoever that is." She laughed at the thought. "Even I don't know what my new name will be—how do you like that? I'll be on top again, at some other university, maybe in Europe. I've always been fascinated by Germany, and I'm fluent in the languages, you see . . ."

Without moving her lips, Tessa prayed fervently. She kept her gaze fixed on Jasmine, but the eyes of her heart were on her Savior. Only He could help. The words flowed freely through her innermost being, welling up from deep within her, followed by a sense of calm. A verse from Psalm ninety-one now quickened her thoughts, affording her strong reassurance and fortitude:

"He that dwelleth in the secret place of the most High shall abide under the shadow of the Almighty. I will say of the Lord, He is my refuge and my fortress: my God; in him will I trust." Warmed by a sudden and perfect peace, Tessa knew He would help, that He was right there, in that cold, dark room with her.

Jasmine screamed, "Stop praying!" With her lips pressed firmly in place, she jerked the handgun, motioning with it toward the door. "Let's go."

Tessa hesitated. "Where?"

Jasmine smiled sinisterly. "Oh, just a little sightseeing. You drive."

"You'll never get away with this, you know that," Tessa said, matter-of-factly." You have to know that . . ."

Jasmine laughed. "I already have. You're worth a million bucks to me, sweetie. Nobody's taking it away this time." Then she paused, regarding Tessa with an immensely sad expression, then smiled wanly. "Even if what you say is true, it doesn't matter, really," she said. Her eyes glazed over as she looked right through Tessa. "Nothing matters anymore. The old me . . . is gone . . . you see."

She gestured again with the revolver, and Tessa led the way out the door. Jasmine directed her to the light green, two-door sedan parked in a stand of cottonwoods just out of sight behind the house and ordered her into the driver's seat.

As they pulled out of the driveway heading north, inordinately out-of-place yet happy glockenspiel ice-cream truck music filtered through the trees, its volume fading in and out in the howling wind, like part of a soundtrack from a B-grade horror movie.

A Buffalo County Sheriff's Department cruiser skidded to a stop in Ellen Davis' dirt driveway in a spray of muddy water. Jacob and Deputy Akim bolted from the parked vehicle and, in the wash of headlights, ran to the house—pounding on the door, peering through darkened windows, and rushing around back. Through the peals of thunder and the torrential rain came the sound of glass shattering. A few moments later, they exited the front together and raced back to the cruiser, the wind grabbing at a nun's head dress clutched in Jacob's hand. Shrouded in darkness, the car peeled out of the driveway, as they headed south along the highway.

Tessa's mind raced but her mouth could not find the words. *I'm going to die*, she thought, and images of Jacob, Margaret, and Nathan flooded her mind. *Oh God*, she prayed, *please take care of them* . . .Tears streamed down both sides of her face. From the corner of her eye, she looked at a stony-faced Jasmine, the cold, black gun clenched tightly in her deceptively delicate hand, the barrel tilted sideways at Tessa's midsection. "Faster," Jasmine ordered.

"We'll hydroplane if I do," Tessa cried out, her voice shaking as Jasmine laughed at the irony. Here Tessa was about to be murdered in cold blood amid misplaced concerns about road safety.

Miles out of town, the sedan began the ascent into the mountains, the high beams piercing through the heavy rain to the road ahead. The sign, "Cutter's Pass—8 Miles" whizzed by, the white lettering brilliant in the headlights.

As they rounded a curve, a massive fork of lightning flashed across the sky directly in front of them. In the sudden illumination, both Tessa and Jasmine gasped at the form of a blacktail deer standing directly in the car's path. Tessa yanked on the steering wheel sharply, and the vehicle's tires spun out of control on the wet roadway, wildly fish-tailing the car toward a badly damaged guardrail bordering the edge of a ravine.

Tessa slammed on the brakes, but the car glided across the road and over the rail. The sickening crunch of metal now yielded to the terrifying sensation of the car plunging headlong, weightlessly toward the unseen ravine below. Just before Tessa passed out, she heard Jasmine's scream as a faraway sound. Then, darkness claimed her.

Through closed eyelids, the brilliant light appeared ethereal, and when she opened her eyes, she recognized the double headlights of an ice-cream truck parked just a few feet from her prone form. The high-pitched, tinny, contrived music was surreal, to be sure. But never before had it been more welcome. Even its repetitive nature went surprisingly well with the incessant drumming of rain on the cold asphalt. She shivered from the rain, the cold, and the shock. As Tessa lay on the ground, a worried face hovered over her, one side lit up and discernible by the headlights, the other side obscured in the gloom. Suddenly, she recognized him. "You. From the library."

The little man nodded sympathetically and implored, "Are you hurt little lady?"

"I'm not sure . . . I think I'm OK." Tessa's voice was shaky. The man gently helped her into a sitting position. He then urged, "If you think you can get up, let's get to my truck. The heater's on. We need to get you out of this rain."

Shaking from the cold and the aftershock of the accident, Tessa leaned heavily on the man and stumbled to the truck while "Pop Goes the Weasel" played preposterously in the background. To her left and far down the ravine, a ball of flame that even the rain couldn't put out ravaged the trees, and the smell of burning rubber and spilled gasoline mixed strangely with the fresh scent of mountain wind and rain. Nearby and off in the distance, thunder rumbled.

Inside the vehicle, she huddled on the seat, leaning close to the floor heater, continuing to shiver and shake while the man quickly threw an old woolen jacket over her shoulders. He slid the side door shut and ran around the front of the truck to get into the driver's seat. Sliding his own door shut, he gently said, "You'll be okay now. Just hang on. I'm taking you to the hospital. Then," he said with a sigh, "I've got some explaining to do to the police."

"We have to call 911," Tessa said, almost frantically. "The woman I was with—she could still be alive."

"I highly doubt that, but I already called, just before I got out of my truck. They should arrive soon."

He put the out-of-place ice-cream truck in gear, and as the truck began inching forward and picking up speed, he swung it around onto the highway and headed back toward town. How strangely ironic that a small plane had landed on the same highway only a few hours earlier. The rain pounded on the thin roofing, nearly drowning out the sound of the truck's motor. Tessa bounced on a seat cushion barely upheld by ancient springs. Her voice trembling, she asked, "You put that note in my purse, didn't you? Who are you? And how did you know I was here?"

The light from the dashboard was just enough for Tessa to perceive a hint of a thin-lipped smile come over the man's face. "And that, dear niece, is the million dollar question."

For thou hast been a shelter for me,

and a strong tower from the enemy.

(Psalm 61:3)

CHAPTER

18

"I'm afraid it's all my fault." Wind-driven, sideways rain battered the hospital windows, and the dark, ominous clouds had, an hour or two before, brought on an early evening. The room was filled with the heavy scent of wet clothing. The man did a thorough sweep of the room, looking out at everyone apologetically and taking into account those who wordlessly stared back—Jacob, Margaret, and Nathan—all clustered together sitting on one side of the hospital bed—and sheriff deputies, Akim and Crandle, standing to either side of the doorway watching the odd little ice-cream man coldly but expectantly as they dangled damp hats in their hands. Akim and Crandle had been to the accident scene and returned now. Between the crash and the fire, the wreckage and everything in it was unrecognizable. "There's no way anyone survived being in that vehicle," Akim had said grimly when he first came to the hospital.

"Well?" Akim insisted, "What's all your fault? We're all waiting."

The small man let his gaze revert back to the injured and exhausted Tessa, who, from her reclining position, regarded him with eyes full of questions. He smiled vaguely. The overhead fluorescent light gleamed against his bald head. *He does look rather harmless, come to think of it,* Akim thought.

"No need for a defensive posture, gentlemen," the man said. "The time has come for me to speak openly of many things." Moving to the other side of Tessa's bed, he pulled a chair over and sat beside her, reaching out a tentative hand to pat hers. "Please understand," he said, his voice quiet, "I had no idea you were alive all these years."

Looking around the room, he swallowed hard and let his gaze rest once again on Tessa. "My name is Theo Macklin, brother to James J. Macklin . . . your biological father."

Tessa gasped, and Margaret looked like she was going to faint.

"Macklin . . ." Akim mused aloud. "I've heard that name. Some big corporation or some such thing."

Theo nodded. "A financial empire, actually," he said. "Macklin Enterprises. Steel, mining, electronics, the whole nine yards as they say here in the States."

"The States?" Nathan queried. "Does that mean you're not an American?"

Theo waved a hand at the air. "Oh, as American as apple pie and all that," he said. "But let me back up. None of that is going to make any sense unless I tell you the whole thing. And all I can say is . . . brace yourselves. You may have a hard time believing it at first—I have trouble believing it myself, and I lived it!"

Filling his lungs, he let out the air in a quiet "whoosh" through puffed cheeks, and from their vantage point, they could visibly see the wheels of his mind turning, sorting, and prioritizing. "It's hard to know where to begin," he said reflectively. He stood up then began to pace back and forth. "But I'll try to explain. I know you'll have questions, but please let me tell it all first from start to finish while I still have both the courage and presence of mind to do so."

Akim gestured, more amicably this time, with his hat. "We're listening."

Theo nodded, looked at Tessa, took another deep breath, and let it out by starting with, "Your father was the good one. Me, I was the proverbial 'black sheep,' the big spender who was so much better at spending money than I was at earning it. I suppose every rich family has one, and the lot fell to me . . . or, rather, I happily chose the lot. While James was busy building his corporation from the ground up, I was actively engaged in sponging off friends and relatives—while any remained—in order to accommodate a rather hedonistic lifestyle. Simply put, I was a bum and liked being that way. I spent nearly all my early years freeloading off of others and hooking up with pretty much anyone who would support me."

Theo's eyes fell to the floor, and he stared, saddened by the memory. "It's a shameful thing, I admit," he said. "But there it is." He resumed pacing and continued by saying, "When Jimmy met Elena and they married, I at least had enough decency to pull up stakes, head for Mexico, and leave them to a happy married life without me as an encumbrance."

"Why Mexico?" Jacob asked.

Theo shrugged. "I'd never been there, and I'd heard through the hippie grapevine that the place I was headed for was especially welcoming of 'free spirits.' The cost of living there was a pittance compared to the United States, and, although the accommodations were equally low-income, it allowed me the opportunity to indulge my indolence with little thought for what the consequences might be. At any rate, I knew my brother, ever the loving one, would insist on either me coming to live with them or would insist upon routinely taking a monthly portion from their own savings—not a lot in those days—and hand it over to me. He knew well what I was but could not bring himself to make me work or starve. I was the only blood relative he had left after our parents died, and he felt responsible for his little brother. So, I packed it up and moved across the border to Baja where I could surf, lay in the sun, and drink cheap margaritas.

"But despite his being a sucker for a hard luck, bad news story, Jimmy was gifted with a business acuity that surprised even him. Taking a little of their savings a bit at a time, he wisely invested in growing industries, took those dividends and applied them to his own business, and in the space of several years' time was heading up a corporation that had its fingers in a wide variety of pies, so to speak. It didn't take much more time before he extended his reach overseas and rapidly gained a name for himself in both high society and politics. He went from poverty to staggering wealth nearly overnight. God blessed him wonderfully.

"With his newly acquired fortune, he lavishly increased my monthly stipend—which I now see as a foolish move because it enabled me to live literally carefree in plush surroundings. Taking stock, I thought Rio de Janeiro to be the perfect place to spend the rest of my days. Ever the opportunist, I could shed the hippie look for one of affluent society, which, of course, would open doors for me to enjoy the finer things in life. I cleaned up, put myself through finishing school, bought expensive clothes, advertised my name as the brother of steel magnate James Macklin, and voilà! Socialites fell all over themselves to accept me as one of their own. I was introduced to big stakes gambling and, much to my amazement found out I was good at it. I routinely walked away from private poker games with a considerable bankroll. This form of income, coupled with the money James continued to send, earned me yet a more prominent position among my idle rich peers. I had it all, and was really quite content."

Theo furrowed his brows in deep thought and then his features all but collapsed. He shook his head and almost to himself said, "It all comes to an end eventually, doesn't it?" He looked again at Tessa. "A few years later, I got word of your parents' deaths—and their little daughter's too—in a crash of their private jet as they were coming to visit me in Rio. From the moment I heard of the tragedy, it has replayed in my mind a countless number of times. I was sitting by the poolside amongst 'friends,' and as the waiter brought me another drink, he informed me of a long-distance phone call that needed my immediate attention. It was Eric Staedler, my brother's main business attorney. Brilliant man, but devious. I never trusted him. He gave me the sad news and I went numb, hung up the phone, and got drunk to the point of blacking out. When I came to in my hotel room, I caught the first flight out to Macklin Enterprises' New York headquarters." A sheepish and somewhat pained expression came over Theo's face. "I remained drunk the entire way there too," he recounted.

"So you took control of your brother's corporation?" Akim inquired.

Theo's eyes widened. "Oh, goodness, no!" He laughed. "That's the most laughable thing I ever heard. Me? Spend all my previous life avoiding work only to find myself commandeering a corporation from behind a desk? Nooo, Deputy Akim. Philanderer, hustler, and loafer that I was, that is what I would remain. As ashamed as I am to admit it, my only thought was to attend the double funeral, sell off the business—either piece by piece or in toto, return to Rio—or perhaps the Italian Riviera, and drink myself into oblivion. With Jimmy . . . my only remaining family gone, I no longer had ties to anything of consequence. My life became a massive black hole at that point, and all I wanted to do was to jump headlong into it."

"You said, 'double funeral,'" Margaret interjected. "You mean 'triple,' don't you? Tessa was supposed to be in that crash too, right?"

Theo grinned big, thrust a forefinger into the air, and with an "aha!" look, replied, "Now, as Shakespeare put it, 'Ay, there's the rub.'" He pointed at Tessa and shook his head. "The child's body was never recovered, either in the wreckage or in the area surrounding it. It was presumed by the authorities that, as the plane exploded in mid-air, from a mysterious—to this day—mechanical failure, they believe, that somehow the child, who was only a year old at the time, was ejected from the aircraft and the body forever lost to the jungle below."

"Me," Tessa replied breathily, her voice far away.

Theo nodded. "Exactly. But, you see, you had actually been left behind in the care of a trusted nanny. Jimmy and Elena originally meant for it to only be a short trip. They were scheduled to return to the States after spending only two days with me. You, dear niece, had been recovering from a mild cold, and your parents thought it wise to leave you at home. It proved to be a wise decision indeed. No one knew that except the nanny who had her own small, private residence on the estate tucked away and out of sight from the Macklin mansion."

Nathan frowned. "But if the nanny knew Tessa was alive, why didn't she come forward long before the funeral?"

Theo's face sobered. "She disappeared," he said. "And . . . so did the child."

Tessa gasped.

Theo raised an eyebrow. "What is it, Tessa?"

"I recently ran across a letter that my mother, I mean, Mrs. Dawson, had written to me. I found it inside the inner lining of the volume of Shakespeare she'd given to me when I was very young," Tessa explained. "In it, she spoke to me of some man who refused to reveal his identity, bringing me to her and her husband for a secret adoption, then giving them new identities. I was given a new identity, too. And she warned me in the letter, 'Be very careful'—the same thing you wrote in that note you left in my purse."

Theo nodded. "Some man," he said. "I'm guessing that would be Harkness—all business and cold as ice. He would have made a good Nazi. 'Just following orders' and all that. Very by-the-book and to-the-letter."

Crandle cocked his head. "So where's the nanny?"

Theo shrugged. "Maybe bought off, given a different name, like Tessa, or maybe . . . you know. These people will stop at nothing. But I'm getting ahead of myself.

"The point is, with the Macklins buried and Tessa vanished (he looked at her apologetically)—not your birth name, I'm afraid—I was the sole heir to the corporation. It had all been spelled out in the will. However, although I craved the wealth, I didn't want the responsibility that went with it. Staedler offered me a buyout—a compromise that would put him in the driver's seat and let me off the hook. One million tax free dollars a year for the rest of my life. No strings, no responsibilities. I could resume my carefree lifestyle and drink and party into oblivion. I didn't need convincing. I signed the documents transferring ownership and flew back to Rio the next day. It was all quite legal.

"Funny how things don't work out quite as planned. I returned yearly as Staedler's guest at the former Macklin mansion, of which the property had been part of the deal for Staedler. I don't know whether he invited me as a joke or to keep up the appearance of being good-hearted or to simply be able to ascertain firsthand that I was still the same old harmless drunk he'd always known—and to assure himself of my continued cooperation. I accepted his invitations because, in my Rio circles, it seemed appropriate, expected of me, and more than fitting to maintain the illusion of close connection to one as powerful as Staedler.

"But once, several years after Jimmy and Elena's deaths, during my last night at the Macklin mansion, he and I spent hours downing round after round of drinks. He was being so personable and affable that I began to doubt my own doubts of him. We laughed together that night as old friends. As always, I consumed more than my share then wandered aimlessly through the many hallways and eventually passed out on the sitting room couch.

"In the middle of the night I awoke to Staedler and Harkness consorting with one another. The lawyer had apparently stopped by after I'd succumbed to drink. They had entered the room through a side doorway and, from where they stood in relation to the couch, could not see me, nor I them. But I listened as they congratulated each other and themselves, then mentioned something inconceivably fantastic—that baby Elizabeth, once adopted out to a childless couple named Dawson, was doing well in her foster care environment. They joked about the child 'evaporating into the backwoods of Idaho,' and Harkness ended with a confident, 'No loose ends.'

"I mulled over that conversation the rest of the night and in the morning went to Staedler's office and, in private, confronted him with the truth." The room fell completely silent. "The truth is," Theo said to himself, "I was a fool."

"Then, he must've been scared," Nathan urged. "You could've blown his whole set-up."

Theo laughed bitterly. "Scared?!" He walked over to Nathan still sitting on the bed. Nathan looked up at him. "You have to understand these people," Theo implored. "Their arrogance is monumental. When I went into that office with all the pomp of the Macklin name preceding me—or so I thought, I expected him to cower. Instead, he merely laughed in my face and told me that if I didn't want to end up like my brother, to just keep my mouth shut, go back to Rio, and stay drunk.

"I was dumbfounded, but being sober that early in the morning gave me the presence of mind to not argue with him. As owner and C.E.O. of Macklin Enterprises, Staedler was now one of the most powerful men in the world of industry. To quote an old adage, 'You don't spit into the wind.' I slunk out of there and caught the next plane back to Rio, fully intending to take Staedler's advice. His attitude suggested he knew more about my brother's 'accident' than he was telling me, and I figured that if I made waves the same thing could happen to me."

Theo's eyes fell to the floor, and he stared a moment, remembering. "What a coward I was," he said slowly. "I knew he had orchestrated my own brother's death and the death of his wife—your birth mother, Elizabeth . . . Tessa. And the only thing I could think of, pathetically enough, was saving my own skin.

"I never saw Staedler after that. I refused to go back, which suited both of us just fine, since we shared a mutual contempt for one another from that point on. That yearly million dollars helped me to live in unstinting debauchery for years after that, but Staedler's words continued to haunt me. I couldn't drink or party enough to forget the ramifications or the possibility that one day he might get a notion to do the same to me, even if I continued to keep my mouth shut and continued to stay away. There was no way of knowing when he might suddenly consider me a 'loose end' that needed tying up."

Theo brightened. "Then, without warning, everything changed—one of the few days of my life that I remained sober the entire day. I went for a walk in the nearest park, wanting to be alone. I felt the weight of the world on my shoulders, not to mention the full import of my sham of an existence, but also, the full brunt of the cowardice I exhibited daily to the extent that it made me consider taking my own life. I had purchased a handgun earlier in the day from a rather shady character I knew from my social contacts, and I spent half the day envisioning putting it to my head and blowing my brains out. I just couldn't take it anymore. I was a pathetic excuse for a human being, and by this time, both I and everyone else knew it.

"I sat on a park bench, and a man passing by, who seemed to be a businessman because of his tailored suit and attaché case, noticed me sitting like death and stopped to ask me why I was so depressed. I don't know why, but for some inexplicable reason, I lost all inhibition with this stranger. Leaving Staedler out of the equation, I told him the all of it—my wasted life, the debauchery that was so part and parcel of my existence, my binge drinking, my tireless, hedonistic pursuit of pleasure . . . and my consummate unhappiness with life at that moment. He listened patiently, smiled, reached into his attaché case, and produced a Bible. He asked if he could read me some things, and as I listened, something incredible happened. It was as if a light went on, in my soul, and I saw things from a completely different perspective. I didn't know what this man had, but I knew I wanted it. Right there on that lonely park bench . . ." Theo stopped as he choked on his words, and tears began streaming from his eyes . . . "I realized what a truly wretched sinner I was and that there was nothing I could do to help myself. That man explained the Gospel to me, and there on the spot, I accepted Jesus Christ as my Lord and Savior and was born again. I looked up at the clouds and felt as if I could see into heaven itself. My new friend gave me his own Bible and, with his reading suggestions, I began my journey through the Gospels. I learned how prayer is a lifeline to our Father, and for the first time in my life I experienced the 'peace that passeth all understanding.' I never learned my friend's name. He disappeared into the crowded plaza, and I never saw him again.

"In just two short weeks, I read through the entire New Testament, praying all along the way. The change in me was dramatic. I lost all desire for alcohol, and I turned down one high society party invitation after another. Amazingly, those things didn't even interest me anymore. I began giving some of my money to the poor I met on the streets and also to a local evangelical mission. I lost a lot of 'friends,' who didn't want to be seen associating with a 'religious fanatic,' and that suited me just fine. When I read the last verse of the book of Revelation, I knelt and prayed, and right then I knew what I had to do.

"I called Staedler long distance," Theo said, and chuckling, added, "collect, no less, and told him in no uncertain terms that unless he surrendered his position as C.E.O. and deeded the corporation back to me, I'd go to the authorities with what I knew. Without being explicit—we were speaking over the phone, after all—he attempted to bluster and posture his way through it, but I was unmoved. Either he abdicated, or I'd see him in jail. Those were my terms, and he knew I meant it. I gave him twenty-four hours to arrive at a decision. When I hung up that phone, I finally knew what it felt like to be a man."

Akim looked at Theo sideways. "So, why didn't you just turn him into the police first and without giving him time to dream up some kind of subversive scheme?" he asked, still somewhat suspicious. "Why first have him step down as C.E.O.? Seems your priorities were a little out of whack."

Theo smiled faintly. "With all due respect, deputy, you have no idea what goes on in the corporate world. These kinds of men have unimaginable and almost unlimited power. I did not wish to expose Staedler without first securing the corporation and the clout that went with its ownership. It seemed to me like a good maneuver to first remove him from the driver's seat, and then and only then bring in the police. Having assumed his pre-existing and yet illegitimate position of authority, I would then have been taken seriously. At least that was the plan. As it was, and as I'm sure you can well imagine, it backfired terribly and almost tragically.

"The next day, as I prepared to phone Staedler for his answer, it all began falling apart at the seams. I had just turned the knob of my hotel room door and opened the door a crack, but the toe of my shoe caught on a section of loose carpet before I could enter. Curiously, instead of falling forward, I fell to one side with the hallway wall between me and the inside of the room, and that's what protected me. That, and a big angel, I'm sure. The room exploded, blowing the door to splinters. I couldn't hear anything for five minutes. I spent the night in the hospital, for observation, and when two policemen arrived, I privately told them of the circumstances surrounding the attempt on my life. They took notes, told me to keep the story to myself while they checked it out, then left. The next morning, as I left the hospital grounds I crossed a busy avenue to hail a cab to a different hotel, and a car came out of nowhere and nearly mowed me down. It sped away before I could get the license plate number. The police were in on it, I knew, and from that point on, I was deathly afraid to trust anyone.

"I hurried to the bank, cleared out my safe-deposit box, which contained about a hundred and fifty thousand American dollars, and fled across the border into Columbia—a most dangerous country for Americans but one where money can buy anything, including a fake passport and a clandestine flight back into the U.S. under an assumed name. Once in the U.S., I traveled to Boise. I thought that one of the state's larger cities might have more resources for a discreet missing person's search.

"It was there I hired a private detective, and after considerable effort on his part located the burial plots of the deceased Dawsons. He tracked the child into the social services system, discovered that Jacob and Margaret Brown of Birch Valley were currently fostering her, and that she—you, Tessa—were on a missions trip to Spain and due to return shortly, as reported in the local newspaper. The investigator turned in the results to me, which presented me with a new dilemma—how to infiltrate Birch Valley and keep an eye on you. I hid out for two months, waiting for your return, pouring over my Bible, and praying for guidance."

Tessa smiled, but appeared noticeably confused. "But an ice-cream salesman? How in the world . . . ?"

Theo grinned and shrugged. "Standing on a Boise street corner trying to come up with ideas, I spied Ned's Frostees around the corner and bingo! I ran after the truck like a madman, managed to catch his eye, and nearly knocked him senseless with my offer of thirty thousand dollars in cash for the truck and all the ice cream in it. He didn't believe me until we returned to my motel room—a cheap little place in the low-rent district, perfect for a hideout—and I went into my bedroom and came out with the cash in hand. He looked at me suspiciously, and I assured him it was neither laundered money nor was it counterfeit. He chose to believe me, shook my hand, and danced out of the room. I threw my suitcase into the truck, gassed up, and drove to your quaint little village."

Theo smiled sheepishly at Akim. "I . . . ah, never did apply for a business license, Deputy Akim, just in case it's an issue later . . ."

Akim chuckled. "Given the extenuating circumstances, I don't think that will be a problem."

Theo continued, "The beauty of the ruse was that nobody paid any attention to me. I was just 'the ice-cream man,' and being a somewhat nondescript individual anyway, in a starched white uniform and with a little hat, I blended right into the community. Just another new businessman trying to make ends meet. I was only concerned that my sudden appearance might spark some queries, but nobody seemed to notice or question my presence. It was a perfect disguise." Theo grinned awkwardly, "You, Tessa, even bought an ice cream from me once, a few days after I bumped into you at the library. You never gave me a second glance. So, you're partial to chocolate-chip mint ice cream, are you?"

"Oh yeah!" she said, remembering, "I never even bothered to look closely at you when you stood in the truck window selling ice creams. And, now that I think about it, I do remember hearing the ice-cream truck's music when Jasmine forced me into her car." She gave Theo a quizzical look. "How did you know about her?"

"Jasmine. Is that her name? Anyway, I didn't know, at first," Theo admitted. "I only knew that once Staedler committed to having me killed, he would certainly make arrangements to do away with you, too. I first became alerted in my spirit that something was very wrong when I noticed the Way of the Master mission posters all over town. Something about the nun really nagged at me. There were so many red flags, to my way of thinking. She appeared suddenly in town, just like I did. No one really knew her, as they didn't really know me either. She had no indigent traffic at her so-called 'mission' nor was there any ongoing renovation at the old diner, in preparation for opening. I decided to play detective and began following her from a safe distance." He smiled, conveying how happy he was to be used of God to be as "innocent as a dove but as wise as a serpent."

"Again, nobody notices the ice-cream man. All day long, I could circle that street where the mission is located, and it would just look like I was trying to drum up business.

"Well, I began noticing a strange pattern—the nun would go into the mission, usually by the front door then, sometime later, a different woman would come out and leave the building by the alleyway exit. Now, after this went on for a time, I reasoned that, unless there were a variety of women inside the building, who never actually returned to the mission once they left, then all the women had to be the same one. And, they all went to the same rented garage at the edge of town and all drove a green, two-door sedan. I know because the flea-bitten hotel room where I was holed up a half-block away from the garage gave me a view of them coming and going."

"The same kind of car Jasmine forced me into," Tessa gasped.

Theo nodded. "Right. And the same one that chased that biker gang member and rammed his motorcycle. I had followed another woman from the mission who was following that biker gang member. My truck could not keep up with her, but I came upon the aftermath of her murder attempt just before the police arrived. I'm ashamed to admit I did not assist Pastor Davis, but I couldn't afford to have my cover blown, as they say. And it was a good thing I returned to town when I did. The last time . . . what was her name—Jasmine?—left the mission, she left as a nun and went directly to the garage in her habit. I followed her because this was the first time she'd done that, and it seemed like at that point she was having to finish something important and had neither the time or inclination to change disguises."

"Maybe I shouldn't tell you this," deputy Akim cut in, "but since I'm buying your story, you might like to know that the biker guy is going to be okay. He's pretty beat up, and they say it's a miracle he's alive. And . . ." he smiled and raised both eyebrows, "he's singing like a bird. Says he was approached by a woman in disguise who hired him for five thousand dollars."

Jacob frowned. "Hired him for what? I don't think I'm going to like this."

"Well, to, ah, 'remove' Tessa. Permanently."

Tessa's mouth fell open. "Him? He really scared me. I thought he was going to kill Chip that night I got really sick from the poison. But I had no idea he was after me."

Akim shrugged. "According to him, he wasn't. Not towards the end, anyway. He claims he accepted the money (from a little old lady at the Birch Bark Bistro—does that sound familiar?) but changed his mind. He couldn't bring himself to do it. He also couldn't bring himself to give the money back, so he blew out of town with the cash and was followed by a brunette in a green sedan. She wasn't dressed like the old lady or like the socialite who pulled a gun on Morrison at a downtown bar, but he recognized her all right. She nailed his bike and almost bought him a slot in a stretcher trolley at the morgue."

Jacob shook his head in total shock and disgust. "Jasmine's been busy—hiring a hitman and slipping arsenic in your chai tea, not to mention everything else she's been up to since she came to town. I knew she was a very troubled person. I knew that back at Flat Plains, but I had no idea she could go this far."

Nathan looked at deputy Akim. "What's going to happen to the biker?"

Akim shrugged. "Well, he's admitted to conspiracy to commit murder but can't tell us who paid him. He never saw Jasmine's real face, you know. And he seems to have had some kind of change of heart. My guess is he'll turn state's evidence, and they'll be easy on him or at least easier than he deserves." Shifting his focus from Nathan to Jacob, Akim went on to say, "By the way, your homeless buddy has been preaching to Hub Morrison, the biker, and reading to him from one of the hospital Bibles."

Jacob perked up, and he grinned from ear to ear. "Our Ezekiel? He's preaching and reading Scripture out loud? To a gang member?"

Akim nodded. "Yep. Now, Morrison's got religion too and won't shut up. I got a guy in there taking a lot of notes."

Jacob slapped his knee and laughed out loud. "God bless them both!" he exclaimed. "Couldn't be more fitting! You know, it was Ezekiel the prophet who said that if the wicked will turn from his sins and do what is right, he will live and not die.* Praise God!"

Margaret reached over to hug him and planted a kiss on his past five o' clock shadow face. "J.B., you've been praying for Ezekiel for a long time, and you didn't think you'd ever see the day God answered." Margaret then whispered in his ear, "I think maybe later tonight you'll be doing some repenting yourself of not trusting the Lord." Tessa couldn't hear those words, but she had a pretty good feeling she knew exactly what Margaret was saying— the humble (and grateful) look on Jacob's face gave it away.

"So," Nathan added soberly, "Jasmine hired the biker to do the dirty work, but Jasmine was hired by Staedler to execute the

---

* Ezekiel 18:21

job. And Jasmine did all this with the intention to destroy or wreak revenge on Jacob for getting her fired? Boy, this is getting more complicated by the minute . . ."

Akim nodded. "Looks that way, although we'll more than likely never know the whole story unless Staedler or one of his cronies decides to spill it as part of a plea deal." He thought a moment and looked at Theo. "One question. The one thing I'm most curious about is how you planned on protecting Tessa? No offense meant, but you don't look very threatening."

Theo timidly slid his hand into his jacket pocket and produced a snub-nose .38, carelessly swinging the short muzzle toward the deputy. Akim's eyes opened wide, and he motioned to Theo to point the barrel downward. He then crossed the floor with an outstretched hand. Theo dutifully handed the gun over. "The man I bought it from loaded it for me. I've never even fired one of these things," he said. "I was hoping I wouldn't have to."

Akim examined the revolver and sighed. "Foreign make. Please," he said, "please don't tell me anything about this. I'd hate to have to mention illegal importation of firearms in my report."

Jacob grinned. "We didn't see a thing."

"I have a question, too," Nathan said, rubbing his jaw line and chin. "I hate to sound mercenary, but curiosity is killing me. Who owns Macklin Enterprises now?"

Theo took a deep breath, thought about it for a moment, and looked over at Tessa. His eyes twinkled, and he smiled. "She does . . . technically speaking anyway," he said. "Lock, stock, and barrel. It was all spelled out in the will. Any deal Staedler and I made is null and void because it was ratified with illegal intent on his part. Tessa is the lawful heiress."

Tessa had remained rather quiet during Theo's presentation of facts. Now, hearing these words, that she was a "lawful heiress," she looked almost vacantly about the room. "I . . . I don't know what to say . . ."

"I know what to say," Jacob cut in. "What is the net worth of the corporation as it now stands?"

Theo pursed his lips, squinted with one eye, and looked toward the ceiling. "I haven't seen the books for some years," he noted, "but the corporation has grown some since then—this I know. So, estimating on the low side, I'd guess my niece is worth somewhere in the neighborhood of several billion dollars."

A hush fell upon the room. Every mouth except Theo's was agape.

"That's including real estate and personal properties around the world," he hastily added. "And there is a little island in the Mediterranean . . ."

Tessa's eyes glazed over. "I think," she said, haltingly, "I think I'm going to . . ." and she seemed to be on the verge of fainting.

Theo quickly moved to sit beside her and took her hand in his. "Dear girl," he said, soothingly, "you have just been through so much and in such a short period of time. Give yourself some time. It will come out all right in the end. And I have a feeling you might be getting married soon."

Akim pushed off from the wall and positioned his hat on his head. "Congratulations, Tessa," he said. "I'd feel like passing out too if somebody told me I owned billions." He sighed, pointed at Theo, and said, "You . . . need to come with me now. I've got a report a foot thick to fill out, and I'll need your statement. You can ride in the cruiser."

"I'll take my own truck, if you don't mind," Theo said, standing. "I kind of like running my own business." He began following Akim and Crandle but paused for a moment right before the doorway. "Oh," he said and reached into his back pocket for his wallet. He flipped it open and walking back toward Tessa's bed pulled something from the clear plastic shield. With a sad look on his face, he smiled and extended his hand. "I think you might like to have this," he said. "You were such a beautiful child."

Tessa reached out and with trembling fingers took the photo. Her eyes blurred, and she bit down hard on her lower lip to keep it from trembling. James and Elena Macklin stood posed in formal attire and smiling, Elena cradling an infant.

"I'll tell you all about them, Tessa," Theo said kindly. "You'll grow to love them as I did."

As he turned to move for the door, Tessa grabbed his hand. She held it to her cheek while her tears ran freely over his fingers. Theo swallowed hard and cried tears of joy inwardly. It was a healing moment for him. He thanked God for a longing fulfilled.

"Thank you," Tessa said, her voice shaking, "Uncle Theo."

Theo fought back his own tears thanking God for having family ties again. "I've waited a long time to hear that," he confessed. "When I looked out of the window and saw you coming into the library that day, it was all I could do to not panic. So I wrote out a quick note of warning and was so flustered I . . . I'm sorry for knocking you over. It was an unexpected meeting, and I was stunned at the likeness. You look just like Elena." Theo pulled his shoulders back, smiled, then followed the deputies to the door. Akim and Crandle moved in lockstep, but just outside the door, Akim turned. "We'll need a statement from you, Tessa," he said, "in the next day or so, when you feel up to it, okay? Oh, and I'll be calling in the feds, since kidnapping is a federal offense. Anyway, they'll want to storm Staedler's New York headquarters. Wish I could be there to see the look on that guy's face when they bring charges against him." He paused with a look of self-congratulation. "You know, this'll be a feather in my cap," he said. "Maybe next year, *I'll* run for sheriff." He exited the room and made his way down the hallway with Crandle and Theo in tow.

"Wait!" Jacob said suddenly. "What about Jasmine?!"

Akim poked his head back inside. "Her car was completely demolished. Gas tank blew. We've got a team out there now, but so far they haven't found her. There's a river running through the bottom of that ravine. With all the rain we've had, it's pretty swollen. Chances are the body was thrown from the wreckage and carried away by the current. We'll likely find it hung up on rocks downstream. Won't be much left of her at that point, I'm afraid."

Margaret's face took on a distinct pallor as she turned away. "How awful," she murmured. "Poor, lost Jasmine."

Akim shook his head in disbelief. "Beats me how you can feel sorry for her," he said matter of factly. "She got what she deserved. As it is, the state will likely have to pick up the tab for her burial. Wherever she was hoarding her money, it's still a mystery. She's sure not worth much now."

Warmed by the early morning sun, Tessa stood at the shoulder of the road overlooking a steep ravine. To one side, skid marks, like black graffiti, snaked their way across the asphalt toward the guardrail roping off the cliff. A new section of rail now replaced the former torn-out section, but the limbs and bark of trees clinging to the steep slope bore the gouge marks of shredded metal. Her eyes followed a downward path of shattered trees that marked the trajectory of the vehicle that should have been her own coffin a week earlier. The charred wreckage was gone now, lifted from where it had been wedged between two old growth conifers. In a circular pattern all around that spot, blackened bark and limbs showed the perimeter of the fireball. Far below, she could see the river, a silver thread snaking through dark spruce forest. From her vantage point, it appeared subdued—tranquil even. Beside her, Nathan slipped an arm around her waist and drew her close. Tessa leaned into him, her eyes following the outline of the mountains, rising and falling, all the way to their furthest horizon.

"Wow." Tessa's voice sounded incredulous, humbled but steady. "Peace and tranquility, and justice . . ." Her words trailed off as she let a huge sigh carry them away like dead leaves swirling in a downdraft.

"I'm not sure I understand," Nathan said, his voice soft. "This is a place of sadness. You almost died here."

Tessa nodded then shrugged. "Jasmine's infamous catchwords. Remember? I can't explain how I feel right now. I had to see. To remind myself that it was all real and not just some bad dream."

For a moment neither spoke, then Nathan said in an ever-so-gentle manner, "You'll have to let her go, Tessa. None of us are guaranteed to win everyone to the Lord. Jasmine had one opportunity after another, and in the end, it caught up with her."

"I wish I could have helped her," Tessa murmured. "I feel so bad . . ."

Nathan squeezed her lovingly. "It's not your fault. We're not responsible for other people's decisions."

"They never did find her," Tessa said, staring at the river below.

"Now they don't think they ever will." She shuddered. "And I know it's not my fault. But I can't help feeling sorry for her. Such a waste of a life."

"Yeah," Nathan agreed. "Chip, too. I don't know if he'll ever get it. He still insists, like the worst of the two thieves on the cross, that he's the one who's been wronged."

"It's good for him they're not pressing charges," Tessa said. "No one can prove he knew anything about Jasmine's intentions. And he's not talking. But his reputation's destroyed. Everybody knows he's nothing but a fake now. It's his grandmother I feel sorry for the most. She feels like a real failure, Jacob tells me."

"It's not her fault, either," Nathan said. "Everybody makes their own choices. It's just a shame that most people would just as soon keep going their own way that seems right to them . . . but actually leads to death . . . instead of trying God's way for a change. Chip could have gone far, especially with Christ leading him. But I don't know if he'll ever understand that good looks, charisma, charm, and uncommonly good manners won't make up for ungodly character. Like Jacob said, he sowed the wind and now he's reaping the whirlwind. At least the Sheep Gate Lane Church board came to their senses. How's it feel, by the way, to have Jacob as its new pastor?"

"I'm so proud of him—especially for seeing his way through the spiritual rut the enemy had him in," Tessa said, smiling. "He'll be a shot in the arm to that church, and he won't let any smooth talking conman teach heresy again."

"Yeah," said Nathan, regarding Tessa through smiling eyes. "Especially to the good-looking young ladies."

Tessa smiled but looked embarrassed. "I guess I deserved that. What can I say? Chip was very persuasive at first. And he seemed to know all the right things to say. He sure conned me."

"I think he left town yesterday," Nathan said. "No fanfare, nothing. Just kind of sneaked out. I hope he learned something from all this. And I really hope one day he repents and truly commits his life to the Lord. What a testimony that would be." He shook his head, incredulous. "It's almost too much to grasp," he thought out loud. "Somebody ought to write a book about this."

"I know," Tessa said and shuddered again. "It's enough to make a girl's head spin—mine especially. So much has happened; it doesn't even seem real sometimes."

"C'mon," Nathan said gently. "Let's go back into town. You don't need to rush anything. There's plenty of time to get used to your new life." As they walked to Nathan's jeep, he added, "Like your name. Tessa . . . I don't even know if I should call you that anymore. I'd hate to give it up, but . . ."

At the jeep, Tessa leaned back against the hood. "You won't have to," she said with quiet reserve. "It's the only name I've ever known. I don't think I could answer to anything else. Maybe a lot of other things have changed for me, but not that."

"Good," Nathan said. "Elizabeth is a nice name, but you'll always be Tessa to me. And, I've been thinking and praying a lot in the past few days, and you know, God answered our prayers with our being able to reach you in time. It's pretty amazing. All of us—Jacob and Margaret, me, even Theo, were always just one step behind. But God watched over you when we couldn't."

"That reminds me of Psalm ninety-one," Tessa said. "'He shall give His angels charge over thee, to keep thee in all thy ways'. I guess He had a lot of them working overtime. I still don't remember how I got out of the car as it went over the embankment. I was just, suddenly, out, and lying on the road, and the car was at the bottom of the ravine. Angels again. It had to be. I just can't fathom it all."

"And," Nathan added, "it says in Romans that God works all things together for good to those who love Him and are called according to His purpose. One thing's for sure, God is faithful to His promises."

"That's a truth I'll carry with me for the rest of my life."

"Me too," Nathan said. Taking her gently by the shoulders and turning her so that they faced each other, Nathan placed a soft kiss on her forehead. "Look," he said, meeting her questioning gaze with his own direct one, "I never asked you properly. There was so much going on, you know, and things kind of got sidetracked . . ." He took a deep breath. "We have tomorrow," he said, smiling, "and, by the grace of God, many more tomorrows. I want to spend every one of them with you. For the rest of my life. Do you understand what I'm saying?"

Tessa smiled, her eyes misting. "I think so. But I'd like to hear the words."

Nathan took her small hand, lifted it to his lips, and leaned to kiss it tenderly. With her hand still in his, he knelt down on one knee and raised his eyes to meet hers. In a quiet but strong voice, he asked Tessa, "Will you marry me, my dearest, loveliest Tessa and give me the chance to make your life as rich as you've made mine? I love you with everything in me, and I promise I'll do my best to be all you need in a husband. From this day on, I want to commit my life to you."

Tessa reached over and took hold of the Stetson he was now holding in his hand and placed it on her own head. "Nathan Shepherd, you are the man of my dreams. I love you too. Yes, I will be your wife and stand beside you always." Nathan stood, and Tessa threw her arms around his neck. He wrapped his own arms around her waist and lifted her off her feet. With a sweet Tessa smile and a look of tenderness in her eyes, she said, "Seal that proposal, cowboy."

And while both of them were bathed in the golden light of a new day, Nathan went ahead and did just that.

For we wrestle not against flesh and blood, but against principalities, against powers, against the rulers of the darkness of this world, against spiritual wickedness in high places. Wherefore take unto you the whole armour of God, that ye may be able to withstand in the evil day, and having done all, to stand. (Ephesians 6: 12-13)

EPILOGUE

ERIC STAEDLER was arrested and indicted on multiple charges, including suspicion of murder, conspiracy to commit murder, attempted murder, and fraud. At his trial, he was found guilty and given a life sentence with no possibility of parole.

ALEXANDER HARKNESS turned state's evidence when offered a plea deal. According to Harkness, Jasmine was never to be paid the $1,000,000 but was set up, with Hub, to take the fall. With no knowledge of who her "employer" was, Jasmine would have had no evidence of outside accomplices and would appear to be acting alone in her recruitment of Hub.

HUB MORRISON testified openly of his part in the murder conspiracy, and thanks to endorsements by Jacob Brown and John Akim was miraculously sentenced to only five years probation. With the court's permission, he returned to California to witness to the members of his former biker gang and won a handful of converts to Christ.

ZHANNA HARGRAVES took notice of the change in Hub and with Nathan and Tessa acting as mentors, began reading the Bible and gave her heart to Jesus. She and Hub eventually became engaged. Not long after, Zhanna learned through an elderly aunt who was dying that Zhanna has a twin sister who was adopted out at birth. Only Hub knows about this so far and has promised to help find her twin.

EZEKIEL HAZLETT reunited with the son he had not seen in fifteen years and was belatedly awarded the Congressional Medal of Honor for his Vietnam War rescue of two wounded comrades while under enemy fire and subsequently leading his men to safety despite his own wounds. The people of Birch Valley celebrated his return with a parade in his honor and awarded him a hand-sewn banner reading, "Welcome Home, Zeke."

WILLIAM ("CHIP") DAVIS was never formally charged and quietly left Birch Valley. He was arrested a year later for running a low-level church scam operation and sentenced to fifteen months in state prison.

FRANK JOHNSON disappeared. The police are searching for the driver of a stolen car found at a rest area in the Montana Rockies after a hiker discovered a baseball cap and a passport near a protected grizzly bear habitat.

JASMINE WINTERS' body was never found. The only trace that remained was a tattered strip of a bloodied nun's habit hung on a spruce bough not too far from the wreckage.

JACOB BROWN was instated as pastor of Sheep Gate Lane Church. Attendance by visitors dropped dramatically in the first few months, then rose again with the influx of congregants hungry for the Word of God.

BUD CLEMENT AND HENRY BEAM stepped down from eldership after a public repentance. They were later voted in a second time by the congregation.

ROB CARLTON was removed as elder by a vote of the congregation. He and his wife left Birch Valley to join the ministry team of an emerging church in Colorado called The Journey. The last thing anyone heard about him was he was helping to build a labyrinth on the church grounds.

NATHAN AND TESSA married the following spring. They had a small but beautiful ceremony in a little rustic chapel in the Rocky Mountains with sixty people in attendance. They purchased and renovated the diner Jasmine Winters had used for her headquarters and opened with Ezekiel as minister and manager of the Birch Valley Recovery Center, a biblically based half-way house for those struggling with addictions and other destructive behaviors.

Tessa, by proxy, assumed the helm of Macklin Enterprises, liquidated many of her land holdings, and used the proceeds to fund struggling Bible-based missions worldwide. She also paid to have Jacob and Margaret's home fully renovated including updating the plumbing and reinforcing all the outbuildings. She and Nathan purchased a small ranch close to Jacob and Margaret Brown, where they continue to hold weekly Bible studies.

THEO MACKLIN was named the silent partner in Macklin Enterprises but continued with his ice-cream truck business. His kindness and joviality to Birch Valley children earned him the nickname, "Uncle Theo."

ENDNOTES
Chapter 13
1. Neal Donald Walsch, *Conversations With God,* Book 2 (Charlottesville, VA: Hampton Roads, 1997), p. 56, as quoted in Warren B. Smith's book, *False Christ Coming: Does Anybody Care?*

BEFORE *DANGEROUS ILLUSIONS,* THERE WAS *CASTLES IN THE SAND*—THE FIRST NOVEL EVER TO WARN OF THE SPIRITUAL FORMATION MOVEMENT

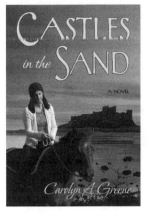

CASTLES IN THE SAND BY CAROLYN A. GREENE

When the horse-loving, day-dreaming Tessa Dawson enters a Christian college, she is introduced to the writings of 16th century Teresa of Avila by her spiritual formation professor. Soon Tessa's life is dramatically affected as she delves headlong into "Christian mysticism." When she ventures deeper into this spirituality, her grandfather and a mysterious young man set out to reach her. But will they be able to help her before it's too late?

This "fiction with a message" takes a compelling and thought-provoking look at the true nature behind contemplative spirituality, which has impacted Christian churches, colleges, seminaries, and universities across the globe.

> [A] believable, action-packed plot . . . [a] fantastic effort. *Castles in the Sand* is definitely an eye-opener! . . . Lighthouse is now a leading publisher of conservative Christian titles and serves a key role in a dwindling class of [publishing] houses that are not afraid to be politically incorrect. Major kudos to Lighthouse Trails Publishing for taking on this important project.—Jim Fletcher, free-lance reporter

Castles in the Sand is Carolyn Greene's debut book. Carolyn has studied the New Age movement and the contemplative prayer movement for several years. She lives in Canada with her husband and two children. Carolyn A. Greene is the author's pen name.

SOME OF THE TITLES BY
LIGHTHOUSE TRAILS PUBLISHING

BOOKS

Another Jesus (2nd ed.)
by Roger Oakland, $12.95

A Time of Departing
by Ray Yungen, $12.95

Castles in the Sand (a novel)
by Carolyn A. Greene, $12.95

Faith Undone
by Roger Oakland, $12.95

For Many Shall Come in My Name
by Ray Yungen, $12.95

Foxe's Book of Martyrs
by John Foxe, $14.95, illustrated

How to Protect Your Child From the New Age & Spiritual Deception
Berit Kjos, $14.95

In My Father's House
by Corrie ten Boom, $13.95

Let There Be Light
by Roger Oakland, $13.95

Muddy Waters
by Nanci des Gerlaise, $13.95

Out of India
by Caryl Matrisciana, $13.95

Seducers Among Our Children
by Patrick Crough, $14.95

Stolen from My Arms
by Katherine Sapienza, $14.95

Stories from Indian Wigwams and Northern Campfires
Egerton Ryerson Young, $15.95

Strength for Tough Times
by Maria Kneas, $7.75

The Color of Pain
by Gregory Reid, $10.95

Things We Couldn't Say
1st Lighthouse Trails Edition
by Diet Eman, $14.95, photos

The Other Side of the River
by Kevin Reeves, $12.95

Trapped in Hitler's Hell
by Anita Dittman with Jan Markell, $12.95, illustrated, photos

For a complete listing of all our books, DVDs, and CDs, go to www.lighthousetrails.com, or request a copy of our catalog.

To order additional copies of:

Dangerous Illusions or *Castles in the Sand*
Send $14.95 ($12.95 for *Castles in the Sand*) plus shipping to:

Lighthouse Trails Publishing
P.O. Box 908
Eureka, Montana 59917

For shipping costs, go to
www.lighthousetrails.com/shippingcosts.htm
($3.95/1 book; $5.20/2-3 books; $10.20/4-20 books)
You may also purchase Lighthouse Trails books from
www.lighthousetrails.com.

The bulk (wholesale) rates for10 or more copies is 40% off the retail price.

For U.S. & Canada orders, call our toll-free number: 866/876-3910.
For international and all other calls: 406-889-3610
Fax: 406-889-3633

Dangerous Illusions, as well as other books by Lighthouse Trails Publishing, can be ordered through most major outlet stores, bookstores, online bookstores, and Christian bookstores in the U.S. Bookstores may order through: Ingram, SpringArbor, Anchor, or directly through Lighthouse Trails.

Libraries may order through Baker & Taylor.

For more information on the topic of this book:
Lighthouse Trails Research Project
www.lighthousetrailsresearch.com

You may write to Carolyn A. Greene or Zach Taylor care of:
Lighthouse Trails Publishing
P.O. Box 908
Eureka, MT 59917

Lighthouse Trails has a free weekly e-newsletter and a bi-monthly subscription-based 32-page print journal. Visit www.lighthousetrailsresearch.com, or call one of the numbers above to sign up for the free e-newsletter or to subscribe to the print journal. ($12/year for U.S. | $24/year for CA | $36/year for international).